# The Batiandi Li Family

## 八天地

Xi Fu

Zea Books
Lincoln, Nebraska
2025

ISBN 978-1-60962-356-2 paperback
ISBN 978-1-60962-357-9 ebook
doi: 10.32873/unl.dc.zea.1513

# Preamble

The novel tells the story of six generations of the Li family over the course of nearly a century and a half, a legendary saga. The protagonists of the Li family in various historical stages of the book are searching for their own identity and the position of the family on the road of life. Sometimes they seize opportunities and create temporary brilliance for the benefit and glory of the family, while at other times they submit to fate and follow the tide of history, content to live ordinary lives like common people.

# Table of Contents

## Part Four: Stories of the Li family sons of the generation named "Zhen"



## Part Five: Two daughters of the Li family: intelligent Yaozhi and virtuous Yaoxian

## Part Six: The turbulent life story of Li Yaoxin



## Part Seven: The Li family sons of the generation named "Yao": Yaoguo, Yaoyou, and Yaowei

## Li Family Branch that Migrated to Northeast China from Pingdu, Shandong,

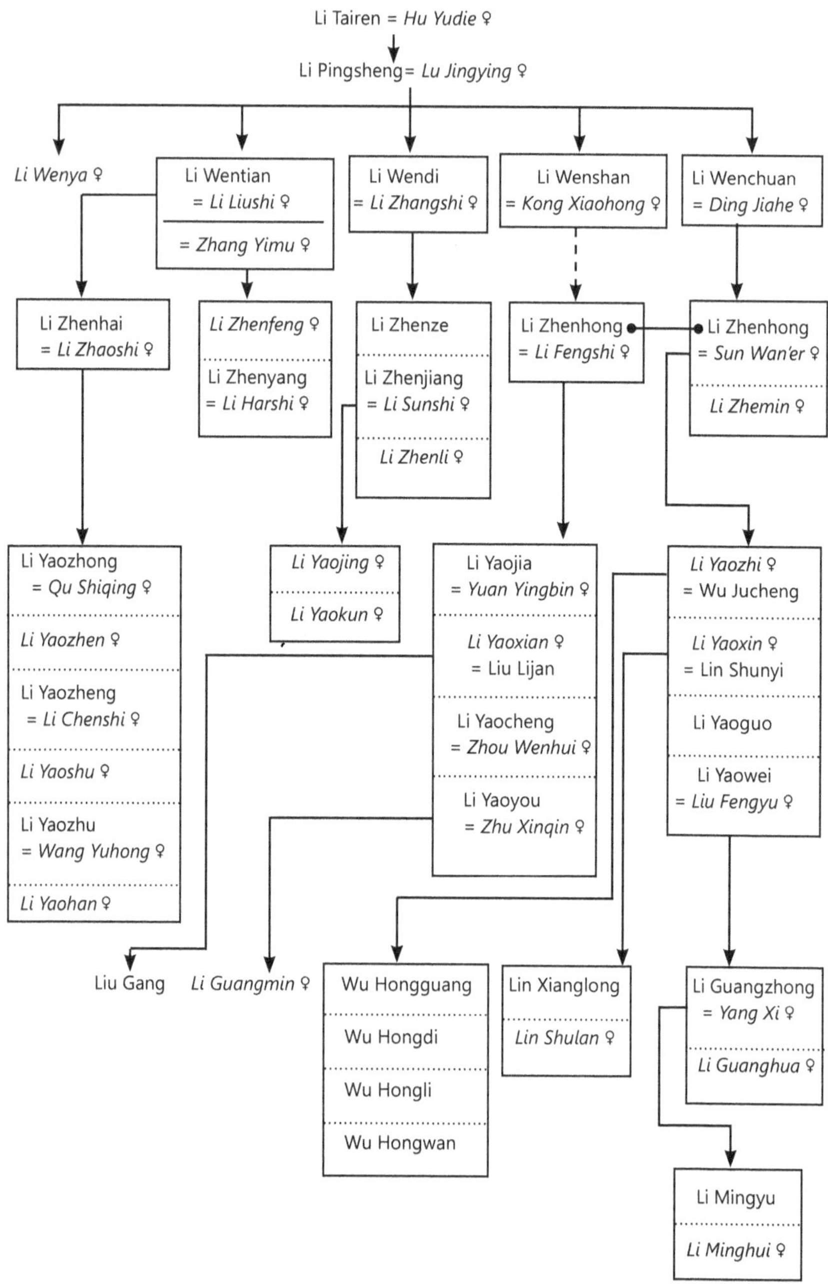

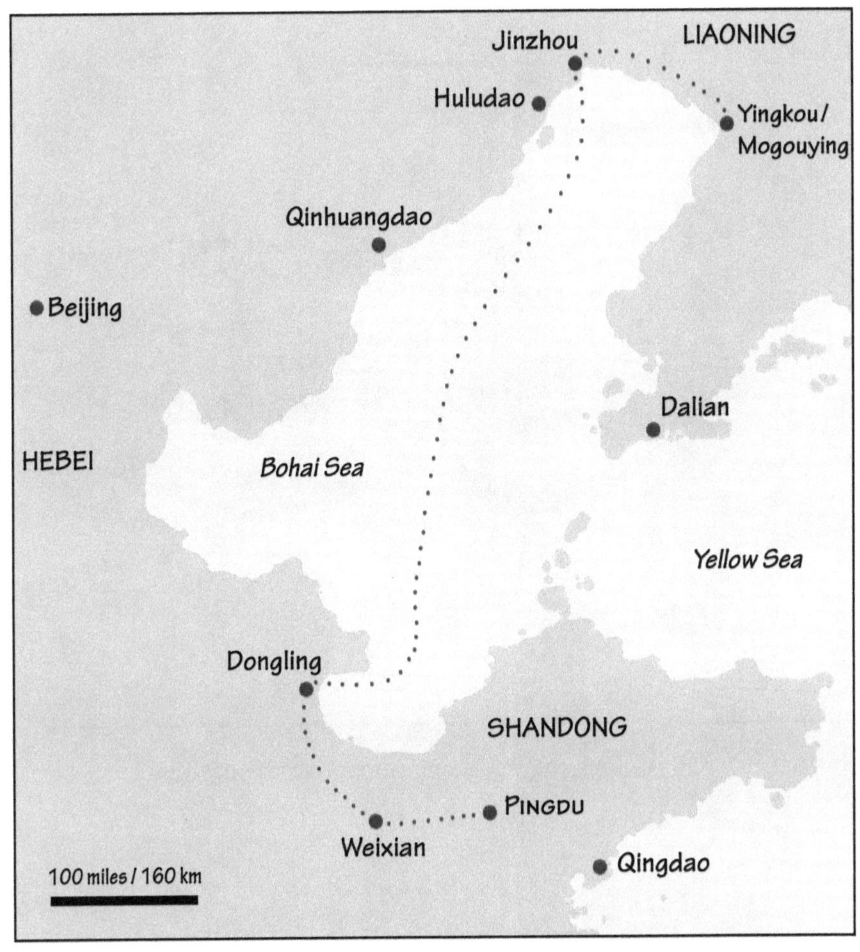


Li Tairen's route from Pingdu, Shandong, to Yingkou, Liaoning

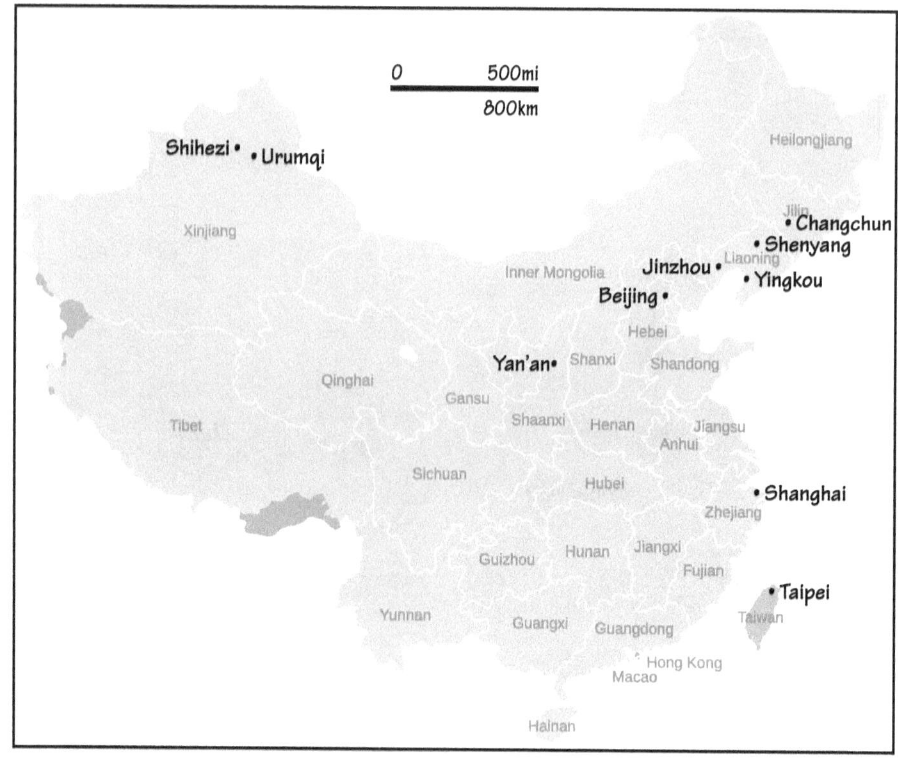


Cities where the Yao generation found themselves.

*This book dedicated to my father-in-law, Li Yaowu, who passed away on July 5th, 2021. The character Li Yaowei in this book is based on him.*

## Introduction

# My trip to China

In 2015, I went back to mainland China with my parents to visit my grandparents and great-grandparents. This was my third trip back since my parents and I had left 23 years ago when I was just a child. Now, I was 25 years old! When I was young, my dad was pursuing his PhD and my mom was always busy with work and business trips, so they left me with my grandparents until the end of 1993 when my mom took me to Germany to see my dad who was doing his post-doc there. Later, our family moved to many countries, and finally settled in the United States when I was ten years old.

Before this trip, I tried hard to recall my memories of the days when I was with my grandparents. I remembered that my grandparents were both university professors, and at a university Sports Meet, when I was three years old, I ran on the 400-meter track with my grandpa's encouragement. I finished the entire run for the first time in my life amid the applause of a group of university students. Now, I know that my grandpa was teaching me that with effort, anything is possible in life.

I'm back again! My first hometown! I can never forget it! This time, I also learned that my family has so many stories on this land! It all starts with a family genealogy book that my grandpa brought out.

That day, I was jet-lagged and lazily lying in bed refusing to get up. Grandpa said, "Mingyu, wake up and eat breakfast, I'll tell you about our family genealogy. It's time to tell you! I'm getting old, if I don't tell you, some stories will be buried with me."

When I was young, I saw some old family photos. In the summer of 1990, when I was only a few months old, my aunt from Taiwan returned to the mainland for the first time. My grandpa and grandma, as well as my uncles, stayed in Beijing for about a week. Of course, I have no memory of that. It wasn't until 1999 when I returned to China at the age of ten and met my aunt again that I became curious. The Li family had so many stories!

After breakfast, Grandpa and I sat on the sofa, and he took out a black-covered "Li Family Genealogy". As he flipped through the pages, tears shimmered in his eyes. After taking a sip of water, Grandpa began to speak.

It was during the tenth year of the Qing Dynasty, during the reign of Emperor Daoguang, when Shandong province experienced four years of continuous floods and droughts, with starving people everywhere and people barely surviving. To survive, my ancestors, like many Shandong villagers, sold their properties, took their elderly and young and headed north. In the 14th year of Daoguang (1834), they set out from Laiyang, Shandong (now part of Pingdu) and began the difficult journey to cross the Bohai Sea to the east. It took my ancestors more than a year to finally cross the Bohai Strait, landing in Huludao, and eventually arriving at the mouth of the Liao River in the Liaodong Peninsula, now known as Yingkou City, Liaoning Province. After coming ashore, my great-grandfather built a house and started a business, and later cleared and cultivated the land, which is now the famous "Eight Fields" of Yingkou City, known as "Batiandi" by the locals.

At that time, my ancestors were the first to cultivate vegetables in Yingkou, and naturally the fertile land that was developed belonged to our old Li family. At that time, because the area of this vegetable garden was exactly eight "tian" (a unit of land area in old China, with ten mu being one tian), it was named "Ba Tiandi".

In the age of the internet, I easily found out online that there were several households surnamed Li living in Yingkou, who cultivated vegetables and were known as the "Li Family Vegetable Garden", and their area was exactly "Ba Tiandi". Sure enough, it was BaTiandi, so I named my book on the Li family genealogy "BaTiandi".

Up until 1949, our old Li family was a well-known and respected family in Yingkou's "BaTiandi". My ancestors not only had several properties and large tracts of farmland for rent, but also engaged in the trade of seafood, hardware, banking, and several jewelry stores.

My grandfather had never told me the story of the Li family in detail before, but this time he spoke for more than three hours.

Yaowei, Yaoxin, and Mingyu in 1996

It turned out that our old Li family had a family genealogy passed down through the generations, consisting of only twenty words, from which we could trace our ancestors and descendants. These four lines of words were: "When the sky is high, there is peace on the left; when the river is calm, there is brightness in the east. With sincerity, the branches will flourish and forever have peace and tranquility."

In Chinese:

天高左太平，汶振要光明，诚心繁枝茂，永世得康宁。

My four-great-grandfather, Li Tairen, only had one son, my three-great-grandfather Li Pingsheng, when he went to Northeast China. Li Pingsheng had four sons, and my great-great-grandfather was the youngest, Li Wenchuan. Li Wenchuan then had four sons, and my great-great-grandfather was the youngest, Li Zhenhong.

The four brothers were all named “Zhen” in their generation, and the eight boys and eight girls they fathered were all named “Yao” in their generation. The Li family did not separate, and this large family lived together in a large courtyard. Because my great-grandfather Li Zhenhong was the youngest brother in the “Zhen” generation, his four children were all ranked lower. The eldest sister, Li Yaozhi, was considered the most outstanding and experienced the most hardships. She was the fifth oldest in the “Yao” generation of girls. Her sister, Li Yaoxin, who went to Taiwan, was the second oldest in the “Yao” generation of girls. Her brother, who sacrificed his life in the Korean War, was the third oldest in the family and the fifth oldest in the “Yao” generation of boys. Finally, my grandfather, Li Yaowei, was the youngest brother in the “Yao” generation of boys.

I learned later that my great-grandfather, Li Zhenhong, actually had eight children, because one of my great-great-grandfathers, Li Wenshan, had no children. The Li family tradition would not allow a family line to end, so my great-grandfather, Li Zhenhong, took a second wife and had two sons and two daughters in the Li Wenshan family line. They were my grandfather’s half-brothers and sisters.

My grandfather took out a few military medals from an old wooden box and said to me, “These are the rewards I received for fighting in the Korean War. They will belong to you in the future.” He also took out an old paper that looked like an award certificate from behind a picture frame and said to me, “It’s been 64 years. This is the award certificate that my brother received, your great-uncle, sacrificed his life in the Korean War.”

He spoke as he unfolded the yellowed paper that had been rolled up like a tube. In 1950, my grandfather, who was only sixteen years old, and his nineteen-year-old brother, Li Yaoguo, went to the Korean battlefield together to fight against the Americans and help North Korea. Li Yaoguo was sent to an infantry unit and unfortunately died in early 1951.

I was born in mainland China in 1989 and have been living with my parents in various places overseas ever since. Later, I settled in the United States for a long time. Although my way of life has been completely westernized, I still vaguely feel that my roots are in China, where I have an unbreakable emotional attachment and my ancestral history. I have always been fascinated by that period of history.

After that day, whenever I had time, my grandfather would tell me about the Li family's genealogy and stories. Time flew by, and half a month had passed. One morning, my grandfather said to me, "If you have the opportunity, you should visit these relatives who are the same age as me. Each of their histories is full of hardships and stories. Some of them have passed away, and some are still alive with good memories. You should go and listen to their stories. They are all very valuable! Mingyu, if you have the opportunity, write their stories into a book and publish it for the world to know about the history of struggle of our Li family, which is also a microcosm of that era. Speaking more specifically, I believe you can write the genealogy and stories of our Li family, so that our Li descendants will not forget their roots.

To fulfill the task given to me by my grandfather, I began traveling back and forth between the two sides of the Taiwan Strait and the Northeastern region of China in the summers of 2015, 2016, 2017. I visited these elders and recorded their stories.

**Part One**

# *How Li Tairen took his family on a journey to Manchuria*

## Chapter One

# Fleeing from locusts and separating from the family

### 1

When I was a child, my grandfather often told me that our ancestral home was in Shandong, but I saw on my father's household registration that his ancestral home was in Yingkou, Liaoning. This mystery wasn't solved until I returned to mainland China in 1999 and met my Paternal Aunt Yaoxin, who had returned from Taiwan.

Paternal Aunt Yaoxin had a kind and friendly face, and she was very capable and efficient. She would always pat my head and speak softly and gently to me, saying, "Mingyu, when I first came to the mainland, you were only half a year old. Now you're almost as tall as me." She even made me stand up to compare our heights. This made me feel a strong sense of closeness to her, and from then on, my fondness for her came from the bottom of my heart.

I remember one time when Paternal Aunt Yaoxin was chatting with my grandfather like a child. She said, "I really want to go to the big courtyard of our family in Yingkou, take a stroll in the Li family's vegetable garden, and go to the fields on the ridges of LiJiaGu Village in Pingdu, Shandong to shout loudly, 'I'm back!'"

Pingdu, Shandong! So that's where my Li family's roots are! Today, I heard about the history of the Li family's hardships in pioneering the northeast.

The story goes back to the 14th year of the Daoguang reign (1834 AD). Starting from Guizhou in the south, a severe drought caused a locust plague that swarmed to Hunan, Hubei, Henan, and Shandong. In LiJiaGu Village, Pingdu, Shandong, the fields were devastated, the crops were almost completely destroyed by locusts that darkened the sky, and the withered seedlings swayed weakly in the breeze.

Sitting on a distant field ridge was a man of twenty-six or twenty-seven years with a lean and sturdy figure and a handsome face. He was Li Tairen, a member of a local wealthy family. His wife Hu Yudie had just given birth to a chubby baby boy named Li Pingsheng a few days ago. However, due to several years of disasters and almost no harvest in the fields, and the locusts and sandstorms covering the sky and blocking out the sun for the past two years, almost all the tenant farmers had left their hometowns to go to Northeast China. With no income at home, they were forced to rely on their savings, and life had already become difficult. Now with the addition of another mouth to feed, Tairen sighed! A few days ago, several of his cousins left to go to Northeast China, but his elder brother Li Taihong and younger brother Li Taihe were determined to stay and guard the ancestral farmland that the Li family had cultivated for generations.

The Li family had farmed the land since their ancestor Li Ren Mei fled to North Guancun, Laiyang County, Shandong Province, during the invasion of the Jin Dynasty at the end of the Northern Song Dynasty.* After the Li family's many years of hard work by, the place was named LiJiaGu Village in their honor! They were so proud! But it seemed their family's glory would have to fade while in the hands of Li Tairen's generation?

In the past, Shandong Pingdu had vast fertile fields and an ever-flowing Bohai River in the northeast and a gurgling Jiaolai River in the west. The mountains in the north blocked the cold north wind and allowed the sun to warm the vast and flat plains in the south. Farming there was almost always successful, yielding bumper harvests of soybeans, peanuts, wheat, and corn. Pingdu was often called the granary of the homeland. During the harvest season, people would celebrate the rich harvests by jumping on stilts and dancing the candlestick horse dance! Candles were placed on the front and back of their chests and bottoms, riding on the candlestick horse, and people would sing and dance, longing for a harmonious and prosperous life.

Pingdu's abundant resources and happy people made it a frequent battleground for military strategists. From the Song Dynasty,

* In the 12th century AD.

there were records of military troops stationed and cities built there. Today, if you visit Pingdu City, you can still see the remains of the earthworks of the past buildings, and in some places, there are earth walls two to three meters high that stretch for several miles.

During the Jin Dynasty, the Li family's ancestor came to Shandong to take refuge, and he immediately chose this place. From then on, the Li family multiplied and thrived from generation to generation.

But after years of drought, the rivers dried up, and large areas of once fertile land cracked open. Tairen couldn't bear to look at it anymore. The past two years of drought and sandstorms had made survival difficult.

Tairen sat on the ridge of the field, smoking his fifth bag of tobacco, but he hadn't yet come up with a good solution. He looked at the setting sun and the evening glow spreading slowly from the west sky to the distant ridges. Tairen stood up, brushed the dust off his buttocks, and slowly walked the path leading back home, leaving behind a trail of the evening glow.

As soon as he entered the village, he saw a grand courtyard to the southeast with a tall gate painted in red and the golden characters "Li Family" carved on the lintel. The glazed tiles on the walls had been transported from the capital years ago and had now become somewhat weathered, but they still displayed the magnificence of the Li family.

Tairen walked past the first two courtyards, belonging to his older brother Taihong and younger brother Taihe. Taihong's two children, Pingshui and Pinglu, were playing in the courtyard, while Taihe's daughter, Pinghui, was nearby. Although Tairen was only the second son in the family, he and his wife had produced a son Li Pingsheng after four and a half years of marriage; that made him highly valued.

Tairen saw his older brother helplessly digging out the remaining soybeans from a once bulging bag, now flat and empty, and shook his head. It was as if Taihong was speaking to himself and Tairen at the same time, "How are we going to survive? We adults can bear, but the children can't!"

Tairen didn't respond and just walked straight back to his own courtyard.

The servant Juanzi was washing the baby's diapers while Tairen's wife Yudie was resting with her eyes closed. She had experienced a difficult childbirth and lost a lot of blood, making her already pale face even more colorless. Her delicate features, with curved eyebrows, a straight nose bridge, and tender skin, indicated that she came from a wealthy family. Her maiden name was Hu Yudie, and her family made tofu and pancakes. They were a wealthy family from a neighboring village, located ten miles away from the Li family. They employed many laborers, especially during the soybean harvesting season, and sometimes hired additional temporary workers. The Hu family's soybeans were supplied mainly by the Li family, which led to the two families becoming in-laws. Their business dealings eventually turned into a family relationship, making them even closer. Hu Yudie became the second daughter-in-law in the Li family. A few years earlier, when the old master Li Zuoxiang and his wife were still alive, they were unhappy because their second daughter-in-law was not able to conceive. And now that she had finally given birth to a chubby grandson, they had passed away without seeing him.

Hearing the door, Yudie opened her eyes and said to her husband, "What are you thinking? You've been gone all day, and my family has already left. I have nothing else to worry about. After a few days, when I recover from childbirth, let's leave too!"

Tairen scratched his head and said, "I have no other choice. I'll just have to be an unfilial son and leave the family to my older brother and younger brother. I'll start packing up our valuable belongings these next few days, and we'll leave in a month."

At that moment, Juanzi came back with the dried diapers and overheard the master and mistress talking about heading east to break through the barrier. She interjected, "If you leave, I'll follow you."

Juanzi was bought by the Li family from the servant market two years ago. She was orphaned at a young age and was now sixteen years old. Tairen and Yudie treated her as their own family. Juanzi was not tall, and she had long black hair that reached her waist. Her almond-shaped eyes, thick eyebrows, and rosy cheeks, made her look quite charming. There was also a boy named Shi Tou in the family who was picked up by Li Zuoxiang from Ji Zhou. He was only eight years old at the time, seven years younger than Tairen, but now he was nineteen years old and taller than Li Er Ye ("Second Master Li"). In these years of famine, the long-term workers in the family were all laid off. Many of these workers had been eating from the same pot for so many years, and it was really hard to let them go. But Shi Tou and Juanzi were treated like family members. Shi Tou has said where was the Li family going? Where was he going?

Tairen told Juanzi and Shi Tou to prepare for a farewell banquet after his wife finished her confinement and invited the eldest and third uncles over. Li Er Ye said, "There's nothing much to eat. Take out the sorghum wine from the cellar. We won't be able to drink pure Shandong sorghum wine in the future! And use some good fabric from the house to exchange for some rice in GuShan town and buy some meat."

Time passed quickly, and a month passed just like that. Tairen sold what needed to be sold and gave out what needed to be given. The eldest brother and third brother each took some of the things they couldn't take with them. The oxen used for farming were also given to Taihong and Taihe's families, and some calligraphy, antiques, and the like were sold. These things were really worthless these days! It was a pity that the old master had paid a lot of money for them, but in times of famine, grain was still the most valuable thing. Yudie insisted on bringing her pancake stall, saying that it would come in handy on the way to Dongbei. She was right; it really did come in handy!

The farewell banquet was also the full moon banquet for the little master's birthday. It was called a banquet, but there was not much to eat. Some fried soybeans were considered a big dish! After the children finished eating, they let out loud farts. There was a bit of braised tofu and vegetables, eggs and scallions, some stir-fried sweet potato shoots, Yangshu money bag dumplings, three per person; pan-fried cakes, one per person; roasted corn, half a cob per person. There was also a big pot of red sorghum porridge from Yudie's stall, which was enough for everyone. This was the most luxurious family banquet of the past year. Now, people were starving to death everywhere, and rice was worth a thousand qian per bucket! Five years ago, this was Shandong's vegetable garden, but now, even a small family banquet like this was unaffordable! However, the children, Pinglu, Pingshui, and Pinghui, were thrilled, running around the table with big cakes in their hands and roasted corn.

Taihong, Tairen, and Taihe sat at one table, drinking sorghum wine and saying goodbye, discussing their plans for the future and how they would meet again. Tairen said, "At present, the imperial court does not allow large-scale conversion of land to cultivation, which is not good for the people! The restrictions outside the Great Wall should be relaxed. After settling in the north, I will send a letter to you, and we will go beyond the Great Wall to reunite!"

Eldest brother Taihong shook his head and said, "I will die here in our ancestral home!"

It came to pass as he said: he died early, but his son Pingshui later became a county magistrate, and then his grandson passed the imperial examination and became a *jinshi.* His great-grandson Li Zhenting really turned his family's fortunes around; he became the county magistrate and drafted the first genealogy and family tree. The eldest branch had guarded the old house in Shandong and revitalized the surviving remnant of the Li family in LiJiaGu.

That night everyone slept very late, feeling uncomfortable—after all parting is painful.

## 2

Two days later, the Tairen family woke up early in the morning just as the sky was starting to brighten. If it had been a year earlier, they would have heard roosters crowing and dogs barking in the village, but now it was very quiet, feeling almost like death. Most of the people in the village had already left, so there was no more liveliness. Almost all the chickens in the village had been killed for their meat, so there were no more crowing roosters.

Taihong, Taihe, and their cousin Taile also got up to help load the carts. They hitched a horse-drawn carriage, and Tairen and Shi Tou took turns driving on the way. The person driving had to sit at the front of the carriage. The horse was very thin, so only two women, Yudie and Juanzi, and the young son, Pingsheng, could sit in the carriage. Taihong suggested bringing another helper, but the horse didn't have enough strength to pull more people. If they hitched another ox cart, it might attract unwanted attention on the road and could be unsafe. Moreover, people might not have enough food to eat on the way, and there would be no grass to feed the animals.

Juanzi took care of most things inside the carriage since Yudie's health was not fully recovered, and she was still weak. She could only eat a little bit of food, which was converted into milk to feed Pingsheng. Juanzi laid a dog skin mattress on the carriage and covered it with a cool mat. She also put a duck-feather pillow inside a reed mat for Yudie and Pingsheng to lie on. Tairen made a clever cradle out of reeds that he had salvaged them from a riverbed several villages away. After cleaning and drying them, he split them into thin strips and used them to weave a beautiful and sturdy cradle that would not be uncomfortable for Pingsheng. They lined the cradle with a new blanket that Juanzi had embroidered and a flower-shaped pillow that she had made. The young master slept comfortably in the cradle. A few nights earlier, Yudie had not slept at all. She stayed up to sew a money pouch that slanted across the shoulder and waist, where Tairen could carry silver notes. Yudie also brought some gold, silver, and jade ornaments just in case they were needed. Additionally, they took a pancake stand and some rice, noodles, oil, and salt, which they stored in the compartment under the big cart.

As the sun rose over the mountain, it was time to go to work in the fields, although there were no longer many people left to work. The parched land seemed to be shouting desperately, "I'm thirsty!" The Tairen family bid their relatives farewell and began on their journey to northeastern China.

On the road out of the village, there were only a few scattered pedestrians, since many families had left already with no intention of returning. The road was dusty and the dust made people cough. The prolonged drought meant there was no rain to moisturize the land. The sun in the sky was scorching hot, and the heat rising from the ground was burning. The young master Peng Sheng kept crying, while Juanzi kept rocking the cradle and fanning him with a big fan. When they turned onto the main road to Dengzhou, the road became smoother, and more people appeared. There were porters, cart drivers, and pedestrians everywhere, all in a hurry. Occasionally, one could hear parents scolding their children for not walking fast enough.

The Tairen family followed the crowd southwest because people said that going northeast would be difficult due to the river's windings, and there were few major roads. Moreover, the furthest northeast was the bay where the legendary Bohai Penglai was located, a place where mirages were common and not a place for ordinary people to visit. Therefore, Tairen and his family decided to follow everyone else and head southwest first.

At noon, everyone was in a hurry and ate their pancakes with big scallions and pickled vegetables. They had covered more than twenty *li* (10 km), but the sun was about to set, and they were nowhere near a village or a store. Tairen estimated that they had walked at least forty to fifty *li* (20–25 km) that day! He began to worry as everyone was getting hungry. He suggested, "Let's find a place to rest, eat something, and spend the night; then continue our journey tomorrow."

As they were trying to figure out which direction to take, two young men came walking down a small road from the west. Shi Tou had sharp eyes and said, "Look, isn't that Hu Zi and Liang Zi from our village?"

Tairen took a closer look and indeed it was them, the two brothers who were known for their acrobatic performances and often went to town to make money. They were wearing only shorts and a worn-out rope as a belt, and Liang Zi was wearing a tattered melon-shaped hat. They had not been to the village for a while. In the past they had sometimes escorted important people as bodyguards. They said there was a broken temple a little over two *li* ahead where they could stay the night.

As they descended the hill, they saw many people walking towards the southwest, where there were scattered adobe houses. When they reached the ruined temple, they saw a crowd of people sitting on the ground outside. Many elderly people and children lay on the ground, and Tairen's heart sank. Nevertheless, Tairen had the large pot unloaded from the cart and dug a hole nearby. He gathered some dry twigs and set up the pot. Hu Zi and Liang Zi helped fetch water and they cooked a pot of porridge, which they shared, along with the leftover dry rations they had brought from home. Tairen thought this would suffice for one night. Just as Juanzi had served a bowl of porridge to Yudie, a group of people suddenly rushed over to snatch it, causing Tairen to protect the pot and burn his hand in the process. Hu Zi then picked up a thick wooden stick, and Liang Zi untied his hemp rope to use as a whip. They both shouted loudly for everyone to step back, and only then did the crowd disperse. Later, there was still some porridge left, which they distributed to the elderly and children. Tairen realized that at this rate, their food supplies would soon be depleted, so he decided to set off again in the cart that night.

As they started their journey, however, a group of three black-clothed youngsters suddenly jumped onto the cart and snatched Tairen's money bag before fleeing in a frenzy. It happened so suddenly that Tairen was stunned for a moment! Liang Zi scolded the thief: "Little bunny! where are you going!"

As he said that, he rushed out to chase, but the children ran really fast like rabbits as they passed the purse from hand to hand. Then all of a sudden, Liang Zi flicked the hemp rope and made a crackling sound with it. The rope entangled the money bag and flung it back to him while the boys stood for a while dazed. Liang Zi cracked the hemp rope and said loudly: "Go away!" and the black-clad boys quickly disappeared from sight.

Juanzi leaned out of the cart and stared blankly, her eyes full of surprise and affection. Tairen and Yudie saw it, and they asked Liang Zi where he was headed. They proposed that they travel together for mutual assistance.

Liang Zi said: "We are home all over the world. We will walk together as long as we can survive."

With Hu Zi and Liang Zi accompanying them, their journey became more lively, and they were able to move faster with more food supplies. Hu Zi and Liang Zi were skilled at climbing trees, and often found scattered fruits at the top of trees after others had already picked them clean. They found hairy peaches, haws, sour dates, and more that everyone else didn't know how to get.

After walking for over a month, they covered a distance of forty to fifty *li* each day. At this pace, it would take them another two months to reach Weixian. Tairen was looking forward to arriving in Weixian soon because his father, Li Zuoxiang, had told him before, "If you want to do business, you should consider going to Weixian. They say 'It's like the Suzhou of the South and Weixian of the North.' You can imagine how prosperous the business is there."

Tairen thought that Weixian might be better than his hometown and they might not have to walk so far.

There were still many pedestrians on the road, and every day, some would collapse; these were known as "roadfall." Nobody cared how many people fell on the road to Northeast China. They might have been lonely individuals or entire families that collapsed. How many unwilling souls had fallen on the road to Northeast China!

One day, they arrived at a bridge over the Dagu River, but it had been crushed by the people traveling the road. Looking at the deepest part of the river, it was only up to one's ankles. After years of drought, the riverbed had dried up, and only a few small streams struggled to flow.

Tairen looked at the riverbed and said, "It's probably a sandy road or a muddy pit underneath that the cart could get stuck in."

Shi Tou rolled up his pants and was about to jump into the riverbed when Liang Zi stopped him and said, "Don't be in a hurry. Find a stick and test it how deep."

Stone and Hu Zi went to explore the road, and Liang Zi stayed with the rest. Now that the second master Tairen no longer needed to drive the cart, Shi Tou and Liang Zi took turns driving, while Hu Zi followed the cart. Er Ye would occasionally sit in the cart for a while. Juanzi and Liang Zi got along well, and the two of them talked a lot. Juanzi liked to learn stick skills from Hu Zi and whip skills from Liang Zi. Hu Zi with a tiger head and a tiger brain, still young, didn't have a thought about girls.

After a while, Shi Tou and Liang Zi came back and said that it was indeed a sandy pit, and the cart could not pass through. But according to the information they received, they would have to detour about twenty to thirty li ahead to find another place to cross the river. It seemed that they would have to spend the night in the wilderness tonight!

In the evening, Yudie Butterfly personally made pancakes for everyone, and the dough was almost gone. They should have reached the boundary of Weifang County by now, and there was still more than half the journey to Dengzhou before taking a boat to the Customs. After finishing making the pancakes, Yudie Butterfly rushed into the shed and didn't come out to eat. Juanzi called her, but she only said she would eat later.

At night, the forest was full of rustling sounds, and hungry wild beasts were howling in the distance. However, Tairen had Shi Tou and Hu Zi gather a pile of firewood, as animals were afraid of fire. By midnight, Xiaoping kept crying nonstop, and Yudie Butterfly still hadn't eaten anything, holding and feeding Pingsheng milk all the time. Listening to the cries of the young master, Juanzi felt helpless and said, "Give him to me."

She reached out to take the young master, but when her hand touched Yudie Butterfly's body, she shuddered! It was so hot, like touching hot charcoal! It turned out that after several days of traveling on foot and sleeping rough, Yudie had almost no milk left. She was now running a high fever, and the young master had become thin. Juanzi was so worried that she almost cried and said, "Madam, why didn't you say anything if you were feeling unwell? What if something bad happens!"

Yudie Butterfly said weakly, "I'm fine, but I have no milk left. Pingsheng is gnawing on my breasts, and I'm afraid he'll go hungry."

Tairen was anxious and felt guilty. If something happened to his wife and child in this wilderness, how could he live with himself! So he made a quick decision and said, "We can't wait until dawn. We must leave now and find a place with people to get you treated and get some milk for Pingsheng to drink."

Everyone agreed, realizing that staying here was useless, and so they decided to leave.

In the quiet night, the moonlight poured onto the ground, leaving their uneven shadows. They occasionally saw the light of campfires where people were camping in the wilderness, heard moans of hunger, and cries of children.

Tairen remembered a poem by Meng Haoran:

> The bright moon hangs in the clear autumn sky,
> Its light shining on the dew-wet ground.
> Startled magpies have yet to settle,
> Dancing fireflies enter the room along with the rolled-up window blinds.
> Sparse shadows of the cold courtyard trees, coming clear and urgent night sounds of a neighbor's pestle.
> The sound of the night neighbor's pestle clappers is urgent.
> What a long wait for our next meet!
> Stand there gazing into the emptiness.

In Chinese:

> 秋空明月悬，光彩露沾湿。
> 惊鹊栖未定，飞萤卷帘入。
> 庭槐寒影疏，邻杵夜声急。
> 佳期旷何许！望望空伫立。

## Chapter Two

# Kindness of Jinghui's family and a temporary stay in Weixian

### 1

Tairen's family dared not rest, and at dawn they finally saw a village. It seemed that some of the houses were no longer inhabited, with their doors wide open and small animals coming in and out. Juanzi saw smoke was rising from several chimneys and pointed with her finger, saying, "Great! There are still a few households left. I'll go and ask for help."

Tairen immediately let Liang Zi accompany her and instructed them to be polite and make requests.

Juanzi and Liang Zi left the cart and went to ask for help. Hu Zi guarded the cart, and Tairen was anxious, but he didn't show it on his face. He knew that he was the backbone of the family at this time, and he couldn't show his emotions. Yudie was still sleeping in the cart, and Pingsheng seemed to have cried enough and fell asleep in his mother's arms.

Juanzi and Liang Zi saw a house that was not too dilapidated, with two courtyards, one large and one small. They walked up to the door of this house, and the main gate of the courtyard was not locked. They pushed it open and knocked on the door directly. A man in his forties or fifties opened the door. Before they could speak, he said, "There's no food here. You can go!" With that, he slammed the door shut. No matter how hard Liang Zi and Juanzi knocked on the door again, there was no response from inside.

They went to several more houses and were turned away at each one. They were about to despair when they finally arrived at a high-walled courtyard with two majestic lion statues at the gate and a large Buddha statue. Liang Zi walked up to the gate to knock, and an old man walked out from inside, chanting "Namo Amitabha Buddha" in his mouth.

Juanzi immediately knelt down on both knees and pleaded, "Grandpa, you are a Buddhist, please save our lady master and young master! Saving one life is better than building a seven-level pagoda!" She kept bowing continuously as she spoke.

The old man helped her up and said, "Don't rush, girl, take your time and tell me what happened."

Juanzi cried and said, "Our lady master is seriously ill, and the young master has no milk to drink. We came from LiJiaGu village in Pingdu state, which is more than 700 miles away in the south."

The old man was surprised and asked, "LiJiaGu? Do you know Li Zuoxiang ?"

"Of course, he was our master! But he passed away, and his son Tairen is here." Juanzi replied.

Upon hearing this, the old man asked Liang Zi and Juanzi to lead the way to Tairen's family.

Most of the trees in the village were dead, and even the ones that survived had lost their leaves. Hungry people were eating whatever they could find. Without the shelter of tree leaves, the sun was scorching, and people were getting dizzy from the heat.

As Liang Zi and Juanzi returned the same way they came, they couldn't see the cart anymore. While they were standing there puzzled, Tairen and Hu Zi appeared from behind a house and waved at them. They had been hiding in the shade behind the house.

When the old man saw Tairen, he went up and shook his hand, saying, "You look so much like him! You look just like your father."

Tairen asked, "Do you know my dad?"

The old man excitedly said, "Not only do I know him, but we were also young together. I was trying to do some business and had saved up some money to go to JiNan to buy goods. But I lost my money bag, and I was desperate. I lived on Qiandi Street and stayed in the same guesthouse as your father, Li Zuoxiang. At that time, your father lent me some money, and I was able to expand my business! I always wanted to repay him, but we were in different parts of the world and never had a chance. Now he's gone!"

As the old man spoke, his eyes welled up, and he wiped his tears with his sleeve.

This was a pleasant surprise for Tairen. They followed the old man back to the village.

The Tairen family sat down at the elderly person's home and took a sip of water. It turned out that the drought had also affected this place, and the water in the large bowl was murky. Tairen and his family were extremely thirsty, so they drank the water along with the sediment, feeling the unpleasant taste in their mouths only after finishing it.

The elderly person's name is Chen Jinghui, a name that Tairen had heard his father mention when he was alive. Chen Jinghui used to be in the cotton business and later switched to the fabric trade. They had a fabric shop and a clothing workshop at home, employing dozens of skilled embroiderers who were renowned for their embroidery in Weixian County. Their eldest son married the daughter of a famous blacksmith in the county. In recent years, the Chen family was even livelier than the prosperous Li family in LiJiaGu. However, both sons have now left home to seek their own fortunes, and their daughter got married to the son of the county magistrate.

Chen Jinghui's wife, Chunni, suffers from arthritis and has small feet that prevent her from walking properly or leaving the house. She sits on the kang bed even during the scorching summer days, wrapped in a thick quilt. Chunni is quite talkative and was delighted to have Tairen's family visit their home. She held Yudie's hand, asking about their well-being. She instructed the only servant in the house, Shun Zi, to go five miles away to ZhaoJiaWan and fetch a doctor to examine Yudie's illness while suggesting that Yudie lie down comfortably.

Yudie said, "I'm fine, but is there any milk for my son? He's starving." Chunni heard this and said, "How lucky, we do have some! Your little master has a fortunate face with thick earlobes and lips, he will have great blessings in the future."

Chen Jinghui continued, "A few days ago, we saved a woman. Her husband died, and their newborn daughter also died of illness. She wanted to die too, but we saved her. Her milk hasn't gone away yet, so let her come and breastfeed the child." Juanzi and Chen

Jinghui went to the backyard to call Lixiang to come and breast-feed Pingsheng.

At this time, Shun Zi led the doctor Zhao back. Zhao checked Yudie's pulse, tongue coating, and prescribed some medicine. As they were leaving, the doctor whispered to Tairen, "Her condition is not very good. If you have any food to give her, please help supplement her diet. I have some donkey-hide gelatin that you can boil and let her drink first." Tairen gave the doctor a gold chain. Money was no longer useful in those days.

A moment later, Lixiang arrived. She had thick eyebrows, big eyes, and large hands and feet. She looked like a worker. She picked up Pingsheng and immediately unbuttoned her shirt, revealing her snow-white breasts to feed him. Pingsheng eagerly sucked on her nipple, and soon fell asleep, satisfied. Lixiang then buttoned up her shirt and smiled at the sleeping baby. She should be satisfied, as she had seen a child's face again since losing her own little girl.

Tairen looked on happily and thought to himself, it looks like we'll be staying here for a while.

## 2

Chen Jinghui was a practitioner who recited scriptures in front of the Buddha statue in his home every day to pray for peace. Recently, he prayed to the Buddha to bless them with sweet dew. Tairen was also a believer in Buddhism, so the two of them naturally met in the Buddhist hall every morning.

Hu Zi and Liang Zi helped to clean up the courtyard and were always looking for something to do. They begged Master Chen to find them some work. Master Chen hesitated and said, "There is indeed some work, but I don't know if you have any taboos."

Liang Zi said, "We'll do any job!"

Chen Jinghui said, "According to my uncle, the government wants people to clean up the "fallen roads" dead bodies people who died on the East Pass Road " and dig deep pits to prevent an outbreak of disease. The people who collect the fallen roads will be provided with three meals a day and an extra corn bun each day."

Hu Zi hesitated, but Liang Zi was determined and said, "Let's do it!"

Shi Tou also said he would go.

In the following month, Hu Zi, Liang Zi, and Shi Tou would leave early and return late to help the officials' family clean up the fallen roads. Every day, they would bring back some cornmeal steamed buns, sometimes accompanied by pickled vegetables or green leafy vegetables like scallions. These provisions were greatly appreciated by the women in the household, and Yudie's face gradually regained some color as she began to recover her ability to breastfeed. However, Lixiang was unwilling to let go and continued to come to the main house every day to breastfeed Pingsheng. Yudie didn't say much, but she felt that her milk was insufficient, so it was better for Lixiang to continue. Besides, she had been feeling more comfortable lately and enjoyed chatting with Chunni every day. The two even became like mother and daughter, forming a close bond.

Yudie did indeed want to stay and not leave. However, something unexpected that occurred later forced her to leave.

## 3

One day, Hu Zi came back wearing a luxurious satin gown, looking quite impressive. Juanzi teased, "Oh, look who's back, Master Hu Zi!"

Hu Zi felt embarrassed, and Liang Zi spoke up for him, saying, "He took it off a body found on the road."

Shi Tou, always practical, said, "I told you not to wear it, but you insisted. Now, look at the trouble it caused!"

Juanzi fell silent for a moment and her eyes welled up with tears. She said, "Hu Zi, how could you do this? That master disappeared under mysterious circumstances, and you won't even let him leave in decent clothes. I think of my father, he left wearing tattered sackcloth, and it breaks my heart."

Juanzi asked Hu Zi, "Do you remember where they buried him?"

Hu Zi scratched his head and said, "I don't know. He didn't have a name, and they took him away on a cart to the barren land west of here and buried him in a pit."

At that moment, Master Chen and Tairen happened to pass by. Master Chen clasped his hands together and chanted, "Amitabha Buddha."

Tairen suggested to Hu Zi, Liang Zi, and Shi Tou that they should create a burial mound and erect an unnamed tombstone overnight. Tairen said, "Let's name it after the place where it happened!"

Hu Zi said, "It happened below the bridge slope."

Tairen replied, "Then let's call it Bridge Slope."

He took out some silver coins and gave them to Shi Tou, instructing them to go to the county town of Wei County and find a craftsman to engrave a tombstone to send off the late Master of Bridge Slope.

From then on, Liang Zi and Hu Zi continued to wear hemp ropes around their waists, long shirts and trousers, tied their legs, and wore the large hats made by Juanzi as they protected themselves while cleaning up the fallen roads. Shi Tou also followed suit and dressed the same way.

Hard work paid off, and perhaps Tairen and Master Chen's devout prayers for rain touched the Avalokitesvara Bodhisattva. On this day, a few scattered raindrops fell, bringing joy to Tairen as he wondered if the drought situation would improve. May the blessings of the Buddha be upon them!

However, the rain would only come down in a few drops. No matter how much Master Chen and Tairen prayed to Avalokitesvara Bodhisattva, it seemed that the heavens were not granting their request. The days remained tight, with a lack of food and difficulties in obtaining drinking water. Jinghui family's well had already dried up, and now the water storage pit was also running low.

A few days ago, they still saved the vegetable washing water to wash dishes, but now they wiped the plates with a handkerchief and continued using them. Moreover, everyone skipped washing their faces in the morning to save water.

Tairen came up with an idea. He instructed Shun Zi and Shi Tou to dig a deep well in the lowest part of the village. These two had been busy these past few days, and by the time they reached the tenth day of digging, the soil they excavated had formed a small hill. Suddenly, a gush of clear water emerged! Shi Tou couldn't dodge in time and got soaked. Without hesitation, he immediately knelt down and began drinking the water! That greedy fervor resembled Pingsheng's first taste of Lixiang's breast milk.

Shun Zi quickly ran to inform Master Chen, Madam, and Yudie. Everyone gathered in the backyard, joyously dancing and celebrating beside the deep pit.

## 4

Lixiang would request Yudie's permission every day to bring the child back to where the servants lived in the backyard and feed Pingsheng there, claiming it would be more convenient for breastfeeding. Initially, Yudie would accompany them, but over time, she realized that Lixiang genuinely loved Pingsheng and stopped joining them. Juanzi, of course, insisted on going along, and Lixiang couldn't refuse. This continued for another half a month, during which whenever Pingsheng was in Lixiang's arms, he wouldn't cry or fuss. He became extremely calm, as if he had found a very secure embrace.

Usually, as soon as it became light outside, Juanzi eagerly volunteered to massage and do acupressure on Madam Chunni's legs. She had been doing this for about ten days. Typically, Pingsheng would sleep until the sun rose about one rod high before Lixiang would take him to be breastfed. However, on that day, Lixiang took him away early, claiming her milk was abundant and engorged, and that Pingsheng needed to feed. Juanzi was massaging Madam Chunni's legs, and Yudie was squatting in the outhouse. Neither of them accompanied Lixiang to the backyard. By lunchtime, Lixiang had still not returned. Juanzi went to call her, but there was no response from inside the house. Juanzi pushed open the door and found a mess, and the baby's cradle was nowhere to be found! Juanzi panicked and ran back to inform Yudie: "Lixiang and the young master are both missing!"

This was a firecracker that exploded in the heart of Tairen. Yudie had always been weak, and she had three pregnancies that ended in miscarriages. This was the only precious child left. Master Chen also became anxious and asked Shun Zi to seek help from his son-in-law, the county official, to post notices and search for the child. Tairen also instructed Juanzi to call Liang Zi, Hu Zi, and Shi Tou to go and search immediately.

Lixiang had already regarded Pingsheng as her own child and couldn't bear to be apart from him for even a day. She had been planning to take him away for several days, and today was her chance. A few days ago, she took some silver coins from Madam Chunni's jewelry box, and this morning she took some food from the kitchen stove and filled a gourd with water, preparing to drink on the way. Holding the cradle, she braved the scorching sun and walked quickly on the road from the village to the county. After a while, she became exhausted and out of breath. Villagers from the village came towards her, greeting her. They all assumed she was a servant from the Chen Jinghui's family.

Lixiang had no family here, so she wanted to inquire in the county town of Weifang to find out how to get to her maternal hometown, Haojia Town in Dongying at the mouth of the Yellow River. She missed her family very much and longed for the Baiyu Feast of her hometown! How magnificent the seawall there was! There was the awe-inspiring sight of the Yellow River flowing into the sea for thousands of miles. There was also the TieMen Pass of LiJin County, the most famous commercial customs dock, where the ships of the big-nosed merchants gathered, creating a bustling scene. But now, it was unlikely to be the same.

It took Lixiang three hours to reach the county. She rested in a guest inn, fed Pingsheng, and had something to eat herself. She inquired about the route back to her hometown from the innkeeper. Without wasting a moment, she picked up the cradle and set off.

## Chapter Three

# Searching for Pingsheng in Dongying; a typhoon and the tragic fate of Liang Zi

### 1

All of these stories were told to me by my great-aunt, and she spent three days telling me the story of the Li family. At that time, my Chinese wasn't very good, so my mother Yang Xi helped me translate.

Upon hearing this, I became very nervous, because according to the family tree, my great-great-great-grandfather Li Pingsheng was from a single male-lineage. He had four sons, and the youngest was my great-great-grandfather, Li Wenchuan. My grandfather, Li Yao-wei, was the youngest son of my great-grandfather, Li Zhenhong.

I anxiously asked my grandmother, "How did we find our way back to our ancestral roots if our great-great-great-grandfather was lost?" She took a sip of water, looked at my anxious face, and smiled. "MingYu, these stories were also told to me by my grandfather when I was young. Let me continue."

The household was so busy that pots were boiling over, all in a rush to find Li family's young master Pingsheng. According to the people who had returned from the county, they had seen Lixiang carrying a cradle on the way to the county.

Chunni had heard from Lixiang that her maternal family was in Haohuajia Town, Dongying, at the mouth of the Yellow River. A messenger sent by Chen Jinghui's grandfather-in-law's county had returned and said that a 25 or 26-year-old woman, who was breast-feeding a child, had inquired about the route to Dongying in the past. She has already taken a donkey cart to Dongying for about two or three hours now!

Realizing the urgency of the situation, Tairen and the others quickly expressed their gratitude to Chen's family, promising to meet again in the future. They immediately hitched the carriage and set off for Dongying overnight. Tairen estimated that it would take about five or six days to travel 100 miles from Weixian to Dongying. Yudie felt anxious in her heart. She wanted Lixiang to bring the child, but she was unsure if she had enough money to sustain them during the journey. Additionally, she needed to breastfeed Pingsheng. Without food for herself, Pingsheng would go hungry. This was a worrisome predicament.

The next day, while on the way to Dongying, they encountered Lixiang resting in a village. She had suffered from heatstroke and was unable to continue walking. Thankfully, Pingsheng remained unharmed under her protection. From then on, the group traveled together to Dongying, escorting Lixiang back home.

Upon returning to Lixiang's hometown of HaoJia Town, Yudie formally asked Lixiang to become Pingsheng's godmother. It is said that later, my great-great-great-grandfather even visited Lixiang's hometown in Dongying, HaoJia Town, with the intention of paying her a visit. However, he learned that she had passed away. She was a good person, but she was born in a time of famine where she lost her husband and children. Later, she placed her hopes on Pingsheng, and eventually she entered a monastery, living a melancholic life. Pingsheng honored her as his godmother in their hometown, placed her memorial tablet alongside his biological mother's, Li Hu Yudie. He said that without Lixiang, there might not have been Pingsheng, as he was nourished by the milk of both mothers.

As he looked at the memorial tablets of his birth mother and godmother Lixiang, Pingsheng thought to himself:

The fragrant and enduring jasmine,
Like nourishing milk for the infant me.
Butterfly wings gently fluttering,
Ever soaring in every corner of my life.
Mother's love, like the flowing Liao River,
Flows through the river of my memories.
Her words, like a whispering spring breeze,
Reveal the mysteries of my life.

I grasp a gust of wind, kneading in my longing,
Sending a message to her in the breeze.
The continuation of life can never be severed,
Pingsheng follows in the footsteps of mother,
seeking the journey back home.

Note: Yudie (玉蝶) means Jade Butterfly in Chinese; Lixiang 莉香) means the fragrance of Jasmine.

## 2

The original ocean terminal in Dongying used to have hundreds of boats of various sizes docking here every day for ocean fishing and salt trading. However, nowadays, there are only a few boats left, and the locust plague has also reached here. People have all crossed the East through sea routes. For the sake of Lixiang's feelings, the Tairen family stayed here temporarily and lived off fishing for ten months until Pingsheng turned one year old. During this period, Yudie had another miscarriage. Her body could no longer withstand any long journeys. However, Dongying is no longer a good place to live for anyone. Lixiang became a Buddhist nun and said she no longer wanted to think about worldly affairs. Tairen and Yudie could finally let go of their guilt towards her emotionally. So they decided to continue their journey of exploring the east by sea.

The sea route to the Northeast passes through Tiemen Pass in LiJin County. It used to be a famous commercial customs wharf during the Qing Dynasty, a bustling hub for both water and land transportation and salt trade. In the last few years, it had become deserted. Tairen sent Liang Zi, Hu Zi, and Shi Tou to gather information about the situation at the pass.

Liang Zi was a sociable person, and as soon as he arrived in Dongying, he found Da Linzi, the leader of the escorts they used to work with. This guy still had some skills and was now the leader at Tiemen Pass. They arrived at the pass. It was located by the sea, with a natural trench and a massive solid salt mine weighing trillions of tons. The pass was known for its abundant sea fish and solid salt, attracting domestic and foreign merchants every day. From a distance, Liang Zi and his companions saw the vast seawall encircling the sea, with several boats moored there. The Jin people had built an earthen fortress here, with a large city gate in the east, south, west, and north, adorned with countless iron rings and nails. Everyone called it Iron Gate Pass! To go out to sea or leave the city, they had to pass through Iron Gate Pass.

After listening to the story of my great-aunt, I looked up some historical legends on Baidu Baike. According to the legend, there was a Dragon King Temple in the earthen fortress, housing a statue of the Dragon King. During the Ming and Qing dynasties, many of the hundreds of households here made a living through fishing and salt drying. At that time, the sea route between TieMen Iron Gate Pass and the outside world was not well-developed. However, the transformation began with a widely spread saying, "Iron Gate Pass is a divine pass."

The legend goes like this: "One year, a storm arose at sea, and a southern merchant fleet lost its direction. Fierce winds whipped up enormous waves, towering several 丈 zhang high, crashing against the ships. It seemed that the vessels would be swallowed by the sea. At that time, there were no navigation lights, and the sea was pitch black. Suddenly, someone noticed a red light in the western sky not far away. The fleet desperately steered towards the direction of the red light. Strangely enough, as they rowed, the wind gradually subsided, and eventually, the sea became calm. The fleet followed the guidance of the red light and reached a safe harbor, where they landed. However, the red light in the sky had disappeared. When dawn came, they realized that they had arrived at Iron Gate Pass. The people on the ships sincerely believed that the Dragon King in the Dragon King Temple of Iron Gate Pass had shown them mercy by sending a "divine light" to save their lives. Several ship captains rushed to the Dragon King Temple to burn incense, kowtow, and make vows to rebuild the temple after their safe return."

Since then, Iron Gate Pass gained fame, and the number of ships docking here increased day by day, greatly driving the economic development of Tiemen Iron Gate Pass.

Later, those merchants fulfilled their promise and rebuilt the Dragon King Temple. The temple was built entirely of rectangular stones with a black fish-scale tile roof, and the interior walls were covered with variously-shaped divine dragons.

With the presence of the Dragon King Temple, people began to come and offer incense and make wishes. Later, on both sides of the Dragon King Temple, temples dedicated to the local deities and the God of War, Guan Yu, were established. As the people in the city became more prosperous, they donated money to build a grand theater, standing over three meters tall. Skilled craftsmen coated the roof of the theater with gold powder, and the backdrop featured a painting of a group of dragons. In previous years, theater troupes from thousands of miles around would come to perform, with at least 200 shows per year! The combination of these three temples and the spacious courtyard became a natural and excellent open-air theater!

However, in the past year, Tairen and his family only had the chance to watch a play once. They were experiencing a famine, and people couldn't even eat their fill, let alone have the inclination to watch a play! The theater stage had been neglected in recent years, with some areas of the gold powder on the top of the stage peeling off or being scraped away. The wooden structure of the stage was also deteriorating, posing a risk of collapse. Moreover, Yudie's health was deteriorating, and she grew thinner and weaker each day, needing support from Juanzi to walk. The family's livelihood depended on Liang Zi and a few others going out to sea to fish. The money they brought with them was mostly depleted, with only some gold and silver jewelry remaining.

It's strange, not only Pingsheng but also Juanzi became close to Liang Zi. Every time Liang Zi returned from fishing, he would deliberately bring some rare items like seashells and sea anemones for Juanzi. Similarly, whenever Liang Zi went out to sea, Juanzi would go to the pier every day to watch the docked ships, hoping for Liang Zi to come back soon!

Tairen and Yudie had long noticed this and were considering giving their blessings to the two of them. However, no one could have expected that Liang Zi would encounter a sea disaster!

Liang Zi saw Da Linzi under TieMen Iron Gate Pass. Da Linzi had become much thinner recently. He used to be muscular and had trained in martial arts. Liangzi noticed his sunken eye sockets and protruding cheekbones, giving him the appearance of someone who hadn't eaten enough.

Liang Zi asked him, "Doesn't the Iron Gate administration provide meals for you? How come you look hungry?"

Liang Zi sighed and said, "Ah, these days, where can you find a proper meal to eat? Next year, I won't do it anymore!"

Da Linzi patted Liang Zi's shoulder and asked, "What's the matter?"

Liang Zi proceeded to explain his plan to travel to Dongguan by water route. Liang Zi scratched his head and said, "I can arrange for tickets for you guys. But, Liang Zi, you know how difficult it is, especially currently! So many people are waiting!"

Liang Zi understood what Da Linzi meant and quickly responded, "Of course, I know. That's why I came to you! If we succeed, my master Tairen said he would give you one-third of the Li family's wealth."

Da Linzi nodded and said, "It's a deal. There's a ship heading to Huludao in half a month, and I'll get you the tickets."

## 3

The half-month wait felt incredibly long. Liang Zi continued to go fishing at sea with Hu Zi, while Shi Tou stayed at home to harvest and process salt to support the family. Second Master Tairen was skilled with his hands and made many tools for Liang Zi and the others to use while fishing. The neighbors praised the usefulness of his tools. He also started growing soybeans and corn on a piece of barren land near the coast and planted some melons and vegetables in the backyard. The crops didn't grow well, resulting in a meager harvest. Unfortunately, the government still sent people to collect taxes, taking a whopping forty percent! This further strengthened Second Master Tairen's determination to venture to Dongguan and go beyond the pass.

In private, Yudie discussed with Tairen the idea of arranging Liang Zi and Juanzi's wedding before they left. Tairen said, "We shouldn't shortchange them; we should do it properly! But we don't have much to offer in terms of wedding items."

Yudie said, "Juanzi is just like my own sister, and Liang Zi is like a brother to me. They won't mind. I have a gold pendant and a jade bracelet; I'll give them to Juanzi. I also have two sets of clothes from when we got married; I can alter one set for Juanzi. As for Liang Zi's clothes, let Juanzi make them."

Tairen replied, "Then you take care of it."

Yudie secretly informed Juanzi about the plan, and Juanzi felt a bit embarrassed, blushing. On that very day, she started working on making her own red jacket and Liang Zi's long coat!

Eight days remained until their departure. Juanzi had finished making the clothes and was waiting for Liang Zi to return from his final fishing trip so they could proceed with the wedding. This time, Liang Zi and Hu Zi had been gone for five days and still hadn't returned. It wasn't until the sixth day that the fishing boat they were on returned, with Hu Zi onboard. However, Hu Zi came home in silence, looking dazed and lost. The fishing boat that returned with them was also severely damaged. They told Tairen that they encountered a typhoon, and Liang Zi's boat capsized. Hu Zi, being a good swimmer, was saved by the others, but Liang Zi was lost. Hu Zi said he wouldn't leave and would stay there. Juanzi, for two days, neither ate nor drank. She was disheveled, holding onto Liang Zi's wedding clothes, refusing to leave. On the day they were supposed to depart, she couldn't bear it anymore. In a dazed state, half asleep, she was carried by Shi Tou and Tairen onto the crowded double-decker wooden passenger ship.

The family that once had seven members suddenly found itself missing two. Juanzi lay in a daze on the crowded ship, deprived of fresh air, for two days, while Yudie comforted her. Shi Tou was not good with words, he simply watched. Over the past year, he had learned a few martial arts moves from Liang Zi and Hu Zi. He was eager to learn and hardworking, a reliable helper. Tairen admired his sincerity, and both Master and Mistress had already treated him like their own brother.

On the ship, meals were like a scramble. If you couldn't get there in time, there would be nothing to eat. Shi Tou was tall and skilled in martial arts, and he always led Master in the front to secure their portion. When the food was distributed, it would first go to Pingsheng, then Yudie, Juanzi, Master Tairen, and Shi Tou. There wasn't much variety—just leftovers porridge with pickled radish and sometimes a small amount of minced meat. They couldn't eat their fill, and Yudie no longer had milk. Little Master Pingsheng didn't like the leftovers porridge, but Juanzi would coax him to eat, and it always took great effort.

Due to serious overcrowding, the sailing ship had a very slow speed, barely reaching two knots per hour. Sometimes they encountered storms at sea and had to sail against the current. Although the ship had a square sail that could be adjusted for different wind directions, the large size and heavy body of the ship made it feel like they were going in circles at times. After sailing for about ten days, people on board started developing symptoms like corneal inflammation, angular cheilitis, and severe cases of bleeding gums and tooth loss. Some attributed these symptoms to a deficiency of vitamins. Yudie was one of the first to show symptoms, with pale complexion and dark brown gums. After another four or five days, the remaining four people also started experiencing these symptoms. Tairen had no idea how many more days it would take to reach land. After enduring three more days, the ship finally arrived at the first market town past Shanhai Pass in northeastern China — Huludao!

Huludao is the pearl of western Liaoning, located on a peninsula on the northwest side of the Liaodong Bay. Huludao was originally the name of an island, which was first mentioned in the "Complete Liaoning Chronicle". It was described as follows: "Forty miles from the coast, with half the mountain extending into the sea." It is surrounded by sea on three sides and connected to the land on one side, and because the part that extends into the sea is relatively small, while the area connected to the land is relatively large, it looks like a big gourd. Over time, people began to call it Huludao. In fact, according to local legend, it was really transformed from a treasure gourd.

Many people who disembarked from the ship decided to settle down right there. The nearby Tashan Mountain was a crucial strategic point for both domestic and foreign transportation throughout history. In the third year of the Xuande era of the Ming Dynasty (1428 AD), in order to defend against disturbances from Mongolian and other minority ethnic groups and strengthen the defense of Liaodong, Tashan City was established. At that time, there were three city gates: Yicang Gate in the east, Haining Gate in the south, and Anping Gate in the west. Later, in the forty-second year of the Jiajing era (1563 AD), Tashan City was rebuilt, with the city walls raised an additional three feet on the original foundation.

Arriving on this island, they finally witnessed the sight of greenery! Large tracts of land were covered in lush green carpets. They could finally see birds soaring in the sky and squirrels chasing each other in the trees! And there was a vast expanse of blue sky! No more scorched earth, no more tax collectors! Tairen took a deep breath of fresh air and said, "Is this the legendary paradise?!"

Shi Tou was astonished. He had grown up in the Li family and had never seen such a scenery before! Yudie was too weak to walk more than a few steps, and Shi Tou supported her. Juanzi held Pingsheng in her arms. The family had finally been liberated! They later went through several twists and turns and arrived in Yingkou, Liaoning, which was initially known as Mogouying and later as Yingkou. It was a famous waterfront trading port during the Qing Dynasty, where various ships anchored. The Li family eventually engaged in fishing as a secondary business, while growing vegetables and crops became their main occupation! Thus began the story of the Li family's Batiandi and their vegetable gardens.

# Part Two

## *The Li family settle in Mogouying*

## Chapter One

# The Li family settle down and establish the Batiandi

### 1

My grandfather gave me the contact information of his cousins. My grandfather was the youngest among all his cousins, who were my great uncles and great aunts, ranging from the first great uncle to the seventh great uncle and eight great aunts. However, either they had passed away or were too old to remember many of the past stories. I collected fragmented pieces and pieced them together into these stories.

They stayed in Huludao for a little over four months. Tairen had never made up his mind to settle there, to establish a new home. He always felt unsettled inside. Huludao was quite windy, and in the summer, especially in July and August, there were many days with heavy rainfall due to typhoon impacts. Tairen told his family that he still wanted to find a safe harbor as a permanent home. He asked everyone to rest for a while, especially since Yudie was severely sick and would need another one or two months to recover and be able to move.

Tairen was a Buddhist and often went to Ling Mountain Temple to listen to the abbot's preaching and sermons. He also accompanied the temple monks in performing acts of releasing animals and giving alms. He heard from one of the abbots at Ling Mountain Temple that he had traveled with his master to Mogouying in the past. It was over 400 miles away from Huludao, following the Liaodong Bay eastward. It was a port city without disasters or difficulties, with a pleasant climate. Upon returning home, Tairen lit incense and made a vow, firmly believing that Mogouying was the new home for the Li family branch!

On this day, the sun shone warmly on Tairen, while a gentle breeze brushed past him. The clouds in the sky floated gently. Tairen looked at the white clouds and observed Yudie basking in the sun, as well as Juanzi playing with the little master, Pingsheng. Juanzi was singing a song while Pingsheng chased after butterflies, filling the air with laughter. As Tairen gazed at this beautiful scene, he was reminded of the description in Tang dynasty Han Yu's "Sending Li Yuan Back to Pangu Preface": "With curved eyebrows and plump cheeks, a clear voice and a graceful figure, beautiful on the outside and wise within."

Juanzi truly lives up to these poetic lines! Tairen realized that Juanzi was indeed his capable assistant. She was intelligent and kind, with proper and graceful manners in her speech and behavior. It's no wonder that Liang Zi had such deep affection for her back then.

Tairen suddenly found himself missing Liang Zi, as well as Hu Zi, and his eldest brother and third brother who were still living in their ancestral home in PingDu, Shandong. Tairen, who rarely shed a tear, felt his eyes moisten! Suddenly, Shi Tou, in a rush, came over and said, "Master, you always talk about leaving. When are we going to go?"

Shi Tou was eager to see what their future new home would be like. Tairen snapped out of his thoughts and smiled, "Soon, you see, everything is moving in the right direction! May the Buddha bless us!"

They looked forward to a better tomorrow together.

After leaving Huludao, Tairen led his family through another half year of travel and finally arrived at Mogouying, now known as Yingkou.

Mogouying was the earliest developed port in the Kanto region, located at the lower reaches of the Daliao River and adjacent to the Bohai Sea, with a unique and advantageous geographic location. The inscription on the monument of Tianhou Palace and Xidamiao Temple during the reign of Emperor Yongzheng recorded that "Mogouying, a hub for county and river crossings, where numerous boats and ships gather, numbering in the thousands."

In the 11th year of Xianfeng (1861), British merchants conducted a survey of Yingkou and proposed to develop Mogouying as a port. Subsequently, the British established a trading port in Mogouying, and built docks and berths on the south bank of the Liao River for shipping and trade. On April 3rd of the same year, Mogouying officially opened as a port. Later, Japanese, Germans, Americans, and local merchants successively built docks along the river in Mogouying. Southern merchants and northern travelers also gathered here, making it the busiest port for shipping in the Kanto region. By the reign of Emperor Daoguang, Mogouying had become a well-known water transportation hub where large and small boats could dock.

The bustling scene of the docks immediately captivated Tairen and his entire family as soon as they arrived. There were numerous docks of varying sizes at the entrance of the Liao River. The largest ones included the British-owned Tongfu Dock and Dagudong Dock. There were also the Japanese-owned Sanjiazi Dock and Xiaosi Dock, as well as the German-owned Deshigu Dock. On the northern bank of the Liao River, there was the American-owned Meifu Dock, the Zhaoshang Bureau Dock acting as an agent for the government, and the Xiqichang Dock jointly operated by the government and foreigners.

There were all kinds of ships moored at the docks, with steam-powered ironclad ships generally used by foreigners and rented out to local merchants. Most local civilian ships were wooden sailboats, and as far as the eye could see, sailboats with white sails were preparing to set sail, with the triangular white sails making a "Hualala" sound in the sea breeze. There were neatly arranged large trough ships, cow ships, towing boats, and small sampans.

Ocean liners shipped large quantities of Northeastern specialty products such as coal, firewood, salt, soybean oil, grains, and beans every day, and brought in foreign goods such as cosmetics, Western medicine, daily necessities, and even opium. There were also food products such as soybeans and sorghum transported from upstream on the Liao River. Traders from various East Asian countries conducted trade here, and people of different cultures and languages met here, making this a vibrant and enticing treasure trove of multiculturalism!

Not far from the docks, there was a street called Xinshi Street, where numerous small shops selling various types of food were concentrated. There were shops selling fish and meat, fruits, vegetables, and daily necessities. At that time, there was a very famous market called Dong Market, and at the northern end of the market, there were the Hanyamaya Trading Company and Yamashita Trading Company, both operated by the Japanese.

Tairen and Shi Tou explored every corner of Mogouying and found a lush hillside location, which later became the famous Bada Field. With the help of their fellow Shandong villagers, Tairen and Shi Tou cut down trees from the surrounding area to use as beams and rafters. They used a makeshift brick kiln to fire the clay they dug out into bricks. They built four rows of single-story houses, with five rooms on the north side (three main rooms and two side rooms) and a porch not far from the northern side, which led to the Liao River. On the south side of the house, there were also five rooms (three main rooms, two side rooms), and a gatehouse. There were two main entrances on the east and west sides, each with a storage shed on either side. The houses formed a square courtyard, creating a "口" shape, with a central courtyard resembling the quadrangles of Beijing's royal residences. There was a side gate in each direction, and all the houses within the courtyard opened towards the courtyard. The family lived happily and harmoniously inside, enjoying their time together. This house gained a reputation in Mogouying.

During the construction of the house, Shi Tou worked diligently, doing the work of two people. He was simple-hearted and honest, never speaking and always working hard. Tairen and Yudie liked him for this. However, not long ago, the local authorities recruited patrol officers, and because Shi Tou had some martial arts skills, he became interested in joining. Tairen saw this and didn't stop him; instead, he encouraged and supported him. Before leaving, Shi Tou bowed and expressed his gratitude to his Tairen Uncle and Yudie Aunt. Now, Shi Tou had gained some status in the yamen (government office) compared to his time with the Li family. However, Shi Tou still often came back to visit them and would buy things for the family. Not long ago, he even got married, and the house was provided by Tairen and Yudie.

People still called Tairen "Second Uncle (Ye)", although no one knew why he was called that. Tairen, Yudie, and Juanzi knew about it. In their hometown of LiJiaGu in Pingdu, Shandong, Tairen's eldest brother and third brother were still there, but they had no idea how they were doing. Sending letters back home now took about a year to arrive, and many letters seemed to disappear without a trace. The whole family deeply missed their Li family brothers in their distant hometown in Shandong.

Over the years, Tairen never forgot to send a family letter to Pingdu, Shandong. After sixteen years, they finally received a reply. His eldest brother, Taihong, had passed away, and his son, Pingshui, became a county magistrate. Pinglu also took on responsibilities at home. The situation with disasters had improved over the years, and the occasional small calamities were no longer worth mentioning. Calculating the years, Pingshui should be around twenty-five now. He was married and had a son named Li Zhenting, who was seven years old. Surprisingly, the daughter of his third brother, Taihe, had married and moved to Hunan. She married a salt transporter, and their son was already fourteen years old. When Tairen received the family letter, tears flowed freely, and he hurriedly wrote a reply, informing his brother Taihe that everything was fine except for Yudie's poor health and her inability to bear children. Pingsheng, who was raised by Juanzi, was very close to her and called her Aunt Juanzi. Pingsheng was now fourteen years old, and they had a private school at home. Every day, a teacher would come to teach Pingsheng and a few other children how to read and write. He was already involved in the family's affairs. This year was the 28th year of the Daoguang era (1848).

## 2

Over the past decade, Tairen had been engaged in the salt transportation and seafood business. The geographical location of this area is excellent, with Mogouying relying on the Liaohe River pier and providing access to ports such as Yantai and Dengzhou along the Liaodong Bay. The shipping industry was flourishing at that time.

When Tairen first arrived in Mogouying, he knew the hardships of life and had to count every penny. After building the house, there was only a little savings left in the family, but fortunately, they had the house to rely on. The pier owner told him that if he rented the house to them as a tool warehouse, they would provide him with free boat rentals. Soon, Tairen discovered that most of the fishing families in Mogouying used their small fishing boats individually, which was not very efficient. Almost all the coastal fishermen were also involved in salt production, but they hadn't been combined into a large-scale industry. So Tairen sent Shi Tou to purchase salt and seafood, centralized those resources, and then used the rented boats to sell them along the Da Liao River to inland cities such as Panjin, Shengjing, Jilin, Inner Mongolia, and southern cities like Beijing, Shijiazhuang, and Shandong. This brought considerable profits and laid the foundation for the early-stage salt and seafood transportation business of the Li family. After a few years, the Li family owned their own cargo ships and reclaimed the houses that were previously rented as warehouses.

In recent years, the Qing Dynasty had initiated reforms in salt administration and governance, aiming to address corruption issues. However, corruption remained prevalent among officials at all levels, and the opium problem persisted. Increasing amounts of opium were being transported by British merchant ships, and recent years had also seen the emergence of heroin, a refined product of opium. Opium dens could be found everywhere in the county town, with emaciated opium addicts puffing clouds of smoke there. The situation was disheartening.

Tairen now employed two helpful assistants, a Shandong man named Wu Zhenshan and a local man named Guo Kangning. Wu Zhenshan was 35 years old. He became separated from his wife and children during their escape, when his son was only four years old at the time. He had been searching for his wife and children for nearly ten years, inquiring about their whereabouts everywhere, but there had been no trace of them. He said he was working here with Master Tairen because he believed that Tairen was a person capable of achieving great things, He wanted to earn money to find his wife and children. Guo Kangning had a family, including two young girls and a son. They all lived at the Li family's house, and Mrs. Guo was a sharp-tongued and fierce woman who worked in the Li family's kitchen. Guo Kangning became the Housekeeper of the Li family. All three of their children studied for free at the Li family's private school.

Tairen smoked dried tobacco with a long tobacco pipe. It was much colder here in winter than his hometown in Shandong. He would sit around a brazier on the heated kang bed. Northeastern rooms typically had a heated kang bed, and on top of it, there was an exquisitely crafted kang cabinet adorned with plum blossoms, orchids, bamboo, and chrysanthemum patterns. The kang cabinet was primarily used to store bedding for different seasons—folded during the day and taken out at night to be spread on the kang bed.

In the outer room, there was a hearth with added firewood. If the bellows were pumped, the fire would blaze and crackle, creating a vibrant flame. A large pot for boiling water was usually placed on the stove. The people from the firewood room would add firewood and cook meals at mealtime. Next to the hearth, there was a large water tank, and the water ladle was made from a hollowed-out gourd split into two halves.

In the main room, there was an octagonal table and chairs, all painted in red lacquer, used for family discussions. When it was time for the family to eat, they would go to the kitchen adjacent to the main room. Tairen's house had a connecting door that provided direct access, ensuring they wouldn't catch a cold during the winter.

The calligraphy, paintings, and ceramic ornaments in the house were Tairen's collection and his pride. There was always an ancestral hall, also known as the ancestral shrine, in the house, where the ancestral tablets were enshrined. Tairen would never allow Pingsheng to forget his roots and would often take him to pay respects at the ancestral shrine. Tairen believed in Buddhism, and the family's Buddhist shrine was always open. He would not forget to offer incense and recite scriptures every day. As for Juanzi, ever since she had a falling out with her family, she began devoutly believing in Buddhism. It was Tairen who introduced her to Buddhism, and she believed that having the opportunity to be associated with Tairen in this lifetime was the result of her past life's blessings.

The people from Northeast China had a tradition called "Mao-dong (cat winter)," but Tairen didn't have this habit. In the winter, he loved tinkering with small gadgets, making music boxes, fixing locks, repairing watches, and so on. He thought Pingsheng really resembled him in some ways! They both loved tinkering with small tools and trying out new things. In the past few days, Tairen had been contemplating developing one or two new ways to earn a living and support the family. He called Pingsheng into his room and asked him to sit down. Then he filled a small copper tobacco pipe and brought it close to the burning coals in the brazier. With a satisfying click of his mouth, he took a few puffs from the pipe, and the tobacco inside turned red.

He exhaled a puff of smoke and said to Pingsheng, "Pingsheng, you are almost eighteen now, all grown up! It's time for me to gradually pass on the family business to you. Your mother and I used to spoil you, but now that you has reached adulthood, I want to talk to you about the family's affairs."

Pingsheng liked managing the family business. He had been helping his father with the business since he was around ten years old. Pingsheng had a knack for calculations and was skilled for math and was good at keeping track of accounts. Tairen always told Yudie, "Look at our son, he's a born businessman."

Yudie said, "I still prefer our son to be an official, with a salary from the court, not having to worry about livelihood expenses."

Tairen would say, "You don't understand! If the times change, everything could go wrong! It's better to rely on our own business."

And so, Tairen and Yudie decided to entrust the family business to Pingsheng. Today, Tairen was going to discuss some important matters with Pingsheng regarding business and the impact of the imperial policies on family enterprises. He looked at Pingsheng with seriousness, took a puff of his tobacco, and said, "Sheng, do you know how our family makes money?"

Pingsheng replied earnestly, "Shipping?"

Tairen nodded and then shook his head, saying, "Shipping is just one aspect of our family business, but we need to have a broader perspective."

Tairen pondered for a moment and then continued speaking, "The salt policy of the court has changed, making it difficult to do business. Fortunately, we have found your uncle and third uncle's families. Your cousin, Pinghui, has married a salt transport official, so we can expand our business in the future, focusing more on the regions of Hunan, Jiangsu, and Zhejiang. However, the Li family cannot rely solely on salt and seafood. I'm thinking of clearing the wood on our northern land and cultivating crops and vegetables. We are sure to have a good harvest, and after all, people always make food their top priority!"

Pingsheng listened attentively and nodded. "I understand, Dad. You want to revive our family's traditional farming skills?"

Tairen continued, "Yes, Sheng, farming is our family's expertise. Our ancestors built wealth and status for our Li family through their farming skills and wisdom. With the changing policies of the imperial court and the instability of businesses nowadays, we need to diversify our operations and not rely solely on shipping and the salt trade. Farming is our traditional strength, and we must utilize this advantage to secure our family's livelihood and future. I hope you can inherit the wisdom and skills of farming and become a pillar of our family's business."

Next, Tairen discussed with Pingsheng many recent regulations regarding the salt policy of the imperial court, as well as important matters to consider when cultivating the land. This included how to coordinate with the government officials and how to handle corrupt officials.

Pingsheng looked at his father's serious expression and became nervous. His father had never talked to him so seriously before. He didn't spend much time with his father and was a little afraid of him because Tairen always asked him if he could do accounting. Pingsheng was closer to his mother Yudie. He sat quietly on the edge of the kang, listening and without interruption.

Tairen added, "Pingsheng, you're still young. I won't let you go into the restricted area alone. I'll send Wu Zhenshan to support you. He has been with me for a long time, and he is careful and capable. He can help you and let me rest assured. And if there are people causing trouble when opening new land and you need the help of the police station, go to your uncle Shi Tou. He is the leader of the patrol there now."

Tairen recalled his family's traditional occupation of farming. He took another puff of his tobacco and said, "In the future, I want to open a hardware store. I enjoy working with these tools. You will manage the farmland, and I will tinker with things I enjoy!"

Pingsheng listened attentively, feeling deeply his father's expectations and responsibilities. He responded solemnly, "Dad, I will strive to learn and carry on the knowledge and skills of farming. I am willing to take on this challenge and contribute my efforts to the prosperity and development of our family."

On that day, Pingsheng felt that his father had treated him like an adult. The way his father talked to him was different, he suddenly felt a heavy burden on his shoulders!

Tairen not only asked Wu Zhenshan to help Pingsheng with the clearing work but also assigned the head butler Guo Kangning to assist Pingsheng. Over the next six months, they cleared a large area of barren land. Transforming this type of ground into arable fields would take a long time because the trees that were cut down still had their roots, and without chemicals, it was almost impossible for Pingsheng to accomplish. However, Pingsheng marked all the places with tree roots and, in addition to digging them up one by one, he also burned them directly with fire. Tairen came up with an idea for Pingsheng to plant mushrooms in the areas with tree roots. This method proved to be very effective; the decomposing tree roots gradually became nutrients for the mushrooms. The Tairen family could sell the mushrooms to sustain their livelihood, and after several years, the barren land was completely transformed into farmland. Tairen proudly declared that his family were pioneers who had developed 80 mu* of new farmland, which came to be known as "BaTian" or "Eight Fields." Later, people in the surrounding areas also started referring to it as such, making it the earliest "Batiandi."

* Approximately 13 acres or 5 hectares.

# Chapter Two

## Pingsheng meets Jingying (Crystal); a grand wedding in the first year of the Xianfeng Emperor

### 1

From the time he was seven years old, Pingsheng had studied at the private school in his home. The teacher, Mr. Huang Yongxiang, was a scholar who had not passed the imperial examinations, but he had extensive knowledge and taught seriously, demanding strictness from his students. He made his students study new books and recite them a hundred times every day. The number of students in the school had increased from the initial five to over twenty during the previous two years.

When Pingsheng was thirteen years old, Lu Shunqi, a dock owner, sent his daughter Jingying (Crystal) to the private school at Pingsheng's home. Jingying was two years younger than Pingsheng. Previously, girls in her family were not allowed to leave their homes, so Jingying had studied at home with a scholar. In recent years, some wealthy households had begun to send their daughters to private schools to study. Lu Shunqi was a relatively open-minded person, so he sent his daughter to the Li family's private school to broaden her horizons.

Jingying was fair-skinned and had a pair of big eyes that twinkled as though they could speak. Her cherry lips were painted red, and her face was lightly powdered, making her look extremely charming. What was more important was that she was smart, gentle, and poised. Whenever Pingsheng saw her, his heart would race as if he were holding a small rabbit in his arms.

Pingsheng had previously been a private school student who was unparalleled in his knowledge, had a photographic memory ,and wrote long articles. When Jingying was added, they became a perfect match! Jingying had beautiful handwriting and enjoyed discussing school matters and memorizing books with Pingsheng.

On the evening of the Dragon Boat Festival, after watching the play "Legend of the White Snake," Pingsheng held Jingying's hand in the darkness. Jingying hesitated and then withdrew her hand. However, Pingsheng felt keenly that Jingying was both eager and hesitant. So he invited Jingying to try some Xiong Huang wine at his home and joked, "In the story of the 'Legend of the White Snake,' Bai Suzhen transformed after drinking Xiong Huang wine. I wonder what it would look like if Jingying, who is even more beautiful than Bai Niangzi, transformed into her true form after drinking it?"

Jingying said, "My father will send someone to pick me up soon. We need to hurry!" Taking advantage of the darkness, Pingsheng held hands with Jingying again. This time, Jingying also held Pingsheng's hand tightly. Pingsheng's hand was thick and warm, while Jingying's hand was small and gentle. The two hands grasped tighter and tighter.

Instead of going to the Li family's kitchen with many people to drink, the two went to a small hill in the south of the city. Standing on the dirt slope, Pingsheng was a little excited. He pointed to the sky and said, "Jingying, my heart is as bright and transparent as this moon, but it shines for you." Jingying pursed her lips, lowered her head, and remained silent, but her heart was filled with joy. She ignored the pain, ruthlessly pulled out a strand of hair, opened Pingsheng's hand, and placed it in his palm. Jingying said, "I don't have the moon to describe myself, my hair is me. You have to keep it safe!"

Pingsheng tightly held the hair in his hand and pulled Jingying towards him with the other hand, and the two hugged each other.

After finishing his studies at his family's private school, Pingsheng spent some time working in the Li family's vegetable garden. But every day when he returned home, he couldn't stop thinking about Jingying. Two years went by quickly, and Jingying also finished her studies at the private school. Whenever Pingsheng went to the school and couldn't find Jingying, he felt a bit disappointed.

Recently, attentive Yudie noticed that her son had something on his mind, so she asked Pingsheng privately if he was interested in

Lu family's daughter. In fact, over the past year, several matchmakers had come, but neither Tairen nor Yudie had made up their minds. Yudie said to Pingsheng, "If the second daughter of the Lu family is good, then I will find someone to arrange a marriage for you."

Pingsheng immediately said, "Other than Lu Jingying, I won't marry anyone." The next day, Yudie discussed the matter with her husband. Since Tairen favored Pingsheng, there was no objection. Moreover, Tairen had seen Lu Shunqi's daughter in school before and had a good impression of her. Coincidentally, Lu Shunqi had visited the Li family recently for some small talk, and Tairen discussed calligraphy and painting with him. As luck would have it, Lu Shunqi came to the Li family again today and brought Jingying with him. Jingying said she came to see Mr. Huang, so Tairen had someone call Mr. Huang to come to the South Courtyard.

Yudie complimented Jingying on her tasteful clothes and beautiful appearance. Jingying felt embarrassed and fidgeted with her handkerchief, not saying a word. Tairen took Mr. Lu to admire his precious belongings. At that moment, Mr. Huang Yongxiang arrived, and Pingsheng and Jingying greeted them. Tairen gave Huang Yongxiang a reward, and Mr. Huang thanked him and went back to teaching. Before leaving, Mr. Lu received a Qingzhou black mountain red silk inkstone from Tairen as a gift. Although Lu Shunqi did not have much education, he was a person who loved Buddhism and calligraphy very much. His calligraphy was famous in the area, and even the magistrate had asked him for a painting. He loved the red silk inkstone so much that he stroked his beard and asked Tairen with a smile, "This gift is too precious, what can I exchange for it?"

Pingsheng pulled his father's sleeve and Tairen laughed, saying, "Then promise to give Jingying to Pingsheng as my daughter-in-law."

To his surprise, Mr. Lu readily agreed and laughed, "Our two families will join hands in this alliance!"

Then it became Yudie's matter. Yudie asked Mrs. Guo for help, and Mrs. Guo found the most famous matchmaker in the area to arrange the marriage between the two families. They compared the birth dates, exchanged horoscopes, and waited for the wedding day.

It was then January 1850, the thirtieth year of the Daoguang Emperor's reign, and he had just passed away, so no red wedding ceremonies were allowed. It was not until the new Emperor Xianfeng ascended the throne the following year that Pingsheng and Jingying had their wedding ceremony.

## 2

In the first year of the Xianfeng Emperor's reign (1850), Pingsheng, who was eighteen years old by traditional reckoning, married Jingying.

During the wedding, Tairen and Yudie chose an auspicious date for the couple, which was the eighth day of the eighth month. Guo Kangning and the staff prepared a new bed, with fresh bedding adorned with a dragon and phoenix pattern. The bed was filled with peanuts, dates, longan fruits, lotus seeds, and more, symbolizing the wish for the newlyweds to have children early. The Li family also paid a formal visit to the Lu family, signifying the official engagement. After the ceremony, Jing Ying's dowry was sent to the groom's house by carriage. The Lu family was wealthy, owning half of the warehouses at the wharf. The dowry was complete, including a ruler with pure gold and silver lettering, symbolizing vast fertile land; various types of shoes, symbolizing a lifelong companionship; and sparkling silver-plated spittoons, symbolizing a household filled with descendants. There were also countless items of clothing and accessories.

On the wedding day, before dawn, Jingying got up and had a full-fortune woman to help her shave her face, comb her hair, draw her eyebrows, apply rouge, and paint her lips. This full-fortune woman used a shiny silver comb while shouting: "Combing your hair until a long and prosperous life, combing your hair until offspring fills the land, combing your hair until your white hair reaches your eyebrows, combing your hair until your family line is long-lasting."

In the Li family, there was also a similar ceremony for Pingsheng. Tairen had instructed Guo Kangning to invite the full-fortune woman to the house the night before. In the Qing Dynasty, men also braided their hair. The next morning, Pingsheng anxiously waited for the moment while combing his hair. However, they had to wait until the auspicious time at dusk for the "wedding ceremony" of the couple to take place. By this time, the Li family compound was shining with red decorations both inside and outside, with red lanterns hanging high in the gateways and halls and a large red "Double Happiness" sign pasted on the doorpost and windows of the new house in the east courtyard. The red color enhanced the festive and auspicious atmosphere. As the sun was about to set, the evening glow reddened the western sky, and it was getting closer to dusk.

As the sun began to set, the western sky was painted with the hues of the evening glow. The hour was nearing dusk. Finally, the sound of suona (a traditional Chinese wind instrument) echoed through the streets, announcing the arrival of the bridal procession! An eight-person sedan chair covered with a red auspicious carpet arrived at the doorstep, and celebratory firecrackers were set off! In those times, only the bride and high-ranking officials of the third rank or above were allowed to ride in such a grand sedan chair.

When the bridal sedan chair descended, the bride, Jingying, alighted from it. The sedan chair's door was facing the direction of the auspicious deity. Jingying carried a jar filled with golden and silver rice, symbolizing wealth and abundance. She wore a red embroidered jacket, red trousers, and embroidered floral shoes adorned with peony patterns. Her headdress was a red embroidered cap with silk tassels that swayed elegantly with each step. Bridesmaid Xiao Cui held a red umbrella over Jingying, symbolizing the blossoming of branches and leaves and bringing prosperity to the family. Jingying had to step over the fire basin in the courtyard, signifying warding off evil spirits and also symbolizing a future life filled with prosperity and happiness for the newlywed couple.

Then Jingying crossed the threshold, paid homage to heaven and ancestors. When the auspicious time arrived, the groom and bride, holding a red embroidered ball, were sent into the bridal chamber.

A red couplet was pasted on the door frame of the bridal chamber, with the top line reading "The wind is harmonious, and the sun is bright, peaches and plums are fragrant," and the bottom-line reading "Pearls meet, birds mate for life," and the horizontal scroll read "Companions for a thousand years."

The red bedding embroidered with phoenixes was spread on the new bed, and dragon and phoenix-shaped mosquito nets were hung on both sides of the bed. The doors, windows, boxes, cabinets, and tables were all covered with large red characters of joy, and the festive atmosphere in the room made Pingsheng extremely excited.

The red candles illuminated the room, giving it a crimson hue. Pingsheng held a small delicate pole with red tassels in his hand. His heart was pounding as he slowly walked towards his bride, who was veiled in a red cover, dressed in a red jacket, red trousers, and red shoes. He took a deep breath, gathered his courage, and lifted Jingying's veil. It was revealed that:

Jingying's (Crystal) clear pupils shining bright,
Wearing a red cotton coat so tight,
Rosy-Red make-up on her face,
Smelling sweet, with every pace.
She walks with grace, so gentle and meek,
Beauty enhancing, never bleak,
Like peach blossoms in the spring,
In full bloom, beauty and charming.
In an instant, as the veil was lifted,
A powdery scent wafted, so sweet and gifted.
Crystal's face blushed red,
Pouting lips, eyes closed, in ecstasy, she led.
Pingsheng lifted his wife up high.
He placed his lips upon hers, a passionate sigh.
On a bed draped in red satin at night,
Crystal spoke, fearless, to her husband, in sight,
"Sheng, I want to bear you three children."
Sheng replied, "Three aren't enough, let's have five then."

And so, as planned, Crystal bore five children.

The next morning, Jingying went to the main hall to pay respects and offer tea to her father-in-law, Tairen, and her mother-in-law, Yudie. Tairen and Yudie sat upright, and Jingying held a tea cup with both hands, raising it above her head while kneeling on one leg. She said, "Father, Mother, please have some tea!"

Tairen accepted the teacup first, followed by Yudie, taking a sip to signify their acceptance of their new daughter-in-law. Then, Yudie handed a red envelope to Jingying, who expressed her gratitude, officially becoming a daughter-in-law of the Li family. From that day on, everyone in the Li family addressed Jingying as "Madam."

## 3

Since the marriage with Jingying, the Li family began to address Tairen as the head of the family and called him "Lao Ye". He mainly ran the hardware store business and helped Pingsheng with the salt business in Haiyan. However, it was a difficult time during the Taiping Heavenly Kingdom, with war and chaos making transportation challenging, especially in the Grand Canal section, where anti-Qing rebels and the Yihetuan (Boxers) would gather to block the waterways and loot goods. Therefore, the salt business was not doing well.

In addition, during the reign of Emperor Xianfeng, the Eight Banners nobility in the Guannei region began occupying the farmlands of the peasants, making their lives even harder. The wealthy landlords used their money and power to buy up small plots of land, resulting in excessive land concentration. Tairen and Pingsheng insisted on developing new farmland without encroaching on the peasants' land. With the help of Wu Zhenshan, they recruited many laborers and opened a piece of good land. The Li family's farmland grew to more than double what was known in the past as Ba Tian, and since "Ba Tian Di" had already become a well-known name, the name continued to be used.

At that time, the court proposed a land consolidation system and increased taxation. Still, for the past two years, the weather had been favorable, and there was an increase in tenant farmers. The Li family treated their tenants well, and despite the increase in their land holdings, their additional revenue was offset by Tairen's insistence on keeping the rent for the tenants unchanged for ten years, so their annual income did not double. There were four major landlords in Mogouying, and the Li family was the largest. Despite the increase in taxes, the Li family's rents remained the same, giving them a good reputation, and the tenants were willing to rent land from them. In addition, Mogouying was on the frontier, and the government had to rely on the Li family's tax revenue to pay its expenses. This created a balance, and everyone was at peace.

More than six months had passed since Jingying entered the Li family. Every day she followed her mother-in-law and Juanzi to learn how to manage household affairs and sometimes even how to manage accounts from Pingsheng. Fortunately, Jingying also did these things often in her own home, and she was smart and eager to learn. She quickly became familiar with these tasks. During the day, Pingsheng was either in the vegetable garden or in the accounting room with the head butler, Guo Kangning, and rarely at home. The newlyweds were inseparable. Jingying would go to the fields to see Pingsheng. She would ride her bike to the Batiandi vegetable garden three miles away from Mogouying to see Pingsheng. It was quite unusual for a woman to ride a bicycle in Mogouying.

The Batiandi vegetable garden became the main industry of the Li family. In the summer, several cargo ships full of fresh vegetables and fruits were sent to the markets in nearby towns every day. When Jingying arrived at the field, she would put down her bike and look at the wheat fields. It was the golden autumn season, and the fields were golden. That was the ripe wheat. The autumn wind blew, and the heavy wheat ears danced in the breeze. It was beautiful! Soybeans and corn were also at the harvesting season, and many tenants were busy harvesting. After harvesting, the threshing and winnowing would take place beside the wheat fields, followed by loading the bags into the granary and waiting for a good price to sell! Jingying learned all the steps involved in this process. At this moment, Pingsheng was wearing a large bamboo hat and holding a wheat ear, talking to Zhenshan. Jingying went over, and it turned out that they were discussing the wheat in this field that was going to be harvested in the next day or two because it looked like there would be heavy rain.

When Pingsheng saw his wife, he turned around and half-blamed and half-flirted, "Didn't I tell you not to come? How come you're here again? Don't let your mother-in-law say anything about you. She doesn't like women running around outside."

Jingying hooked her arm around Pingsheng's arm and said with a smile, "Doesn't someone miss you?" Zhenshan looked at them and smiled without saying a word.

On that day, Jingying returned home and as soon as she entered, Xiao Cui anxiously told her, "Miss, you need to go to Lao Ye and Mistress's room. They're looking for you."

Jingying quickly took off her pants and changed into the dress that she wore at home and went to the master's room. Lao Ye Tairen and Mistress Yudie were talking, while the maid Juanzi was cleaning the hall.

Jingying timidly asked, "Father, Mother, did you look for me?"

Tairen had a dark face, while Yudie said, "Lao Ye heard that you rode your bike to the vegetable garden, and he's afraid that people will gossip about it, so I'm reminding you not to do it again in the future!"

Jingying was a bit unhappy, but she didn't say anything. Juanzi spoke up for her and said, "Er Ye, let her go!"

She still couldn't change her habit of calling Tairen Lao Ye because many people in the house still addressed him that way. Juanzi continued, "Just don't ride your bike in the future. Let Xiao Cui follow you, and the family can provide a carriage. How about that?"

Jingying saw that Tairen was considering it, so she said, "How about I deliver the food to Pingsheng? I'll make sure he eats well."

Tairen didn't want to refuse Juanzi's face, so he said, "Okay, but don't ride your bike alone. It attracts gossip."

Jingying nodded and agreed not to ride her bike anymore.

I think my ancestors were very feudal. Women were best suited for staying at home, taking care of their husbands and children, doing housework and embroidery, and that made them good daughters-in-law. However, in that era, most women did indeed do so, especially Han women who had bound feet. Jingying had her feet unbound when she was five or six years old and had argued with her mother about it, and so it turned out she had a pair of big feet.

Later, the family had a carriage, and Jingying began to deliver food to Pingsheng in the fields every day. She persisted for two years. The car the family provided was not like today's cars, but a covered horse-drawn carriage with a canopy. As the carriage traveled along the dirt road, the swirling dust behind it resembled a soaring yellow dragon, obscuring any signs of human presence for a while. Fortunately, Jingying and Xiao Cui were inside the carriage shed, shielded from the discomfort. However, the person driving the carriage did not have such a pleasant experience.

## 4

In the early autumn of the third year of the Xianfeng era, Jingying had been feeling unwell for some time and hadn't been going to the fields on certain days. After a busy day in the fields, Pingsheng returned to the eastern courtyard. Juanzi was in the yard, airing and sunning the quilts. Over the years, Er Ye had tried to arrange a good marriage for her, but she said the bond had been broken, and her heart had gone with Liang Zi. She had no intention of marrying anyone anymore. She now lived in a side room of Er Ye (Second Master) and Er Nai's (Second Madam) residence, ready to serve them at any time. She was devoutly Buddhist, reciting scriptures daily. Firstly, she prayed for the Buddha's blessings on the prosperity of the Li family for generations to come, and secondly, she sought the Buddha's salvation to guide her to the Pure Land in the afterlife.

The kitchen at home was already filled with the scent of cooking, and Guo's wife saw Pingsheng enter the courtyard and quickly urged the kitchen staff to work faster. Turning back to Pingsheng, she shouted, "Young Master, the food will be ready soon!"

Pingsheng greeted Aunt Juanzi and Guo's wife, then pushed open the door. Inside, he saw Jingying's maid Xiao Cui holding a spittoon while Jingying was retching. Pingsheng quickly walked over and asked what was wrong. Xiao Cui mischievously smiled and said, "Young Master, don't you know? Madam is pregnant!"

Jingying felt somewhat better and breathed a sigh of relief. She lightly patted Xiao Cui's shoulder and said, "You silly girl, only you understand!"

This great news gave the Li family reason to celebrate for three days. Since Pingsheng was born, no one had been added to the Li family. Upon hearing the news, Tairen walked in circles in the courtyard of his own house and immediately went to the pier to tell his in-laws. The two families discussed and agreed that the Li family would host a grand banquet to celebrate.

Tairen asked Pingsheng to make a list. Guo Kangning sent invitations to prestigious families in Mogouying who had no affiliation with the government, as well as friends who had previously traveled with them in the Northeast and neighbors. The Li family hired four well-known chefs from De Xin Restaurant, along with their personal cook, Laiwang, making a total of five chefs. Additionally, they hired several temporary helpers. They constructed four stoves in the courtyard and borrowed a bellows. They arranged more than a hundred tables, extending all the way to Xinshi Street near the dock. Each table had four plates and eight bowls. The men drank from big bowls and talked loudly, congratulating the Li family on the forthcoming addition to their family. Tairen and Mr. Lu greeted the guests, while the women dined in the Li family's courtyard, with Mrs. Guo as the hostess. Yudie wasn't feeling well, so she ate in the small kitchen inside the house, where Juanzi looked after her. She was happy and even had a few glasses of wine even though she had a low tolerance of alcohol. Jingying couldn't drink alcohol, and Mrs. Guo prevented her from doing so. She could handle one jin of white wine. Mrs. Lu welcomed guests into the courtyard. Mr. Lu's wife was a competent woman. Her family owned around a third of the dock warehouses, and most of the ships that came in and out of the dock had to store goods in her family's warehouses, including the Li family's ships, which were frequently managed by the Lu family.

This was a significant occasion for Mogouying, and almost all its prominent figures were in attendance. This was all thanks to Guo Kangning, who had been assisting Tairen and Pingsheng with various matters both inside and outside the house for many years, honing his skills in dealing with people from all walks of life. Earlier, Tairen had sent Guo Kangning to inform the local magistrate through invitations and requested the assistance of the patrol officers in maintaining order. Now, Shi Tou had become the head of the patrol officers, assisting the county magistrate in handling cases with great proficiency. He also had a son now, and upon hearing the good news about Pingsheng, he had made a special trip back home a few days ago. He personally brought a congratulatory gift and extended his wishes to Pingsheng in advance, addressing him as his nephew.

In the summer of the fourth year of the Xianfeng reign (1854), Jingying gave birth to a daughter and named her Wenya. Four years later, in the twelfth lunar month of the eighth year of Xianfeng (1858), Li Wentian, the first grandson of Tairen from the Li family, was born in Mogouying. Over the next decade, during the reign of Tongzhi (1861–1875), the Li family's vegetable garden became famous far and wide, offsetting the difficulties in shipping. These were tumultuous years filled with crises and changes, as the Taiping Rebellion grew increasingly fierce. A ship carrying salt was looted by the Taiping peasant army in the south. Although the Li family paid tolls and protection fees to the local officials every year, it was all in vain. The officials were unable to resist the Taiping army. Recently, there was a Hunan army, but they suffered repeated defeats.

Wu Zhenshan went to Beijing to transport seafood, but the goods never returned. He said that the Xianfeng Emperor had encouraged the army to fight against foreign invaders in the Second Opium War. They shouted the slogan "Support the Qing, exterminate the foreigners," and claimed to be invulnerable to knives and guns. However, they fell in droves when facing the artillery of the Anglo-French coalition forces, who took Beijing and burned the Summer Palace.

With the country in turmoil, after several unsuccessful shipments, the Li family's salt business came to a halt. Pingsheng told his father that his father's expedition to the northeast was the most magnificent feat of his time. The situation had become unstable in the north and south, and everyone lived in fear and anxiety. Compared to that, the situation outside the Great Wall was much more stable. Over the past decade, Pingsheng had grown from a teenager to a tall and sturdy man, with thick eyebrows, big eyes, a square face, and a deep voice. In recent years, he had also managed the vegetable garden with precision. Jingying had also been very fertile, giving birth to three more little masters in succession: Li Wendi , Li Wenshan, and Li Wenchuan. Li Wenchuan was born in the eighth year of Tongzhi (1869). Thus, a branch of the Li family from Pingdu, Shandong, became prosperous and developed in Mogouying (Yingkou), Liaoning!

## Chapter Three

# Staying together and parting with regret: the souls of Tairen and Juanzi

### 1

In the 13th year of the Tongzhi reign (1874), Tairen's eldest grandson Wentian went to study in the United States for five years. Later, he heard that the children sent out during the Westernization Movement were being called back, and Tairen looked forward to his grandson's return every day. But Wentian wrote a letter saying that he was not coming back and that his host family had helped him with the formalities to continue his studies. That year was also the first year of Emperor Guangxu's reign, and the summer was very hot. Yudie suffered from heatstroke and then pneumonia and she passed away in less than a month.

Yudie's passing left Tairen feeling like half of his life was missing. He experienced a fear he had never felt before, and he was afraid to enter his own bedroom. As soon as his head touched the pillow made by his late companion, he would start dreaming. In his dreams, he would see Yudie walking in front of him like a young girl. Looking at the arrangements in the house, Yudie's belongings, and all the good things his companion had done, each one flashed through his mind. The bickering between the two and the words of concern from Yudie echoed in his ears. He plastered Yudie's portrait everywhere and would get lost in a daze whenever he saw it.

Seeing that Tairen was grieving excessively, Juanzi tried various ways to prepare dishes that he liked. However, Tairen said he had no appetite. Juanzi then suggested, "How about we go out for a trip and relax?"

At the age of seventy, Tairen had never ventured outside the Yingkou area since moving to the region. However, Juanzi's suggestion sparked some ideas in his mind. So, Juanzi made arrangements, and Tairen and she embarked on a trip to the city of Shengjing (now known as Shenyang). Accompanying them were Tairen's son, Pingsheng, and his grandson, Li Wenshan.

The population here was much larger than that of Yingkou, and it was bustling with traffic. There were many people riding bicycles here, and the earliest three-wheeled motor vehicles were running faster than horse-drawn carriages. Many people pulled rickshaws in the old city, and going out was also convenient. The streets were all in a cross shape, with the imperial palace in the center of the cross-shaped avenue. Tairen looked at the solemn and magnificent palace with rows of glazed tiles.

The most eye-catching were two big gates, Wende Fang and Wugong Fang, followed by the Meridian Gate, and then the Great Qing Gate written in Manchu. There were guards there. But when there were cars and people coming and going, you could see the magnificent Hall of Supreme Harmony (literally "Golden Luanyuan Hall") inside. Now the Qing Dynasty has its capital in Beijing, and Shengjing is only a palace. During the Tiancong reign, Shengjing City had only one wall, also known as the inner city. In the nineteenth year of the Kangxi reign, a second earthen wall was built around Shengjing, which was 16 kilometers in circumference, and it was called the border wall. Eight border gates were also established. There were also four tower temples built on the four sides of Shengjing, each with a large Buddha inside. The Yongguang Temple was in the east, the Yanshou Temple was in the west, the Guangci Temple was in the south, and the Falun Temple was in the north. The four tower temples symbolized the four great vajras guarding the four directions, protecting the country and the people, and ensuring "no calamities or disasters for the nation" and "Five blessings come together."

Tairen's main purpose for this visit was not primarily to see the Imperial Palace. He came to conduct an on-site investigation of the hardware stores in the area. He had opened a hardware store in Yingkou, initially managing it himself, but later he shared the responsibilities with Pingsheng. Currently, Pingsheng was busy taking care of the vegetable garden and couldn't handle the workload alone. In recent years, Tairen discovered that his grandson, Wenshan, was a mechanical genius. He wanted to nurture and train him well, with the intention of having him inherit the family hardware business in the future.

They stayed at an inn next to the Imperial Palace. For three consecutive days, they would walk along Hanlin Road, pass through Tianshuijing Hutong, and turn onto Tianjing Street, which led them to a market street. There, they found the largest hardware trading firm in Shengjing. The owner of the firm was surnamed Qian, of medium build, fair complexion, and slightly hunched posture. They exchanged greetings and bows, and then took their seats to enjoy tea. Pingsheng handed Mr. Qian a cigarette, a rare foreign novelty. It was a gift from an English merchant at the dock, and there were only ten of them. Pingsheng also used the Western-style lighter he had repaired himself to light Mr. Qian's cigarette. Speaking of this lighter, it was obtained from a British merchant who visited their hardware store in Mogouying. His camera was broken, and Tairen and Pingsheng worked on it for half a month to help repair it. The British gentleman was very pleased and said, "My lighter is also broken. If you can fix it, I'll give it to you as a gift, along with ten cigarettes that Pingsheng has never seen before."

And so, Pingsheng acquired these foreign novelties. Qian was very interested in lighter and cigarettes, and suddenly developed a good impression of this grandfather, father, and grandson. After hearing them talk, he realized they were all well-educated, especially Wenshan, who had seen the world and fallen in love with the hardware industry.

Tairen felt that he had someone to carry on his legacy. This trip also brought another gain as they visited the famous "Eastern Ruhr" industrial zone in the western outskirts. The "Eastern Ruhr" truly lived up to its reputation, with factory buildings standing side by side, densely interconnected, stretching all the way to the outskirts of Shengjing. Mr. Qian's small-scale hardware stamping and processing machine factory was among them, and his workshop had indeed taken on a bit of industrialization! Wentian and the others placed orders for several machines with Mr. Qian and also signed contracts for the processing of the machines upon delivery. They also visited the Fengtian Machinery Bureau and gained a lot of knowledge from the experience. Later on, a branch of the Li family's hardware store was opened in Shengjing.

## 2

As they were about to return home, Juanzi noticed that the soles of Tairen's shoes were frayed. For over twenty years, Juanzi had personally made a pair of shoes for Tairen every year. Tairen had grown accustomed to wearing shoes made by Juanzi. Shoes made by others didn't fit well and were uncomfortable. Juanzi made paste by herself, then glued together the leftover scraps of fabric from making clothes layer by layer, brushed them onto the panel to dry, cut them into the shape of shoes, and finally sewed the soles onto them. Sewing the soles was a labor-intensive task, involving thousands of stitches, one by one. Juanzi would weave the shoe soles herself, carefully selecting high-quality hemp and hand-twisting it into a rope. In recent years, her eyesight had deteriorated, making it difficult for her to weave the shoe soles by touch, but she never failed to make a new pair of shoes for Er Ye (Tairen, second master) each year.

On Tairen's 80th birthday, he gathered his children and grandchildren in the ancestral hall to pay respects to their ancestors. Now, he had a son, four grandsons, and two great-grandsons. He could be considered the contented patriarch of a happy and complete family. The Li family's branch, led by Tairen's ventures in the Northeast, had flourished once again! Tairen felt that he had lived up to the expectations of his ancestors!

Beside the memorial tablet of Li Hu Yudie, there was Juanzi's spirit tablet, named Li YuJuan, taking the character "Yu" from Yudie's name. Two years earlier, Juanzi had fallen ill, and before her passing, she expressed her innermost thoughts to Tairen. As he held Juanzi in his arms, she softly said, "Er Ye, don't let my soul wander aimlessly after I die. In truth, all these years when I said I didn't want to marry, it was all excuses because of Liang Zi. My heart has belonged to you for over fifty years. I don't care if I'm your mistress. Even if I marry you as a concubine, I am willing to do so. It is you who taught me how to live and face setbacks with unwavering determination."

Tairen choked with emotion upon hearing her words. Indeed, the human heart was made of flesh. Over the years, Juanzi had already done everything a wife could do. She had a kind heart, was efficient in her work, and had become Tairen's reliance.

Two days later, Pingsheng organized a simple wedding for Tairen and Aunt Juanzi. It was still a bit chilly that day, and it was already the Qingming Festival, but there was still a layer of hard, crunchy white snow covering the ground, over the tender shoots of grass that had just emerged. When people stepped on it, it made a pleasant "crunching" sound. There was a gentle breeze that day, and it was a truly comfortable feeling. Tairen only invited some of his old neighbors and friends of the same generation to celebrate. Juanzi was supported by her grandsons Wentian and Wendi , and she greeted everyone with a smile on her face. She looked beautiful that day, beaming with joy.

A few days later, Juanzi passed away peacefully with a smile on her face in Tairen's embrace. Her departure was very peaceful.

After the funeral, Tairen locked himself in his room for a day or two, showing no interest in food or drink. No matter who tried to persuade him, it was to no avail. He wrote numerous lines, with the most prominent being Su Shi's "Song of the River City":

> Ten years of life and death, a boundless expanse,
> Unforgettable, thoughts persist and dance.

On the third day, Tairen emerged from his room, dressed very neatly and even shaved his beard. He leaned on a cane and looked dignified. He asked Pingsheng to arrange for a middleman to draw up his will. In the will, he stated that his eldest grandson, Wentian, should study industrialization in the United States during the Yangwu Movement, work at Mobil Oil upon his return. In last year he had already built him a courtyard with five large gates. Tairen privately told him not to take anything else from the family.

For his second grandson, Wendi, who had just married at the age of seventeen, he left some gold, silver, and valuables. He also entrusted Wendi with the struggling shipping business because of his business acumen. Tairen believed that Wendi could revive the salt and shipping business. As for Wenshan, who was only thirteen and a mechanical genius, Tairen had already established a small-scale hardware store for him. He would inherit 80% of the business. The remaining 20% was designated for the youngest grandson, Wenchuan, along with the vegetable garden. After writing the will, Tairen stamped it with his personal seal and pressed his handprint as well. He said to Pingsheng, "It's settled. After my death, no one should fight over the family property."

After settling his affairs, Tairen expressed his desire to return to his ancestral hometown, LiJiaGu in Pingdu, Shandong. This posed a challenge for Pingsheng, as the southern region was currently chaotic, and it wasn't suitable for travel, especially considering Tairen's age of over eighty. Seeing Pingsheng's lack of enthusiasm, Tairen became a little upset and insisted that they wait for the situation to improve before going back. Pingsheng and Jingying coaxed him, assuring him that they would definitely take him back when the situation stabilized. Tairen responded, "As long as I'm alive, I'll be waiting."

Actually, my great-great-great-great-grandfather did not live to see that day. He passed away in the spring of 1890, during the 16th year of the Guangxu reign. Before he passed, he expressed his wish to have his bones buried in his ancestral homeland in Shandong. However, my great-great-great-great grandfather's wish was not fulfilled by my paternal great-great-great grandfather, Pingsheng, and maternal great-great-great grandmother, Jingying, as the Qing Dynasty was embroiled in the Boxer Rebellion at that time. It seemed that the Emperor was confused and declared war against the eleven countries that had established diplomatic relations with the Qing Dynasty.

As a result, those powerful nations formed the Eight-Nation Alliance and invaded Beijing, occupying the city. They looted the treasures from the Imperial Palace and set fire to the Summer Palace, reducing it to ashes and ruins, destroying its beauty. Subsequently, the Emperor and the Empress Dowager sought refuge in Xi'an. Pingsheng said that it was not suitable to travel during such chaotic times, so we had to wait. However, there was no specified timeline for this wait.

My great-great-great-great grandfather had a long life due to his longevity genes, and my paternal great-great-great grandparents also lived a long life. Thinking back to the time when my great-great-great-great grandfather, Tairen, braved hardships and brought along my newborn great-great-great grandfather, Pingsheng, to venture into the Guandong region, it was through his efforts that the Li family bloodline was passed down in Yingkou (which was renamed from Mogouying at that time). This has allowed our Li family descendants to thrive and enjoy a prosperous and harmonious life together.

**Part Three**

# *The Li family ancestors of the generation named "Wen" and their stories*

## Chapter One:

# Li Wentian dedicates himself to industry, and achieves success studying in the United States

### 1

Li Wentian, the great grandson of Tairen, was not content with studying in a private school. After studying at home for five or six years, he went to a foreign missionary school. Tairen was extremely unhappy about this, as the Li family had always been Buddhists, and he could not understand why his grandson wanted to attend the Catholic St. John's School.

Both Tairen and Pingsheng strongly opposed this. Wentian persisted for a few years, and finally convinced his mother when he was nine years old. A year later, his mother persuaded his father, and two years after that, his grandfather, who had come around to the idea. Wentian's roundabout tactics finally worked, and at the age of twelve, he began attending the church school.

At first, Tairen and Pingsheng only agreed to let him try it out, but Wentian's academic performance was excellent, so they stopped objecting. Although Wentian was a good student, he was also sickly since childhood. Pingsheng and Jingying were afraid that he might have an accident, so they arranged for him to have a child bride.

Li Liu, the child bride, was fifteen years old when she came to the household, while Wentian was only seven. She came from a tenant farmer family and was the oldest of many girls. She was born to take care of people. She never had a name, and everyone called her Liu Daya (the first girl). When she married into the Li family, she placed her husband's surname before her own, so she became Li Liu. She wasn't considered beautiful, but she was still pretty. She had narrow, slit-like eyes, a straight nose, and slightly upturned corners of her mouth, always giving people a smiling feeling. Since Li Liu became the daughter-in-law, she took care of Wentian meticulously. Previously, whenever he ate something he couldn't handle, Wentian would vomit incessantly. At the beginning, Li Liu would go to the kitchen herself to make millet and lotus seed porridge for Wentian, and she would feed him spoonful by spoonful. Sometimes, it would take two hours to finish a meal. Li Liu was never tired of it. Under her attentive care, Wentian's weak stomach gradually improved, and he gained weight. Wentian had a habit of occasionally wetting the bed at night, but since Li Liu came, she would wake up little Wentian every night. She would softly hum a nursery rhyme with modified lyrics: "TianTian, every night, pee on the bed, wake up and pee, the bedding will be dry."

She hummed while blowing her whistle. Holding the chamber pot in her hand, she was ready to catch Wentian's urine at any time. She was like a mother. At first, Wentian was unwilling, but over time, he got used to it. As time went on, Wentian's bedwetting problem miraculously improved.

This daughter-in-law was honest and quiet, always keeping her head down and working. She had bound feet, and Wentian complained about her foot odor. Whenever she unwrapped the foot bindings, there was indeed a faint unpleasant smell. Looking at her feet, except for the big toe, which remained normal, all the other toes were fractured and bent, tucked under the sole of her foot. One can imagine how painful it must have been for her to walk. Her shoes were tiny with pointed toes, and her instep was high, so the shoe upper was slightly elevated. The heel of the shoe was of regular adult size. The overall size of the shoes seemed to be meant for a four or five-year-old child, but with a peculiar shape. Bearing the weight of an adult on such small feet must have created significant pressure. It's no wonder that women in those days seldom left their homes or took small steps when they did.

Wentian was intelligent and had a strong personality. He never saw Li Liu as his wife, especially since he left home at the age of twelve to attend a church school. It was at the church that he met a girl named Zhang Yimu, who was an orphan from a young age and didn't have a surname. Later, a kind-hearted person surnamed

Zhang adopted her. However, because the person was too poor and had to go out to work frequently, unable to take care of the child, he wrote a note explaining the situation and left the child at the church door. Missionary John took her in. Previously, everyone called her Yimu, which meant "bathing in the rain and dew of God." However, to be more subtle, the priest changed her name to Zhang Yimu. She was also the priest's goddaughter, a devout Catholic who could speak English and had an English name, Elizabeth.

When Wentian was fourteen years old, a teenage boy going through puberty, he grew tall and was arranged to sleep with Li Liu, who was twenty-two years old. Although Wentian had not lived with the woman who was like a mother to him for two years, he was reluctant. But recently, he had begun to experience puberty and sometimes woke up with wet underwear. He was curious about what sex was, so he wanted to try it. As a result, Li Liu became pregnant.

Li Liu happily hummed a folk song as she went in and out of the door, "The rooster crows loudly, the husband and wife lie in bed, lazy on the kang. You are my good gentleman."

Wentian covered his ears tightly and didn't want to listen to her.

Except for Wentian, everyone in the Li family was overjoyed, burning incense to worship their ancestors and going to temples to offer prayers to Guanyin for the birth of a child. But Wentian didn't care at all. He didn't know what it was like to be a father. He was still just a child. Occasionally, he would think of Zhang Yimu. When Li Liu gave birth to a boy named Li Zhenhai after a ten-month pregnancy, Wentian was out on a spring outing with his teachers and classmates. Li Liu's delivery went smoothly.

Since the birth of Tairen's great-grandson Zhenhai, Wentian didn't dare to go back to his own room when he returned home. He always went to sleep in the room of Wu Zhenshan, an elderly relative from his ancestral home. Wu Zhenshan was now hunched over and had never found his own wife and children. Tairen had allowed him to stay and retire at the Li household. Later, Wentian decided to move to the church school to live.

In private, Zhenshan spoke to Tairen, saying, "Master, it seems that this child has some emotional issues. Perhaps we should find a doctor to have a look."

Tairen agreed that it was a matter of concern. They sought out a few local doctors, who all diagnosed Wentian with marriage phobia. They believed that the sudden change in his perception of Li Liu as his spouse, after never seeing her in that light before, made it difficult for him to accept. Wentian had been away from home for six months, so Tairen and Pingsheng went to the church school to find him.

## 2

This church is located next to the Guan Sheng Ge, which is dedicated to Guan Gong and Guan Yin, in the center of the old camp. Its name is not very pleasant, it's called "Rooster Tower," adjacent to the bustling West Street. After the opening of the port at Mogouying, Western missionaries came here to preach and built this church. The church was funded by missionary John a few years ago, and he gave it the name "St. John's Cathedral". At that time, he preached to everyone, but people didn't like him and accused him of having ambitions for building the church. So, they mocked him. During the day, the workers he hired dug the church's foundation, but at night, the townspeople filled it up. Later, he took the lead in giving food and warm clothing to the poor in winter. Over time, some people did convert to Christianity.

St. John's Cathedral is different from the Buddhist temples. It has a gray-black exterior and a pointed roof, as if it could reach the sky. It is located on the south bank of the Liao River, with a weathervane erected on the roof that looks like an iron rooster. Therefore, people gave it the nickname "Rooster Tower." The church worships Jesus Christ, and a large cross is placed next to the pulpit. There are candlesticks and a tall pipe organ with two rows of keyboards. The sound of the pipe organ comes from the metal pipes standing behind the keyboard. Each metal pipe is connected to the pipe organ. So, when a nun presses the black and white keys, beautiful music floats out from the high pipe organ, filling the spacious church. The Venetian-stained glass windows in the church have colorful pictures that seem to tell the stories of God and Jesus to the faithful believers.

John was tall with a full beard, deep-set eyes, a high nose, and cheekbones. Many children called him a foreign devil because he looked different from the Han Chinese. John got up and sent someone to call Wentian from the dormitory behind, but after a while, the person came back and said that Wentian didn't want to come to see his grandfather and father.

Tairen and Pingsheng explained their intention, and Pingsheng said, "Now we are really worried about Wentian. If he doesn't want to go home to live, he doesn't have to take care of the child either. Can't he at least come home to see the child?"

John hesitated for a moment and revealed that the church school now supports the Westernization Movement promoted by the Qing government and plans to send some young students to study in the United States at the expense of the Qing government. In fact, they are not currently recruiting students in the Northeast. I have a St. John's Church School in Guangdong, and I will have Wentian enroll as a student from Guangdong."

John stroked his beard and further explained, "After going abroad, he will live with an American family, complete his school first, and then study industrial manufacturing at the university."

This situation came as a sudden surprise! Tairen disagreed. He paused for a moment and said, "What kind of place is America? How to get there? How can we trust that?"

Pingsheng, on the other hand, didn't oppose the idea. He said, "We can give it a try."

He felt that this was a good opportunity for Wentian to get out of this environment, and it was a good opportunity for him to heal.

Ignoring his father's opposition, Pingsheng went to the church school several times and finally saw Wentian in class. The last time he went with his wife, Jingying. When they came back, Jingying said to Pingsheng, "Where is America? I heard people say it's a wilderness, thousands of miles away, across the ocean?"

Pingsheng had talked to Father John when he went to the church. He had seen the world map and knew that even if they took a boat, it would take more than a month to get there. It was much farther than their previous journey when they migrated to Northeast China across Liaodong Bay. But there were thirty children going together this time, and he wasn't worried. Some people said that within a few years, the Hundred Days' Self-Strengthening Reform Movement would send a total of 120 children between the ages of ten to sixteen to study abroad in America, and some would go from Hong Kong. Pingsheng comforted Jingying, saying, "There shouldn't be any major issues. Wentian is one of the older children among them. Moreover, in the past two years, many children have already gone, and this is the fourth year of the program."

## 3

In 1875, 15-year-old Wentian went to study in the United States. A group of boys, aged ten to sixteen, dressed in new Chinese-style suits and shoes, wearing black conical hats and braided hair, boarded a ship in Shanghai. After a journey of over a month, they arrived in San Francisco, USA. Then, they were packed into black, rumbling steam trains and traveled along the recently completed transcontinental railroad, built with the hard work of Chinese laborers. After a long journey, they reached the New England region on the East Coast and began their study abroad.

However, the good times didn't last. With the death of Zeng Guofan, some people began to complain that these young students had become too Westernized, too enthusiastic about playing baseball and football, and demanded their return. Several years later, most students went back to China, but Wentian stayed abroad, studying for more than a decade.

When he first arrived in the United States, Wentian couldn't get used to the food, the beds, or the language. He also faced teasing from American children who pulled his braided hair and called him "Chinese girl." Wentian felt helpless and shed tears. He sensed the stark contrast between the Qing Dynasty and America—cleaner air, abundant living conditions, cars running in the streets, towering buildings, and a market filled with a wide variety of goods. He called this place "Greater Shanghai of America." Wentian loved it there and saw it as a direction for his future endeavors. He wanted to return to China and build a better China, believing that human civilization belonged to all humankind.

Wentian graduated from high school after four years abroad. He was fortunate to have lived with Jack, a high-ranking executive of the Standard Oil magnate. Jack had no children of his own and treated Wentian as his own child. Wentian was intelligent and responsible, often helping with household chores whenever he had free time. Jack would take Wentian to play ice hockey whenever he had time. Ice hockey was Wentian's strong suit. Growing up in the frigid winters of northeastern China, he enjoyed ice skating, ice sliding, and even speed skating on the frozen surface of the Liao River, wearing ice skates made from his father's two vegetable knives.

Although Wentian had poor health as a child, Li Liu took care of him and improved his condition. However, he still suffered from occasional gastrointestinal problems, headaches, and fever. But ever since he fell in love with speed skating, he would break out in a sweat after each session, and his health problems disappeared. He also noticed that his physical strength had increased, he had a better appetite, and his body had developed muscles. When Jack introduced him to ice hockey, Wentian immediately fell in love with the intense and exhilarating sport. He became a key player on the team, displaying exceptional dribbling and maneuvering skills, adept at quick stops and changes of direction, and rapidly improving his puck control, passing, and shooting techniques. Jack was one of the club's founders and always brought Wentian along for matches, contributing to his joyful and happy growth.

Later, Jack encouraged him to participate in more school activities, such as joining the school's drum corps. However, during that time in America, there was extreme racial discrimination, with black and white students attending separate schools and not being allowed to use the same drinking fountains. Chinese students also faced discrimination, and the school initially refused to let Wentian join the drum corps. So, Jack changed Wentian's name to "Ethan Jackson," a purely American name, and Wentian adopted Jack's surname. Jack made Wentian wear Western clothing and cut his braids.

As Wentian's guardian, Jack persisted in applying for his rights, and with his local reputation, the school eventually agreed to let Wentian participate in various activities.

Wentian also faced his own troubles. One time, a young player of English descent from the ice hockey team invited him to his birthday party at his home. Wentian carefully prepared a gift and wore the black suit that Jack had bought him, filled with excitement.

This team member's home looked very wealthy. The furniture was all jaw-dropping and magnificent. There were two high-backed chairs that look like they were influenced by Asian furniture design. The backs of the chairs were engraved with peony flower shapes and dyed with bright color of pink. The chandelier in the home was as dazzling as a gem, hanging high on the ceiling beams of the middle hall. Wentian was dazzled by what he saw. He felt that Jack was also very rich, but the furniture at home was very ordinary. In contrast, Jack was not a person who was greedy for pleasure.

It was time to blow out the candles and eat the birthday cake. Wentian and other team members gathered around and sang happy birthday. At this time, a fashionable middle-aged white woman came down from upstairs. She was wearing a tight-fitting blouse inlaid with pearls and lace, a round long skirt. She also wore a top hat. She stared at Wentian as soon as she got downstairs, then called her son aside and asked, "Who have you invited to your house? Next time, please don't invite these random people."

His friend, apologizing repeatedly, His friend listened to his mother's words and told Wentian that he couldn't stay any longer. Then he hastily stuffed a return gift bag to Wentian and reluctantly escorted him to the door, apologizing repeatedly , "I'm sorry, really sorry!"

But Wentian walked out alone, gazing at the beautiful house, and hearing the laughter of his teammates from inside. He felt a profound sense of racial discrimination.

This party was a humiliating experience for Wentian. He left early and walked back to Jack's house on foot, without waiting for Jack to come pick him up. He didn't tell Jack about it afterward because he didn't want to make a big deal out of it. After that incident, whenever there were student parties, he would usually decline, using the excuse of having other engagements.

Meanwhile, at school, Wentian's English proficiency improved rapidly. He participated in school speeches, math competitions, and drumline performances. He felt like a caged bird set free, soaring freely.

Later, when the Qing government called back the young students studying abroad, Wentian informed Mr. and Mrs. Jackson that he was determined not to return. If he didn't have money for college, he would work and save up before pursuing higher education. Seeing his strong resolve, Mr. Jackson decided to financially support Wentian's enrollment at Rensselaer Polytechnic Institute. At this point, Wentian was no longer just a small student from the Qing Dynasty studying abroad.

## 4

When he graduated from high school, Wentian saw so many diesel cars on the streets and immediately fell in love with this convenient and efficient mode of transportation. At the time, with the development of oil, Jack had already started to pay attention to the automotive industry. He said to Wentian, "You came abroad to study mechanical engineering. Now that you love cars, why not study the automotive industry?"

Wentian nodded in agreement. He knew that without petroleum-powered cars, he couldn't go anywhere and he also needed to study the petroleum industry. He was fortunate to have such a good teacher, as Jack was a high-ranking executive at Standard Oil. Four years of high school passed year after year, and Wentian became closer and closer to Jack, who had already regarded him as his own child. He often unconsciously called Wentian "son"!

Upon receiving the acceptance letter from Rensselaer Polytechnic Institute, Wentian wrote letters to his family and John. In his letter to John, he also sent his greetings to Yimu.

Beautifully situated next to New England in eastern New York state, Rensselaer was located in a vibrant region with rolling hills and a thriving population. It was the most developed center in the United States, densely populated and bustling with activity. When Wentian first visited the school, Jack drove him to see the ocean, following the New Jersey coastline all the way to the school. The vast ocean, with its endless expanse, was never calm. It surged with immense power, evoking a sense of passion and mystery in Wentian.

He said to Jack, "Is the sea of knowledge in front of me as boundless and unfathomable as this vast ocean?"

Jack replied, "There will certainly be endless challenges, son. Are you ready?"

Wentian raised his arms and shouted towards the ocean, "I, Ethan Jackson, Li Wentian, am here to take on the challenge!"

With Jack's help, Wentian smoothly moved into the dormitory at the school. At that time, over 80% of the teachers and students lived on campus. The student population numbered in the hundreds, while there were only dozens of teachers. The school had extracurricular clubs, and Wentian discovered that there was even an automotive manufacturing interest club. Without hesitation, he signed up. However, once he joined, he realized that many of the students were children of wealthy families, most of them members of fraternities, and they spent money extravagantly. Building car models required purchasing materials, and Wentian was already a self-funded student. He knew that if he told his father he needed money, his father would find a way to send it over. However, at the moment, Wentian only informed his father that he needed some living expenses, and Jack took care of his tuition. He didn't want to trouble his family, nor did he want to tell Jack, so he chose to quit the club. Wentian worked on his car models in the dormitory, resulting in a messy room with his homemade car parts scattered everywhere. He tinkered with them until late at night, making him a night owl. He wouldn't sleep until past midnight, never before twelve o'clock. His roommate, on the other hand, was an early bird who woke up early in the morning for exercise. The two of them had limited interaction each day, respecting each other's routines without causing any disturbance.

Despite facing financial constraints and limited resources, Wentian's perseverance allowed him to pursue his passion for automotive engineering and develop his skills while studying at the university. Wentian purchased several electric toys from a flea market and dismantled the engines, bearings, and wheels from them to use in his car model's power system. Despite using scrap tin sheets, nails, and inexpensive paint, his model was able to run when connected to electricity.

With his resourcefulness and creativity, Wentian was able to transform discarded items into functional components for his car model. He carefully assembled the engine, bearings, and wheels, ensuring they were properly connected and aligned. Using wires and a small battery, he created a simple electrical circuit that powered the model when activated.

Although his model might not have had the sleek appearance or high-quality materials of commercial models, it had the essential components to move and function. Wentian's passion and determination drove him to create something out of limited resources.

Studying at an American university was indeed demanding and fulfilling. In his first semester, Wentian (Ethan) achieved four A's and one B. Apart from academic courses, the school offered various sports teams and activities, although ice hockey, his favorite, was not available. As he had no interest in other sports, Wentian (Ethan) chose cross-country running. This sport tested his endurance, and he would run around the campus every day. However, his expensive shoes quickly wore out. To avoid spending money on new shoes, Wentian (Ethan) decided to quit cross-country running.

The winters in that region were bitterly cold, with heavy snowfall. The school was situated on a small hill, and after snowfall, students would slide down the hill. However, the price of skiing equipment and boots was too high for Wentian (Ethan) to afford, so he refrained from participating. Consequently, his daily routine consisted of eating, sleeping, tinkering with his car models, and focusing on classes and studying. He was like a thirsty sponge, eager to absorb the vast ocean of knowledge.

Despite being in a foreign land, Ethan yearned for someone to accompany him and add some color to his monotonous study life. He longed for a companion or friend who could share the little moments of life and provide warmth and care. Although he had a close relationship with Jack, he also desired to establish his own social circle at the university, connect with other students, and experience college life together. Perhaps, he yearned even more for someone who truly understood him to be by his side.

Several months after sending his letter about starting university, Wentian (Ethan) excitedly received a reply from Yimu one evening. He was thrilled to see that it came all the way from the United States, and he couldn't wait to open and read it. Yimu had already arrived in the US and was living near Chinatown. However, it was already late in the day, so Wentian (Ethan) had to endure his anticipation and stay awake. He couldn't help but think about Yimu throughout the night and hardly got any sleep.

Three months after Wentian (Ethan) and Yimu met, on that particular day the sky was a beautiful shade of blue, as if painted with a magnificent stroke. Wentian (Ethan) had arranged to meet Yimu on the university campus, and as he spotted her from afar, she looked nothing like the typical Li Liu from back home. She stood tall and graceful, dressed in a sea-blue traditional Chinese jacket with deep blue lantern pants. Her naturally curly hair flowed elegantly, and she truly looked like a heavenly beauty.

As Yimu walked towards him, Wentian's (Ethan) heart raced, and his face blushed. He was twenty-one years old, with a height of 1.78 meters, exuding charm and sophistication. With his fair complexion, sharp eyebrows, and shining eyes, he seemed like a young man. At that moment, he felt like a little boy, unable to meet the gaze of the girl in front of him. He took out a red rose he had hidden behind his back and proposed to Yimu. Lowering her head, Yimu accepted the flower and swiftly ran off like the wind.

From then on, they did everything together—watching movies, buying groceries, cooking, doing laundry, and going on outings. They were inseparable, like two souls stuck together with glue. However, they never crossed that boundary between friendship and something more.

One day, in Chinatown, two small-time thugs attempted to harass Yimu. Wentian (Ethan), alone, confronted the two of them, but ended up getting injured and hospitalized. It was at that moment that the two of them truly came together. It was a classic tale of a hero saving the damsel in distress and capturing her heart.

## 5

Fifteen years later, he returned to his hometown as a successful and knowledgeable man, full of vitality. He came back to assume the role of the Chief Representative of Chevron Oil Company in China, and Yimu accompanied him. They had been married for three years now and brought back their second son, Zhenyang, whose English name was Philip. Wentian now changed his American name (Ethan) back to Wentian.

Despite his gratitude towards his first wife Li Liu for taking care of him in the past, he still couldn't bring himself to face her. He appreciated her kindness but did not love her. The old lady understood and didn't want to force him, so she let him go his own way. He built a grand mansion with five large gates near Dalian, in a town called Dashiqiao. These five tall and wide wooden gates were arranged in a straight line, painted in vermilion, exuding a solemn and dignified aura. The courtyard was concave in shape, and each gate had six rooms, consisting of east and west wings and a main hall. It was known as the renowned "Five Great Gates" in the area. Because of his work, Wentian traveled in a carriage; the distance was not an issue, since he had the means to afford it.

As for Mrs. Li Liu, she continued to live in the Li family house and did not live with Wentian. She stayed with her son Zhenhai. She appeared very old, and many people compared her to a servant in the household. In reality, even the household servants mistreated her, and Zhenhai witnessed it all. The servants would distribute provisions to the masters of the house, always leaving Mrs. Li Liu for last and giving her whatever was left over. Because of this, when Zhenhai got married and had three sons and three daughters, he chose to stay in the Li family mansion to take care of his mother.

Mrs. Li Liu experienced loneliness and sadness, but she endured it. She believed that heaven had given her a son, and she witnessed her son become the head of the Li family, bringing honor and glory to their ancestors. She was happy! She considered herself fortunate, saying, "I have descendants to bring joy under my knees, and my family is flourishing. Others envy me."

Afterwards, Li Wentian treated Mrs. Li Liu with respect and courtesy. Their relationship was delicate, but they still treated each other with great respect. Another significant reason for this was that Wentian and Yimu's second child, Li Zhenyang, had no offspring. The exact details are unknown, but it is possible that he was not included in the family genealogy. According to family tree, Zhenyang disappeared after 1944, and no one has seen him since. More precisely, he vanished after the dissolution of the Communist International on May 15, 1943. Some say he joined that organization. Later, according to Zhenyang's younger sister, Zhenfeng, he went to the United States to find Jack, which was something their father had instructed him to do before his passing.

Before Wentian's return to China, Pingsheng and Jingying had become dissatisfied with him as the eldest son and unhappy with his childhood wife Mrs. Li Liu. So they arranged a marriage for him and sent multiple letters asking him to come back and get married. However, he didn't return and took matters into his own hands by privately marrying Zhang Yimu without the family's approval.

Things became complicated. When Wentian brought Yimu home, there were many unpleasant incidents arising from cultural differences. Yimu grew up in a church and didn't speak Chinese well. She also had not been exposed to traditional Chinese customs and etiquette, so in Jingying's eyes she seemed a bit ignorant of the rules. When they entered the house, Yimu didn't address Pingsheng and Jingying as father and mother, nor did she kneel down and acknowledge them as her elders. This made Pingsheng and Jingying feel uncomfortable.

During their first meal, after food was prepared in the kitchen and everyone gathered to eat, by custom Grandfather Tairen would take the first seat, followed by Pingsheng and Jingying, and then Wentian and Yimu. However, before Jingying was seated, Yimu took a chair and sat down, leaving everyone feeling awkward and unsure how to react. At first, Jingying didn't pay too much attention to it. She understood that Yimu didn't come from a Chinese family, so she was understanding of the situation. But Wentian noticed everyone's reaction and pulled Yimu up, asking her to stand. However, Jingying said, "Yimu, please sit. We don't have so many rules at home."

Yimu, feeling embarrassed, asked, "Did I sit in the wrong place? Where should I sit?" Yimu hesitated, unsure of what to do. Wentian still pulled Yimu up, but after Jingying took her seat, Wentian and Yimu finally sat down.

As the dishes were served, Jingying asked Yimu, "What kind of dishes do you like? I'll have them placed next to you when they bring the food."

Without much thought, Yimu replied, "I love fish."

In a traditional family banquet, it is customary to have a fish dish, as fish symbolizes abundance and prosperity. The fish should be placed in the center of the table, with the fish head facing the head of the family, who is usually the eldest member. Additionally, it is customary for Tairen (the grandfather) to raise his cup, lead the toast, and start eating the fish with his chopsticks. Others are not allowed to start eating until Tairen gives the signal.

However, Yimu initially moved the fish closer to herself without considering the direction of the fish head. She then began to pray, seemingly disregarding the presence of the elders. Furthermore, she inappropriately took the first bite of fish, even though that was intended for Wentian's grandfather.

These actions were considered serious breaches of etiquette. Sensing the awkward atmosphere, Wentian moved the fish platter to the center of the table, with the fish head facing Tairen.

Chinese dining culture is vast and profound, with specific customs for various occasions, such as festivals and celebrations. The main purpose is to foster family harmony, but this particular meal created prejudice against Yimu within the Li family.

Consequently, Yimu became unwilling to visit the Li family. Wentian, who had received a Western education, also disliked these traditional formalities. So they began to live according to their own rules, which further deepened the rift between them and the family. Even Pingsheng and Jingying stopped acknowledging Yimu as their daughter-in-law.

## Chapter Two:

# Li Wenchuan, the Vegetable King, devotes himself to farming

### 1

Li Wenchuan is also my root great-great-grandfather. He was the fourth younger brother of Wentian. Before reaching adulthood, Wenchuan had little contact with his elder brother Wentian because he was nine years younger than him. When Wentian went abroad to study, Wenchuan was only six years old.

Compared to Wentian, who was weak and sickly, Wenchuan was a strong young man. From a young age, he had a preference for working shirtless, even in snowy weather, wearing only a small padded jacket and no hat or gloves. His rosy cheeks resembled red apples, but he never complained about the cold. He rarely fell ill and enjoyed accompanying his father to work in the fields.

He had a natural talent for farming. He excelled in various agricultural tasks, such as nurturing seedlings, grafting branches, loosening soil, applying fertilizer, pruning, and dealing with plant diseases and pests. Even in his early teens, he provided his father with insightful suggestions on intercropping and crop rotation based on the height and maturity period of different vegetables. These ideas significantly improved the land's utilization, resulting in a 20% increase in crop yield and vitality. Wenchuan was knowledgeable enough to educate others, often sounding like a small expert. He knew which vegetables had medicinal properties, which ones were good for mental alertness, and which ones had aphrodisiac effects. Sometimes, while discussing these topics, he would pluck a handful of greens and taste them, savoring their flavors. He enjoyed looking at the greenery he had planted, seeing the different varieties of vegetables added vibrant colors to the landscape, like a colorful quilt spread out over the land.

Wenchuan seemed simple-minded, but he was very intelligent. In the past, his father allocated land for crops based on the existing seed situation, as well as the approximate income and demand of different crops from the previous year. However, Wenchuan said that method was not accurate. He told the servants, "We are implementing new rules. Every winter, before spring plowing, all of you will go to the nearby markets in the counties and towns to assess the situation and find out what the demand is there. What is the saturation level?"

He also requested, "Furthermore, for the grain crops harvested each year in the autumn, we need to see who bought them. Apart from individual buyers, we should maintain contact with the larger buyers and persuade them to sign contracts. The earlier they sign the contract and the more they purchase, the more favorable prices they will receive."

He also set a rule for the accountants: "After checking the market, assign tasks to each person. If any worker's contract brings in more than 20% of the expected income in the fall, in addition to their annual bonus, they will also receive a percentage of the Li family's annual income, up to 2%. This is very attractive, as 2% of the Li family's annual income is a substantial amount. A generous reward inspires bravery!

The workers were all enthusiastic and went out to conduct surveys, no longer spending their winters playing mahjong and lazing around at home like previous years.

Master Pingsheng was pleased with the work of the Li family's vegetable garden, which had become well-known in the region due to Wenchuan's efforts. He raised his thumb proudly and said, "We have a successor for the Li family's vegetable garden."

Jingying also looked at Wenchuan, who had become tanned from the sun, and smiled, "I have two sons that I'm most proud of. One is Wenshan, as you said, he's a mechanic material and perfect for the hardware store; the other is this little black guy Wenchuan, the king of vegetable growers!"

In addition to these, Wenchuan did something even more out of the ordinary. His worker, Ding Er, bought back some blue, fragrant rice from near DaShiQiao, and brought back a few rice stalks. He showed Wenchuan the heavy and plump rice grains and said, "Boss, look at this rice, it's all tribute rice! Why don't we try growing it? Rice is much more expensive than sorghum or corn."

Wenchuan looked at the inexperienced Ding Er and found that his own idea for many years coincided with the young man's suggestion. He took the rice stalks, peeled off the rice husks, and looked at the white and plump rice grains inside. He said, "This is a new variety. We need to conduct experiments first. We have no experience in growing rice fields and no full confidence."

Wenchuan rewarded Ding Er and told him to prepare to plant rice in the spring. Then he immediately went to the hardware store to discuss it with his father, Pingsheng. While smoking a cigarette and tinkering with an old clock, Pingsheng looked up at his son Wenchuan and said, "I don't agree with growing rice fields. It will completely change the planting structure of the Li family's vegetable garden."

But Wenchuan still wanted to try. He said to his father, "Let's try planting a few mu first, enough for ourselves to eat."

Pingsheng didn't argue with his son. Smoking his cigarette, he casually said, "Then you can try? That's a good thing. If you succeed, we can eat rice all year round!"

Turning dry fields into paddy fields is not an easy task. In order not to destroy their eight fields, Wenchuan rented two mu of land by the Liao River. He learned how to build water supply and drainage systems and used pressure difference to directly pipe water from the Liao River into the field. This method really worked, and within a day or two, the water in the field was ten centimeters high.

Then Wenchuan called Ding Er and two other young men. They wore water boots and planted rice seedlings, fertilized the field, and Ding Er was responsible for taking care of the two mu of paddy fields. As they watched the seedlings grow taller day by day, they encountered a problem. Their rice was infected with a disease, with many seedlings wilting shortly after sprouting. Those that didn't die had slender leaves, pale yellow leaves, and withered before flowering. Wenchuan noticed that there were red mold spots at the junctions of some of the rice husks that had sprouted early.

Wenchuan went to ask the rice farmers in Dashiqiao himself and learned that the prevention and control of rice viruses were very important. Just like the dreadful disease that he had experienced, it could reduce rice production by half or even result in no harvest at all! He listened carefully as the rice farmers explained how to prevent such diseases. He also heard that rice likes acidic soil, so Wenchuan planned to adjust the soil acidity when he returned, hoping for a great harvest next year!

The next year, unwilling to give up, Wenchuan tried planting four mu* of rice in his own eight fields. However, as soon as the rice began to flower, someone came to his door to order his rice!

But one night, all the water in the field dried up. The next day, Wenchuan and Guo and workers blocked up all the leaking spots and refilled the field with water. When they checked the field during the day, the water had all flowed away again. What was going on? Wenchuan was a little angry. He hired some people to keep watch at night, but they were unexpectedly beaten up. The attackers warned him that if he tried to plant rice again, they would burn the fields down!

It turned out that it was the people from Gou Qingshan who planted rice nearby who did it. They saw Wenchuan as a threat to their livelihoods, so they acted out of desperation. Wenchuan wanted to report it to the authorities, but his father, Pingsheng, stopped him. Pingsheng said, "We have enough to eat and drink. Planting rice will affect others. We won't do it."

Wenchuan couldn't let it go and was unwilling. Guo the Steward said to him, "Master, if you can't let it go, we can teach them a lesson."

Wenchuan shook his head and said, "I'm really annoyed, but it's not right to retaliate with resentment. Let's do something else first." But what to do?

In the past, every household in the north would dig a cellar in the winter to store vegetables like cabbage, radishes, potatoes, as well as meat and fish. The Li family would also dig a large-scale cellar. Wenchuan came up with the idea of enclosing a space with

* 4 mu ≈ 2/3 acre

wooden boards and adobe on the ground and opening a skylight to let in more sunlight. There, he could use a stove to keep it warm and grow vegetables, creating a greenhouse-like space. This was a great improvement that allowed northerners to enjoy seasonal vegetables and fruits. Although the quantity was limited, my great-grandfather began to use similar greenhouse vegetable planting techniques at that time.

When Wenchuan first started working on a vegetable greenhouse, his father, Pingsheng, said, "Chuan, have you forgotten the lesson of growing rice? This idea is even more uncertain."

Wenchuan replied, "Dad, you didn't used to doubt me like this. You always said I could do anything! How come one failure with rice has made you lose confidence in me?"

Upon hearing his son's words, Pingsheng walked around the space enclosed by Wenchuan using wooden boards and adobe several times. He confidently told his son, "Chuan, I'm afraid this won't work! Think about it, vegetables, just like trees, have a dormant period. It will be futile to plant them."

Wenchuan tried to reason with his father. He said, "Dad, you don't know. I've been reading a lot lately. With sufficient nutrients, sunlight, water, and temperature, vegetables will sprout and grow."

Pingsheng still didn't believe it. Shaking his head, he said, "I've been growing grains and vegetables for so many years, and I've never seen you try something like this. Don't deplete the soil, or we won't have a good harvest next year."

Wenchuan remained steadfast and said, "No, it won't happen. I believe it will succeed. Besides, by next spring, we can plant sorghum on this piece of land again. By properly timing the seasons and fertilizing appropriately, we will have a good yield."

Seeing his son's determination and considering his recent studies, Pingsheng said, "Alright, I'll trust you once again. Let's give it a try. Just don't end up with empty hands like fetching water in a bamboo basket."

Wenchuan felt somewhat disappointed with his father's attitude and said, "Dad, just watch. I'm at least 80% sure of success."

Pingsheng thought about how over the years, this son of his had truly dedicated himself to farming, rarely engaging in disputes over family property or pursuing high-profit ventures like his second and third sons. He didn't want a share in the banking or shipping business; his whole focus was on farming. He rarely even paid much attention to the hardware store. He would say, "Everyone needs to eat, right? They need vegetables!"

This time, this clever lad, Wenchuan, didn't speak empty words. He grew some cold-resistant vegetables. The radishes in the heated greenhouse just started sprouting, the spinach was vibrant green, the celery stalks were straight, the small onions lined up neatly, and the cilantro was fragrant. For the first time, the Li family produced fresh vegetables in winter. Although the costs were higher, the prices for winter vegetables were quite good. The family was also happy because they didn't have to rely on cabbage, radishes, and similar vegetables for the entire winter.

Wenchuan's steadfastness, simplicity, and efficiency in his work earned the trust of the tenant farmers and merchants. His reputation spread far and wide, and Pingsheng constantly heard praises about him. In fact, the most important aspect of the Li family's assets to Pingsheng was the Li family vegetable garden because his ancestors were originally farmers. It was the foundation of the Li family and must never be abandoned. Previously, Pingsheng and the former estate manager, Guo Kangning, took care of the vegetable garden. Now that Old Guo had passed away, his eldest son, Guo Yunsheng, took over his position. The two of them, along with Wenchuan, managed the vegetable garden, and it thrived more and more.

After graduating from the Li family private school, Guo Yunsheng began working alongside his father, Old Guo, learning bookkeeping and managing the accounts. Old Guo also introduced him to officials, merchants, and tenant farmers, familiarizing him with various matters related to government affairs, tenancy, and commercial activities. Then Guo Yunsheng came to be considered Wenchuan's right-hand man.

The Li family's accounting department had grown significantly from the simple scale during the time of their benevolent ancestor. A row of three rooms in the western backyard of the house was designated for the accounting department's use. It consists of the estate manager, Guo Yunsheng, a head accountant, an external accountant, a consolidation accountant, and a junior accountant, making up a team of five individuals. Their role is to ensure timely and accurate bookkeeping, handle any losses or bad debts promptly, and reconcile the accounts with foreign banks on the last day of each month, issuing silver to the tenant farmers.

Additionally, the accounting department handled matters related to hiring workers, all economic transactions of the Li family, including weddings, funerals, marriages, celebrations, land buying and selling, land tenancy, rent collection, and grain distribution.

From this point onwards, everything about the Li family was handled as a family business.

During the late Qing Dynasty, when the Eight-Nation Alliance invaded Beijing, Qing officials began to realize the shortcomings of the corrupt imperial examination system. They started to recognize the importance of establishing schools and cultivating talents in various fields such as education, military, and diplomacy as the foundation of the nation's development and the path forward for China.

Later, Emperor Guangxu of the Qing Dynasty issued an edict ordering the establishment of modern-style schools in all provinces, which would be centrally managed by the Ministry of Education, similar to present-day national universities. From then on, the trend of establishing schools spread throughout major cities in the Qing Empire, and new-style schools were established one after another. As one of the important political and economic centers of the Qing Dynasty, Shengjing (Shenyang), also known as the "secondary capital," naturally kept pace and took the lead in establishing higher education institutions.

Wenchuan valued education and later sent his only son, Zhenhong, to study in Shengjing, where he also studied business for a year. Wenchuan believed that agriculture was the foundation of the Li family, while knowledge served as the capital to ensure the family's prosperity. All descendants were expected to be diligent, frugal, avoid extravagance, treat others with generosity and live in harmony. Only by following these principles could they uphold the family legacy and prevent decline.

The private school called "Ningren Study Room" in the family had closed because intense competition from other schools made it difficult to find qualified teachers. However, the family established an "Ancestral Precepts Hall" in the home, which became a place for family members and shareholders to discuss important matters. Tairen and his sons educated their children not to be proud of wealth but to conduct themselves with integrity and kindness in business. Any child who violated the family rules would be punished according to family discipline, including being beaten with a paddle, whipped, or kneeling in the ancestral hall for a day without being allowed to eat.

## 2

When Wenchuan was nineteen years old, the local matchmakers flocked to the Li family's doorstep, one after another, proposing marriage.

In the 14th year of the Guangxu reign (1888), at the age of eighteen, Wenchuan had a grand wedding and married Ding Jiahe, the second daughter of one of the famous Four Families of Yingkou. Unfortunately, their first son died in infancy, but three years later, they had a son named Li Zhenhong.

Speaking of Wenchuan, one must mention his third elder brother, Li Wenshan. When Li Wenshan's first wife passed away during childbirth, leaving no child behind, Pingsheng and Jingying were worried that it would have a negative impact on him. To divert his attention, they let him learn to sing opera. Wenshan had been playing the erhu since he was young and sometimes went to the opera house as an audience member. It was there that he became infatuated with Kong Xiaohong, a performer. From then on, he rarely stayed at home and followed the opera troupe everywhere, listening to opera and generously rewarding the troupe, especially Kong Xiaohong. When Kong Xiaohong performed, Wenshan would sit in the front row, sipping tea, enjoying the show, and occasionally shouting "bravo." He would throw silver coins, gold hairpins, and opera costumes onto the stage. In short, he seemed to have taken up residence in the opera troupe.

When Pingsheng and Jingying realized that Wenshan had become obsessed with opera, they decided to confine him. However, Wenshan resorted to a hunger strike and refused to eat for three days. Jingying felt deep sympathy for her son and managed to convince Pingsheng. Together, they gradually persuaded the patriarch, Tairen, as well. After a couple of years, Tairen finally agreed to let Kong Xiaohong, the opera performer, enter the household. However, their relationship was not formalized through a proper wedding ceremony. And so, Kong Xiaohong became part of the family. Unfortunately, Kong Xiaohong was unable to conceive a child of her own. Two years later, her belly gradually began to grow, but she did not show any signs of morning sickness. The hired doctors were unable to detect any signs of pregnancy, despite changing several doctors. Everyone assumed that Kong Xiaohong was simply indulging in excessive eating, which caused her belly to expand. Although Kong Xiaohong did not have a child of her own, Wenshan loved her dearly, and they remained a loving couple.

Later, Kong Xiaohong's belly grew to an astonishing size, making it difficult for her to walk. Eventually, she had to undergo surgery at the affiliated hospital of the Medical University in Shengjing, Yingkou. It was discovered that she had a benign tumor weighing ten kilograms in her uterus, which had caused her infertility.

Subsequently, Jingying gave her personal maidservant, Xiaowen, to Wenshan, but Xiaowen only gave birth to two girls.

Since Wenshan did not have any children, his nephew Li Zhenhong became his adoptive son and followed the tradition of marrying two wives. One wife was named Li Fengshi, and she and Li Zhenhong had four children: sons Li Yaojia, Li Yaocheng, and Li Yaoyou, and daughter Li Yaoxian, the fourth in girls birth order. These were the grandchildren of Li Wenshan. The other wife of Li Zhenhong, Sun Wan'er, gave birth to four children who were the grandchildren of Li Wenchuan. The grandsons were Li Yaoguo, the sixth in birth order, and Li Yaowei, the eighth and youngest in birth order. The granddaughters were Li Yaozhi and Li Yaoxin, the fifth and sixth in birth order, respectively.

During the Republican era, Pingsheng grew older, and watched all five of his children establish their own families and careers. Wentian worked as an agent for the American Standard Oil Company in Northeast China. During the Republican era, Pingsheng also held the honorary position of district head in Xingren District. His family operated gold shops in Yingkou and Changchun. Pingsheng's second, third, and fourth sons, as well as his eldest daughter Wenya, had all grown up and established their own families and careers

During the Republican era, on the Mid-Autumn Festival of 1914, Pingsheng, the patriarch, celebrated his 80th birthday. He led the members of the Li family from Batiandi in a grand ancestral worship ceremony. The ceremony usually took place at dusk. In the front hall of the Li family's ancestral hall, there were three large tables with red lacquer. On the offering table, there were five bronze incense burners, nine fruit plates, and ten plates of scattered cakes. On the ground table, there were three wine cups filled with Qing wine. During the ceremony, one cup was offered to the heavens, two cups to the earth, and three cups to the ancestors. Then, the wine was poured towards the sky and splashed on the ground, and the last cup was consumed to demonstrate respect and nostalgia for the ancestors and the determination to carry on and glorify the family in the future.

A portrait of Tairen hung on the main wall of the ancestral hall. Pingsheng knelt at the forefront, accompanied by his four sons, brothers Wentian, Wendi , Wenshan, Wenchuan, and his daughter, Wenyu. Behind them, four grandsons (later totaling eight) and five granddaughters (also later totaling eight) knelt. Following them were the wives of the Li family, who paid their respects to the ancestors by kowtowing and offering incense. Pingsheng's descendants behind him performed the grand ritual of worship, earnestly saying, "Ancestors, please accept our worship."

Pingsheng's descendants behind him performed the ceremony with great piety, saying loudly, "Ancestors above, please accept our worship."

During the ancestral worship ceremony, the Li family's history was recounted, from Li Tairen's pioneering of Guandong to Li Pingsheng, and then to the four sons of the Li family and their descendants. The lengthy text described Li Wentian's enormous contributions to the automobile and petroleum industries in Northeast China, documenting his later travels to Heilongjiang, Jilin, Liaoning, and other places, and his dedication to the automobile and petroleum industries, which contributed to the development of the automobile industry in the three northeastern provinces. The text mainly recorded the contributions of Li Wenchuan, the fourth son of the family, to the Batiandi vegetable garden in Yingkou. The Li family's reputation was widely known, mostly because of this vegetable garden, and when it was mentioned, everyone knew Li Wenchuan, who was the pride of the Li family. Pingsheng let Wenchuan sit next to him, and solemnly handed over the Li family's accounting seal, the keys to the Li family's business and property, to Wenchuan's hands, and Wenchuan accepted them by kowtowing.

Speaking of Li Wendi, the second son, his achievements are not so impressive. His family owned a shipping company and a bank in Yingkou, and he had a son named Li Zhenjiang. However, there is little description of him in the family genealogy because his education was very ordinary. Zhenjiang attended private school and was an average student since childhood. His father did not expect him to achieve great success, so he just hoped that Zhenjiang would inherit the family business and the bank. However, this son was somewhat mediocre and conservative, and he lacked the ability to think creatively. He liked to play with grasshoppers and keep small animals. The house was full of cats and dogs, and he often ran hundreds of miles away to buy a purebred hunting dog, causing his family to lose money. Other businesses took advantage of the situation, and the bank was squeezed out.

Whenever that happened, the employees would run back home from the back door of the bank to find Zhenjiang for a solution, but they couldn't find him.

Second brother Wendi would go to the flower and bird market in a hurry, shouting for Zhenjiang, cursing, "Where did this useless brat go again? What should we do now?"

When they couldn't find Zhenjiang, his brother Zhenze would be scolded by his father, but it seemed that he was only part of the

Li family business for a short while, and as an adult, he left home because he fell in love with a courtesan and had a child. Finally Wendi had no choice but to ask his elder sister Wenya and her family to help manage the businesses, and from then on it no longer carried the Li name.

Speaking of the third son, Li Wenshan, he had the potential to become a skilled mechanic. If he had reeived the same opportunity as his elder brother, Li Wentian, to study abroad in the United States, he would have been equally successful. Li Wenshan's family lived in the Li family's large compound, where they had a hardware store. He had a passion for cars, and his elder brother Wentian provided him with a source of goods. He also enjoyed collecting cars and spent all his money on them. Even their father, Pingsheng, would say, "This third son, his mind is all on cars. He neglects his work, and the family's money is spent on buying cars. But having so many cars doesn't put food on the table."

There was also another thing: Wenshan did not have a son. This was something that Pingsheng didn't like to mention because of an ancient Chinese saying: "Three unfilial acts bring dishonor, and the greatest is having no descendants."

The Li family remained united in one place until the generation of my grandfather, the one with the "Yao" generation name, when due to social turmoil, they had to separate. It wasn't really a split, but a confiscation and redistribution of their property for the common people to live in. After the Cultural Revolution, some of it was returned to the descendants of the Li family. But by then, the Li family had already been divided into four or five parts!

Three years later, the 83-year-old Li Pingsheng passed away, and he should have been satisfied with his life. It is said that he passed away with a smile on his face. The children knelt down at his bedside, and they chanted Buddhist sutras for one day and one night to deliver his soul. He was very influential in the local community, and both government officials and business tycoons set up mourning halls to send him off.

His coffin was made of "sandalwood," which is highly resistant to decay.

There was a lot of controversy among the family members about choosing this type of coffin. Wenchuan proposed, "Use golden silk nanmu, it is the best wood for making coffins, and it is said to attract good feng shui."

However, Wendi disagreed, saying, "Golden-threaded nanmu wood represents power and royal lineage. It is generally considered a material used by members of the imperial family. We should not use such material for our ancestor's coffin."

After hearing Wendi 's words, some members of the Li family expressed their opinions, saying that they loved Pingsheng, but they didn't want to cause trouble.

Wenshan suggested, "How about using cedar wood? It's very common, has strong anti-corrosion capabilities, and is also much cheaper."

Wenchuan was dissatisfied with his brother Wenshan's proposal. Was this the time to be cheap?!

Wendi said, "Dad mentioned using rosewood for his coffin before he passed away, so why don't we use rosewood?"

Looking at the stalemate situation, Wenchuan waved his big hand and said, "Let's draw lots and vote."

So, a dozen lots were prepared, with several types of coffins written on them: nanmu wood, rosewood, sandalwood, and cedar.

Someone prepared a writing brush, paper, and ink, and as Wenchuan expected, the children and grandchildren of the Li family hoped to represent the symbol of the Li family — Li Pingsheng's body that would never decay!

Eight out of ten people agreed to use the precious "sandalwood." Then Wenchuan announced, "Sandalwood has a rich fragrance and can purify and eliminate impurities. No matter how expensive it is, we'll use it!"

Finally, Li Pingsheng was buried in the Li family ancestral tomb, on a hillside near Li family's Batiandi, located by the mountains and water.

Wenchuan led the children and grandchildren of the Li family in raising their wine cups to pay tribute to Li Pingsheng, reciting:

The waters of the Liao River flow endlessly,
Life's path soars with determination.
Once the flowing water is gone, it never returns,
Once a lifetime passes, there is no starting anew.
Rest in peace, Li Pingsheng!

Wenchuan reflected on the passage of time. The rushing waters of the Liao River never turn back once they reach the sea, and once a person's life disappears, it never returns. Life is transient and fleeting, and all worldly wealth and prosperity are not eternal. How should one live so as not to have wasted this life? Although his father, Li Pingsheng, was not a prominent figure, he provided a foundation for the family, ensuring its continued prosperity and living up to the ancestors. In the hearts of the descendants of the Li family, Li Pingsheng had already become a great figure.

After 1960, seriously overestimating the threat of the international situation, Mao Zedong issued a call to carry out extensive construction of bomb shelters and trenches among the masses nationwide, advocating for "digging deep tunnels, storing grain widely, and not seeking hegemony."

I have heard from great Auntie Yaozhi that in these years, she went back to Batiandi several times to visit her ancestors' graves. During the 1960s and 1970s, however, some ancestral graves were destroyed, both by the preparations for the feared nuclear attacks and by the campaign against the Four Olds* during the early period of the Cultural Revolution. As a result, the tombstones are incomplete, and the exact locations of the burial sites are unknown. This historical account is based on the memories of my grandfather Yaowei, great Auntie Yaozhi, and great Auntie Yaoxin. I am grateful to them for leaving us with valuable memories of the past.

* The Four Olds were 'old ideas', 'old culture', 'old customs', and 'old habits'. The campaigns against them began in summer 1966 led by the Red Guards. Actions included the desecration of graves and shrines and destruction of antique artifacts.

**Part Four**

# *Stories of the Li family sons of the generation named "Zhen"*

## Chapter One:

# Li Zhenhai tries to exclude Li Zhenyang

### 1

The Li family kept adding new members one after another. First, Wentian had his eldest son Zhenhai and second son Zhenyang, then Wenshan had the third grandson Zhenjiang, and finally Wenchuan had the fourth grandson Zhenhong. Zhenhai and Zhenyang had a significant age gap and didn't spend much time with each other. Wentian himself didn't live in the Li family's main courtyard but built a large house outside, rarely returning to the family estate. He lived there with his second wife, Yimu, and their second son Zhenyang. Wentian opened a jewelry store in Yingkou and later opened a branch in Changchun.

Zhenhai was a reliable and just businessman, which pleased Wentian. However, Zhenhai was very deeply dissatisfied with his father because he showed little concern for his mother and caused her to feel sad and neglected. She had recently developed Parkinson's disease and walked with a tremor due to her bound feet. To take care of her, Zhenhai continued to live in the Li family's compound.

The Li family's jewelry store later opened another branch in Changchun, and Zhenyang became the manager there. Zhenhai became the head of the original store and occasionally visited Changchun to oversee business matters. Although Wentian's two daughters-in-law never met, the half-brothers still had a good working relationship.

Wentian always took Yimu with him wherever he went. They appeared dignified during his official visits. Yimu was capable of giving him advice, and they traveled together to many cities in the Northeast. Initially, Zhenyang also accompanied them. Following in his father's footsteps, Zhenyang studied automotive manufacturing in college. He was meticulous in his work, and Wentian intended to groom him as his successor. Zhenyang often acted as a liaison between his parents and accompanying officials, arranging accommodations, meals, and other details. However, over time, he grew weary of the formalities and politics of the government and the overwhelming workload. This caused a rift between him and his father. Eventually, Wentian had no choice but to let Zhenyang manage the jewelry store in Changchun.

Zhenhai made the original jewelry store prosperous, and the family's expenses were mostly covered by the income from the store. Even Zhenjiang and Zhenhong benefited greatly from it.

Later, Zhenhai's son, Yaozhong, took over the jewelry store in Changchun. Filial Zhenhai continued to return to his hometown in Yingkou to accompany his elderly mother until her final days. However, when Wentian, their father, passed away suddenly during his official trip to Harbin, Zhenhai was not present. It was only Zhenyang who handled this unexpected event, arranging for the transportation of their father's coffin back to the Li family. Zhenhai, however, refused to let Zhenyang have any involvement in the burial arrangements because he adamantly opposed the idea of his stepmother, Zhang Yimu, wearing mourning attire to bid farewell to his father. He insisted that Zhang Yimu should not be part of the funeral because she had never acknowledged her role as the second wife. If Zhenyang would not agree, Zhenhai said he would handle everything himself and even exclude Zhenyang from participating. Indeed some family members also doubted Zhenyang's full acceptance within the family.

## 2

At this time, all the family affairs were controlled by Zhenhai, the eldest of the Zhen generation. Any decision had to be made by a family meeting and vote. Zhenyang couldn't persuade the clan members, nor could he outsmart his older brother Zhenhai. Moreover, his father's sudden passing left no evidence that he wanted Zhenyang's mother to accompany him on his final journey. Additionally, during the preparation of the deceased, the previous generation's clan leader had to accompany the eldest son, who would smash a basin from a roof tile and clear the way. Therefore, Zhenyang had no choice but to let his mother be inconvenienced and not attend the burial of her husband.

During the funeral procession, Zhenhai and Zhenyang cried while throwing money into the river using a water gourd. This water represented their last gratitude for their father's kindness. The flowing water symbolized the kindness of nurturing and the emotion of missing. The procession carried banners with words like "Li Wentian, the ancient patriarch," and the funeral car was decorated with paper men and horses. They cried and scattered paper money along the way to the Li family ancestral tomb. The age of Li Wentian was written on the front of the car, and male descendants walked on the left side of the car, while female descendants walked on the right side. When they arrived at the cemetery, the family members crawled around the coffin once to perform the "coffin crawl" ritual to bid their final farewell to their deceased loved one.

The coffin was coated with shiny black paint on the outside to prevent body fluid from leaking. Inside the coffin lay Li Wentian, dressed in a blue longevity gown, with a jade bead in his mouth and surrounded by his daily necessities such as handkerchiefs, wine pots, and tobacco pipes, to be enjoyed by him in the underworld. At the time when the sun set, it was also the moment when the coffin was lowered into the soil. Amidst the sound of crying, Zhenhai and Zhenyang added soil onto the coffin, and then the coffin was laid to rest.

Yimu followed the funeral procession from a distance, wearing a white mourning robe with a white flower on her head, crying all the way. She didn't eat or drink anything for a whole day, waiting until the coffin was buried and everyone had left. Then, she threw herself onto Wentian's grave and cried herself to sleep in the Li family ancestral tomb.

At night, Zhenyang was worried that his mother couldn't handle the grief and went to the Li family mansion to see her, but she wasn't there. He searched for her all night and finally found her and carried her back home.

It was heard that Zhenhai later demanded a division of the family assets, stating that the grand estate of Wentian couldn't be solely controlled by Zhenyang and his mother. However, this time Zhenhai and the others were powerless. It was then that Yimu presented the will that Wentian had written long ago regarding the distribution of the mansion's assets. Clearly written on it was: "Li Wentian, after my passing, the 'Five Great Gates' mansion and everything within it shall be managed by Li Zhang Yimu!" Unexpectedly, Wentian, who deeply loved Yimu, had already made arrangements for her to handle everything after his death.

The "Five Great Gates" estate covered an area of more than 5,000 square meters [1.2 acres]. Whenever Yimu thought of Wentian, she sat in the empty courtyard, looking at the stars in the sky, feeling incredibly lonely.

Later, she rented out the houses of the "Five Great Gates", which were then sublet to the public by middlemen, and it developed into a lively and bustling place with various vendors and residents. It became known as the "Five Great Gates" (Wu Da Men), a famous large courtyard.

# Chapter Two

## Li Zhenze runs away for love; Li Wendi regrets losing his son

### 1

In addition to his eldest son, Li Zhenjiang, Li Wendi had a second son named Li Zhenze. He was always a troublesome child, known for his rebellious nature. At the age of seventeen, his father arranged a marriage for him with a girl named Lingling. The betrothal gifts were exchanged, and the wedding date was set. However, on the day of the wedding, the groom Zhenze was nowhere to be found. It was an embarrassing and humiliating situation for the parents. The wedding procession arrived at the doorstep, but the groom was absent, leaving all the relatives and friends witnessing a brideless ceremony.

Several days later, Zhenze returned and gave the girl a divorce letter. The girl was only fifteen years old and had a charming appearance, but her life was ruined. In traditional Chinese society, once a woman crosses the threshold of marriage, she is considered married. According to customs, no one would marry her again, despite her being still unmarried. It was rumored that she suffered mental distress after returning to her parents' home, but the details are unknown.

Li Wendi asked his son Zhenze why he didn't like the girl, and why he had caused her so much harm and damaged the relationship between the two families. However, Zhenze remained silent as a clam and didn't give any explanation. Unable to get any answers from his son, Li Wendi found a young man named Xiao Du, whom Zhenze didn't know, to secretly keep an eye on him and report on where he went and who he met.

Xiao Du noticed that young master Zhenze often went to a brothel called Chun Hua Lou in the town. Before he went there, he would dress up neatly, comb his hair, and put on his new clothes, even his shoes were new. Xiao Du followed him from a distance, and when Zhenze hailed a yellow cab, he also called one, as instructed by Li Wendi, so that he could keep track of the expenses and report back.

Zhenze went to Chun Hua Lou, but instead of going through the main gate, he went to the corner gate at the back. He paid the coachman, got off the carriage, dusted himself off, and knocked on the small gate a few times.

Xiao Du heard a creaking sound as the gate opened. A charming girl, dressed plainly with two braids and wearing an apron, opened the door. Zhenze immediately embraced the girl, and they entered the courtyard together. Xiao Du watched as Young Master Zhenze seemed to transform into a different person, no longer reserved or shy.

For a month, Zhenze visited this courtyard regularly, staying for two or three hours each time. Sometimes they even went to the market together to buy groceries. Xiao Du didn't dare to keep it a secret and faithfully reported everything to Master Wendi upon his return.

Upon hearing the information, Master Wendi became somewhat angry and sent someone to find out more about the girl. It turned out that she was the child born over a decade ago to Xiao Chunhong, the top courtesan of the Chun Hua Lou. Originally, they intended to give the child away, but Xiao Chunhong threatened to kill herself, which frightened the madam of the Chun Hua Lou. The child appeared to be pitiful and had to rely on Xiao Chunhong's earnings, so the madam agreed to keep her. The child was named Xiao Luzhu and grew up in the brothel, learning singing, playing instruments, and assisting in cleaning at the Chun Hua Lou. She came from a humble background and nobody knew who her father was. Her mother had passed away ten years ago for unknown reasons, and thus no one paid much attention to her. However, as she grew up day by day, she blossomed into a beautiful and charming young woman, captivating the hearts of anyone who saw her.

One day, when she went out to buy groceries, she met Zhenze, who instantly fell in love with her. Zhenze figured out the timings of when she went out and when she returned. He tried various ways to make Xiao Luzhu like him, gifting her earrings, a golden hairpin, and other attractive accessories. Through their interactions, Xiao Luzhu, who had never experienced someone loving her before, gradually developed feelings for Zhenze.

When Second Master Wendì found out, he went to Chun Hua Lou and told the madam, "If you make Xiao Luzhu leave, I'll agree to any conditions."

The madam, playing with her gold bracelet, said, "I spent a lot of money raising this child. Now she can earn money for me. I can't just let her go because you said so."

Wendì knew she was bargaining and said, "I know your secrets. I know how you forced Chunhong to commit suicide ten years ago."

In fact, the incident of Chunhong's suicide caused a stir at the time and was ultimately deemed a suicide. But Wendì had found out from Chunhong's closest sister that Chunhong had seen something shameful that the madam didn't want her to know.

The madam knew she couldn't negotiate a good price with Wendì and so he offered to buy her a new outfit and a pair of gold bracelets. The madam agreed to chase Xiao Luzhu away.

The girl Xiao Luzhu disappeared soon after, and no one knew which brothel she had been sold to. Poor Zhenze left home to search for Xiao Luzhu, and he returned home once a few years later, dressed in ragged clothes and holding a begging bowl. He knelt down and kowtowed a few times in front of the Li family's courtyard before leaving. There was no news from him ever since. Therefore, Zhenze was never recorded in the family genealogy.

However, in the following years, Wendi also suffered greatly. His son never returned! According to the seniority of the "Zhen" generation, Zhenze should have been officially recognized as the fourth son, but after his departure, his name was also removed from the family genealogy. Wendi repented before the Buddha, confessing his momentary confusion, blaming himself for losing his son. He sought to make amends for his mistakes in every possible way.

Eventually, Wendi became somewhat eccentric and would constantly talk to his younger brother, Wenchuan, saying, "Fourth brother, you see, I can't really claim to have two sons, Zhenjiang and Zhenze. Zhenjiang has no descendants, and Zhenze left without saying goodbye. Is this punishment from the heavens for me? Perhaps I was too harsh on Zhenze! I am nothing but a lousy father!"

Wenchuan comforted his second brother, "This is not entirely your fault. Everyone's ideas cannot be changed by you alone. Even you were blinded at the time, like a blind man!"

Wendi nodded and stomped his feet, saying, "I am not only blind but also blind in my heart!"

Wendi then asked Wenchuan, "Brother Four, what was I thinking when I let Xiao Luzhu disappear? I have carefully considered it, and it should be because of the face, the false sense of pride! If Zhenze had really married Xiao Luzhu and had children for the Li family, I might have hugged my grandson long ago. How happy that would have been!"

Wendi saw his nephew Zhenhong coming in from outside, and tears streamed down his face.

Before his passing, Wendi told Wenchuan not to engrave any words on his tombstone. He felt ashamed to face his ancestors and was afraid of not being able to explain himself when he met his son in the afterlife.

# Chapter Three

## Loved and hated, fighting injustices; Zhenhong's life of trouble

### 1

Zhenhong has always been a mischievous and restless child since birth. When he was born, he had a large head, and the midwife struggled for four or five hours to deliver him. His mother, Jiahe, was exhausted from the ordeal, and Fourth Master Wenchuan immediately rushed to the town to bring the renowned doctor, Xu Zuming, to assist with the delivery. However, Dr. Xu was not at home, so Wenchuan and his companions hurriedly went to the neighboring village to fetch him. By the time they returned home, Jiahe was in critical condition. However, Dr. Xu miraculously saved her life and safely delivered the nine-jin [12-pound] baby Zhenhong into the world.

As Zhenhong grew older, he noticed how respectful his father and mother were towards Dr. Xu Zuming. They never forgot the doctor's kindness and were grateful for his life-saving actions. Zhenhong silently kept this gratitude in his heart.

There was another incident when eight-year-old Zhenhong skipped school and dragged Zhenjiang along with him. They walked to the riverbank, took off their outer clothes, and threw them by the river before Zhenhong dragged his cousin up the hill to pick wild fruits.

The two cousins didn't go to school, and by noon, Wendi and Wenchuan started to worry. They sent people to search and found their clothes by the river. This was a serious matter! The members of the Li family mobilized and searched downstream along the river, but even as the afternoon sun began to set, there was still no sign of the two boys. Everyone was getting anxious. Meanwhile, the two cousins had filled their pockets with wild fruits and strolled back home confidently. This made Wenchuan, Fourth Master of the Wen family, furious. He gave Zhenhong a sound beating, and if it weren't for Jiahe's intervention, he would have thrashed the young boy until his bottom was red and swollen. Zhenjiang, being obedient, was scared and stood aside without making a sound. However, Zhenhong, while getting spanked, still laughed and said to his cousin Zhenjiang, "It feels like scratching an itch."

Zhenhong led his little friends to climb walls, catch grasshoppers, crickets, peel off tiles on the roof, and catch fish in the river, causing trouble along the way. On one occasion, Zhenhong led a group of children to climb over a wall. They ran along the top of the wall one after another. However, his cousin Zhenjiang slipped and fell from the high wall. His leg was cut by a broken piece of tile, leaving a large gaping wound that kept bleeding and oozing pus without healing.

Zhenhong went to a witch named Luo in the town dozens of miles away for advice. Everyone said that the witch Luo was specialized in treating difficult and complicated diseases. However, many people didn't believe her methods and thought they were frightening. Zhenhong wanted to try, so he walked for a day to Luo town and got a prescription that said the parasites on toads could be used to treat wounds. From then on, he would look for toads with maggots after school every day. If he couldn't find one, he would catch one, knock it to death with a stick, and put it in a bottle, then catch flies and put them in the bottle too. Several days later, he really found toad maggot larvae. He put the white larvae into his brother's wound. As it turned out, a few days later, Zhengjiang's wound started growing new granulation tissue. Zhenhong had done many things that defied common sense but turned out to be unexpectedly effective.

All the little friends on the street elected Zhenhong as their leader, and everyone called him "Big Head." He held an inauguration speech in earnest. Zhenhong chose a plot of land in the fields of Batiandi, stood on a high hill, and tied red silk around his wrists and head. He didn't need a script and as soon as he got up there started his speech, which was very infectious. He said our primary task was to form a youth group to help poor children. They couldn't eat enough or keep warm, and we couldn't just sit idly by. Those who have resources at home need to work harder! Everyone needs to bring what they have at home and bring it to me for centralized distribution to poor children. He said the youth group needed detailed division of labor, and nobody could take more than they should. He also came up with a way to save resources.

Back then, there was a branch of the Northeastern Peking Opera called "Beng Beng Xi". Xue Shiliang, the deputy of this branch, had a father who was the foreman in the theater and was also fond of singing and playing the erhu. Shiliang often went to the theater with Zhenhong, and after watching the performances, they would teach the children in their youth group to sing and practice martial arts with wooden sticks. Zhenhong ordered Shiliang to talk to his father and collect some old costumes for their group. Shiliang did not disappoint and brought back several sets the next day. Zhenhong had his mother Jiahe modify the costumes, and their youth group began to wear them to perform and sing around the town, attracting a crowd of people who even threw money after their performances.

After the show, the children counted their earnings and distributed them according to the amount of effort they had put into the performance. However, children from poor families who couldn't sing could only act as assistants and didn't receive much money. Zhenhong gave his share of the earnings to them and asked everyone to vote to contribute 30% of their earnings to a fund for needy children. They continued to sing for a while, but some parents of the children felt ashamed and did not allow them to perform. Moreover, their performances were subject to the limitations of weather and venue, and eventually the group disbanded.

The youth group lasted for several years until Zhenhong was 14. During this time, he had taken things from his home, but his father Wenchuan turned a blind eye because he was doing good things. However, some affluent families said they were unwilling to help poor children anymore, and some adults even kept their children away from Zhenhong. Zhenhong continued with the children of the other three wealthy landlords in Yingkou for two more years, but as they grew older and had more responsibilities, their focus shifted away from the group.

Even though many young people had given up, Zhenhong did not. He began to let poor children come to his horse stable to clean up the manure and allowed them to clean up chicken manure in his chicken coop. Then he had them deliver the manure to the manure pit on the Li's fields, and he would give them a note indicating how much manure they collected and how much money they could get from the accounting office of Li Cashier. In the Li family's accounting department, Guo Yunsheng was the head accountant, while Liu Lianxing handled the financial records. Because he had a long beard, everyone referred to him Liu Dahuzi as "Big Beard Liu."

Liu Dahuzi was sitting in the accounting office wearing glasses and calculating the accounts when he saw Liu Laobie's son, the poorest in the village, come to redeem a two-ounce silver coin with a small master Zhenhong's note. He handed the note to Liu Dahuzi, expecting to receive the money. Liu Dahuzi looked at the poorly dressed child from head to toe, ripped the note to pieces, and said, "Go away, go away, don't cause trouble here! If the accounts are wrong later, I will say you stole it."

At that moment, another child entered, also looking to cash a note. Liu Lianxing became somewhat annoyed. His authority was being challenged. He shouted at the two children to leave, just like shooing away chickens.

Zhenhong happened to come to the account room at this time. He wanted to see his teammates happily taking the money home, but he didn't expect to see this situation. Zhenhong said to the two wronged companions, "Don't worry, come to my room, and I will exchange it for you."

That's how the matter was resolved! However, Li Zhenhong looked down on Liu Dahuzi's appearance and his contempt for poor people made him angry!

Zhenhong came up with a malicious trick. One day when Liu Dahuzi was dozing off, Zhenhong snipped off his stylish long beard with a pair of scissors!

Angry Liu Lianxing went straight to Wenchuan's place. To save face for Liu's account room, Wenchuan slapped Zhenhong. However, right after he slapped him, Liu Lianxing begged for mercy for

Zhenghong. He said, "The child doesn't understand anything. If he understands now, it's fine!"

Liu Lianxing was very slick. He knew that this young master was not easy to provoke. He was the master's own son, and the father would always side with his son. This slap was enough to save face. If the master continued to beat the young master, not only would he be unhappy, but Zhenhong might also have other tricks waiting for him. A slap was enough to have a deterrent effect!

Wenchuan told Zhenhong, "Your children can use the receipts that Zhenhong gave them to receive money."

But Wenchuan also told Liu Lianxing, "Put a limit to how much they can exchange once, a maximum of one silver coin."

The two men were even, but Zhenhong was not satisfied. At the dinner table, he said to his father, "Dad, I can tell that Liu Lianxing is not a good person. Don't use him!"

Wenchuan looked at his son and asked, "Tell me, how did you come to that conclusion?"

Zhenghong said, "He is a petty person who looks down on others. I'm afraid you might be deceived."

Actually, Wenchuan was also evaluating Liu Lianxing. The account room really needed someone with good character to manage it, and recently, some other things that Liu Lianxing had done had made Wenchuan worry. So, Wenchuan still decided to replace him.

This incident clearly marked a complete victory for Zhenhong! All the children in the group now admired him as their leader, and from that day on, Zhenhong's words were law among the children of Batiandi. And so, Zhenhong grew up stumbling along like this! His father Wenchuan remarked, "This child really makes people worry!"

## 2

In 1908, the fourth son of Pingsheng, Wenchuan, who always advocated education as the foundation of the country and the savior of the nation, sent his 16-year-old son Zhenhong to study at the first Fengtian University in Shenyang. He personally accompanied his son on this journey to Shengjing (the old name for Shenyang). They took the newly opened small train to Shengjing, which, in Zhenhong's words, was remarkably fast, reaching their destination in just a few hours. This was the second time in Wenchuan's life that he came to Shengjing. The first time was when he came with his grandfather and his third brother to purchase small hardware machinery for Fengtian.

This time, he saw the tragic situation of Shengjing's Forbidden City being occupied by the Russians and then being smashed and looted. The wall plaster fell off, some places were in ruins, and the buildings collapsed. But later he heard that the "Provisional Regulations for the Surrender of Fengtian" signed by Zeng Qi on behalf of the Qing government had been declared invalid, and Zeng Qi had also been dismissed from office. Moreover, on April 8, 1902, China and Russia signed the "Treaty on the Transfer of the Northeast", which stipulated that the Russian soldiers would withdraw from the Northeast in three batches within one and a half years, and now there were not many Russian soldiers to be seen on the boundary. Wenchuan saw many soldiers standing guard on the city walls of Fengtian and heard that they were under the command of Zhang Da and Zhang Zuolin.

The newly established modern Fengtian University was located outside the Small West Gate (Xiao Xi Men), surrounded by several pavilions and temples, creating a beautiful scenic setting. In fact, Zeng Qi had done some commendable things. This university was established by utilizing various temples and shrines outside the provincial capital, making it the first institution of higher education in the northeastern region of China during the Qing Dynasty.

Wenchuan accompanied his son to the school for registration. Inside the school, the male students were dressed in long robes and jackets, with most of them still sporting long braids, while some had adopted the trendy parted hairstyle. Even the schoolteachers wore long robes and round, shiny spectacles, giving them a scholarly appearance that was vastly different from the traditional rote-learning academies. The curriculum at the university included courses such as Chinese literature, English, Manchu language, various philosophical schools, history, geography, mathematics, and more. The total tuition for three years of university education amounted to twelve thousand taels of silver.*

For sixteen-year-old Zhenhong, it was his first time in Fengtian, and everything seemed fresh and exciting to him. He remarked that even the sky in Shenyang was bluer than in Yingkou, and the water tasted sweeter. As they walked along the wide streets of Fengtian, they passed by Fengtian Financial Street and even the Fengtian Police Station. Zhenhong wanted to go inside and take a look, but Wenchuan pulled him away. Along the way, Zhenhong was captivated by the grand buildings of the Great Qing Bank, Buddhist temples, pagodas, and the Tongshan Hospital in Fengtian's Da Xi Men (Great West Gate). They were particularly surprised to find that the Fengtian Machinery Bureau they had visited before had transformed into the Fengtian Mint and was now off-limits to visitors.

Later, Zhenhong wrote to his parents saying that their school was managed by the Education Administration Office, and that meals and accommodation were managed centrally. He mentioned that there were also female students at the school, some of whom wore braids in a unique style called "sheep horn braids." It was all so fascinating to him! There were blackboards, and the teachers would fill it up with dense notes in every class, so they had to take good notes and review them later. There were more than twenty students in each class, and every two students shared a desk. Everyone was very diligent in their studies, so he had to work even harder. He also said that he enjoyed listening to Mr. Xia Jingren's English classes, who had returned from studying in the United States, and that he could now speak English with his uncle Wentian.

In another letter, he mentioned that during his free time, he visited the banks of the Hun River, the Southern and Northern Pagodas Temples, and the vicinity of the Imperial Palace, among others. It seemed like there was an endless array of new experiences and discoveries for him to share.

Three years passed in the blink of an eye. In 1911, Zhenhong graduated from Fengtian University and returned to Yingkou at the age of nineteen. Upon his return, the Xinhai Revolution broke out, and

* Approximately $6,000.

the Republic of China was established. On January 1, 1912, Sun Yat-sen announced the founding of the Republic of China in Nanjing, marking the first year of the Republic. At that time, the government of the Republic of China implemented a series of policies to protect national capitalism and encourage the shipping industry. Wenchuan wanted to revive the Li family's shipping business although he was not successful in the end. So he sent his son Zhenhong to study at Yingkou Business School, the first business school in Yingkou (predecessor of Liaoning University), established in May 1905. Zhenhong studied business here for one year. In the second year of the Republic of China, 1913, Zhenhong officially took over the Li family's eight fields vegetable garden.

## 3

Zhenhong, the only son of Li Wenchuan, was the perfect example of the phrase "the son carries on the family business". He was hardworking, resourceful, and persevering, and he spent more time in the fields than even the tenant farmers. He enjoyed improving the soil and implementing rational land use practices, resulting in bountiful harvests in the Li family's eight fields vegetable garden each year after he took over. The tenants were also very pleased because Zhenhong did not ask them for money to improve the soil, yet the crops grew exceptionally well! Their income also increased significantly. It was also a stroke of luck that those years had favorable weather, which was just as delightful as Zhenhong's vegetable garden.

Zhenhong was mischievous when he was young, but as he grew up, he became very steadfast in his work. He was like someone who had grown up in the fields and wouldn't come home until it was dark. His naturally dark skin became even darker from sun exposure, resembling the black soil.

After the National Protection War in 1916, China descended into a state of chaos and warlordism. For a time, there were some rogue soldiers who appeared in the northern cities. A Captain Zhang whose mother became seriously ill, sent his soldiers to take Dr. Xu

Zuming to their temporary headquarters at gunpoint. The doctor had never encountered such a situation and was sweating nervously. Captain Zhang's mother had an intestinal obstruction, and because the treatment was delayed, part of her intestines had already necrotized and her face had turned black and purple. It was too late, and even the renowned physician Xu Zuming was powerless to save her. Nonetheless, the brutal and rude Captain Zhang threw Xu Zuming into prison.

Xu Zuming's son was a royal physician who had received his father's medical skills. He had no idea what had happened and was still treating the abdicated Emperor Puyi and members of the royal family in the capital. At that time, the emperor was confined within the Forbidden City but still retained the title. Xu Zuming's son had asked his father to go with him to the capital, but Xu Zuming had said that fallen leaves would return to their roots, and he would guard his hometown and treat his fellow villagers.

When the servants who delivered food to the town came back to report that Doctor Xu was in trouble and had been thrown into prison, Zhenhong was very anxious and immediately tried to find a way to help.

He managed to bribe the soldiers guarding the prison and finally saw Xu Zuming, who was sleeping on straw in the dark cell. When Xu Zuming saw Zhenhong, tears welled up in his eyes. He reached out his hands through the prison bars, and Zhenhong grabbed onto them. Xu Zuming said, "I knew you would come. You are a righteous and sincere person. I have been waiting for you."

The prison guards opened the cell door, and Zhenhong handed over the food he had brought. He also brought good wine for Xu Zuming. The two sat on the straw, drinking and talking.

Xu Zuming said, "Seeing you, I can rest assured. I have something to entrust to you. Today, after drinking your wine, I have no regrets."

Saying this, Xu Zuming unbuttoned his inner garment and tore open the lining, revealing densely written words inside. He pointed to the words and said, "I was afraid that if I died, this ancestral secret formula would be buried with me in the coffin. So, these past few days, I have been waiting for someone trustworthy to come and take it away."

Zhenhong felt sorrow in his heart because he knew that he couldn't save Xu Zuming with his own power. Before coming to the prison, he had sought help from the county magistrate and even offered money, but it was of no use. In these times, the military officers held true power, and everyone feared them to some extent.

Zhenhong said, "Times are tough, and there's not much I can say. I will risk my life to protect what you have entrusted to me."

Then Xu Zuming told him, "You keep this secret formula for two years, and when my grandson turns sixteen, let him take over. Just don't give it to that imperial physician's son. He doesn't treat common people; once the secret formula enters the Forbidden City, it will never return to the people."

Zhenhong deeply respected Xu Zuming and nodded vigorously, saying, "Rest assured!"

Then the two men changed their clothes. Zhenhong was afraid that something might happen to the garment, so he immediately went back.

Less than a week after Zhenhong returned home, he heard that Xu Zuming had died in prison. He sent someone to the capital to deliver a message to Xu Zuming's son, Xu the physician, and together they took care of Xu Zuming's affairs. They erected a tall tombstone with the following inscription:

> Bringing back the dead, healing the sick;
> Saving lives, miraculous hands that revive.
> The tomb of the divine physician Xu Zuming.

Xu the physician took his fourteen-year-old son to the capital, but Zhenhong followed Xu Zuming's wishes and didn't give him the vest with the formulas written inside.

One day, when Zhenhong's nephew was cleaning out a chest, he found the garment and discovered the secret formula. He asked his uncle several times to copy the formula, but Zhenhong refused. He waited for two years until Xu Zuming's grandson, Xu Yimin, turned sixteen.

Two years later, Zhenhong went to the capital several times to look for Xu Zuming's grandson Xu Yimin, but he was unsuccessful.

Later, by chance, he learned from a patient who had been rescued by Xu Yimin that he had been practicing medicine and treating people since the age of fifteen and had later enrolled in the National Beijing Medical School to study Western medicine-pathology. This school is the predecessor of the current Beijing Medical University. Zhenhong found him, and the secret recipe finally fell into the hands of Xu Yimin, who was dedicated to integrating Chinese and Western medicine and helping the people.

As the saying goes, good deeds are rewarded. After this incident, the villagers and neighbors in the community had even more trust in Zhenhong. Traders and merchants flocked to the Li family's vegetable garden to buy vegetables. In addition to regular workers, there were also many temporary workers in the Li family. During the busy autumn harvest season, the farm was particularly bustling.

During the other seasons, the Li family employed fewer temporary workers, and the regular workers would dry the fresh vegetables and make them into pickled and salted vegetables. They made soy sauce with pig ears and broad beans, pickled radish strips, and preserved mustard greens, among other things. This business was also thriving.

## Chapter Four

# Wan'er marries into the Li family. Zhenhong loses Batiandi at the gambling house

### 1

Another troublesome matter was that Zhenhong was not in a hurry to get married, which worried of Wenchuan. He was looking forward to holding his grandchild! The matchmaker said, "Many families' girls appreciate Zhenhong's masculine and impressive demeanor."

With so many people urging and pressuring him, Zhenhong reluctantly agreed to get married. But he ended up getting married twice. In the autumn of 1920, the 9th year of the Republic of China, 29-year-old Zhenhong married a girl from the Feng family. This marriage was a traditional custom of the Li family, where Zhenhong, as the (adopted) son of Uncle Li Wenshan, married his daughter-in-law. This was because Uncle Li Wenshan had no son all these years. This matter was decided by Uncle Wenshan and Zhenhong's father, Wenchuan, of course, with Zhenhong's consent. Uncle Wenshan watched Zhenhong grow up and valued him the most. He had told his fourth brother Wenchuan several times that he wanted Zhenhong to be both of their son. To show his sincerity, Uncle Wenshan even had a will draw up, stating that half of his estate would be given to Zhenhong after he passed away! At that time, the Li family's hardware factory and store were managed by the Wenshan family. In this way, Zhenhong married Fengshi to continue Uncle Wenshan's family line. A year later, in the 10th year of the Republic of China, Zhenhong got married again, this time with the daughter-in-law entering the Wenchuan family. He had finally been looking forward to this day!

Sun Wan'er was of average height, with a beautiful appearance, arched eyebrows, delicate eyes, not particularly big, but slightly drooping at the corners. Her embroidery was famous far and wide, and everyone praised the jackets, vests, and even the linings she embroidered! What's more, she was literate, wrote excellent calligraphy, and could even paint. Later, she had great influence on their children. After she married into the family, Zhenhong wrote her a poem in the style of Tang Yin, titled "Jealousy of Flowers Song":

> Last night, the Begonia bloomed in the rain,
> Several delicate buds, charming as if to rain.
> In the morning, the beauty rises from her inner chamber room,
> Picking flowers and comparing her red attire in front of the mirror.

This made the elder daughter-in-law, Li Fengshi, most angry, because Zhenhong did not write a poem for her.

The two wives had different personalities. Li Fengshi did not talk much, but she had a quick temper and got angry easily. She often competed with Sun Wan'er over which room Zhenhong would sleep in at night. If Zhenhong spent too much time in the backyard and neglected her, she would not try to win him over, but instead ignored him for several days out of anger. Whenever she encountered something that displeased her, Li Fengshi would quarrel with Zhenhong. However, this only made Zhenhong prefer to be with Wan'er in the backyard even more.

Nevertheless, Li Fengshi was very fertile and gave birth to four children in quick succession. Her eldest son, Li Yaojia (later changed his name to Li Feng), was the fourth in line among the male descendants of Tairen and Pingsheng, and her eldest daughter, Li Yaoxian (who later changed her name to Li Wen), was also the fourth in line for the female descendants. Her youngest son, Li Yaoyou (a professor at Tsinghua University, later changed his name to Li Da, following his fourth elder brother), was the seventh in line for the male descendants. She had another son, Li Yaocheng, the fifth in order, who had seen through the mundane world and was content to be an ordinary person.

Sun Wan'er, who was loved by Zhenhong, gave birth to daughter Li Yaozhi in 1922, who was clever and smart and deeply loved by the patriarch. Then another granddaughter, Li Yaoxin, was born. She was kind-hearted and hospitable, and eventually became a Buddhist. Then in 1931, Wenchuan, the patriarch of the Li family, welcomed his first grandson, Li Yaoguo, who unfortunately would shed his blood on the Korean battlefield at the age of twenty. Finally, three years later in 1934, the youngest of the fourth generation of the Li family, Li Yaowei, was born, who is my grandfather. In that year of 1934, Zhenhong became a father twice. During the Lunar New Year in February, Fengshi gave birth to a boy named Li Yaoyou, and in May, Sun Wan'er gave birth to a child named Li Yaowei. Their names were quite similar, making them the "You Wei" brothers. The implication is "brothers with accomplishments."

Since Wan'er had entered the Li family, Zhenhong favored her because of her literacy, and he eventually gave Wan'er the keys to the household management. One day, during a family meeting, Zhenhong suddenly said to Li Fengshi who was dozing, "Wake up! From now on, the keys to the house will be entrusted to Wan'er. It's been hard work for the ex-housekeeper Fengshi, so we'll give the Feng family elders extra silver for the new year."

This came about very suddenly, and Fengshi had no idea it was coming. She wanted to protest, but seeing the seriousness on the master's face, she reluctantly took off the keychain from her waist and handed it over to Master Zhenhong.

Zhenhong handed the keys directly to Wan'er, who was unprepared and hesitant. The master tied the keys around her waist without any further thought. It's not that Wan'er was completely unprepared. Lately, the master Zhenhong had been complaining to her about Fengshi's management skills, how the costs were not distributed fairly and the house was full of complaints. Especially in the kitchen, since she brought in her own younger brother to manage it, the money allocated to the kitchen staff had been increasing, which was unfair.

Wan'er was always gentle, and she urged the master not to be too hasty, and she didn't want to create conflict with Fengshi. Besides, the master could have reminded Fengshi to pay more attention so she would be more restrained. But today, the master had simply demanded the key. Seeing Sister Feng's expression, Wan'er felt a little guilty.

Wan'er began to draft household rules and rectify the family's discipline, which inevitably involved reducing the allocation of silver to the kitchen. Lately, the master often visited the backyard and rarely went to the front yard, and Wan'er was busy, so she rarely saw Fengshi. But one day, Fengshi turned to Wan'er with flashing eyes and said, "The jade ruyi hanging on the corner of the ancestral cabinet in the house is missing! Someone in the house is stealing. Whoever has the key knows who did it."

This was clearly pointing the finger at Wan'er, but even if the key to the ancestral hall was in her hand, everyone could freely come and go until the lights went out at ten o'clock at night, and Wan'er would then lock the door. With so many people going in and out of the ancestral hall every day, how could it be said that it was Wan'er who took it?

Fengshi shouted in front of everyone, "Wan'er, do you dare let us come to your yard and search your house?"

Wan'er, who was usually mild-mannered, became serious and said, "If we want to investigate, let's investigate together, go door to door, and find out who did it."

Zhenhong was a bit annoyed, he raised his cane and pointed at Fengshi's forehead and said, "What are you all making a fuss about? I trust Wan'er, she didn't take it, no need to investigate. It's just a jade ruyi, forget it. If someone took it, they would return it if they have a conscience."

However, Fengshi was not satisfied and a few days later, she brought up the idea of splitting the family, saying, "If we keep losing things like this, we'll eventually bankrupt this family."

Zhenhong frowned and said to Fengshi: "What's the point of making a fuss? Haven't you had enough? Do you want to make people laugh at us?" Fengshi had been throwing a tantrum for a while, but she couldn't shake Wan'er's position. Zhenhong was also a little annoyed with Fengshi, but he knew that the scale in his heart was a bit off-balance, and Wan'er weighed a little heavier.

The next day, the shopkeeper Liu, who ran a pawnshop in town, came to the Li family with a jade Ruyi that Zhenhong recognized. Old Liu said, "You better keep an eye on your servants! I saw you with this jade Ruyi before, so I took it."

Old Liu handed the jade Ruyi to Zhenhong, who looked at it carefully and said, "It's mine. There's a deep green mark on the handle of this jade Ruyi, and no two pieces of jade are the same."

Zhenhong asked in confusion, "How did you get it?"

Old Liu sat down, crossed his legs and said, "How are you going to thank me? Do you remember Chen Cuozhi?"

Zhenhong waved his hand and repeatedly said, "Old Chen, impossible! Impossible! I've known him for so many years, I know him too well. He's a skilled worker on my land."

Old Liu stood up and said, "This is your family's matter. I have things to do. You investigate it yourself!"

After seeing off Old Liu, Zhenhong was puzzled. Chen had always been very loyal and never lied. However, Zhenhong thought that Chen was nicknamed "Chen Cuozhi" because of his short stature and had never married because of it. Maybe he was short of money and went to find girls in the brothel. He couldn't get it out of his mind and went straight to the workshop. Chen was not there, and everyone said that there was a big event in his family recently and his father had passed away.

Zhenhong had never heard Chen mention the death of his father recently. He took a hundred taels of silver in the account and took a carriage to the Chen village thirty miles away. Chen's parents lived at the west end of the village, the closest to the inside of the village. Chen was the only son in the family, and he had two sisters. From the small, low house of Chen's family, Zhenhong could tell that Chen had not taken much money from the Li family. Zhenhong felt that he had not misjudged Chen.

There was a white cloth hanging outside the door, and the sound of crying could be heard inside. Zhenhong pushed open a door following the crying sound and saw Chen Cuozhi, who had a short stature, keeping vigil for his father. His two sisters were crying beside him. Zhenhong saw that Chen Cuozhi became even smaller at once, and more importantly, he saw that the coffin for Chen's father was made of thin and cheap wood for children. Zhenhong felt very sad. Chen Cuozhi looked up and saw Zhenhong, he was somewhat surprised and did not dare to face him.

Zhenhong walked to Chen Cuozhi's side, squatted beside him, and said, "You, a silent pumpkin, why didn't you tell me?"

Chen Cuozhi lowered his head, blushing and said, "When Liu boss asked me that day, I knew you would come. I originally wanted to buy a decent coffin for my father so that he could rest in peace. I thought that since I became a lucky man and had money, I would buy the coffin first, and then slowly redeem myself. I didn't expect... sigh, I really shouldn't have thought like that."

Chen Cuozhi cried silently. Zhenhong self-blamed and said, "Seeing your home, I know I should give you a raise. You need more money to support your family. For now, let's give your father a decent funeral."

Zhenhong handed the money bag to Chen Cuozhi and said, "It was my fault. Go buy a pine coffin for your father. I will send someone over in a few days to give you some more money and renovate your house."

Zhenhong added, "Don't go to brothel too often in the future, better forget about the brothel from now on."

Zhenhong left the house, and Chen Cuozhi saw him off at the door. He knelt at the door and shouted, "Fourth Master, Chen Cuozhi will be your man from now on!"

Later, with the help of the Feng family, Chen Cuozhi found a good woman and had a son the following year. When they held a one-month-old celebration for his newborn son, they specially invited Zhenhong to give a speech. Later, when the Li family was in trouble, Chen Cuozhi behaved very honestly.

## 2

Zhenhong was indeed a very restless and active person. Since he had married two wives, Li Fengshi and Sun Wan'er, he had become a proud father of eight children. What had made him even prouder was that his vegetable garden had thrived. Sometimes Zhenhong took a break and went to the town to have some fun.

Recently, Xue Shiliang, who had been Zhenhong's assistant in the youth group when they were young, had come to buy vegetables in Zhenhong's green vegetables garden and had told him about a new game called Pai Gow introduced by foreigners at the Qingfeng Casino in town. Xue Shiliang had said, "Big Head, you are doing serious business now, but you should also have some fun when you have time."

Zhenhong had said, "What can we play? We have a big family to support."

Xue Shiliang replied, "Let me tell you about a fun game. It's called Pai Gow, and there's not much to lose or win."

Xue Shiliang had added, "Your brain works well. When should we go and check it out?"

Zhenhong had really itched to go because he had dreamed of becoming a gambling god since he was a child. He stepped into the Qingfeng Casino for the first time.

The storefront of the casino was small. Although gambling had been prevalent from the late Qing Dynasty to the Republic of China, the government still cracked down on it. Therefore, most gambling venues had a small storefront that was a combination of a tavern and a snack bar.

A guide led the gamblers inside, and the lobby inside was lively, with rows of card tables surrounded by some high-pitched gamblers. Some even lost their pants and had to walk home in their underwear in the middle of the night during the winter. As everyone knew Zhenhong, his arrival had caused quite a stir. The casino owner, Hou San'er, ran over and led Zhenhong and Xue Shiliang to a private room inside. Inside, there were several square card tables with purple satin tablecloths covering them. There were several stacks of chips and a deck of poker cards with jokers on the table.

After they sat down, the dealer asked Zhenhong what he wanted to play, and he chose the easy game of blackjack. In addition to Xue Shiliang, there were several other players, including the dealer's son and nephew, making a total of six people. At the beginning, Zhenhong was cautious and won most of the time, rarely busting when his cards exceeded 21 points. He won for several days in a row and was happy. Whenever he was having fun, he drank several bottles of wine.

Then, in recent days, Zhenhong seldom went to the vegetable garden. He left the family affairs to the steward and went to the casino almost every night, winning small amounts of money every day, which had all been recorded on the casino's account. It was already late one night, and Wan'er had been sewing clothes while waiting for Zhenhong to come back. Then the door opened, and Li Fengshi came in and asked Wan'er, "Has Zhenhong come to your place yet? He has gone crazy lately, still gambling so late!"

Wan'er looked at Fengshi and calmly said, "He should be back by now! I'm a little worried too!"

Fengshi only shouted loudly, "This won't do, we can't let Zhenhong go on like this!"

Wan'er comforted her, "Let's wait a little longer, Zhenhong has had a difficult few years and is very worried. He has never had any bad habits. Let him play this time, and when he's done playing, he'll come back."

Zhenhong didn't come back that night until dawn. As soon as he entered, Wan'er, who had stayed up all night, immediately brought him some water to wash his face, and then brought him a bowl of freshly cooked millet porridge. Zhenhong, who was drowsy, washed his face and drank the porridge. Wan'er helped him take off his clothes, hung them up, took off his shoes, washed his feet, and then made his bed. Zhenhong got into bed and fell asleep. He slept until almost noon, and Wan'er had prepared lunch by the time he woke up.

Wan'er watched Zhenhong eat and asked him, "Zhenhong, you've been playing outside for a long time recently. This thing is addictive, like smoking opium."

Zhenhong said while eating, "It's okay, I know my limits. I can control myself and not play big."

Wan'er wanted her man to turn around and advised him, "Sister Fengshi also asked me to persuade you not to gamble. How about we play mahjong at home if you want to play? It doesn't matter if we win or lose."

Zhenhong readily agreed, “Okay, I’ll listen to you. My luck has been good lately, and I’ve been winning! I’ll play a few more days, satisfy my cravings, and then quit playing big.”

Wan’er still wasn’t reassured, “If you win from those people, will they let you go?”

Zhenhong said confidently, “Wan’er, don’t worry, nothing will happen.”

And so, Wan’er spent several days on edge, with Fengshi coming to her house every day to nag. Wan’er and Fengshi became comrades in the same struggle, both worrying together. One night, it was past midnight and Zhenhong had not yet returned. Wan’er and Fengshi went together to the courtyard where their parents lived. Their parents lived in the largest south room facing the sun inside the courtyard. Wan’er and Fengshi knocked on the door, and their parents lit the lamp and came out wearing their clothes.

The two daughters-in-law knelt as soon as they entered the door. Wan’er said, “Dad, Mom, I think it’s better for you two to talk to Zhenhong. He has recently become addicted to gambling and hasn’t come back yet.”

Jiahe asked nervously, “Did he lose?”

Wenchuan said to Jiahe, “What are you thinking? In ten bets, nine will lose. There is no undefeated gambling god.”

Wan’er said in a pleading tone, “He hasn’t lost until yesterday. But we think it’s not a good thing, so we disturb you, Dad and Mom.”

Wenchuan said, “What’s the trouble? Let’s pull him back together.”

He turned around and asked Wan’er and Li Fengshi, “Which casino is he in?”

Wan’er immediately answered, “Qingfeng.”

Wenchuan left leaning on his crutches. Jiahe urged from behind, “Speak nicely, respectfully, he is an adult.”

Wenchuan told the two daughters-in-law to go back. He went to the backyard stable, had a servant harness the carriage, and went to the town. When he arrived at Qingfeng casino in the town, it was past one o’clock in the morning, and the casino was still brightly lit. But after inquiring, he learned that Zhenhong had left. However, Zhenhong did not return home, which made the old man very anxious. He woke up the butler and the servants in the house to look for him. Everyone searched all night and finally found Zhenhong by a reservoir next to a sorghum field. Fortunately, the water was not deep and he was not drowned. His bike was damaged and one of the wheels was missing.

Wenchuan woke him up and immediately smelled the alcohol on him. Zhenhong was half awake and said slowly, "Dad, I was winning all day today, but later they teamed up against me, and I lost half of our family's land."

Wenchuan widened his eyes and asked, "What did you say?"

Zhenhong raised his voice and said, "I lost half of our family's land." Wenchuan felt a buzzing in his head, and his blood surged. His eyes widened, his lips trembled, and he collapsed into the ditch where Zhenhong had just been lying.

Fourth Master Wenchuan fell ill, with some parts of his body not under control. Zhenhong's mother, Jiahe, who was taking care of Wenchuan, had always had poor health, and she also fell ill. Wan'er thought it was Zhenhong's fault that their parents were like this, so she often served them, helping with meals, cleaning, and even taking care of their bodily functions. Six months later, Wenchuan was able to walk with a cane, but Zhenhong's mother's condition worsened.

Half of the Li family's land was lost to the Hou family's gambling house, and they took the best land from the Li family. Since losing the ancestral land, Zhenhong had no face to see his parents. He only asked Wan'er how they were doing privately and gave her some medicine to boil for them. He was delighted every time Wan'er told him that his father's condition had improved. However, every time he heard that his mother was not doing well, he felt a pain in his heart. He thought that when he was born, he almost killed his mother, and now he had caused her to have a serious illness again.

In the end, his mother passed away, and before she left, she told Zhenhong: "You always loved to cause trouble since you were young, and this time you did the most outrageous thing. Get yourself together, and you still have to support the Li family's eight acres of vegetable gardens."

Zhenhong nodded tearfully. His mother's last words were resolute: "Not even one acre of the Li family's eight acres of vegetable gardens can be lost!" Zhenhong hugged his mother's ear closely and said, "Mother, I will bring it back."

## 3

As soon as his mother Jiahe was gone, Zhenhong threw himself into soil improvement again. He was determined to use soil improvement and reasonable planting to produce the same amount of grain and vegetables on half the land. When he saw the Hou family planting soybeans on the land that used to belong to his family, he felt uneasy. He partly resented Xue Shiliang for taking him to the gambling den. But when Xue Shiliang lost all his money and begged Zhenhong to take him in, he knelt in front of Zhenhong and said, "Li Laosi, my Master, it was my fault for being so blinded by money and causing you so much trouble. You can punish me however you want, but please don't chase me away."

As Xue Shiliang spoke, he burst into tears, but Zhenhong was not one to be swayed by force. He went up to Xue Shiliang and pulled him up, saying, "It's okay, you didn't do it on purpose. We were both blinded by money and tricked."

Xue Shiliang said, "Master, just tell me what to do, and I'll do it."

Zhenhong said, "I have an important task for you. Let's be partners again and work on improving the soil."

Xue Shiliang didn't hesitate and moved into the work shed on the land with his luggage. He ate and lived with the tenant farmers and didn't even ask for any compensation. He worked tirelessly alongside Zhenhong.

Zhenhong's farming got better every year but compared to the Hou family on the other side of the ditch, they were not doing well. The Hou family had a stroke of bad luck - their gambling den was shut down by the government after a fatal fight. They then relied on their vegetable garden to support the family, but they lacked the knowledge and experience to run it properly. They didn't carefully select seeds with full grains and attractive appearances to ensure a high germination rate. Moreover, the Hou family didn't remove damaged, insect-infested, and withered seeds, so the seeds they planted were already subpar. The seeds were not soaked before planting, and the spacing was not considered, resulting in their beans growing with shriveled pods and thin stems. In addition to beans, the Hou family also planted some sorghum, but the ears were not upright, and the yield was not high because they didn't beat the grains before they matured. In fact, this was a mutated fruit of sorghum, also known as black sorghum, a black fungus that was delicious to eat. Zhenhong picked black fungus sorghum ears every year and used them to stew with potatoes and green beans, which was his favorite dish because of its rich nutrition and delicious taste. However, looking at the Hou family's lack of knowledge in beating the grains, Zhenhong couldn't help but laugh. He saw that the Hou family's grains had turned into black powder, and the fungus had damaged the sorghum ears, resulting in reduced yield. Xue Shiliang pointed at the Hou family's crops and laughed, "Evil begot evil, and they got their just deserts! Master, look at the poor crops that the Hou family grew. They tried to handle delicate porcelain without a diamond-like tool to do so."

While enjoying the misfortune of others, Zhenhong also felt some sympathy. As a farmer himself, he was pained to see the decrease in crop yield, knowing that the same land could not support more people. So, he said to Xue Shiliang, "I feel like I've wasted my good land at the Li family's. But I can't bear it in my heart. You know people from the Hou family, so tell them privately to remind Hou Saner not to forget to pick black fungus sorghum ears next year."

Xue Shiliang nodded, admiring Zhenhong's kindness. Such an employer was worth fighting for. As autumn approached, Zhenhong's land was lush and green, and people came to the Li family to buy vegetables and grain, lining up in queues. People from the Hou family were shouting through a loudspeaker, "The lowest price ever, we're selling at a loss!"

They even went to the village and nearby towns to advertise, but still, not many came to buy. Those who did buy Hou family's food and vegetables were scattered households who wanted cheap prices. It was clear that the Hou family couldn't hold on much longer.

Three years later, the Hou family stopped competing with the Li family in planting crops. They took someone's advice and built pigsties on their land to start pig farming. Unfortunately, they were hit by swine fever and only a few pigs survived. Zhenhong saw all of this and wanted to forgive the Hou family, but the memories of his mother's departure, his father's suffering, and a recent attempt by the Hou family to poach Zhenhong's skilled workers made his heart harden again. The Hou family had really misjudged him. After Zhenhong's actions following Chen Cuozi dad's death, he could never have had any other thoughts towards the Li family.

In the fifth autumn, the Li family had another abundant harvest. Growing spring wheat was Zhenhong's specialty, and in this northeastern land, there were not many who could grow wheat well. This was Zhenhong's proudest achievement. His wheat was plump, with even grains, good quality, and the flour had good gluten, making it chewy and perfect for making noodles. As a result, it was always in high demand. This year's harvest looked promising too. The wind blew the wheat ears up and down, as if singing a song of bountiful harvest.

As the harvest time approached, an unexpected disaster struck. In August, there was a heavy rainstorm, and the Liao River flooded. Zhenhong was anxious, and he called almost everyone in his family and even hired temporary workers to urgently harvest the wheat. But it was still not enough, and it looked as though nearly half of the harvest would be lost. Zhenhong didn't have time to think, and everyone in his family worked tirelessly in the heavy rain. When it got dark, Zhenhong reluctantly called a stop to the work, as everyone was exhausted.

The next morning, Zhenhong was shocked to see the scene in the field. The wheat had been harvested and neatly stacked in the empty grain barn of the Li family. Several men from the Hou family, including Xue Shiliang, had worked all night to transport the wheat. Zhenhong's eyes were a bit blurry, and he ran over to hug Xue Shiliang. Then he shook hands with everyone in the Hou family, without saying a word. The enmity between the two families was resolved.

Later, the two families implemented a profit-sharing system, which was probably the earliest form of a joint-stock company. The vegetable garden was returned to the Li family, and they and the Hou family started growing wheat together and became lifelong friends. Whenever they talked about it, Zhenhong would jokingly say, "who says good things don't come from bad situations? The Hou family raised pigs in the vegetable garden and fertilized the land with manure, and I had been working my whole life to improve the soil. I never expected it would be so easy."

Li Zhenhong with three of his children: Yaozhi, Yaoxin, and Yaoguo

## Chapter Five

# The Japanese occupation, their withdrawal and the Communist public-private partnership; empty results

### 1

On September 18th, 1931, the Japanese launched the Mukden Incident and occupied most of the Northeast region, including Yingkou, within 100 days. This gave rise to a new regime in Northeast China, known as Manchukuo. At the time, Zhenhong was in his forties and full of vigor, just entering his prime. He discussed with Wan'er what to do now that the Japanese had arrived. Wan'er was always calm and steady in her actions, like a reassuring pill. While she was busy stuffing a quilt with cotton, she said, "When the enemy comes, we block them; when water comes, we cover it with dirt. We should sell our valuable possessions for gold bars and store them. Gold will not depreciate and may even appreciate in value. Besides, we will need money no matter what happens."

Zhenhong couldn't help but admire his wise wife's sharp mind. He immediately assigned his eldest son, born to Fengshi's family, to buy gold. Afraid that Wan'er might object, Zhenhong deliberately asked her, "Although he is Madam's child, he is also the person I trust the most. Would you mind if he handles this matter?"

Wan'er was always reasonable and saw money as an external thing. She nodded gently and said, "Of course not, it's all for the good of our family."

Zhenhong's family acquired 20 gold bars and opened a compartment in the wall to hide them away.

Later on, the situation in Yingkou became increasingly worse. Yaojia and Yaoxian were discovered to be members of the Communist Party and were arrested, and Zhenhong was taken to the police station. This time, the Japanese targeted Zhenhong, who had always been the leader of the four major families in Yingkou. They wanted to promote him as the chairman of the maintenance association in Badaichi, to help maintain order and collect taxes. However, Zhenhong refused to agree. The Japanese used both soft and hard tactics, promising to reduce taxes for the Li family as a soft approach, and threatening to take control of the Li family's vegetable garden army in Badaichi as a hard approach. After two or three months of persuasion, the Japanese finally shifted their focus to a Jewish leather manufacturer who was a descendant of one of the four major landlords in the town, and the matter was resolved. However, the Japanese were still not satisfied and wanted the Li family to step forward as the chairman of the association, because Zhenhong was easy to talk to. Zhenhong refused, and the Japanese then turned their attention to Zhenjiang, the third uncle.

The Japanese still wanted to persuade Li Zhenhong and tried again. Li Zhenhong was "invited" to the headquarters of the Imperial Army and the Japanese offered him the position. They promised that if he became the chairman, they would no longer pursue their Communist Party suspicions of Yaojia and Yaoxian. But tough Li Zhenhong was not fooled, and he said, "Find someone else to be the chairman. I'll just farm."

The Japanese became so angry that their mustaches were shaking, and they retaliated by torturing Zhenhong, whipping him until his white shirt was torn apart. When Wan 'er went to visit her husband, she was so heartbroken that she couldn't speak and just cried.

Zhenhong told Wan'er, "Why cry? They can't do anything to me. Don't let the soft-headed Zhenjiang listen to the Japanese and agree to be the chairman."

Wan 'er replied confidently, "Don't worry, even though Zhenjiang is weak, he still has principles. He has promised our family that he will never compromise."

Zhenhong felt relieved and said, "Then I can rest assured. You don't need to come and see me again. They won't kill me; they still need me. They rely on the Li family's vegetable garden to supply them with food and vegetables."

Wan'er wiped away her tears and left behind the good wine and food. After returning home, she used four gold bars to bribe the Jewish man and the warden of the prison. The Jewish man spoke on behalf of Zhenhong to the Japanese, who agreed to let him return home for medical treatment, but he was not allowed to leave the Li family's compound. Wan'er had originally planned to use all of her gold bars to save her own family. In fact, those sixteen gold bars had already been taken by Yaojia to buy weapons and medicine for the Communist Party. This was something that Yaojia's younger brother, Yaoyou, only found out about later. However, Zhenhong didn't say much. He mentioned that the gold bars were used indirectly to fight against the Japanese, so it was worth it. He was worried that Wan'er might get upset, so he bought her a gold ring and two gold bangles. Wan'er looked at these shiny pieces of jewelry and said, "Hong, I don't insist on having these trinkets. Without the gold bars, we won't have a backup at home. I'll keep the jewelry you bought for me, and we can use it in case of an emergency."

With Wan'er's understanding, generosity, and magnanimity, Wenchuan held her in high regard, apparently surpassing his estimation of Fengshi.

During the puppet Manchukuo era, Zhenhong's daughter had to go to Japan to study. The family's vegetable garden business was still running, and the hardware factory and store were also open. However, thirty percent of the vegetables from the garden were bought by the Japanese, who not only paid very little but also often beat people up, and even almost caused a loss of life.

One day, a few Japanese soldiers came to the vegetable garden to transport vegetables. They picked the biggest and fullest Chinese cabbages in the garden and pierced the smaller ones with their bayonets. They also wore big leather shoes to kick the vegetables, making a mess of the garden. Guo Yunsheng's ten-year-old grandson, Guo Tuantuan, tried to pull one of the Japanese soldiers away from kicking the vegetables. The soldier lifted his gun and was about to shoot, scaring Guo Yunsheng who rushed over and hugged the long gun. At that moment, the gun went off, and Guo Yunsheng was injured and fell to the ground. This incident made the vegetable farmers in the garden very scared and uneasy.

Zhenhong confronted the Japanese officer, Mrs. Yamada, about the incident. Yamada did not want to offend Zhenhong, as they also needed vegetables. So, she sent Japanese soldiers to take old Guo to the Hitachi Hospital for treatment. However, his leg remained lame, and not long after, he passed away. This incident left Zhenhong unable to swallow his anger.

From then on, Zhenhong wanted to grow fewer vegetables, but the residents of Yingkou still needed them, and he could not confront the Japanese head-on. The hardware store was even harder to operate, as the Japanese often came to order parts that were used in military machinery. Zhenhong suggested closing the hardware factory and store, but his eldest son sent a message saying that it could not be closed, as it had a significant purpose.

Zhenhong didn't know what his son's grand plan was, but he always felt that this son had some skills, spoke in a progressive way, and everyone in the family was willing to listen to him talk about his concerns for the country and the people. Sometimes, as a father, Zhenhong also had some doubts about whether his son was a member of an organization, and he couldn't quite figure it out.

Zhenhong didn't want anyone to accuse him of being a traitor. As a Chinese person, Zhenhong felt humiliated and helpless. However, after the incident with the Communist Party happened, everything became clear, and Zhenhong felt more at ease. Soon after, the half-paralyzed Wenchuan passed away after a fall, followed unexpectedly by the passing of Wan'er! Everything in the family fell apart.

## 2

At the end of 1947, Yaoxin went to Taiwan. In 1948, after the Communist Party took over Yingkou, they repeatedly talked to Zhenhong, asking him to explain the situation of his daughter going to Taiwan and the issue of his son-in-law Wu Juncheng being a Military Intelligence Bureau spy. Zhenhong understood that the Communist Party did not trust him.

In 1951, the Communist Party implemented land reform, and the people took over the Li family's eight fields and vegetable gardens.

After this land reform movement, in 1953, party representatives began to forcibly invest in Li's hardware factory, adding some "public shares" to the factory and public representatives to participate in factory management. This was an early preparation for the public-private partnership. The newly assigned factory manager to the hardware factory was surnamed Xu, and it was said that he was the son of a big shot in the province. He came to the factory with a group of people, and they walked around the factory with Zhenhong, giving him suggestions. They pointed to a workshop and said, "There are safety hazards here, and there must be a dedicated person to supervise safety production."

So, the staff who followed him wrote it down in their notebook. They went to a storage room, and Comrade Xu pointed and said, "The lighting here needs to be redesigned, and it must be well-lit." The staff also recorded this.

Zhenhong thought to himself, no one usually goes into the storage room, so does it really need to be well-lit? They walked around every corner of the factory, and Comrade Xu proposed about a dozen improvements in total. Finally, Comrade Xu ordered Zhenhong, "You need to prepare for all the improvement measures. The public-private partnership working group will report next week."

Zhenhong said, "Thank you, Comrade Xu. The report can be issued without any problems. But where will the funds come from for so many changes? The factory does not have so much idle capital. Without money, how can we make improvements?"

Comrade Xu became serious and said, "This is your capitalist narrow-minded worldview at work. Not everything can be attributed to capital! What if there is no money?

Comrade Xu responded confidently, "The problems you will face in the future will be considered by our country. That's why it's so urgent to transform private enterprises into socialist ones. If you cooperate, the country will help find ways to solve these specific problems."

From that day on, Li Zhenhong knew that the situation was changing.

One of the Party branch secretaries was named Zhang Geming, and his job seemed to be mainly leading everyone in reading party documents and shouting slogans, as well as doing ideological work with the masses. He spoke forcefully and made the Party's platform his soul! He waved his fists and called on everyone, "Comrades, we must see the situation clearly. The country is calling for public-private partnerships, and this is the trend. You know that land reform has already been completed in rural areas, and farmers now have their own land to farm. So, our factories must also cooperate publicly and privately, which is the country's socialist transformation of the business community, making all of you the new working class of China and the owners of the factory and the country!"

Then the party members below began to chant slogans, "Unite and strive for greater victories!"

Zhong Geming also lifted his hand time and time again, shouting slogans with all his might. In fact, before this, Zhang Geming had already come to the Li family's courtyard and privately talked with Zhenhong, saying, "Comrade Zhenhong, the state will carry out a policy of transforming and redeeming private industrial and commercial enterprises, requiring private business owners to understand the laws of social development, take control of their own destiny, and walk the socialist path. You must also recognize the current situation. Capitalists have a future only if they accept socialist transformation!"

Zhenhong did not argue, only saying, "I will listen to the Country and Communist party's arrangements."

Zhang Geming raised his oily head and laughed, "Comrade Zhenhong, you are the most understanding person, sparing me a lot of persuasion. That's settled then, I still need to go and do ideological work with others."

Zhenhong saw that Batiandi was gone, and he saw through the situation. Later, in early 1956, shortly after talking with Zhang Geming, he took the lead in cooperation. On the day of the cooperation, Director Xu asked the workers to stop working for a day, and he led them to decorate the factory auditorium.

The auditorium was full of red flags, and a large red banner was hung above the stage, reading: "Walk the grand road of socialism! Public-private partnership is glorious!"

The city propaganda team came to the scene with great fanfare to present Li Zhenhong with a certificate for the Glorious Advanced Individual in Public-Private Partnership. The mayor personally pinned a large red flower on Li Zhenhong and said, "Today is a day of great joy. The Li Family Hardware Factory in Yingkou has set an example for everyone in public-private partnership. We hope that from today onwards, other business owners will join the tide of public-private partnership! Let's join together quickly and embark on the prosperous socialist road."

He then led the applause. At that moment, another business owner walked up to the mayor and declared on the spot that they also wanted to participate in public-private partnership. Zhenhong knew him, he was the boss of Zhaoxing Company, and he also had the surname Li. That day, Zhenhong was like a hero. From then on, he became an enthusiastic supporter of the Communist Party of China's leadership and was elected as a member of the Political Consultative Conference.

After the partnership, Zhenhong became the first factory manager of the joint venture, and many unfamiliar people came to the factory. Every day, they would call him "Manager Li!" At the beginning, Zhenhong felt a sense of responsibility as the owner. He participated in the big and small affairs of the factory because the older people in the factory liked to consult him, especially when they encountered technical difficulties that they couldn't solve, they would still come to ask Zhenhong for advice. Some people couldn't see the situation clearly and thought it was unfair that the Party Branch Secretary Zhang enjoyed all the benefits. As a result, some of them were arranged to work in other positions, and some were talked to and forced to resign.

Later on, few people recognized Zhenhong. The new leaders no longer sought him out, and he eventually became a figurehead factory manager. Zhenhong felt heartbroken, as he had lost the factory he had built with all his energy, a factory that was like his own child. But he also thought that he was getting old, tired, and unable to keep up. It was rare to have peace and quiet without anyone disturbing him.

So, Zhenhong decided to hand over everything to the Communist Party. He submitted his resignation letter to the Party branch in the factory and retired a few months later. Later on, he donated his collection of calligraphy and paintings to the Dalian Museum. In 1959, amidst the sound of the national Great Leap Forward, Zhenhong, who had let go of everything, passed away in the tenth year after the establishment of New China, at the age of 68. He had sent his two sons to fight in the Korean War to resist the United States and assist Korea. He witnessed that his eldest son with Wan'er Yaoguo who left was still alive, but when he returned, came back with only a certificate of heroism and a military medal. The most heart-wrenching thing for him was that the Li family's old house was divided among more than a dozen officials to live in, and the old house was no longer called "Li's". The Li family's "Batiandi" vegetable garden also disappeared, and the name of "Batiandi" disappeared too!

> He drove the crane west, with no return journey,
> Once brilliant in his life.
> The fields were gone, the house was empty, and the tree fell, monkeys were scattered,
> Life's various experiences were both bitter and sorrowful.

History has its cycles. In the 21st century, Yingkou finally restored the old name of "Batiandi". People may ask why it is called "Batiandi". Some may say that there used to be a Li family who grew crops and vegetables there.

**Part Five**

# *Two Daughters of the Li Family: Intelligent Yaozhi and Virtuous Yaoxian*

## Chapter One

# Li Yaozhi has innovative ideas and Li Yaoxian follows the Communist Party

### 1

In the 21st year of the Republic of China, Sun Wan'er became pregnant with her first child during her first year in the Li family. In March of that year (1932), the Japanese-supported Manchukuo was established in Changchun and named Xinjing. The deposed emperor of the Qing dynasty, Puyi, became a so-called emperor again with the reign title of "Datong".

At the end of that year, the weather was unusually cold, and Wenchuan, the grandfather, was eagerly awaiting the birth of his granddaughter, who was named Zhi and ranked fifth among females in the generation. This was two years after Li Fengshi had given birth to her only daughter, named Xian, who ranked fourth. The two girls went to school together, learned female skills together, drew and wrote together, and played shuttlecock together. Wan'er's other daughter Xin, who was three years younger and ranked sixth, was considered the younger sister of the family, but Zhi was very close to Xian, and the two girls were inseparable. They spent so much time together that many neighbors thought they were the real sisters.

In the morning, Sun Wan'er was always the earliest to rise in the courtyard. While the other rooms were still quiet and everyone was still asleep, Wan'er had already started to cook and make a fire. Actually, the kitchen servants were responsible for these chores, and everyone in the courtyard would gather in the master Wenchuan's yard for breakfast. However, Wan'er wanted the children to have more nutritious food, so she cooked for them separately.

When smoke from the chimney started to rise, the yard was filled with a pleasant aroma. Yaoxian always arrived early at Er mom's yard to have breakfast with Yaozhi. Big Mom felt guilty that her daughter was running to Er Mom's yard every day, so she offered to give Yaoxian some money for food, but Wan'er refused, saying, "The children can only eat so much, it's just a matter of adding more chopsticks. Besides, it's good for the two girls to be together."

Li Fengshi went along with it and said, "That's fine, from now on, Yaozhi can come to our front yard whenever she wants, the gate will always be open."

Wan'er smiled and nodded, saying, "Then it's settled! Actually, we're all family, there's no need for so much formality."

Today, as usual, Yaoxian walked into the kitchen and sweetly asked, "Er Niang (means second mom), what delicious food are you making today?"

Wan'er was steaming egg custard and she lifted the thick wooden lid, inviting Yaoxian to take a bowl. She said, "Xian always comes so early, my Zhi just woke up; go find her, so you two can have the egg custard."

Yaoxian took a full bowl of custard, picked up two spoons, and walked into Yaoxzhi's room. It was almost the same every day.

Yaozhi's little sister, Yaoxin, was only five years old and had two pigtails and a round face. She was helping her mother add firewood to cook. When she saw Xian, she knew she was looking for Zhi and pointed to the inner room, saying, "Zhi Jie (Means elder sister) hasn't woken up yet, Xian Jie, you're so early!"

Yaoxian replied, "It's okay, I'll lift her blankets and spank her butt." She chuckled as she spoke.

Yaozhi, slender and delicate, didn't like to do kitchen work. She usually practiced calligraphy and drawing in the morning. At only eight years old, she was already the top student in her elementary school in both academics and handwriting. Yaoxian, who was nine years old, used to say that if Yaozhi weren't in school, she would be the top student, but with Yaozhi there, she would have to settle for second place.

When Yaozhi saw Yaoxian coming, she crawled out of bed lazily and put on a small jacket. She moved over to the kang bed to make room for Yaoxian to sit down. The two of them ate egg custard with two spoons from the same bowl, occasionally snatching from each other and laughing. The pleasant laughter of the two girls drifted from the room.

Sun Wan'er could draw, but she drew because she liked embroidery. She would hand-draw the pattern and then stitch beautiful gold, silver, and colorful threads on it, stitch by stitch. At a young age, Yaoxin was too young and not very interested in this, but Yaozhi would always follow her mother to learn women's handicrafts. Because Yaoxian and Yaozhi were often together, they learned together. At first, Yaozhi and Yaoxian learned to sketch patterns and then embroidered them. Later, they began to unleash their creativity. Yaozhi had many clever ideas, and she and Yaoxian bought various paints and colored the patterns. They drew the appearance of New Year's paintings and landscapes, and gradually the house was not only decorated with their embroidery but also with their watercolor paintings!

Yaozhi, Yaoxian, and Yaoxin attended primary school, then middle school, and finally women's high school. They studied and grew up day by day. Women's high school focused on educating girls in household skills, nurturing their moral character and emotional wellbeing, as well as providing a general education. Starting from high school, the education style shifted to Japanese, and students

Yaoxin

Yaozhi with her father Li Zhenhong

were required to greet their teachers in Japanese, bow at a 90-degree angle, and sing the national anthem of Manchukuo. They also had to bow towards Tokyo and Xinjing.

The school was managed by a Japanese man named Takahashi Taro, who wore round-framed black glasses and had a small black mustache above his upper lip. There were Japanese language classes, and students were not allowed to speak Chinese, or they would be reprimanded. The Japanese teacher also gave each student a Japanese name, with Yaozhi being called Yamada Chika, Yaoxian being called Kobayashi Mai, and Yaoxin, still in primary school, being called Tanaka Nobuko. Not only did their first names change, but even their surnames changed to Japanese names. Yaoxian hated it when the teacher called her by her Japanese name and often said to Yaozhi in disdain, "I feel angry when Takahashi calls me by my Japanese name. I wish I could smash his little glasses!"

At this point, Yaozhi would comfort her impulsively and say, "What's the point of plucking his little mustache? Studying is more important."

Yaoxian would say, "Zhi sister, don't you feel angry? I just can't stay calm!"

In this way, Yaoxian often vented her grievances to Yaozhi, who became her punching bag for several years. In the blink of an eye almost, Yaozhi, Yaoxian, and Yaoxin grew into teenagers, and their three younger brothers, Yaoguo, Yaoyou, and Yaowei, were also growing.

The school was full-time, and students were not allowed to go in and out of the school gate during the day. They ate lunch in the classroom. Japanese children had a small stove and ate white rice, meat, and eggs. However, Chinese children like Yaozhi were not allowed to eat rice or wheat flour. They ate millet flour cakes, some vegetables, and tofu, which just filled their stomachs. Yaozhi was always the first in every exam, which made some Japanese students jealous. Yaoxin told Yaozhi that sometimes they needed to pretend to perform poorly in some exams to give Japanese students a chance to get first place. Yaoxian sneered at this and said, "Why should Zhi not get the first place? It's ridiculous. Let's make those little Japanese kids angry."

## 2

During the 12 years of Manchukuo, in the 26th year of the Republic of China (1937), on July 7th, the Lugou Bridge Incident occurred, and the common people said that there would be another change in the world. When will this world ever be peaceful?

On the streets of Yingkou, people often saw Japanese soldiers armed with guns, and the deafening roar of planes flying overhead. There were two more Japanese clubs on the street, and banks and shops gradually increased as well. In fact, many years before this, the Japanese had begun to build railways in the northeast to transport timber and coal to ports, and then ship them to Japan where resources were scarce. Japan's economy also began to enter various industrial fields in Manchuria, opening Manchuria in all aspects.

This began in 1908, the first year of the Xuantong Emperor, the last emperor of the Qing Dynasty.

Yaojia inherited the Li family's hardware factory and hardware store, and his nickname was Si Ge (the fourth brother). Yaozhi often saw people gathering at Si Ge's store and wanted to ask her forth sister Yaoxian what was going on. One time, Yaoxian was scolded by a Japanese teacher for refusing to bow and wearing a school badge, and she impulsively dropped out of school. After that, she went to help at Si Ge's store.

Yaozhi went to find Yaoxian after school. Si Ge's store was not big, but the plaque was magnificent, with the words "Yaozu Hardware Store" inlaid with gold, very eye-catching. The door was double-sided, with two large brass locks in the middle, usually hung on one side of the door. Yaozhi bounced into the door, and at the door was the shop's assistant Mao Chunyu. When he saw Yaozhi, he deliberately shouted, "Yaozhi is here! Is there anything you need, or are you here to buy something?"

Yaozhi was familiar with him. He was Si Ge's assistant and was highly valued by Si Ge. Yaozhi stopped and asked, "Is Yaoxian here?"

Mao Chunyu hesitated for a moment and said, "She went back. I'm watching the store."

Yaozhi was about to leave after hearing that, but she saw a unique silver bracelet inside the counter and walked over to take a closer look. Mao Chunyu was busy taking care of other customers who had just entered and didn't pay attention to her. Yaozhi rarely came to this hardware store and didn't expect that they also sold women's jewelry, such as jade ruyi, gold and silver bracelets, earrings, and so on. Yaozhi looked at them and lost track of time for an hour. When she reached the last row of shelves, she left the store through the back door. Suddenly, she heard Yaoxian talking to several young men, and Yaojia Si Ge was also there. They seemed to be talking about leaflets and protesting Japanese bombings in Guiyang. Curious, she wanted to walk over, but Mao Chunyu suddenly came over and said, "Miss Yaozhi, why did you come here? Do you like bracelets? I have wrapped one for you to see."

Yaozhi was interrupted by Mao Chunyu, so she followed him back into the store.

Yaozhi was a sensitive girl. She remembered over the past year when she went to the front yard to look for Yaoxian at night, she often wasn't home. Every time Yaozhi asked where Xian went, Da Ma (First Mom) always evaded the question. Yaozhi also often heard Xian and Si Ge Yaojia discussing the incompetence of the Nationalist government, as well as the Japanese-controlled Northeast Army in the Mukden Incident last year, which resulted in the Japanese occupation of Shenyang and the entire three northeastern provinces by the end of the year. Yaoxian mentioned communism, the Communist Party, and Mao Zedong more than once. Could it be that Yaoxian was also involved in the revolution with Si Ge Yaojia?

Recently, Japan implemented a policy of one million immigrants, and Japanese military personnel settled in Yingkou with their families. Their women wore kimonos and wooden clogs, making a crisp clacking sound as they walked down the street. Some Japanese-style two-story buildings were built in the backstreets, which had running water and flush toilets, unlike the residents of Yingkou who had to pour their chamber pots every morning and spit into spitting basins at street corners, emitting a foul smell of excrement.

In fact, it seemed that the Japanese and everyone else were living in peace. They organized the people of Yingkou into groups called "Bao," with each group electing a "bao Leader" responsible for collecting taxes, including agricultural taxes, livestock taxes, business taxes, tariffs, tobacco taxes, and household taxes. Since the establishment of Manchukuo, Japanese-style education had been introduced in schools, with the school officials being Japanese. Yaozhi's girls' school advocated for Japanese-Manchukuo friendship, the Greater East Asia Co-Prosperity Sphere, and Japanese-style education. Every year, the girls' school sent exchange students to Japan, and in recent years, the number of students from the three northeastern provinces going to Japan for study had risen to nearly four thousand. Yaozhi's school had not stopped sending students to Japan due to the Sino-Japanese War, but the number had decreased from three a year to just one.

In the beginning of 1939, which was the 25th year of the Republic of China, Yaozhi was 17 years old. Due to her outstanding academic performance, she had repeatedly ranked first in her local school examinations, and she had done so again this time. The principal of the school, Takahashi, personally came to the Li family to deliver good news to Mr. Li Zhenhong — Yaozhi had been recommended to study abroad in Japan at Nara Women's University, where she would study humanities and history.

Nara Women's University, also known as "Nara Women," was established in 1908 (during the 34th year of Emperor Guangxu). It had a very high reputation and was well-known among the Japanese. At that time, Nara Women's University and Ochanomizu University were the only two national universities for women in Japan.

## 3

Mother was always reluctant to let her daughter go. She advised her daughter to continue her college education in Manchuria, where there were already more than ten universities, some of them good schools. She really didn't want Zhi to leave. Wan'er felt reluctant in her heart and asked her second daughter Yaoxin, "Xin, your sister is leaving, are you willing to let her go?"

Yaoxin replied, "Going out to see a different world is definitely extraordinary. Zhi sister is outstanding and has the opportunity, so what's there to be reluctant about? I'm happy for her!"

Mother felt relieved after hearing her daughter's words and said to Xin, "You're usually quiet, but you have a clear mind at critical moments."

Yaoxin added, "Why did the Japanese come to China? They came uninvited, and Zhi was invited by them."

When Wan'er heard Xin's words, she felt that her daughter was clear-headed, thoughtful, and wouldn't be fooled.

In fact, Yaoxin didn't care at all whether Yaozhi went or not. She had always been very independent and liked to play with her three younger brothers Yaoguo, Yaoyou, and Yaowei after school. She wasn't very close to Yaozhi.

At first, Zhenhong was firmly against his daughter studying abroad in the enemy country. He went to consult with his father and third uncle, Wenshan, because the two brothers always played chess and discussed family matters together.

When Zhenhong arrived, the two elders were playing chess, and his son Yaojia happened to be there too. Zhenhong didn't beat around the bush and directly talked about Zhi going to Japan to study.

Wenchuan put down the "cannon" he was holding and paused for a moment before saying, "We're about to go to war with Japan. I can't understand why we would send our child to Japan to study now! It makes me uneasy to do things for the Japanese!"

Wenshan, on the other hand, said, "The Japanese want to train her and send her back to China to work for Japanese. By then, she'll understand both languages and cultures. Japanese education is good, and it won't cost us any money to send her there. I say we should let her go. When her return, she'll serve our Republic of China government."

At this moment, Yaojia walked over, picked up Uncle Four's "cannon," and fired a shot towards his Grandpa's "general". He then spoke with a somewhat authoritative tone, "In my opinion, Sister Zhi should pursue higher education. What a great opportunity this is to learn more knowledge. Our country needs talent, doesn't it? Mr. Zhou Shuren (Mr. Ru Xun) studied in Japan, as did Mr. Li Dazhao. Many knowledgeable scholars from past dynasties also studied in Japan, and they played a very important role in the revitalization of our nation. Sister Zhi should definitely go!"

And so, the decision for Yaozhi to study abroad was made. Since Zhi made the decision to go to Japan, she felt that her cousin Xian visited her home less often, and she had begun to distance herself from her mother and her. The day when her father told her that both he and her grandfather had agreed to let her study abroad, Yaozhi jumped up with joy. She ran to the front courtyard to share the good news first with Yaoxian.

The front and back yards were separated by a wall with crabapple trees on either side and a circular arch in the middle. Crossing the wall was a distance of five or six meters to get to the front yard. Previously, first wife Fengshi had visited the back yard frequently, chatting away. But in recent years, since Xin's father rarely visited the front yard, Fengshi stayed at home and complained a lot, and she visited less often. Zhi had heard her mother refuse to open the door for her father at night, forcing him to go to the front yard. Zhi did not know the awkwardness of two women sharing one husband. She only knew what her father had told her, that he did not get along with Fengshi, who was too stubborn and did not know how to be kind. She did not feel like she had a home in the front courtyard. But because of this, Yaoxian resented her father and said that his marriage to her mother was feudal and lacked love. When her parents quarreled, Yaoxian never tried to intervene and would even secretly encourage her mother to ignore her father.

When Zhi arrived at the front yard, Fengshi was shelling peanuts, and Xian was helping. The peanuts were produced by their own household, managed by her father and grandfather. However, since the Japanese came, they had to pay higher taxes, and her father and grandfather had lost their enthusiasm for farming. So recently, most of their household expenses came from their hardware factory and shop.

Shouting "Elder Cousin", Yaozhi entered the courtyard, sat down next to Yaoxian, and began to help shelling peanuts. Yaoxian seemed not to see Yaozhi, and even turned her head to the other side. Fengshi didn't say anything either.

Yaozhi moved a small stool and sat opposite Yaoxian, happily telling her the news that she was going to study abroad. But unexpectedly, Yaoxian became very excited; she grabbed a handful of peanuts and threw them at Yaozhi, scolding, "Do you know what you're doing? You're selling out your country! Don't you know what the Japanese have done?"

Yaozhi was stunned for a moment. She said to Yaoxian, "Si Ge Yaojia said I'm saving the country through circuitous means. I'm going to Japan to learn more knowledge, not like what you're thinking. Besides, it's not easy for me to get an opportunity like this."

Yaoxian couldn't stop saying, "Going to Japan is selling out the country, there's nothing to argue about."

Then she swore to the sky that she would no longer be sisters with Yaozhi unless she gave up her decision to stay in Japan. Yaozhi was a little confused. She didn't expect Yaoxian to be so radical and ruthless, to cut off their sisterhood over something like studying abroad.

As the study abroad days were approaching, Yaozhi and her mother were excitedly preparing everything they could think of to take on the journey. One day, while Wan'er and Yaozhi were shopping for suitcases, they saw Mao Chunyu and Si Ge Yaojia giving a speech at a market, and everyone was shouting slogans and protesting against the Japanese government's oppressive taxes and so on. Yaozhi saw Si Ge distributing progressive journals to everyone, and some people rolled them up to make a makeshift megaphones to shout slogans that could be heard from farther away.

Just in a moment, a call to assemble came from the north side of the market, and a group of Manchukuo police with long guns ran over. The crowd scattered in all directions, leaving flags, flyers, and people's shoes scattered on the ground. Yaojia, Mao Chunyu, Yaoxian, and others all disappeared in an instant. People on the street were hiding everywhere, and someone bumped into Yaozhi and Wan'er. Yaozhi was knocked down, but she picked up a progressive journal on the ground named "Spark". She remembered that Yaoxian had shown it to her before, and Yaozhi had even teased her, "My dear Xian sister, don't turn yourself red."

Yaoxian proudly replied, "What's wrong with being red? Don't you think red makes people feel passionate? I'm ready to live and die with the nation!"

Yaozhi had said at the time, "I won't let big sister Xian die. You have to live well."

Yaoxian pointed at Yaozhi's head and said, "Zhi, you're so silly. If the nation perishes, I won't live well either!"

While Yaozhi was recalling this memory, Wan'er saw the journal in her daughter's hand and immediately snatched it away and threw it on the ground. At this point, the police started firing into the air, and Yaozhi and her mother hurriedly took refuge in a shop.

In the evening, Yaoxian and Yaojia still hadn't returned, and the Japanese and the police came to the Li family looking for them. There were guards stationed at the entrance, keeping a close watch, and people were not allowed to come and go freely. Li Zhenhong was summoned for questioning at the police station, and it took two days before Wan'er used her own gold and silver jewelry to get him released. However, half a month passed, and there was still no news of Yaojia and Yaoxian. The surveillance at the door gradually eased.

These events took place before Yaozhi left the country. From then on, until 1945, Yaozhi and Yaoxian were not reunited. At that time, Yaozhi learned that both Yaojia and Yaoxian had joined the Communist Party.

## Chapter Two

# Yaozhi studies at Nara Women's College in Japan; her friendship with Kazuko and Mide after returning home

### 1

In 1939, on March 20th, in the 22nd year of the Showa era in Japan, Yaozhi took the ship from Lushunkou to Kyoto, Japan, beginning her one-year-and-eleven-month study abroad.

The morning in Nara was shrouded in mist, and the hazy layer of fog made it feel like a fairyland. Deer occasionally ran over to accompany people, not at all afraid. In the morning, Yaozhi liked to go to the forest surrounding the school and recite loudly. No one would disturb her, only the chirping of birds accompanied her. Life there was not as busy as she imagined, but rather very leisurely and free. Yaozhi didn't like to go out drinking and chatting with some foreign students. When she had free time, she would read and study, and write letters to her family. She stayed in the home of a Japanese woman named Suzuki Mide, who was in her fifties. This Japanese woman was also a Buddhist, ate vegetarian food every day, and seemed to have a son, because Yaozhi saw a photo of a young man in a Japanese military uniform hanging on the wall in her bedroom. Suzuki Mide lived in a two-story Japanese-style house with an upstairs. For herself she only used a 14-tatami-mat-sized room,* and sometimes went to a chanting room. Two other rooms were empty until Yaozhi came and stayed in the south-facing room upstairs. The two seemed not to know each other, and the older woman never spoke to Yaozhi except on rent day.

* About 20 × 12 or 240 square feet.

On rent day, Suzuki Mide would wear a kimono and accept Yaozhi's 50-yen rent. Actually, this amount of money was very little (about $12), and Yaozhi couldn't believe the rent was so cheap at first. So, she introduced another friend to live together, but this Japanese woman said she only wanted one tenant. Yaozhi was very puzzled by this.

After the initial excitement of arriving in Japan passed, Yaozhi felt that the Japanese students didn't like foreign students from China and wouldn't talk to them. In class, the Japanese students sat together, and the Chinese students sat together. Yaozhi did well in her studies, and after a few months, Japanese students came to her for advice, so sometimes Japanese students would come to sit next to her on purpose.

This gave Yaozhi an opportunity to talk to Japanese students and practice Japanese. A girl named Yamaguchi Kazuko even invited Yaozhi to go to Kyoto together. This was exactly what Yaozhi wanted, and she had been planning a trip to Kyoto. She had hesitated however because she didn't have a companion and transportation was not convenient; but now since Kazuko's family was in Kyoto, she could serve as a guide for Yaozhi.

Kyoto, formerly known as Heian-kyo, is a city with a long history. It served as the capital of Japan for a considerable period of time, from 794 until 1869. Over the centuries, Kyoto has become a showcase of Japanese history and culture.

On a crisp autumn day, the two girls took a train together to visit Kinkaku-ji, a famous temple in Kyoto, also known as the Golden Pavilion.

When they arrived Yaozhi saw why Kinkaku-ji was also called the Golden Pavilion. From a distance, the three-story structure shone brilliantly, with the exterior walls of the main hall adorned with gold leaf. The use of gold in architecture is part of the Japanese style. Japanese nobility and the imperial family have a preference for golden buildings, symbolizing power and wealth.

This Zen temple is located adjacent to the Mirror Pond and inherits the aristocratic architectural style of the "Hosui-in" palace from the Fujiwara period. The second floor reflects the architectural style of Kamakura-era samurai, while the third floor surprisingly adopts the architectural style of the Tang Dynasty Zen Buddhist temple known as the "Kyomizu-dera". The temple's roof also features a pagoda-like structure with a golden phoenix perched on top, symbolizing auspiciousness. These three different architectural styles blend perfectly into one building, making it a masterpiece of architecture.

Yaozhi thought to herself, this shimmering golden temple must also have a profound meaning, perhaps it represents the paradise imagined by the Japanese people! Skyscrapers are rare in Japan, and this Golden Pavilion, along with the Ginkaku-ji they visited the day before, are probably considered as representations of paradise. The phoenix at the top is believed to have flown across time and space from Uji.

Yamaguchi Kazuko, the Japanese girl from Kyoto, said that the best food in Kyoto can be found in Kawaramachi. However, it was only when Yaozhi and she arrived at the unassuming Pontocho that she was captivated by the local cuisine. This small street, no more than 500 to 600 meters long, is lined with various eateries, tea houses, restaurants, and izakayas. Almost every shop has lanterns hanging with the words "Delicious Food" written on them, and banners fluttering in the wind, making a rustling sound. Women wearing kimonos and wooden clogs select their favorite clothes and accessories, and when they get tired, they sit down and have a bowl of noodles. However, Yaozhi looked at the prices and found them to be quite expensive. One soba noodle dish could cost as much as her monthly food expenses. As they walked further, Kazuko and Yaozhi saw some performers with their faces painted white like kabuki actors. They were in groups of three to five, with men dressed in traditional Japanese kimonos, some casual and others pretending to be geisha. Kazuko, feeling uneasy, pulled Yaozhi away from there, saying that it was a famous pleasure district called Yaomekai, and they should leave quickly.

They stayed at Kazuko's house for two nights. Kazuko's parents were ordinary Japanese people, and they were of short stature. Kazuko's father had opened a tea house near their home, primarily serving the local neighborhood. Her mother cooked tea and made snacks in the tea house. This small single-story house with two bedrooms, one measuring 10 tatami mats and the other only 8 tatami mats, had been passed down through their ancestors. Kazuko's older sister had gotten married and left, so previously Kazuko and her sister lived in the 8-tatami mat room. During these two nights, Yaozhi and Kazuko squeezed into this small space. Kazuko's parents were very friendly and made natto tofu soup, celebratory noodles, and small snacks from the tea house for Yōchi (Yaozhi) and Kazuko. Two days later, Kazuko and Yōchi (Yaozhi) returned to their school in Nara.

The trip to Kyoto brought Kazuko and Yaozhi closer as good friends. After that, they started sitting together in class, going to lunch together, visiting the mall together, doing homework together, and even going to the restroom together. Yaozhi found a Japanese best friend in Kazuko.

## 2

Time passed by quickly, and before they knew it, the end of the year had arrived, and it was almost New Year's. Since the Meiji Restoration in Japan, the Lunar New Year on the first day of the lunar calendar was changed to January 1st on the solar Gregorian calendar, which is known as New Year's Day. Japanese people are known for their love of cleanliness, and they all participate in a big year-end cleaning. As the New Year approached, Suzuki Mide said she wanted to do a thorough cleaning to welcome the new year. However, Yaozhi noticed that Mide was getting older and didn't like to socialize much, so she voluntarily offered to clean the high places that were difficult to reach with a small ladder. Mide repeatedly thanked her and bowed deeply, but Yaozhi suggested that she shouldn't worry about cleaning and could focus on more important things.

Kazuko also came to celebrate the New Year with Yaozhi. She brought some traditional holiday foods: rice cakes. When she saw Yaozhi cleaning, she spontaneously joined in and she gave Yaozhi a handmade pouch as a gift. Kazuko was easygoing, and in no time, she engaged in a lively conversation with Midi.

Mide, Kazuko, and Yaozhi began to prepare for the New Year meal and made mochi by themselves. Yaozhi, Kazuko, and Mide sat together by the fireplace and enjoyed their mochi and soba noodles, which symbolized longevity and good health. The long noodles were also easy to break, representing the breaking of misfortune and a fresh start for the new year. They also followed the Chinese tradition of eating dumplings. The three of them spent the entire afternoon busy with preparations. During the meal, Kazuko asked Mide a question that Yaozhi had always wanted to ask but hadn't: "Is the young soldier in the photo hanging on the wall your son?"

Mide was silent for a moment and then opened up. It turned out that the young man was her son, a 22-year-old Air Force pilot who unfortunately died in a plane crash last year. Mide wiped away her tears and talked about her son's intelligence and maturity. She said that when he was at home, he never let his mother do any work, and during the New Year, he would clean the house by himself, just like Yaozhi was doing this year. He joined the army at the age of 20 as an infantryman, and later he was selected and trained to become an Air Force pilot. Unfortunately, he went to China and never returned.

Mide said that she didn't like war, which took away so many people's sons, including those from China and Japan. She also said that she kept her son's room exactly as it was when he lived there, and no one was allowed to use it. Yaozhi looked at Mide and realized that ordinary Japanese people were also victims of war.

On New Year's Eve, Mide and Yaozhi passed through the red gates of Todaiji Temple and hung their wishing charms on the ancient trees. Then they went to Kinkakuji Temple, which had a huge Buddha statue. There were many people in traditional clothing at the temple, and Mide also wore a beautiful long-sleeved kimono. Everyone came to pray for blessings in the new year and to listen to the 107 chimes of the bell before midnight. When the 108th chime sounded, both Yaozhi and Mide believed that they could get rid of their 108 troubles, drive away the bad luck of the past year, and bring peace and good luck for the new year! Yaozhi prayed for friendly relations between the Chinese and Japanese people and for peace instead of war.

The next morning, Yaozhi found a beautiful envelope in an elegant and attractive wrapping under her pillow, containing 100 yuan in New Year's money. Looking at the money in her hand, Yaozhi's eyes grew moist, and she missed her mother.

As the delicate relationship between China and Japan evolved, some Chinese students studying in Japan returned to China. In an effort to appease and retain these students, the Ministry of Education decided to allow students who had not returned to school on time to take a leave of absence and retain their student status. However, after Japan's large-scale invasion of China, most of the students were unwilling to stay in the enemy country to continue their studies. Later, the Supervision Office for Chinese Students Studying in Japan was also closed. Then, in March 1940, the Wang Jingwei government became the main force for selecting Chinese students to study in Japan during the period of Japan's invasion of China.

At that time, Yaozhi was studying effortlessly, and by now she often conversed with her landlady Mide, which helped her practice her Japanese speaking skills. However, in February 1941, a student just returning from China brought her a letter. The envelope was drawn with a black border using a brush. Yaozhi opened the letter and saw only a few words: "Come back quickly, mother passed away."

The letter slipped from Yaozhi's hand and fell to the ground, and tears streamed down her face. The next day, she bought a ticket to go home, and three days later, she set off. She never returned to Japan.

## Chapter Three

# Grandpa journeys to the west on a crane; Mother's soul returns to the heavens; and Yaozhi joins the National Government Military Intelligence & Statistics Agency

### 1

As Yaozhi returned home, everything had changed. Grandfather had passed away a month earlier, but Father hadn't mentioned it in his letters for fear of causing Yaozhi to worry. Now, Yaozhi could only go to Grandfather's grave to offer paper sacrifices. Grandfather's spirit tablet was in the ancestral hall, with the words "Li Family Crosses the East, the Fourth Son of Li Wenchuan, the Second Generation of Li Pingsheng" inscribed on it. There were also two lines of words behind the tablet: "Li Wenchuan was born in the second month of the Ji-Si year in 1869 and died in the first month of the Xin-Si year in 1941." It was in the 30th year of the Republic of China, and Yaozhi realized that Grandfather was born in the Year of the Snake and passed away in the Year of the Snake, 72 years later.

Yaozhi's mother had also passed away and her spirit tablet was in the mourning hall, surrounded by black gauze. Her sister Yaoxin was reading scriptures in the mourning hall, her eyes red and swollen, looking haggard. Father's face had lost its radiance, and he had moved to the courtyard of elder aunt Fengshi's house.

Yaozhi knelt in front of her mother's spirit tablet, silently reciting a verse from the Book of Songs: "Oh father, you gave me life. Oh mother, you nurtured me. You raised me, you fed me, you watched over me, you guided me, and you cared for me. I want to repay your kindness. Oh, heaven is vast!"

Unexpected things can happen to anyone at any time. Everything was in vain, and her mother's passing had come too suddenly. Yaozhi was unprepared. She had not repaid her mother's kindness, and her mother was gone. She cried bitterly, regretting that she had not been able to see her mother one last time. Her two younger brothers were also very distant from her, and even Yaoxin seemed to be estranged from her. Her fifth brother, Yaoguo, was already ten years old, and her eighth brother, Yaowei, was only seven. Yaoxin took care of them every day. Whenever they had something to discuss, they talked to Yaoxin, ignoring the fifth sister, Yaozhi.

Yaozhi stayed at home with nothing to do, so she used embroidery and painting to pass the time. Time passed quickly, and half a year flew by in the blink of an eye. Her cross-stitch was very skillful, and anyone who saw it was envious. Yaoxin said to her, "Fifth Jie, can you teach me?"

Without raising her head, Yaozhi said, "It takes a lot of effort, and do you even have the time for it? Besides, you like it, so figure it out on your own. Other than our mom, no one taught me before."

After hearing what Yaozhi said, Yaoxin felt a little uncomfortable. She said, "Actually, Mom taught you carefully at first. She saw that you were meticulous and did things well, so she passed this unique skill on to you."

Yaozhi looked up at Yaoxin and proudly replied, "That's the truth. Mom guided me. She taught me how to choose needles and threads, taught me stitching techniques, and taught me double-sided embroidery. Except for Mom, no one can compare to me."

Yaozhi added with a touch of sadness, "Unfortunately, Mom is no longer with us."

Yaoxin, seeing her fifth sister bringing up their mother again, felt a pang in her heart. She also sensed that her fifth sister had no intention of teaching her, so she went to buy groceries. At that moment, Yaoguo and Yaowei came back from outside with dirty faces and asked as soon as they entered the door, "Fifth sister, where is the sixth sister ?"

Yaozhi, still engrossed in her embroidery, didn't even look up and replied, "She went out, and I don't know where she went."

Yaowei inquired, "Is there any food at home? We're hungry!"

The two siblings entered the kitchen and saw that there was no food prepared yet. They shouted, "Fifth sister, you haven't cooked anything yet?"

Yaozhi, annoyed, said, "What are you making a fuss about? Can't you see I'm busy? Wait for your sixth sister to come back; she'll cook for you."

Yaoguo and Yaowei were a bit displeased. They spotted some pickled vegetables on the cutting board and picked out the hearts to munch on.

After a while, Yaoxin returned, carrying a block of tofu and a bag of loach fish. She entered with a smile and said, "Look at you two covered in mud again. Where did you mischievous kids go?"

The two brothers immediately helped Yaoxin with the groceries and said, "We're starving, and you're back, sixth sister!"

Yaoxin tied her apron while saying, "Alright, today we're having loach stuffed tofu."

Yaozhi, seeing Yaoxin preparing food for her brothers, felt a bit embarrassed and put down her embroidery to help. She assisted with washing vegetables, peeling garlic, chopping green onions, and slicing ginger. In no time, they had a steaming pot of loach-stuffed tofu with pickled vegetables. The brothers washed their faces and hands and were already seated at the dining table. Yaozhi set out the bowls and chopsticks, while Yaoxin served the sorghum rice. The four siblings began to eat together.

Yaoxin, while serving dishes for her younger brothers, asked them, "Is it delicious?"

Yaoguo nodded, and Yaowei chimed in, "It's incredibly tasty!"

Yaoxin patted Yaowei's head and said, "It's delicious, and I'll continue making it for you guys."

Yaozhi looked at Yaowei and said, "Sixth sister is too busy; how about I cook for you guys in the future?"

Yaowei, without hesitation, rejected, "No need, sixth sister's cooking is the best."

Yaozhi felt a bit upset, realizing that she seemed to be growing more distant from her family. Throughout her life, from her family to neighbors, everyone had commented on Yaozhi's cold demeanor, her tough heart, her sharp and sometimes hurtful words. She had a temper she couldn't control; when she got angry, her words could sting. Among her siblings, she was the most headstrong, and no one dared to argue with her. She was well-read, spoke with authority, and could go on at length as if giving a lecture. People didn't say it to her face, but they gossiped about her behind her back, calling her petty and unfair, among other things. Even her father had avoided provoking her in the past.

Yaozhi had grown increasingly resentful of the life of a subjugated nation as she listened to her father and uncles express their deep hatred for it. Everyone wondered when these nightmare days would come to an end. Hearing them recount the atrocities committed by the Japanese — the burning, killing, and looting, and the exploitation of China's resources — filled Yaozhi with anger. In Japan, she had also seen progressive-minded students among the expatriates who distributed flyers, formed alliances, and encouraged resistance against the Japanese invaders. She had come across numerous flyers in her own mailbox, but she had never been a political activist, and she didn't want to get involved. Yaozhi couldn't help but wonder if she had made a mistake in her decision to study in Japan, as her wise sister Yaoxian had suggested.

Then she turned her thoughts back to her friendship with Kazuko and Mide. When Yaozhi was most confused after returning home, she received unexpected letters from Kazuko and Mide, she realized that it was the one thing she cherished the most. It was completely unexpected because when she left Japan, she had discarded all the addresses from Kazuko and Mide's, wanting to cut off all ties with Japan. But their letters made her feel warm and reminded her of the kind side of ordinary Japanese people, leaving her feeling a bit lost.

Recently, from the radio, Yaozhi heard that Japan had launched a surprise attack on Pearl Harbor, and the Pacific War had begun. The United States had joined the European front, shifting Japan's strategic focus from China to the United States. The international situation was changing, and Yaozhi hoped that the Sino-Japanese War would end soon.

Autumn arrived, and Yaoxin enrolled in a national university, commuting daily. In her spare time, she worked at a laundry to earn money. She prepared breakfast for her two younger brothers before going to school, and on her way home, she brought them dinner. Yaozhi had to cook lunch for her two brothers and herself, even though she had never cooked before. In the past, the family's servants had prepared meals, but with the outbreak of the Sino-Japanese War, they had all been dismissed. The family had relied on their mother's support, but now that she was gone, Yaozhi knew that the days of being a privileged eldest daughter were over.

Life had to go on, no matter how difficult. One day, Yaozhi went to the market to buy meat. Prices for groceries had soared recently, especially meat — it could almost be described as exorbitant. While they could pick vegetables from their garden, they had to buy meat. Yaozhi felt the emptiness in her stomach and often felt hungry. Her two younger brothers were going through a growth spurt and were even hungrier. Yaoxin's earnings were clearly insufficient to cover the household expenses. Yaoxin began to sell the family's calligraphy, paintings, and antiques, but in the midst of the chaos, these items no longer held their value. Yaozhi realized that, as the eldest sister, she couldn't rely on others and needed to find a job that would not only support herself but also help the family put food on the table.

## 2

Yaozhi was haggling over the price of pork at the market when someone called her from behind. She turned around and almost didn't recognize her; it was her high school classmate and close friend, Gao Hongying. She was dressed in a Nationalist Military Statistics Officer's sexy camouflage uniform, complete with a beret and a Nationalist Party emblem. She exuded a strong and impressive aura that made Yaozhi envious.

Gao Hongying offered to treat Yaozhi to a meal, which delighted Yaozhi because she was indeed feeling hungry.

The two of them went to a nearby famous restaurant called Xinghua Lou. When they arrived Yaozhi was surprised; in former days her father and local officials often dined at this restaurant and discussed business. Many important deals were signed in this restaurant. Back then, Xinghua Lou had been a flourishing business. Yaozhi even knew the owner, Mr. Hong, who was tall and well-spoken. The Li family often held banquets at Xinghua Lou for significant occasions like baby's first month, birthdays, and elderly birthday celebrations. Today, however, apart from Yaozhi and Hongying, there were only three or four other diners who looked like they were from out of town. Mr. Hong was not welcoming customers at the restaurant entrance, and the waiter was dozing off. It was evident that business was not doing well.

Gao Hongying, somewhat proudly, said, "Yaozhi, you can order."

Yaozhi replied honestly, "I want to eat meat; how about ordering braised pig's elbow?"

Gao Hongying immediately nodded and said, "Then, today we'll go all out and order meat." She then ordered "Guobao Rou."

Yaozhi said, "You really know how to order. Guobao Rou is made with lean pork, and it comes in both sweet and sour flavors. You ordered my favorite dish! Thank you!" Yaozhi even made a playful bow and a funny face. Gao Hongying looked at her and smiled, "You're still as lively as ever."

The food was served quickly, and soon, delicious dishes were placed on the table. The two friends chatted while they ate. Yaozhi shared interesting anecdotes from her time in Japan, and Gao Hongying recounted her experience of becoming a Military Intelligence Statistics agent two years ago. Yaozhi asked her, "Is Military Intelligence Statistics still recruiting?"

Gao Hongying replied mysteriously, "Yaozhi, I'll tell you the truth. We urgently need four female agents, but so far, we've only recruited two, so there are still openings."

Yaozhi excitedly asked, "That's great! How do I sign up?"

Gao Hongying reassured her, "Don't rush. I'll have to put in a good word for you first, and then we'll see how the testing process goes."

Yaozhi nodded and said, "Alright, Hongying, you understand me the best. Say some good things on my behalf."

Gao Hongying patted her chest and said, "No problem; it's on me. Just rely on me."

Yaozhi made sure to serve Gao Hongying some food from her own plate, saying, "Today is my lucky day, and I'll remember your kindness."

Gao Hongying shook her head and said, "Don't be so formal. We're like sisters. Your affairs are my affairs."

Hearing Gao Hongying's words, Yaozhi felt relieved and grateful. She knew she had found a true confidante.

After the meal, Gao Hongying promised to help Yaozhi with the application process for the Nationalist Military Intelligence Statistics Officer's spy exam.

Two days later, Gao Hongying sent a letter to Yaozhi. She explained that Yaozhi's reputation preceded her, thanks to her overseas studies in Japan. Upon hearing that she was applying, the director of the military intelligence Statistics department immediately agreed to schedule Yaozhi for the exam within a week. However, he didn't specify which branch of intelligence she would be tested for. In fact, the director, Wu Juncheng, would later become Yaozhi's husband. He mentioned the content of the exam to Gao Hongying, making it quite clear.

Yaozhi was least worried about exams; she had consistently ranked at the top from childhood to adulthood. However, this time, she was in a dilemma. She didn't know what she would be tested on. How could she prepare? Gao Hongying mentioned that there had been over twenty applicants previously, but only two were selected, and one of them was an older woman who had worked as an independent news propagator before.

Yaozhi asked, "What did you get tested on when you applied?"

Gao Hongying said, "I joined the Military Intelligence Statistics department two years ago, and this year's exam content may be very different."

She continued, "I think you'll be tested on mathematics, typing, English letters, Chinese punctuation, as well as listening and reaction speed."

These pieces of information made Yaozhi read a lot of books. She slept for only four hours almost every day during that week and plunged herself into the sea of books.

On the day of the exam, Yaozhi got up before dawn, and her sister Yaoxin had already started to cook. Yaozhi put on the most beautiful student uniform she brought back from Japan, hugged a pile of books, and walked out of the room. She still had no confidence. When her sister Yaoxin opened her mouth wide, and walked over to her fifth sister, touched her clothes with her hand, and said, "It looks so good! Fifth sister, you look like a princess when you dress up!"

Hearing Yaoxin's words, Yaozhi felt a little more confident. She ignored Yaoxin's call to have breakfast and rushed out.

She took a tram and after four stops, she arrived at the National Government Military Intelligence & Statistics Agency building. She had to show her credentials to enter the building, and she said she was there to apply for the job, showing her invitation letter. A young man at the door led her to room 13 on the 3rd floor, the office of the director of the Intelligence Department.

They had just arrived at the director's office when the door opened. A tall man in a Nationalist Army uniform for the Military Investigation & Statistics Bureau pushed the door open and saw them. He said, "Come in and sit down. I'll be right back."

The young man saw him and shouted, "Director Wu!" He immediately stood up and looked very serious.

Yaozhi went in and sat in a seat directly facing the director's rectangular desk. She looked around and saw a large red flag with a white sun and blue sky next to the desk, which was very eye-catching. On the right side of the desk, next to the window, there was a redwood tea table with a teapot and a teacup on it. Against the wall, there was a row of bookshelves and file cabinets. There were stacks of newspapers and documents on the desk. In the embossed glass cabinet on the left, Yaozhi could clearly see a handgun, which scared her, and she dared not look further. She straightened her clothes and sat up straight.

After five minutes, the door opened, and a tall and handsome officer appeared in front of Yaozhi. He had a dark complexion, small but sharp eyes, a straight nose, and a slightly down-turned mouth, giving him a natural air of dignity. He walked up to Yaozhi and said, "You must be Li Yaozhi! My name is Wu Juncheng. Let's get started!"

Yaozhi felt a little nervous and her palms were slightly sweaty, but she immediately calmed down.

Wu Juncheng, the director Wu, sat down behind his desk in a high-backed leather chair. This young Military Statistics Bureau special agent in his twenties, who had once been the director of the Action Department, looked at Yaozhi with his sharp eyes up and down. Her clothes made her stand out from the ordinary girls in Yingkou, like a beautiful scenery line, especially the blue and white striped top that complemented Yaozhi's innocent and lovely face like a fairy who had descended to earth.

When Yaozhi saw Director Wu, she stood up. Her deep blue dress swayed elegantly, making her look like she was stepping on clouds.

During their first meeting, Director Wu, a man who had previously interacted with various individuals and undergone formal special agent training, unexpectedly developed a strong liking for Yaozhi. He even felt a sense of cherishing and treasuring her, as if she were a delicate flower. He longed to keep this woman and have her by his side.

Director Wu asked Yaozhi about her personal experiences and views on current events while flipping through her file. During the question-and-answer process, which didn't take long, Director Wu gave Yaozhi a case to analyze and write a conclusion on. While Yaozhi was busy answering questions, Director Wu personally sent her file to the archive room and asked the personnel department to check Yaozhi's family background. Wu Juncheng told Personnel Director He, "This Li Yaozhi studied in Japan and has a good talent. Director He, please check her background."

Director Wu took the file and said, "Since you recommended her, Director Wu, I will take care of it."

Half an hour later, Director Wu received Yaozhi's test paper. He quickly skimmed through her answers and gave her some passcodes to memorize. A few minutes later, he brought a letter and asked Yaozhi to mark it with the passcodes she had memorized. Yaozhi had an incredible memory, and in her hands, the letter quickly turned into a string of numbers. Yaozhi felt confident and found the test easy.

A week later, the external personnel handed the external transfer materials directly to Director Wu. From the files he received,

Wu Juncheng learned that Li Yaozhi's half-brother and half-sister had gone to Yan'an and were probably with the Communist Party. He hesitated for a moment but eventually took out the file and burned it. When he first saw Li Yaozhi and her pure, watery eyes, he believed she could be molded into an excellent female spy. Later, Director Wu himself investigated Li Yaozhi's family background and learned that the family was complex, but he didn't think it was a problem since the family had always been engaged in business.

A month later, Yaozhi received a notification that she had been hired! Yaozhi passed a rigorous review and became a spy for the Confidential Affairs Department, and Wu Juncheng, Director Wu, became her husband later.

It was time to go to work! Now Yaozhi could earn seven yuans a month. She knew she was going to have money soon, but before starting work, she prepared some clothes for herself. She also spent a lot of money and to buy a bike. Her own money wasn't enough, so she borrowed some from her sister, who said she was being vain, but still reluctantly gave her the money.

Yaozhi had a drive to do everything well. She learned to ride the bike and fell, scraped her knees, bled, and even developed an infection. She didn't care and practiced all day without eating or drinking. She taught herself to ride a bike in just three days, where it would take others at least a week or two. On the fourth day, she rode her bike on the road all by herself, stumbling and falling along the way.

In the past, there were some men riding bicycles in Yingkou, but it was very rare to see women riding bikes, particular a female soldier riding a bike! Yaozhi had to wear military woman's uniform and she rode her bike to work every day, which became a scene on the street. Many people watched her come and go to work, and almost no one didn't turn their head to look at this beautiful female rider.

Yaozhi and three other newly recruited female cryptographers had to undergo two months of specialized training at the Military Statistics Bureau's training course. The training officer was Director Wu himself, who mainly talked about military statistics discipline, confidentiality regulations, various data and document confidentiality levels, deadlines, and personnel knowledge scope, as well as regulations on designated personnel telegram copying, and so on.

The technical instructor was Gao Hongying! Gao Hongying was one year older than Yaozhi and became an instructor at a young age. Yaozhi felt a little jealous. This was Yaozhi's weakness. People with high IQs like to compare themselves with others. When Gao Hongying was in high school, she was not as good as Yaozhi in all subjects, but now Gao Hongying was giving lectures on the stage, and Yaozhi was taking notes below. Yaozhi felt a bit sour, but she remembered Gao Hongying's kindness. She felt that Gao Hongying was her benefactor. Without her, she would not have entered the Military Statistics Bureau or met Director Wu. She spent some time thinking about how to repay Gao Hongying!

Every time there was a study class exam, Yaozhi felt that her face was shining. Her grades were excellent, and other students could only look up to her. Seeing Director Wu's approving gaze and Gao Hongying's eyes when she collected the exam papers, Yaozhi couldn't be happier.

## 3

Time passed quickly, and two months went by in the blink of an eye. Yaozhi successfully completed her probation period, leading to a secret oath ceremony overseen by Head He from the personnel department. Yaozhi raised her fist and recited the oath: "I, Li Yaozhi, solemnly swear to wholeheartedly uphold the Three Principles of the People, obey the leader's orders, defend the security, strictly abide by organizational discipline, perform my duties with utmost loyalty, and dedicate my life to the organization, even if it requires me to brave danger or sacrifice my life. I willingly accept the most severe sanctions should I ever leak secrets or violate discipline."

After the oath, Li Yaozhi and three other trainees were officially hired as Nationalist Government Military Intelligence Bureau agents. They were arranged to work in the intelligence bureau, earning more than double their previous salary of seven big silver yuans per month; now they got fifteen big silver yuans per month. Yaozhi was so happy she laughed out loud. She was glad she had found a stable job, and her life was finally secure. She gave her younger sister Yaoxin only three yuans per month to support the family, saving the other twelve yuans. She told Yaoxin that she only earned six yuans per month. Yaoxin was honest and trustworthy and after two months, she gave one yuan back to her sister saying, "Big sister Zhi, you've had a hard time too. Keep it as a dowry for yourself. We are motherless children, and Dad has a stepmother, so he can't take care of us."

So Yaozhi managed to save thirteen silver yuans per month.

From 1942 to 1943, there was a severe famine in Henan. The famine spread to 110 counties in the province, and over three million Henan refugees fled to Shanxi, Gansu, and the western region to escape the war zone. There were countless deaths along the way, with people dying from hunger, illness, or falling off overcrowded trains. People were starving, and food was extremely scarce. They had to peel tree bark and eat grass roots to survive. Due to unsanitary conditions, diseases were rampant, and many died or were injured. This exodus was as challenging as when Li's ancestors fled to Northeast China as part of a million refugees during the Taiping Rebellion.

The Nationalist Government had issued clear orders to use military funds for relief efforts. Although the refugees who migrated to Northeast China were in the minority, many soup kitchens were set up, and refugees were given cotton clothes and quilts as aid.

After working for a year, Yaozhi had saved nearly one hundred silver yuans. Yaoxin did not know that her fifth sister was so wealthy. Yaoxin encouraged Yaozhi to use her savings to buy food and winter clothes to help the famine victims. Yaoguo and Yaowei privately told their sixth sister, "Yaozhi would never give her money to help others, she's selfish!"

Whether Yaoxin believed it or not, when she found out that Yaozhi had concealed her income, she believed it.

In fact, Yaozhi didn't really want to give away her money, but she didn't want her younger siblings to look down on her. She gritted her teeth and took out thirty silver yuans. Their dad, Zhenhong, even donated his old leather coat, pants, and leather pad, as well as a few hundred silver yuans.

Yaozhi didn't work in the Military Statistics (Juntong) for long; her time there was relatively short, not even two years. Just as they were considering her promotion to section chief, someone reported her Communist Party-affiliated older brother and sister to the authorities. Wu Juncheng had no choice but to let Yaozhi go. On the same day she left, he took Yaozhi to his home and formally proposed to her. There, he told Yaozhi that Gao Hongying was the informant who had exposed her family's communist connections. Gao had used this opportunity to secure her position as a section chief and even gained the rank of second lieutenant.

Yaozhi cried bitterly upon hearing this and told Juncheng, "I had been planning to express my gratitude to Gao Hongying for her significant help. I even bought the highest-quality cosmetics to give her as a birthday gift. But how did things end up like this?"

Juncheng consoled Yaozhi, saying, "I thought I could nurture you into a true special agent, but it seems you have a different perspective. Perhaps you're not suitable for the spy job. Leaving may be for the best."

Yaozhi nodded and replied, "Maybe you're right. I was too naive."

Yaozhi later learned from Juncheng that Gao Hongying did not serve as section chief for long and left the Military Statistics two years later. Gao Hongying went to Taiwan in 1948, the year before the establishment of the People's Republic of China.

## Chapter 4

# Yaozhi resigns and marries Juncheng; Earning money by painting and writing

### 1

When Yaozhi's mom Wan'er passed away, her father Zhenhong divided the family's assets. The children of the front courtyard's Da Niang (First Mother) Fengshi and the back courtyard's Wan'er each received half. The two sons in the back courtyard, Yaoguo and Yaowei, received properties, some gold and silver jewelry, calligraphy and paintings, and some antiques and furniture. However, the two daughters, Yaozhi and Yaoxin, only received some small items, such as jade tobacco pouches and jade hat buttons, as well as their mother's dowry and clothes. The Li family still valued boys over girls, which Yaozhi hated.

Now that the family was divided, Yaozhi was not satisfied. Her two younger brothers were under legal age, and she took care of the properties they shared. When she married Wu and moved, she took advantage of the situation and moved antiques, calligraphy and paintings, and other treasures from Li's family to her new house. This made Yaoxin unhappy and she went to Wu's house several times to demand her brothers' belongs. However, Yaozhi felt justified in her actions and refused to return the items.

Yaozhi became a wealthy woman and played chess and mahjong every day. She even learned to smoke and always had a cigarette in her hand. After Yaozhi left home, Yaoxin graduated and found a teaching position. She met Professor Lin Shunyi at university and married him. With no one taking care of their two younger brothers, they skipped school every day, played with local hooligans, and often went hungry. If they were hungry, they would go to their sister Yaoxin and her husband for a meal, but they never asked Yaozhi for help. If they were really hungry, they would boldly go to the front courtyard to beg for food from their First Mother Fengshi. At that time, Yaoyou was still studying. Since he and Yaoyou and Yaowei were half-siblings and the same age, they should have had a closer relationship. But because of their mothers' alienation over the years, they became increasingly estranged.

When their Fengshi saw Yaoguo and Yaowei, she said, "You missed the mealtime; your father has already left. Do you want to eat some leftovers?"

Yaoguo and Yaowei were very hungry and didn't care whether it was leftover. They gobbled it up. Yaoyou saw some biscuits and gave a few to his brothers. He proudly said, "These were bought by our mother for me. They are Japanese biscuits, and she told me to eat them when I was hungry at school. I see you two are also pitiful, so I'll give you some."

Yaowei, who was only a few months younger than Yaoyou and had a stubborn temperament, threw the biscuits back at him and said, "Thank you, seventh brother, but I don't need your pity. I'm not hungry, and these biscuits aren't that special."

But Yaoguo, who was three years older, didn't care. He picked up the biscuits that Yaowei had thrown back and put them in his mouth, munching loudly. While he was eating, he said, "They're pretty tasty."

Yaoyou looked at Yaoguo and said, "Eighth brother, you see, Sixth Brother also says they're good. I was just trying to help."

At that moment, Fengshi came over to clean up the dishes and saw Yaoguo eating the biscuits, but she didn't say anything. Just then their father Li Zhenhong came back. He saw the children eating biscuits and said to his first wife Fengshi, "Wow, you're kind! You even bought biscuits for Yaoguo and Yaowei to eat. From now on, give them some money, so they can buy their own food when they're hungry."

Since Wan'er had passed away, the relationship between Li Zhenhong and his first wife had improved significantly. However, Fengshi's personality was not easy to change. Her stubbornness and insistence on being right often reminded Li Zhenhong of Wan'er's gentleness and virtue. To ensure a stable home for the children,

Fengshi often tried to emulate Wan'er's behavior, trying to make Li Zhenhong happy and avoiding arguments. Although she wasn't happy with what Li Zhenhong said, she didn't want to embarrass Yaoguo and Yaowei. During these turbulent times, when every family was struggling financially, she was careful with money, but still managed to give a few coins to the two boys.

Li Zhenhong was initially pleased with Fengshi's generosity, but when he turned his head, he saw a bowl of stewed meat behind the stove. His expression changed, and he picked up the bowl of meat and placed it on the table, calling Yaoguo and Yaowei over. When the two brothers saw the stewed meat, they pounced on it like two hungry wolves.

Their father still loved his sons, and he sent Yaoguo and Yaowei to a well-known Christian boarding school and paid for their tuition and board. The school required students to live on campus, providing security for their lives and studies. Yaowei studied hard and graduated from junior high school, but his brother Yaoguo skipped school shortly after starting, saying that the school was too strict.

## 2

In 1943, the Communist International announced its dissolution and Chiang Kai-shek launched the third anti-Communist wave with the publication of "The Destiny of China". The relationship between the Kuomintang and the Communist Party became even more tense, reaching a critical point.

During those days, Wu Juncheng was very busy, coming home late at night every day and sometimes not returning until dawn. Yaozhi had to stay in a room by herself, and she was already two months pregnant and felt sick and dizzy all the time. There was a Nanny, Mrs. Chen, in the house to cook, do laundry, and take care of Yaozhi. Yaozhi used to play mahjong, go out to eat, and buy clothes with a group of wealthy ladies, and she didn't feel lonely. But recently, because of morning sickness, she couldn't sit for too long and her back hurt. She couldn't play mahjong anymore and her friends didn't come over to chat. She felt very bored. She didn't dare to smoke too much, so she passed the time by writing and drawing.

Nanny Chen used to buy painting tools, paper, and ink for Yaozhi every day. She would take the words and drawings Yaozhi created, frame them, and hang them in the living room. Over time, the living room became filled with Yaozhi's artwork.

One day, Nanny Chen held up a freshly framed painting and asked Yaozhi, "Where would Miss Yaozhi like to hang this painting?"

Yaozhi glanced around the crowded living room and casually handed it to Aunt Chen, saying, "It's for you, Auntie Chen."

From then on, Nanny Chen received many handwritten artworks from Yaozhi.

One day, Nanny Chen mentioned that her younger brother had come to Yingkou and rented a storefront in the city to do business. Yaozhi didn't pay much attention but gave Mrs. Chen some money to help her brother with startup capital.

That day, Yaozhi felt cooped up at home and decided to take a walk in the streets. She invited two of her friends to join her, and they bought candied hawthorns, chatting and walking as they enjoyed their snacks.

The pedestrians on the street were scattered, with groups of three to five people, some were vendors pushing carts to sell goods, some were students riding bicycles in uniforms, and some were cart drivers with their bare backs exposed to the sun on a cold day. At this moment, a group of Japanese soldiers came towards the street corner with their guns. Yaozhi and her companions immediately took refuge in a shop that sold paintings and calligraphy.

Yaozhi was knowledgeable in art, and she started to look carefully at the paintings. As she looked, she was stunned. Some of the paintings looked so familiar! Upon closer inspection, she saw her own signature on them. What was going on? She asked the young shopkeeper for an explanation.

The shopkeeper was quite young, in his early twenties. He felt somewhat embarrassed when he learned of Yaozhi's identity and said, "Miss, I am Nanny Chen's younger brother. She said that your paintings are so good that they take up too much space at home, so she let me bring them here to sell. I didn't expect them to be so popular." Yaozhi asked, "How much for one painting?"

The young man replied, "Two silver yuans each."

Yaozhi not only did not get angry but also said happily, "You sell, and I'll paint. We'll split the income."

And so it was that Yaozhi started her own business selling paintings and calligraphy, as well as some embroidery works, which sold for even more money, especially double-sided embroidery, which was even more popular. Although due to the war, she couldn't persist for long, Yaozhi had her own income and didn't have to be just a housewife anymore. In a few years, Yaozhi became a mother of three sons in the blink of an eye!

## Chapter Five

# Yaoxian pretends not to know Yaozhi; Juncheng is assigned to Changchun

### 1

Wu Juncheng received an order from his superior to search for Communist Party members throughout the city. They were initially successful and captured a high-ranking member of the Communist Party, then the Communist Party requested an exchange of prisoners.

On the day of the exchange, the Communist Party sent a group of five people, including a man named Li Feng and a woman named Li Wen. Wu Juncheng looked through the background files of these five people and learned that Li Feng was the half-brother of his wife, and his original name was Li Yaojia, while Li Wen was the half-sister of Yaozhi, and she was formerly named Li Yaoxian. According to the files, Li Wen (Yaoxian) had studied in the Soviet Union for a year, and had just returned and was being promoted to high ranked officer by the Communist Party.

Juncheng secretly told his wife Yaozhi about this news. Hearing that Li Wen was her own sister Yaozhi. Yaozhi said to Juncheng, "No matter what, you must create an opportunity for me to meet with fourth sister Yaoxian."

This opportunity was not easy to come by and could easily arouse suspicion of collusion with the Communist Party. Wu Juncheng was somewhat hesitant, but when he looked at the mother of his three sons, he made up his mind to help his wife.

The prisoners exchange negotiations were not smooth enough, so they took two days to reach an agreement. On the evening of the second day, both sides were to go to the largest reception restaurant in the city for dinner, and of course, Li Feng and Li Wen would attend.

Wu Juncheng asked Yaozhi to hide in the restaurant's restroom. During the banquet, when everyone was drinking, Li Wen went to the toilet. There were only two squatting toilets in the restroom, each with a half-door. Li Wen saw someone outside, so she opened the door of the squatting toilet, finished her business, and went to the stone bathtub to wash her hands. The door on the other side of the toilet opened, and a fashionable young lady with short hair and a wealthy appearance walked out. Because there was only a simple faucet in the washtub made of stones, Li Wen lowered her head and said, "That's done washing hands."

But the woman walked up behind her and called out softly, "Sister Xian!"

Li Wen turned around and saw that it was Yaozhi! Li Wen looked at her and wanted to embrace her, but just as she was about to step forward, she remembered the strict discipline. The party leadership had spoken to her before she came, mentioning that this was her hometown, and that her brother-in-law was a military intelligence agent. The party organization department head solemnly told her to handle the situation appropriately. He also instructed her to listen to Wu Juncheng's tone, and if she could win him over, she would be sent to liaison with him in the future. But when they stood together and started talking, Li Wen knew that Wu Juncheng was a person of faith, someone who couldn't be won over no matter what, unless something unexpected happened that would force him to abandon his beliefs. But that would take a long time!

So, she stood there and said, "Madam, you've got the wrong person!" Li Wen walked away without looking back!

The door shut with a clang, leaving Yaozhi standing there in a daze, unable to believe this was real. Sister Xian didn't recognize her anymore and even called her "Madam"! Yaozhi felt that they were no longer on the same side. She dressed fashionably and appropriately, but to Yaoxian, who was a proletarian, it might have smelled of petit-bourgeois sourness! Yaozhi saw Yaoxian wearing a washed-out khaki military uniform with creases all over it. Although her clothes were not well-tailored, she had been educated in the Soviet Union. Yaoxian now wore a military cap and belt, and she stood straight with a lively spirit. Although Yaoxian had eaten poorly and done hard labor in Yan'an, she was still full of vitality. Yaozhi thought that if she were still working in military intelligence, she might still compare favorably to Yaoxian, but now she was a full-fledged madam. No matter how good her clothes and cosmetics were, she was still inferior to Yaoxian! Yaozhi watched Li Wen's retreating figure and shed a few tears. She hated the war, and she hated the Communist Party for changing her sister Xian so much that even family members couldn't recognize each other face-to-face. She thought that people said she had a hard heart, but today she had learned that Li Yaoxian-Li Wen was the one with a heart of stone!

In the following two years, many major historical events occurred. In 1945, the Japanese surrendered! But the good times didn't last long before the Nationalists and Communists began fighting again. The Communist Party used its internal contacts within military intelligence to create several incidents that sowed discord and made Wu Juncheng disappointed in the Nationalists. But unfortunately, at the end of 1946, Wu Juncheng was sent to help establish a liaison station in Changchun, in northeastern China. The Communist Party thus lost its internal contact and gave up on developing Wu Juncheng. This also meant that after the establishment of the People's Republic of China, Wu Juncheng would be sent to the Shihhezi labor reform farm in Xinjiang for more than 20 years.

In the months before going to Changchun, Maomao, the eldest son of Yaozhi, went to a small ditch in the east of the city to catch dragonflies, saying he would come back to feed the chickens. However, he did not return by nightfall. As Yaozhi was pregnant at that time, Wu Juncheng sent a few men to the east of the city to look for him. Three of them returned the next morning with a dejected look, saying that they found the body of a boy downstream from the ditch, who was presumed to have drowned.

Yaozhi did not see her son for the last time as Juncheng did not let her go. She was eight months pregnant at the time, and upon hearing the bad news, she held Maomao's photo every night without sleeping. Later, an old Chinese doctor gave her some sleeping pills. She slept for a day and a night, and when she woke up, she was completely fine, starting to take care of the household chores, writing and painting, as if nothing had happened.

## 2

After Yaozhi gave birth to another son, the family took the train to Shenyang. Juncheng took a special car to Changchun, while Yaozhi and the children had to take a long-distance bus. When they arrived in Changchun, they arranged to stay in a small villa, which was Juncheng's special treatment and convenient for the military to monitor and protect him. Yaozhi and Juncheng then had three children, making them a family of five. If Maomao were still alive, it would have been a family of six.

In Changchun, Juncheng completely lost the trust of the Communist Party. He repeatedly organized the destruction of their underground organizations and personally led people to arrest communists and their progressive intellectuals. In two years, Juncheng became a person on the CCP blacklist.

In fact, during his time in Changchun, Juncheng also had doubts about the actions of the Nationalist Army. In the Liaoshen Campaign, the Communist Army won victory after victory while the Nationalist Army suffered continuous defeats, with most of the Nationalist forces defecting. By early 1948, Communist Party controlled most of the Northeast, except places like Shenyang, Fushun, Benxi, Jinzhou, and Huludao.

Although Yaozhi was strong-willed, she was not politically sensitive. Every day, she played a round of mahjong, then took care of her sons, taught them, went grocery shopping, did laundry, cooked, and so on. The youngest son was almost two years old, and the oldest son was already five.

In the spring of 1948 the situation in Changchun became increasingly worrisome. It was rumored that the winter offensive was coming to an end. In March 1948, Chiang Kai-shek established the First Army to defend Changchun, and appointed the Northeastern Bandit Suppression Commander-in-Chief Zheng Dongguo as the deputy chief commander. After arriving in Changchun, Zheng Dongguo issued orders to "strengthen fortifications, control airports, consolidate the interior, and purchase grain".

Changchun is in the middle of northeastern Heilongjiang and Liaoning provinces, in the central part of the Songliao Plain. After the September 18 Incident, it became the capital of Manchukuo. The Japanese Kwantung Army had built many permanent defenses here, and the Nationalist Army strengthened them after taking control of the city. Changchun was supposed to be easy to defend but difficult to attack.

But was it difficult to attack? The Communist Party of China (CPC) began a five-month-long siege of Changchun in May, with 100,000 Communist soldiers surrounding 100,000 Nationalist soldiers. They said they were besieging only the Nationalist Army, but in fact, the civilians were not allowed to leave the city either, so soon the food was running out.

Juncheng told Yaozhi: "The stationmaster told me a few days ago to prepare to die for the country. He told me that I had been promoted to the stationmaster of Changchun Station. But his whole family went to Nanjing before the Communists surrounded the city. I heard they will go to Taiwan from there."

Yaozhi angrily said: "Damn it, he asked you to die for the country, but he ran away. Why should we die for the country!"

Juncheng hesitated and said: "Yes! I have a family too! But how can we get out? We need to come up with a plan."

As luck would have it, Li Zhenhai and Li Yaozhong, the son and grandson of Li Wentian, came to visit Wu Juncheng and fifth sister Yaozhi. Zhenhai said they were leaving the gold shop they owned in Changchun. Now that the city was surrounded, civilians had to pay money and grain to leave the city, and soldiers had to surrender their guns. They had decided to pay the money and leave, first go to Shenyang, and then to Taiwan by plane.

The next day, Juncheng and Yaozhi saw off Li Zhenhai and First Brother Li Yaozhong. Then they sold everything in their home, bought food supplies, and exchanged the rest of their possessions for gold bars. It was a time of war, and the price of gold was rising, and food had to be exchanged for gold. Wu Juncheng hired two bicycle rickshaw drivers, and the whole family got on the carts and disguised themselves as ordinary people. Juncheng hid two guns in his underwear pockets, and they headed to the city gate.

It rained lightly on the day they left, making it inconvenient to travel, but Juncheng and Yaozhi did not want to delay even for a day. They arrived at the city gate and saw crowds of people from all walks of life jostling together.

The voices were noisy, with children crying, adults arguing, and impatient curses mixed. Juncheng gave each of the two rickshaw drivers a bag of cornmeal and urged them to try their best to move forward. The two rickshaw drivers really bent over backwards for five measures of rice and squeezed forward with all their might. Juncheng had hired two young and strong carters, plus a bag of life-saving food each. They had no reason to be turned away.

Finally, they arrived at the city gate. Yaozhi took out their fake documents and fake resident permits, holding them tightly in her hand, while sweating profusely. When it was their turn, the guard asked as usual, "Where are your documents?"

Yaozhi handed him the documents, and after scanning them briefly, the guard returned them to her. He then asked, "How many people in total?"

Yaozhi immediately replied, "Including three children, five in total."

The guard circled around their tricycles and lifted the curtain to see the three boys inside. He then stared at Juncheng and asked, "What did you do before?"

"We were all law-abiding citizens," Juncheng said. "I was a businessman who liked to play around with guns and such."

After speaking, Juncheng pull out a pistol from inside. He gestured with the pistol, and the guard took a step back. Yaozhi's heart almost stopped beating.

Juncheng said to the guard, "I read the notice on the city gate. If I surrender a pistol, we can leave the city. I have reported this cherished and collected pistol."

The guard took the gun and carefully placed it in a metal box, locked it, and said, "Okay, but you have too many people. Only four people can be allowed to leave at a time."

He pointed to Juncheng, who was tall, strong, and had a military bearing, and said, "You stay here."

Yaozhi immediately said, "That won't do. He is my husband! How can a family be separated?"

At this point, the people behind them began to get impatient and shouted, "Hurry up, hurry up!"

Then they began to push forward. The guard waved his gun and shouted, "Whoever pushes forward again, I'll shoot."

At this point, Yaozhi took out a bag of corn with both hands from the tricycle and said to the guard, "Take it. There must be someone hungry in your family."

The guard took the bag of corn and waved his hand, indicating that Juncheng and Yaozhi could pass.

Thank goodness, they finally left Changchun city! It was said that after the five-month siege, the population of Changchun was reduced by two-thirds, from 400,000-600,000 to 170,000.

The tricycle drivers could only send them to the city gate. Juncheng asked them to leave the tricycle there and said, "I'll pay you three times the deposit price."

One of the drivers shook his head and replied, "That's impossible! Even if you have money now, you can't buy anything."

The other driver interjected, "Now gold is valuable, and the price of gold has gone through the roof."

Yaozhi picked a pair of golden earrings from her ear and handed them to Juncheng, saying, "Having fewer material possessions makes life easier!" Juncheng gratefully glanced at Yaozhi and then handed the earrings to two rickshaw drivers, saying, "You two can split them. Leave the rickshaws to us. Nowadays, one jin of cornmeal can be exchanged for a gold ingot!"

The two drivers happily turned around and walked away, discussing how to divide the food fairly. Juncheng let the children and Yaozhi sit on one rickshaw, which he drove himself. They also hired a man from Northeast China to ride the second rickshaw, specifically to transport food and belongings.

The roads from Changchun to Shenyang were rough, and some of the main roads had been destroyed during the Liaoshen Campaign, leaving many bumps and holes on a journey of more than 100 miles. After a few days, the rickshaw wheels became bent, so

Juncheng abandoned them, and the family took a horse-drawn carriage instead. After a few days of rough riding, their youngest son fell ill with a high fever, and they couldn't go any farther. The family was forced to stay with a local villager, which delayed their journey for more than half a month. Next, their second son also fell ill. When they finally arrived in Shenyang after many hardships, it was October, and the last plane from Shenyang to Taiwan had already taken off. Then, on November 2nd, 1948, the People's Liberation Army's Northeast Field Army captured Shenyang.

Wu Juncheng and fifth sister Li Yaozhi stayed some time in Shenyang and later went to Yingkou. Sixth sister Yaoxin and her husband had already gone on to Taiwan. Thus the two sisters became separated by the Taiwan Strait and were not able to reunite for 42 years, until 1990. Sixth brother Yaoguo and eighth brother Yaowei remained in Yingkou, and later went to fight in the Korean War, where Yaoguo died. Seventh brother Yaoyou worked in a factory for a few years and eventually got into Tsinghua University to study automatic control and computer science at a time when the country needed such talent.

Life went on for a while, and Yaozhi was reasonably happy because they no longer had to fight and life was peaceful. She was still a full-time mother. Both she and Juncheng got new identity cards and changed their names.

One day, Yaozhi was cleaning the room at home and saw that the lock on the camphorwood box had been changed. The sweaters and pants she used to put inside were now outside the box, and she was a little angry with Juncheng. A few days later, in the evening, she saw Juncheng take a key from the rafters and unlock the box. He took out a radio from inside, and she was shocked. Was he an undercover agent for the Restoration Movement? She didn't want her husband to do such a dangerous thing! She secretly threw the radio into the Liao River. Juncheng didn't say anything when he found out, but sometimes he came back very late at night.

## Chapter Six

# Juncheng and Yaozhi's endure difficulties and leave the three sons to go to Shihezi together

### 1

Searching for a better life, Yaozhi and Juncheng moved the family to Shanghai. Their street director there was Zhao Dongmei, and she inadvertently learned that Yaozhi and Juncheng had received education and even "drank foreign ink." The city was in the process of establishing primary schools and needed people to write the recruitment advertisements. Yaozhi helped write a few of them, and her writing turned out to be a big surprise! People were amazed by her skilled calligraphy!

Street director Zhao Dongmei's husband was the Party Secretary of the Central Party School in Shanghai. She recommended Yaozhi and Juncheng to him to teach cultural classes at the Central Party School to the leaders of the newly formed Shanghai municipal leadership team. The next day, she told both Yaozhi and Juncheng to go to the compound of the Party School to report to Secretary Qi.

Secretary Qi was of medium build. He dressed in coarse cloth clothes with a belt tied around his waist and wore black cloth shoes with straw soles. He had a serious expression and rarely smiled. Yaozhi noticed that most Communist Party officials dressed this way, without any suggestion of petty bourgeois thinking, appearing simple and austere. Many of the leading cadres who attended the cultural classes at the Party School were dressed like this. In the early days of the Communist Party of China, there were very few cadres with education, and many of them came from backgrounds as peasants and workers. Yaozhi taught them by starting with literacy, teaching them how to read. Yaozhi soon realized that these people had high privileges. They had dedicated vehicles for transportation, and essential supplies such as rice, flour, oil, and salt were delivered to their homes by dedicated personnel, without their needing to purchase them. They also had housekeepers to help with laundry, cooking, and cleaning, just like the neighbor's house, Secretary Qi's. His house had three bedrooms, a flushing toilet, and even a housekeeper. Even its kitchen utensils were provided by the organization. Their family had more food than they could finish. Sometimes Yaozhi's three half-grown children ate so much that there was a shortage of food at her home, and then Yaozhi would borrow from her neighbor, Zhao Dongmei.

Yaozhi taught Chinese language and earned 20 Chinese yuan per month, which was much more than the average citizen. In addition, Juncheng taught mathematics and abacus, earning 25 yuan per month. Together, they were able to save more than half of their combined income each month. Their home, consisting of a front room as the bedroom and a back room as the kitchen, was located inside the Party School compound. Just outside the door was the large playground of the Party School. They also had a backyard adjacent to a large vegetable cellar, separated from their house by a wooden fence.

When the country implemented the rationing system, Yaozhi and Juncheng were classified as state cadres. Each family member received one kilogram of eggs and 30 kilograms of white flour per month. The women received 30 kilograms of rice, equivalent to one kilogram of rice per day, while the men received 31 kilograms of rice, one kilogram more than the women. The family also received one kilogram of cooking oil per month. Everything required coupons: there were grain coupons for food, meat coupons for meat, cloth coupons for fabric, and even soap coupons for soap. To supplement their household income, Yaozhi used the small backyard to grow fresh vegetables like spring onions, garlic chives, and Chinese cabbage. The monthly rent for their house was only two yuan, and the gas, water, and electricity bills amounted to only 2.6 yuan. The children's tuition fees were also modest, only two yuan per semester for each child. Their living was frugal, but Yaozhi believed that as long as the family lived together in peace, it was happiness.

Yaozhi's neighbor, Street Director Zhao Dongmei, was promoted to become the Director of the District Committee. Every time

Yaozhi cooked fresh vegetables, she never forgot to send a bowl and a plate of dumplings to Secretary Qi and Director Zhao's house. Director Zhao was fond of Yaozhi's three little boys because she had a daughter herself. She took a liking to Yaozhi's second son, Xiaodi, and mentioned several times that she wanted to arrange a marriage between her daughter and Xiaodi at an early date.

Yaozhi had actually been trying to avoid Director Zhao bringing up this matter, but it would always get brought up anyway. One day, Yaozhi and Zhao Dongmei went together to their children's school to attend the school sports meet. Yaozhi's second son, Xiaodi, and her third son, Dali, participated in the running events for their respective grades. When Dali took the field to run the 1500-meter race, Director Zhao didn't seem very interested, but when Xiaodi appeared Director Zhao shouted very loudly, "Come on, Xiaodi!"

Xiaodi had always been good at running and playing soccer. He achieved a surprising time of 11.9 seconds in the 100-meter race. He had represented the school multiple times in the city school sports meets and had always finished in the top three.

Yaozhi saw Director Zhao so invested in cheering for Xiaodi and felt uneasy. Director Zhao pointed at Xiaodi and said to her, "Look at your Xiaodi; he's so impressive! I really like this child."

Yaozhi smiled and remained silent.

Director Zhao continued, "He runs so fast. If someone coaches him, there's a good chance he could make it to the national team."

She turned her head and looked at Yaozhi with a smile. "I'll find someone to help him find a good coach. This child will have a bright future."

Yaozhi tried to decline; she said, "It's too much trouble for you. I'll ask the child if he's willing first."

Hearing Yaozhi's luke-warm response, Director Zhao became a bit unhappy. She tried being more friendly and said, "Sister Li, don't take it so lightly. I'm serious. Don't let it hold back the child."

Yaozhi replied, "You're putting in a lot of effort, Director."

Director Zhao waved her hand and said, "That's being too formal. Just call me sister."

Yaozhi didn't want this neighbor to get too close because both she and Juncheng were using names that were not real. Director

Zhao was clearly not very pleased with Yaozhi's coolness, but she still often invited Xiaodi to her house for meals. She also noticed his love for playing soccer and bought him soccer socks and shoes. Yaozhi hesitated a few times but eventually felt awkward rejecting the gestures from both Secretary Qi and Director Zhao.

Beginning around 1952, Juncheng would frequently get up at night, claiming he needed to use the restroom, but then he would spend a couple of hours outside. They had an outside toilet, but it was only just around the corner, so Yaozhi knew there was no need for such a long time. One night Yaozhi pretended to be asleep and secretly followed Juncheng out of the house. Instead of heading to the restroom, Juncheng turned toward the backyard's vegetable cellar. He walked to a low-lying area, opened a small door concealed by some cornstalks, and went inside. The door quickly closed from the inside.

Yaozhi knew what he was doing and felt a shiver down her spine. The next day, when Juncheng went to class, Yaozhi went to the vegetable cellar. There was a small space inside that could only fit one person. In the corner, Yaozhi pushed aside a pile of straw, revealing a radio about the size of a small box. Yaozhi didn't dare stay for long and quickly left. Yaozhi found it hard to believe that Juncheng would have the audacity to do something like that inside the compound of the Party School! She recalled Juncheng had sometimes said, "The most dangerous place is often the safest."

Yaozhi and Juncheng had a long conversation, and she urged him to give up the radio for the sake of their children. Yaozhi said, "Cheng, since 1950, the mainland Party has been systematically purging former members of the Military Statistics Bureau. Once they are exposed, it's either execution or severe punishment. Look, for the sake of our children, please stop!"

Juncheng rested his chin on his hand, contemplating for a while. After consideration, he said, "Okay, Zhi, for you, I'll give it up!"

Juncheng realized a ground-breaking truth: The way to govern a country lies in benefiting the people, gaining their support, and ensuring national stability. It doesn't matter who holds the title of ruler. Throughout history, those who understand the current situation are the true heroes.

Beneath the sky, within the world, emotions of sorrow, compassion, love, and hatred intertwine. From ancient times to the present, the battles of Zhou Yu and Zhuge Liang at the Red Cliffs continue.* A wise mind adapts to changing circumstances, and a person's conscience and aspirations determine their character. Examining history helps one discern right from wrong; it is the path of the noble-minded to understand the times.

A few months later, the small house in the vegetable cellar was filled in. Juncheng then bought a shortwave radio and listened to broadcasts from Taiwan at home. He kept a record of something in a little notebook, including the Voice of America broadcasts. They lived in peace for a few more years.

But in 1957 the Communist Party launched the Great Leap Forward movement, and the children were required to attend school. The schools encouraged students to report on their parents and relatives. Without fully understanding the consequences, Dali succumbed to pressure and reported that his father had previously worked for the Nationalist Party's Military Intelligence Bureau.

Not only that, what scared Yaozhi even more was that Zhao Dongmei once asked Yaozhi: "Do you have an electric box at home? I didn't notice it!"

Yaozhi felt a wave of panic in her heart, but she pretended to be surprised and replied, "No, we don't have one! We can't afford such a thing, it costs over 200 yuan!"

Zhao Dongmei said strangely, "Oh, then why do I always hear noises at night? Secretary Qi even said I have tinnitus."

Zhao Dongmei reported this situation to the Party School's Party Committee and Organization Department, claiming that Wu Juncheng was listening to enemy broadcasts. This caused big trouble! A Kuomintang secret agent had infiltrated the Party School. Secretary Qi planned to suppress the matter at first, since he had allowed Li Yaozhi and Wu Juncheng to join the revolutionary ranks without conducting a thorough investigation. But his wife couldn't keep the secret in her heart and exposed the truth all at once.

* In 208 C.E., at the Red Cliffs on the Yangtze River, forces led by Zhou Yu (175–210) and Zhuge Liang (181–234) defeated the much larger army of the northern warlord Cao Cao and ended his invasion.

The following days were filled with background investigations. When the external investigators returned from the Northeast, Wu Juncheng's true name and identity were revealed. One by one, the facts of his anti-party and anti-socialist activities were exposed. Wu Juncheng's true colors were laid bare. It was discovered that he had indeed been the director of a Nationalist government's military intelligence radio station.

## 2

The days that followed were extremely difficult. Juncheng was thrown into the cowshed, and Yaozhi was dismissed from her job. The children, once the offspring of revolutionary teachers, now became targets of ridicule and contempt. Their classmates, influenced by the teachers, ignored the three siblings and gave them cold glances. During class, they were frequently made to stand as punishment, and after school, other students collectively insulted them, shouting, "One, two, three, spies! One, two, three, counter-revolutionaries!"

The three children huddled together, crying in pain. They dared not walk home with the other students after school. The eldest brother, Daguang, adopted the strategy of hiding. Only when he saw that all the students had left the school did he dare to return home. At that time, he was already in the eighth grade of middle school. One month later, he dropped out of school. Xiaodi, the second child, simply stopped going to school and became the leader of a group of street ruffians, getting into fights every day. Dalie, the youngest, was the only one who continued attending school. As soon as the bell rang, he would run straight home. He kept up this routine for two years, and later, in Yingkou City at a workers' sports event, the young Dalie, who was not particularly good at long-distance running, surprised everyone by becoming the champion in the race.

Juncheng's life was miserable. He received criticism and education from Secretary Qi in the morning, was subjected to public denunciation and humiliation by the propaganda brigade and the revolutionary committee at noon, and then paraded through the streets. In the evenings, he had to confess his crimes.

When Yaozhi went to see him he was sitting on the dark soil of the cowshed. Juncheng appeared to have not washed his face for several days, with a dark complexion and torn clothes. Yaozhi brought him a few clean clothes and some food. There was rice, stir-fried squash with minced pork, and a few dumplings. Juncheng rushed over and grabbed the food with his dirty hands, and devoured it hungrily. He told his wife that if he didn't confess his crimes, they would starve him and force him to eat the paste used for making big-character posters. They would use the soles of their shoes to hit his face and grab his hair, smashing his head against the wall. As he spoke, Juncheng touched his face, lifting his hair to show Yaozhi the scalp bruised from hitting the wall.

Yaozhi was getting agitated, almost on the verge of cursing. But she held back her anger and gently comforted her husband, saying, "Don't be afraid, I'm here. I'll reason with them."

Juncheng collapsed into Yaozhi's embrace and cried, saying, "Zhi, I can't hold on much longer."

And so, Yaozhi held Juncheng tightly as they cried together.

After Juncheng's trial, Yaozhi sat on a tram, the words still echoing in her ears: "Guilty! Kuomintang spy, heinous crimes, death sentence with one-year reprieve."

She didn't know how she had managed through these past few days. On the day Juncheng was sentenced, she took their three sons back to their hometown, Yingkou, overnight. No one from their family lived in the Batian estate anymore. It was occupied by strangers. She and the children lingered there for a while until a woman came by and called out, "Mrs. Wu!"

Yaozhi looked over and realized it was Nanny Chen!

Nanny Chen pulled her aside and said, "You have nowhere to go. Come to my house."

Yaozhi reluctantly looked at the courtyard where she once lived, unable to say a word.

Nanny Chen held her hand and said, "Don't look anymore. The Li family is no longer here. The houses have been allocated to the families of those higher up."

Yaozhi's hand trembled as she held Nanny Chen's. Choking back her tears, she said, "Auntie Chen, our hearts are connected. I was just thinking about how I used to write and paint in the courtyard, selling my artwork to earn money. But all of that is gone forever!"

Nanny Chen's eyes welled up with tears too. She held Yaozhi's hand and said, "Come with me!"

That evening, Yaozhi and the children stayed at Nanny Chen's house. Nanny Chen's younger brother had once sold Yaozhi's paintings, and their families had collaborated before. Nanny Chen was a down-to-earth person. Her two children were grown up, her husband had passed away, and now she lived alone. She resided in a dilapidated apartment building, on the ground floor. In the corridor, each household had a coal stove with some black coal piled next to it. Almost every household had a large water jar, a pickling jar, and a basket for storing vegetables. They arrived during dinner time, and the aroma of various dishes being cooked filled the air.

Inside the house, Yaozhi noticed that Nanny Chen had a sewing machine, a five-drawer cabinet, and a bicycle, but the place was sparsely furnished, indicating that she lived a humble life.

That night, Nanny Chen cooked several dishes: tomato and scrambled eggs, tofu with chopped scallions, cabbage and dried shrimp soup, and a mixture of millet and rice called "er mi fan." The children had been hungry all day and quickly finished their meal. Before going to bed, Yaozhi instructed her eldest son, Daguang, to take good care of Xiaodi and Dali and gave him 100 yuan. While everyone was sound asleep, Yaozhi secretly left 200 yuan under her pillow, along with 50 jin of national grain coupons and some fabric coupons. Then, she picked up her bundle and left Nanny Chen's home, embarking on a journey alone to find her fourth sister Yaoxian in Beijing.

In previous years, Yaozhi had heard from uncle Zhenjiang that Yaojia and Yaoxian had become Party officials in Beijing and were living a comfortable life.

As Yaozhi sat on the tram in Beijing, she watched the continuous flow of bicycles passing by. Most people were dressed in blue or gray-black jackets with blue or dark-colored pants. Red flags were displayed everywhere, and slogans like "Down with the old, welcome the new" could be heard. Some people were even performing the "Loyalty Dance" with the words "Chairman Mao is the ever-bright red sun in our hearts." The atmosphere was very lively.

When traveling by tram in the capital city of Beijing, the fare was always five cents, regardless of the destination. Yaozhi changed trams twice and followed the address that third uncle Zhenjiang had given her to find a large courtyard. The doorplate showed "Building 5, 3rd floor, Unit 2." This was the home of her fourth sister, Yaoxian (now called Li Wen). According to Zhenjiang, her fourth brother, Yaojia (now known as Li Feng), was currently sent as a cadre to the countryside to oversee socialist labor organization. He was expected to return with a golden future and be reassigned to an important position.

Yaozhi could still recall the last time she saw Yaoxian in Yingkou. During that encounter, Yaoxian didn't seem to recognize her, and Yaozhi had sworn afterwards never to see Li Yaoxian again. But now, she had come.

Yaoxian was composed and professional. She didn't show any surprise upon seeing Yaozhi and immediately welcomed her inside. Yaoxian's house was meticulously clean, with a solid and imposing front door. The interior was even more refined. She offered Yaozhi some chocolate, which used to be Yaozhi's favorite. However, over the years, she had gone without chocolate for a long time. Seeing it again, she took two pieces, ate one and put the other one in her pocket. Yaoxian smiled and said, "If you like it, take a few more."

Yaozhi then took a few more pieces.

There was no one else in the house. Yaoxian said, "Zhi, you're lucky. I happened to be home for something. Otherwise, we might not have been able to meet until tonight!"

Yaozhi saw a photo of a family of three. In the photo, Yaoxian's husband was dressed in military attire, looking like an officer. Yaoxian explained, "My husband's surname is Liu, named Liu Lijian. The teenager in the photo is our son, named Liu Gang."

Then Yaozhi could wait no longer. She had hardly sat down, hadn't even taken a sip of tea, and she immediately explained her purpose, pleading with Yaoxian to save Juncheng.

Yaoxian listened to Yaozhi's account without any expression on her face. She set down her teacup and said, "Zhi, it's not that I don't want to help. We have policies, and I completely broke ties with feudal families before joining the revolutionary forces. We are no longer sisters."

Yaozhi stood up in despair, knelt down in front of Yaoxian, and begged her to save Juncheng. She gritted her teeth and said, "Yaoxian, don't you have any old feelings left? Have you forgotten the time we spent together when we were young?"

Seeing Yaoxian's silence, Yaozhi turned and left, saying as she walked away, "I haven't forgotten. It seems you have forgotten everything completely!"

Yaoxian called after Yaozhi's departing figure, "Zhi, go back home first. Let me see what Yaojia has to say. Maybe there will be a turning point in the situation!"

Yaozhi had never been to Beijing before. She had once dreamed of visiting the city, but now she had no mood to appreciate the scenery. She sat on the bus, glimpsing the expansive Tiananmen Square and the still unfinished Great Hall of the People. The Forbidden City, where the emperors once resided, passed before her eyes, but she didn't pay much attention. She only felt that there were many people visiting Tiananmen Square, but this time she wouldn't be one of them.

Upon returning to Shanghai, she went straight to see Juncheng. Strangely, Juncheng embraced her with joy and started crying, repeatedly thanking his wife. It turned out that Juncheng's death sentence had been commuted to a lifetime of labor reform at the Shihhezi Labor Farm in Xinjiang.

## 3

In 1990, Yaozhi finally met her sister Yaoxin, who had returned from Taiwan to visit the mainland. At that time, Yaozhi was already 68 years old, and Yaoxin was 65 years old. Even their younger brother Yaowei, who was born during their separation, had reached his fifties and was 56 years old.

I was only a few months old at that time. Yaoxin and Yaozhi, my great aunts, along with my grandfather, came to Beijing and stayed at our house. Of course, I don't remember anything. But my mother told me the stories she heard from Yaozhi about her time in Shihezi.

Shihezi used to be a desert, where a group of young and vigorous people were striving. They were organized under a military structure and called the Xinjiang Military District Production and Construction Corps. Juncheng and Yaozhi belonged to the labor reform team of the Eighth Division of the Corps. There were fewer women than men there, but they were all required to engage in agricultural labor, to fell trees, and dig trenches to build low and dark underground shelters known as "earth cages" or "earth burrows." Women plowed the land with oxen, sowed seeds, and harvested crops, just like the men. They worked day and night; the only two days off were New Year's Eve and the first day of the lunar year. They had to overcome the challenges of altitude sickness and continue working during menstruation and even a few days after giving birth. Some developed a condition of uterine prolapse due to the constant friction from their undergarments; the bleeding and infection that caused were extremely painful.

Shihezi was a self-sufficient place, and the lifestyle there was simple. For the first two years, Juncheng lived with the male soldiers in the Corps, while Yaozhi lived with the female soldiers. For their food and daily necessities they relied on the supplies provided by the Corps, and they had to work tirelessly every day. However, there were no more extensive confessions of crimes or public humiliations. Yaozhi and Jungcheng became numb to their laborious routine, working from sunrise to sunset, and life became stable.

As the number of families increased, the labor reform team allowed families to live together. Several families would share a living space with cloth curtains for privacy. The thin cloth curtains were not soundproof; at night they became a mere decoration, which everyone understood without saying a word.

But could such a space be called a home? On the barren desert at Shihezi, every home resembled an underground shelter made of thatched grass. To prevent damage from sandstorms, only the triangular thatched grass roof of the house was visible from the outside.

Inside, each of the "earth burrows" had a stove made of mud bricks connected to a heated earth platform, serving the dual functions of cooking and heating the bed platform. The interior of the house was illuminated only by kerosene lamps.

From late autumn to early spring, days grew short and dark in Shihezi. The desert climate was exceptionally harsh, characterized by dryness and cold. Dark clouds often drifted across the sky, and soon large snowflakes would fall, making the roads slippery and the cold wind more piercing. Yaozhi felt that the biting cold wind on this vast desert could penetrate through one's body, break one's bones, and no amount of clothing could provide warmth.

One year the men worked the reclaimed land dressed in military overcoats recently issued by the brigade. They wore military caps and cotton boots; some even had cotton gloves! For the first time in many years the military farm issued complete winter clothing. That year it seemed that both soldiers and labor reform team members gained momentum and no longer worked as timidly.

Out in the bitter wind, everyone dug in soil that was frozen rock hard. They couldn't break loose a clod of dirt without swinging the pickaxe several times. So the soldiers swung their pickaxes time and time again. Sometimes their hands would be shattered, and red blood would stain the handle. But on the ground, there was only a small white mark to be seen.

The wind blew on people's cheeks, making them red like autumn apples.

Shihezi had been a vast desert, but the recent efforts of the military farmers had established some trees that could now be seen. The cold- and drought-resistant pine trees looked like green decorations on the desert, making Shihezi a bit more colorful!

The Subu Road was an important transportation hub being built into Shihezi; once it opened to traffic, Shihezi would no longer be such an isolated place. In spring, the women and girls worked on the road by laying stones and sand. They carried sand from the western Shihezi desert by pushing tricycles. To load them they swung large iron shovels. They would plant their feet firmly, bend their front leg, spring their back leg, and swing their arms with as much force as they could. With a "swish" sound, a shovelfull of yellow sand would fly towards a slanted sieve. Eventually, a hill of tiny grains of sand formed behind the sieve. Then, braving the cold wind, the women loaded and pushed the tricycles across the desert to the Subu Road, where they spread the fine sand and stones. They worked for more than ten hours a day, always getting sand in their eyes. The wind swept up small grains of sand that hit their red cheeks and caused them pain. Sometimes the sand got in their mouths, nostrils, and ears. Each night they returned home and wiped their faces with wet towels, and a layer of fine yellow sand would come off.

Their diet in Shihezi was very simple because the desert soil was difficult to improve and the environment was so harsh. Only crops that preferred sandy soil, required less water, and were drought- and cold-resistant could grow there. They grew peanuts, sweet potatoes, and root vegetables, as well as Hami melons and watermelons. They could also grow grapes, and the grapes in Shihezi, Xinjiang, were really quite sweet.

Yaozhi tried to make the best of the situation and told Juncheng that she loved eating sweet potatoes and Hami melons the most. Juncheng thanked Yaozhi for leaving everything behind and following him to this harsh place. When they finished work, it was already late in the day. They dragged their tired feet back to their small and simple "underground cells" home, which was even darker than the dusk outside. Juncheng watched Yaozhi skillfully light the kerosene lamp, uncover the stove sealed by coal, stretch out her stiff hands to warm them on the stove, and then pick up the aluminum frying pan that appeared colorless in the darkness to start cooking.

Juncheng embraced his wife from behind, taking Yaozhi's cold hands in his, and, touched, said, "Zhi, I'm sorry! In the next life, I will definitely let you live as a queen."

Yaozhi turned around and said, "Actually, if we talk about apologies, the ones I owe the most are our three children! At such a young age, they have to rely on themselves!"

Yaozhi recalled the days before she came to Shihezi. She took two trains and endured a day and night of hard seats to return from Shanghai to Yingkou. As soon as she got off the train, she went straight to Aunt Chen's house. Aunt Chen saw Yaozhi's disheveled hair and pale face, so she cooked a bowl of millet porridge for her and let her rest on her own bed for a while. Yaozhi was really exhausted, and she fell asleep on Nanny Chen's small bed. Over two hours later, Yaozhi woke up, and Nanny Chen was not in the room. Yaozhi saw a note on the table: "Dear Auntie, since you're sleeping so soundly, I went out to buy groceries. When I come back, let's have a good chat and drink a couple of cups. The children have gone to school and won't be back until the afternoon."

Yaozhi looked at Nanny Chen's empty house, opened a drawer, and put her savings passbook inside. Then she tore a corner off the calendar and wrote on it, "My dear Auntie Chen, I dare not go see my sons. If I see them, I'm afraid I won't be able to leave. I've entrusted my bank account book to you, and the password is your birthday. I've also included some national food coupons in it. My three little ones eat a lot, so I'm entrusting them to you. I don't know when I'll be back after I leave. I'll find a way to write to you and send them living expenses. Until we meet again, Yaozhi bows!"

But in Shihezi, Yaozhi's letter-writing was restricted, and she lost contact with Nanny Chen. Yaozhi's thoughts returned to the low and dilapidated kitchen in front of her, and she murmured, "I wonder what the three boys are doing now? How is their life?"

Juncheng comforted her, saying, "We are thousands of miles away, and we can't go back. May Pusa* bless them!"

Yaozhi couldn't hold back her emotions and burst into tears in Juncheng's arms. Over the years, Yaozhi had more than once mentioned the uncontrollable emotions she felt regarding their three sons.

* Chinese Buddhists generally use the term *pusa* (菩薩), a phonetic transcription of the Sanskrit term Bodhisattva or "enlightened being."

## 4

In the year 1964, great-aunt Yaozhi at age 42 gave birth to a son they named Dawan. The child was intelligent, stubborn, hardworking, eager to learn, and diligent. Yaozhi took care of him attentively, fearing that he would suffer some injustice. Dawan also protected his mother in turn. At the age of seven, he didn't hesitate to sacrifice his own finger to protect her.

Yaozhi and the others had a certain amount of work to do every day, and if they couldn't complete it, they often went without food. One cold day in early winter, Yaozhi had a fever and felt sluggish. She woke up late. The squadron leader entered and shouted, "Li Yaozhi, time to work!"

Juncheng pleaded, "Captain, Yaozhi isn't feeling well today. Can she have a sick leave?"

The squadron leader's eyes widened and he said, "Don't pretend to be sick. It's just the stench of the bourgeoisie! Get off the kang (heated bed), stop being lazy, and get to work!"

Juncheng said, "How about I do double the work and cover her part as well?"

The squadron leader waved his hand and said, "No! If she doesn't go today, there will be no food."

Juncheng said to Yaozhi, "You see, I must go to work now. Take it easy when you work, don't exert yourself too much."

At that moment, Dawan said, "I am a man, and I will protect Mom!"

The squadron leader not only did not let Yaozhi have a day off, he also assigned her the heavier task of hauling soil. Dawan worried about his mother and followed her to work, even helping her with the cart.

Yaozhi fell down while pulling the cart with her weakened sick body. The squadron leader came over, forcefully lifted her from the ground, and gave her a hard slap across the face. When Dawan saw the squadron leader hit his mother, he rushed over, grabbed his arm, and bit him.

The squadron leader tried hard to pry open Dawan's fingers, saying, "Let go quickly, or I won't be nice!" But Dawan held on tightly, refusing to let go. The squadron leader struggled to free himself from Dawan's grip, and in his attempt, he applied excessive force and broke Dawan's little finger. Only then did Dawan, in great pain, release his bite. Dawan couldn't sleep that night due to the pain, and Yaozhi stayed by his side all night. His little finger was deformed, bent to one side, indicating it had been fractured. Yaozhi used tape to secure Dawan's broken finger.

Despite his pain, Dawan continued to protect his mother during the day and to study cultural lessons with her at night. He earnestly told his mother, "Mom, I will study hard and when I grow up, I won't let anyone bully you. I will buy a big house for you and take care of you!" When he grew up, he indeed bought a house for his mother.

Soon after, the brigade leader was replaced, and Captain Zhang, who was easygoing and gentle, took over.

While Juncheng and Yaozhi were in Xinjiang's Shihezi, participating in labor reform, Beijing and other cities in mainland China were immersed in the fervor of the Cultural Revolution. Yet the labor reform farm in Shihezi was not completely isolated from the outside world, and the brigade leader often led everyone in giving lectures and engaging in political studies. During the lectures, everyone sat on the ground, and Captain Zhang read aloud the red-bordered documents issued by the Central Committee of the Communist Party of China, urging everyone to always heed the party's call. During political studies the brigade leader read newspapers to everyone, and from the contents of those newspapers, Yaozhi learned that Beijing was undergoing a tumultuous Cultural Revolution.

During the Cultural Revolution, the Red Guards and rebel factions of the Party began campaigns to destroy the old culture, overthrow feudalism, capitalism, and revisionism, and to bring down the "Stinking Ninth,"* referring to those deemed counter-revolutionary. Even the President of the country, Liu Shaoqi, was overthrown! The newspapers depicted Liu Shaoqi as a clown with a big head, big

* The "Ninth" referred to intellectuals, ranked 9th (out of 10) among castes recognized in the Yuan Dynasty (1271-1368), above only "beggars."

nose, red nose, and protruding teeth, with a red rope tied around his neck, while numerous powerful fists rained down on his head, illustrating his unfortunate fate.

Yaozhi sometimes helped with financial accounting, in addition to working in the fields. One day, while Yaozhi was assisting at the brigade headquarters, Juncheng and the brigade leader called her from outside the window. Yaozhi saw two people standing behind them and her heart sank. She couldn't believe her eyes—it was her younger eighth brother, Yaowei, and her older fourth brother, Yaojia!

Yaowei was dressed like a Red Guard from the contemporary newspapers; he wore a yellow military jacket with a black belt around his waist and a military cap on his head. He had on yellow uniform pants and yellow rubber shoes and was holding a copy of Chairman Mao's quotations.

Yaojia appeared to be a high-ranking Party official, and he exuded an air of authority. He wore a gray Zhongshan suit jacket,* gray uniform pants, three-section leather shoes. With his hair neatly parted in the middle, he looked mature and dignified. Captain Zhang seemed to hold a certain degree of respect for Yaojia as well.

Yaowei eagerly approached his fifth sister for a hug. Yaozhi hadn't shed tears for many years, but this time tears of joy welled up in her eyes.

Yaojia, was now called Li Feng; he had been sent to Xinjiang on assignment and was temporarily serving as the Party Organization Department Chief of the Han ethnic cadres in Urumqi, the capital of Xinjiang Autonomous Region. He had stopped by Shihezi to visit Yaozhi and Juncheng. He smiled kindly at Yaozhi and said, "Fifth sister, I always believed that it was wrong for Juncheng to be sentenced to death. The party's policy is to cure the illness and save the person, not to strike with a single blow."

He turned to the brigade leader and said, "You see, my fifth sister and her husband can make contributions to your brigade. They have knowledge and can teach at the military reclamation farm. You should use such talents. Of course, they cannot be allowed to rest on their laurels. They should receive proper reeducation here."

* Also known as a Chairman Mao jacket.

Captain Zhang, the brigade leader, nodded in agreement. Yaozhi remained silent the whole time, feeling that her fourth brother's speech sounded official and lacked warmth. But his meaning was clear: he was recommending her and Juncheng for work they were capable of. Yaozhi felt grateful, suddenly realizing that it must have been her fourth brother who had spoken up to have Juncheng transferred to the labor reform farm in Shihezi!

After only a few minutes, her fourth brother went to the brigade headquarters with the brigade leader and then left Shihezi without saying goodbye. Yaowei and Yaozhi returned to her home.

Yaowei was able to visit because in October 1966 students were allowed to travel by train for free during the mobilization of the masses. Yaowei took a train packed with Red Guards for about ten days and then switched to a military truck that delivered supplies to the military-cultivated farms, arriving at last in Shihezi. Along the way Yaowei coincidentally encountered Fourth Brother Yaojia, who left some money with him for Fifth Sister Yaozhi, along with a bag of frozen dumplings and a bag of sticky bean buns.

At night, lying on the ground with the dim light of the kerosene lamp flickering, Yaowei's face was illuminated intermittently. Yaozhi, his older sister, gave him a freshly harvested Hami melon, a rare fruit in their old hometown. The earthen floor of the cage-like house was compacted soil; sinking and rising with each step. A few tree stumps on the ground served as stools, but they wobbled due to the uneven surface. There was also a one-meter-square dining table made by Juncheng himself.

As Yaozhi cut the Hami melon, she asked her younger brother, Yaowei, "How's Yaoguo doing?"

Yaowei lowered his head and said, "Fifth sister, Yaoguo is no more. He didn't return from the Korean War."

Yaozhi's hands seemed to freeze, suspended in the air. After a moment of silence, she asked again, "And what about Yaoxin?"

Yaowei shook his head and said, "Sixth sister went to Taiwan at the end of 1947. There's no news of her."

Yaozhi gently asked further, "Any news of Yaoxian?"

Yaowei knew that Fifth Sister had always been close to Fourth Sister, so on his way there he had asked Fourth Brother Yaojia about

Yaoxian's situation. Fourth Brother said that Yaoxian was in a certain department of the Public Security Bureau, which he couldn't disclose.

Upon hearing this, Yaozhi fell into silence again, and the air seemed to freeze. After a few minutes, she resumed the conversation, asking, "And how about you? How's life been? Are you married?"

Yaowei replied casually, "After completing my military service in Korea, I attended university. I'm now married and I have a son named Guangzhong. He's two and a half years old."

They continued to talk about their other siblings, reminiscing with a mixture of emotions. Looking at Yaozhi's son, Dawan, sound asleep, Yaowei said, "My son is around the same age."

Yaozhi replied, "Dawan just turned two."

Yaowei remarked, "Oh, then Guangzhong is the older brother."

For dinner, they had naan, a type of bread eaten by the people of Xinjiang, along with grilled lamb buns and barley porridge. Yaozhi bought the lamb buns from the brigade canteen. The pit on the ground served as their stove, and after filling it with firewood, the fire burned bright red. The aroma of the grilled lamb buns was truly delightful! Yaowei wanted Yaozhi to take a break and tried to serve himself, but Yaozhi pressed him onto the wooden stool and snatched the chipped rice bowl away from him. Yaowei noticed that the veins in Yaozhi's hands were exposed, slightly black but with a hint of red, and the fingerprints on her hands seemed blurry!

Yaowei felt that these years of labor reform had changed Yaozhi significantly. In her eyes there was a kind and gentle look, and she had become capable and assertive. She wasn't picky about food or clothes anymore, not like before; and she no longer seemed indifferent to her younger siblings. But she was dark and thin, with a slightly stooped back, indicating that she had endured a lot of hardship. Reluctantly Yaowei bid farewell and left Shihezi.

By the time of his visit, the number of families in the brigade had increased, and the children needed to go to school, and the brigade urgently needed teachers. Based on Yaojia's declaration, Captain Zhang recommended Juncheng and Yaozhi be assigned to teach the students. Yaozhi became the principal of the brigade's school and taught Chinese language and geography; Juncheng taught mathematics and physical education. And so the two of them embarked once again on their teaching careers.

## 5

The nights in Shihezi were silent and pitch black. There were no streetlights, and every household relied on kerosene lamps. Shihezi was self-sufficient, but there were often times when people went hungry, skipping one meal after another. Everyone had a limited amount, and Yaozhi always managed to squeeze out a little extra from her own portion to give to Dawan. He was growing up, and Yaozhi believed that every family's parents did the same.

After teaching for six months, Yaozhi noticed that one of Dawan's friends, Xu Xiaobing, always said that his mom didn't like to eat meat or eggs and gave them all to Xiaobing. Xiaobing enjoyed being with Dawan because Dawan always stood up for others, had a strong sense of justice, and didn't make fun of him like other children did. Xiaobing's father was a Kuomintang officer, and after the liberation of China in 1949, he was sent to a labor reform team for rehabilitation. Once, he argued with the team leader and was punished by being made to stand in the icy snow for a month. Later, he developed frostbite in his legs and couldn't work anymore. He hanged himself on a tree on the labor reform farm using shoelaces. Those who saw it said it was a horrifying sight, with his neck and head almost detached, only held together by a strip of skin. Everyone felt ashamed of the incident, and no one sympathized with Xiaobing and his mother. But Dawan and Teacher Yaozhi were different. They voluntarily helped Xiaobing and provided him with food. Dawan even helped with chores at Xiaobing's home because Yaozhi told her son how difficult it was for a mother and child without a father.

One day, it was getting dark! Xiaobing came crying to Dawan and Teacher Yaozhi, saying that his mom had choked to death on a naan bread. Yaozhi, Juncheng, and Dawan immediately put aside what they were doing and rushed to Xiaobing's home.

Xiaobing's mother's face was already covered with a white cloth, and Captain Zhang was also present. He said, "Xiaobing's mom went to the canteen at the team headquarters to find some food and stole a few naan breads. Maybe she was too hungry and her stomach was empty. She stuffed a whole naan bread into her mouth, but there was no water, so she swallowed it dry. It got stuck, and by the time she realized it, she had no breath left!"

Xiaobing had no parents left. It must be said that Captain Zhang was truly a good person, as he was the one who adopted Xiaobing. Because everyone was afraid of adopting a child with such a disgraceful family background and facing consequences themselves.

Everyone said Captain Zhang was too foolish, that he didn't know how to flatter others and always protected those who were useless. Later, it was heard that he reported the misconduct of the corps commander and was dismissed from his position. Even when he fell out of favor, Captain Zhang still stood by Xiaobing. He took his wife, children, and Xiaobing and left Shihezi, but nobody knew where they went.

## 6

During that time, the red books contained critical texts, such as stories about the wicked landlord Zhou Bapi who was disturbed by a crow's cry in the middle of the night, and the ruthless tyrant Liu Wencai who tortured the farm laborers in a water dungeon, among others. Of course, there were also texts that praised good people, heroic deeds, like the Grassland Heroine Little Sisters and the Red Army climbing snowy mountains and crossing grasslands.

Dawan had a fondness for geography, and he asked his mother to tell him about things other than stories about little heroes like Wang Erxiao. Yaozhi wanted to talk about the beauty of our country's landscapes, but the textbook's content was limited. So Yaozhi went to the only small library in the military reclamation corps to look for information. However, the collection of books there was too limited. She then applied to go to the Xinjiang Uyghur Autonomous Region

Library in Urumqi, which was a three to four-hour drive from Shihezi. But this was not allowed. Yaozhi and Juncheng were political prisoners, so they needed approval from higher authorities to leave the military reclamation compound. It took a year of consideration before they were finally allowed to go, but with Captain Zhang and another organizational committee member, Comrade Chen, as their escorts. Later, Captain Zhang was dismissed from his position, and he was replaced by Captain Wang, who accompanied them instead.

Urumqi was the capital of Xinjiang, and the majority of its citizens were Uyghur people. On the streets, one would often see people dressed in Uyghur traditional attire. Yaozhi noticed that Uyghur women had high nose bridges, deep eye sockets, and large eyes. Their clothes were also very distinctive, with various patterns, bright colors, and exquisite craftsmanship. They commonly wore colorful dresses and embroidered trousers, with a coat and a small vest on the outside. Their dresses came in vibrant colors like red, green, purple, all associated with flowers. They wore embroidered hats on their heads, embroidered clothes, embroidered shoes on their feet, tied embroidered scarves around their heads, and carried embroidered bags. They truly represented a nation that loved flowers and beauty. Uyghur women also liked to wear jewelry—earrings, rings, necklaces, and bracelets that sparkled and dazzled the eyes. Looking at what they wore and adorned, it felt like walking into a splendid little museum! In contrast, men's clothing was more loose, simple, and rugged, mainly in black and white tones. Most of them wore long coats, also called *yaktaik*, and *tooni*, which was a Chinese gown. They tied a very colorful long waistband around their waists, which served as buttons, belts, and pockets. Some people also wore a short coat called *pashmaha* during this season, but it was not common because of the cold weather. Men all wore small hats made of animal fur, mainly sheepskin, which had a column-shaped, bowl-like appearance. After being accustomed to seeing yellow military uniforms and blue and gray uniforms, Yaozhi felt her eyes light up with the vibrant colors and variety of clothing in front of her.

It was early 1967 when the armed conflict erupted in Kashgar, Xinjiang. Yaozhi saw many armed soldiers of the People's

Liberation Army (PLA) on the streets of Urumqi. They were stationed every three steps and there was a sentry every five steps, appearing as if they were facing a great enemy. Yaozhi overheard Captain Wang and Comrade Chen whispering that Urumqi was relatively calm, but they had heard that according to the directives of the Central Committee and the Central Military Commission, Kashgar was under military control, and the atmosphere there was even more terrifying.

Urumqi was very cold. Usually, January and February were the coldest months in Xinjiang, with temperatures dropping to minus 20 degrees Celsius, which could be deadly. However, in the summer, around July and August, temperatures could reach over 30 degrees Celsius, which was scorching hot. Even during the summer, there was a significant temperature difference between morning and evening. People often said, "Wear a fur coat in the morning and a thin fabric in the afternoon, while sitting around the stove to eat watermelon."

In March Urumqi was still very cold. The three of them took a car and arrived at the Xinjiang Uygur Autonomous Region Library on Xin Hua South Road in Urumqi. Captain Wang presented a letter of introduction at the entrance, and the library director personally escorted them to the first-floor book depository.

The construction of this library began in August 1930 and was renamed Xinjiang Provincial People's Library in October 1949. It was later renamed Xinjiang Uyghur Autonomous Region Library in October 1955. The new library building was completed in 1958 and occupied a large area. The library had four floors, with the first-floor housing the book collection and reading area, the second floor housing reference books, copying, and typing rooms, the third floor housing newspaper, literature, and magazine reading rooms, and the top floor serving as the office space for the management personnel.

However, due to design flaws and lack of maintenance, the library had a significant issue of being cold in winter and hot in summer. When searching for information in the library, Yaozhi would become so cold that her hands and feet would go numb. Captain Wang and Comrade Chen, who were also sensitive to the cold, would hide in the office of the staff on the upper floor, where they had electric heaters for warmth. They left a soldier from the corps who had come along to watch over Yaozhi.

Yaozhi noticed that there were Uyghur books in the library, but she couldn't read Uyghur script. Since handwriting the information was too slow, Yaozhi requested to use a typewriter for printing. At that time, not many people knew how to use such a typewriter, but Yaozhi had already used the first one of its kind when she was in Shanghai. During meetings, Yaozhi was in charge of taking shorthand notes. Later, they obtained a typewriter, and Yaozhi quickly learned to use it, achieving a very fast typing speed. However, the typewriter made too much noise, so it couldn't be used during meetings. Therefore, Yaozhi would take shorthand notes in her notebook and then go back to organize and type them using the typewriter.

Secretary Qi greatly admired Yaozhi's efficiency at work and even entertained the idea of appointing her as his secretary.

Since Yaozhi was not allowed to leave for lunch, Captain Wang and the others had their lunch at the staff canteen in the library. After lunch, nearly two hours passed, and Yaozhi finally finished printing the materials. The administrator then took Yaozhi to the fourth floor. Yaozhi informed Captain Wang that time was limited and she couldn't finish the search in one go, so she requested to come back every six months in the future. Captain Wang readily agreed. On one hand, he could visit the big city and buy some local specialties, and on the other hand, his two children were attending a middle school in Shihezi.

For the next decade or so, Yaozhi made multiple visits to the Xinjiang Provincial Library in Urumqi to search for materials. These materials were of great help to her children in achieving high scores in the college entrance examination when it was restored. Dawan benefited greatly from them, and he was admitted to the Department of Geology at Xi'an University in 1982.

Later, I went to Urumqi to visit the provincial library, but it had a completely new appearance. The new library building was located at Beijing South Road # 4 and covered an area of 55 mu, looking quite grand!

At that time, the labor reform team cultivated more than one million mu* of wasteland and transformed the sparsely populated desert into a thriving desert city.

## 7

Entering the 1970s, the older generation of leaders in China were approaching their twilight years. They had fought against nature, against the land, and even against people. Finally, they turned against each other. Vice Chairman Lin Biao, in 1971, did not confront Mao Zedong directly. He fled on a plane to the China-Mongolia border and died in a crash. After that, things calmed down for a few years.

The year 1976 was the most turbulent year when the three giants of the Chinese Communist Party passed away successively. Zhou Enlai passed away on January 8th, Zhu De on July 6th, and Mao Zedong on September 9th. On April 5th, the Qingming Festival, which followed Zhou Enlai's death, large crowds of people spontaneously gathered at Tiananmen Square to mourn him. This led to a massive protest, creating a tense political atmosphere. Then came the death of Zhu De, and two months later, the great leader and helmsman of the Chinese people, Chairman Mao Zedong, passed away at the age of 82, or 83 according to traditional Chinese age reckoning.

After that, Hua Guofeng came to power for a while, but soon Deng Xiaoping emerged. From 1978 onwards, there was a tremendous and transformative change. The Great Debate on the question of truth and standards directly propelled the economic reform of China's social system and initiated a rectification campaign. Yaozhi and Juncheng felt that their lives were no longer under constant surveillance. They could freely enter and exit the military reclamation base, go to the market to buy things, visit the Xinjiang Urumqi Autonomous Region Library for research, and so on, without having to seek permission or report their activities.

* Approximately 160,000 acres, or 67,000 hectares, or 250 square miles.

The period from 1978 onwards witnessed earth-shaking changes, as if undergoing a profound transformation of life's destiny.

In 1980, during the lunar Year of the Goat, on the seventh day of the third lunar month, it was an ordinary day for most people, but for Yaozhi, it was an unforgettable day.

Early in the morning, the weather was exceptionally good. The air was fresh, and magpies sang cheerfully on the branches. Yaozhi was about to go to the nearby grocery store to buy a bottle of soy sauce when the orderly of Captain Wang, from the military reclamation labor reform detachment, appeared at her doorstep, asking Yaozhi and Juncheng to visit the detachment headquarters.

They felt that something was about to change, so they dressed neatly before leaving, feeling anxious as they arrived at the headquarters. Upon entering, they saluted and said, "Reporting!"

Captain Wang smiled and asked them to take a seat, saying, "Don't get too excited and fall over!"

Then he took out a piece of paper and read the lines written on it. Yaozhi and Juncheng were officially informed: they were released upon completion of their sentences!

Upon hearing this news, Yaozhi and Juncheng looked at each other silently, tears welling up in their eyes. Finally, they were liberated, they were free!

When they returned home, the family dared not speak loudly, fearing that the policies might change again. Several weeks later, they disposed of all their belongings and, each carrying only a canvas bag, embarked on a long journey back to their hometown, Yingkou, which they had been separated from for over twenty years.

## Chapter Seven

# Yaozhi returns to Yingkou and Dawan gains admission to the university

1

This is a new beginning, a brand-new chapter for Yaozhi and Juncheng. They carry hope and aspirations in their hearts. They understand that life's path will have many twists and challenges, but as long as they hold onto hope and courage, persistently strive, they will surely be able to achieve their dreams.

Yaozhi and Juncheng believe that the future will be better, and they look forward to new stories and miracles, but reality is harsh. Upon returning to Yingkou, Yaozhi and her family have no place to live, no household registration. Their three elder sons don't recognize them because they had abandoned them years before, without caring or asking about their well-being. The suffering the three brothers endured in those days and nights was indescribable. The eldest son Daguang had recently returned from the countryside and lived in a small flat with no conditions. The second son Xiaodi had a two-bedroom apartment but also had a young child attending school. The third son Dali had recently been married and lived at his in-laws' house.

Finally, the three brothers held a meeting, and it was the second son, Xiaodi, who offered a room for them to live in. Dawan had no household registration and could not attend school, so Yaozhi taught him at home. On the second day after moving in, Yaozhi overheard her second daughter-in-law complaining to Xiaodi in the other room, "Why are you so spineless? Your brothers never step up, and it's only you who can. Our place is just a small two-bedroom, and now you're letting them occupy a room. Our son will have to sleep in the living room."

Xiaodi lowered his voice and said, "Keep your voice down. They are my parents, the ones who gave birth to me, and my biological younger brother."

The daughter-in-law didn't lower her voice, but instead raised it and continued, "I can hear it loud and clear. So what! Yes, they are your parents, but where were they when you were in trouble? Who pulled you out when you were in the police station? Don't forget, it was me! They don't deserve to be called your parents."

Yaozhi lowered her head in sadness, and Juncheng left the house with a birdcage in his hands. Yaozhi knew that this daughter-in-law was not someone to be messed with. When she was young, she used to skip school with Xiaodi, snatch things on the streets, and could handle several men by herself. Many people called her "Mazi," which means "female gangster." She had also been detained for fighting to help Xiaodi. Now, she and Xiaodi were self-employed, going to Guangzhou to buy goods, clothing, and electronic watches, making some money, and buying this unit. Yaozhi was grateful to this daughter-in-law for always standing by her son's side, never leaving or abandoning him.

Yaozhi sat there quietly, deep in thought for a long time. She was relieved that Dawan wasn't in the room at that moment, as she was afraid he would be upset. However, she acknowledged that she hadn't fulfilled her responsibilities as a mother. During all those years in Shihezi, the three brothers had endured the cold eyes and hardships of the world, and she couldn't say anything at this moment.

When it had been three months since they returned to Yingkou, Yaozhi felt that her hometown had changed, changed to the point where she didn't even recognize it anymore. The old Yataji residence had become dilapidated, with several households living in the courtyard. Each family had their own small utility room and kitchen set up at their doorstep. Many partition walls were built inside the courtyard, and the once warm and cozy Li family compound was gone. It was no longer Yaozhi's home. She lingered outside the courtyard for many days, but none of the people entering or leaving the courtyard were familiar to her.

Even the streets and alleys had transformed. The old street names had been replaced by new terms like Shengli Avenue and Wenhua Road. Even the beautiful Yataji, backed by the Liao River and once the financial, cultural, and even political center of Yingkou, had its name changed to Hongqi Commune.

During the ten years of the Cultural Revolution, people's wages didn't increase, the population grew, and housing didn't expand. The per capita living space became smaller and smaller. In the past two years, wages started to rise, and everyone's pockets became slightly fuller. Many new residential buildings sprang up, and the old ones were demolished. Walking on the streets of Yingkou, Yaozhi felt the significant changes that had taken place.

Due to the implementation of central policies, Yaozhi and Juncheng received retroactive salary adjustments. After all those years of teaching in Shihezi, their years of service were also considered under the new policy. A few months later, their household registration was officially established in the local area.

Recently, Yaozhi had been in a very good mood. She enjoyed buying rice and flour in the free market, exchanging ration coupons for eggs, and she was delighted to be able to buy fruits and vegetables that were not restricted by coupons. Moreover, China at that time was in the early stages of opening up, and for Yaozhi, it was an era that felt novel, tolerant, exhilarating, and exciting! She experienced changes every day, and the air was filled with the power of progress. Perhaps people had emerged from the turbulent and chaotic era of the Cultural Revolution, and had started to liberate their previously closed and confined thoughts. Literature flourished during this period, with emerging newspapers, magazines, and films enriching people's leisure time. At that time, there was no internet, no stock market, and no futures market. Everything was still in its nascent stage. The commodities in the free market were numerous but not yet considered abundant. Color televisions appeared in the market, and TV programs began to feature new films by Xie Jin, breaking away from the repetitive model operas.

One morning, as Yaozhi was out for a stroll, she saw a group of girls passing by, carrying school bags, flipping through the June 1980 issue of "Popular Movies" on a street stall. These girls were about thirteen or fourteen years old. Some of them had their hair tied in ponytails, while two girls had beautiful red and purple scarves tied around their braids, looking vibrant and eye-catching. One girl with braided hair was exceptionally pretty, and her clothes were the most colorful. She wore a yellow dress, tied with a floral scarf, and white plastic sandals on her feet. The girls chatted and laughed, each buying a copy of "Popular Movies," and they continued on their way to school. Just then, a group of young boys in their teens whizzed by on bicycles, intentionally slowing down as they approached the girls. A few girls jumped on the back seats of the bicycles, and within moments, they disappeared from sight.

Yaozhi recalled her younger days when she used to ride a bike to work at the Military Statistics Bureau, reminiscing about those memories. She snapped back to reality, flipped through the pictures in "Popular Movies," looked at the back cover, and grabbed a copy of "Reader's Digest" for three-mao* and "Reference News," which Juncheng liked to read, for four-mao. Then she went to buy breakfast.

Recently, the ration coupons for grain and cloth had disappeared. Farmers could come to the city to sell their vegetables and fruits, while city residents could buy two *youtiao* (deep-fried dough sticks) and have a bowl of wonton or tofu pudding from roadside stalls in the morning market. Yaozhi would get three bowls of soy milk in her lunchbox, buy a jin of *youtiao*, and sometimes purchase some small vegetables and a few deep-fried cakes. Then she would go to the free market to buy vegetables. There were plenty of fresh vegetables available, and the prices were very cheap. She could also buy pork, beef, mutton, fish, eggs, tofu, and more. Every time Yaozhi bought eggs, she would always choose the cracked ones first because those eggs that had been chipped or had minor flaws were one-mao cheaper per jin. Yaozhi still had to count her money tightly since her funds were very limited, but she had to buy some nutritional supplements for Dawan because he was going through puberty and growing taller. Cracked eggs still provided protein, so they were just as good to eat. Overall, life was convenient and casual, and Yaozhi enjoyed such days.

This was something she didn't dare to imagine twenty-something years ago. Back then, forget about not being able to buy these eggs,

"mao" is slang for jiao.

even if someone wanted to sell them, it had to be done secretly, for fear of being labeled as "taking the capitalist road" or "undermining socialism."

On her way home, Yaozhi passed a movie theater. There was a large poster with photos of Zhang Yu and Guo Kaimin. The theater was showing "Love on Mount Lu," produced by the Shanghai Film Studio. Dawan had told Yaozhi that this movie was very popular, and China had started celebrating love again. It was said that the film even featured a rare kissing scene at the time! Yaozhi noticed a trendy girl standing in front of the poster. She had two black braids, was wearing bell-bottom pants, and had a yellow scarf on her head. She was holding a point-and-shoot camera, taking pictures of the poster. Yaozhi felt that this was something she could not have seen than twenty years ago.

As Yaozhi walked on the sidewalk, she saw various motor vehicles darting past her. Most of them were blue-and-white or red-and-white minibusses and public transport vehicles, occasionally accompanied by trucks, sedans, and tricycles. It was evident that China was in a period of vigorous development, with everything waiting to be revitalized.

## 2

Students could now take the college entrance examination and no longer need to participate in the "Up to the Mountains and Down to the Countryside" movement to receive reeducation from poor and lower-middle-class peasants. Admission to university was also no longer primarily based on family background but mainly on academic performance. This change was highly advantageous for students like Dawan who came from humble backgrounds.

Yaozhi's family of three squeezed into a tiny 12-square-meter room, with both Juncheng and Yaozhi smoking cigarettes, causing the room to be filled with smoke. Next door, they often heard the sound of their sister-in-law scolding, and sometimes their older brother and sister-in-law would visit, with the sister-in-law's words becoming even more offensive. Dawan lost his enthusiasm for studying and preparing for college in such an environment.

During this time, Juncheng became somewhat lazy, neglecting his responsibilities and engaging in activities like playing chess, cards, and bird-walking. Whenever he heard his daughter-in-law's scolding, he would escape from the house, and Dawan would follow suit. Dawan, a thoughtful and filial child, would feel compelled to confront his older brother every time he heard his sister-in-law berating him, criticizing their parents. However, whenever he saw his mother shaking her head and pleading with him through her eyes, he held back. And when he saw his father carrying a birdcage and walking out the door, he went along. In reality, Dawan felt suffocated hearing those voices every day at home, so going out with his father was quite relaxing. He spent two months accompanying his father, spending his days strolling through the flower and bird market. He even bought two pots of kumquats, hearing that they could be sold at sky-high prices once they were well-cultivated.

However, Yaozhi had high expectations for Dawan, and she became extremely worried when she saw him losing interest in studying while following his father. One day, taking advantage of Juncheng's absence, she said to her son, "Wan, you're catching a good opportunity! Look at your older brothers, they were born in an unfortunate time and didn't have a choice. But you're different. The college entrance examination is something you must take seriously. Once you enter university, you'll enjoy the benefits of state job placement and have a good career and life in the future."

Dawan replied, "Mom, I know you want me to succeed, but there are so many subjects in the college entrance examination, and I haven't studied many of them before. And the review materials are incomplete. I'm afraid I won't do well."

Yaozhi firmly said, "You must take the exam. How will you know if you'll succeed or not if you don't try?"

Helpless, Dawan said, "Mom, do you know how people describe the college entrance examination? It's like walking on a tightrope, like crossing a single-plank bridge. And the admission rate is so low. I really lack confidence! Besides, look at us living here, dependent on others. I hate myself for not being able to provide you and dad with our own apartment."

Yaozhi followed her son's train of thought and said, "That's right. If you want to repay me and your dad, you need to go to university, get a good job, and stand out so that we can have the money to buy us an apartment."

Yaozhi has always had such a temperament since she was young, and once she sets her mind on something, not even eight oxen could pull her back. When she saw small advertisements on the street for college entrance exam tutoring classes, she wasted no time in enrolling Dawan in one. She even enrolled herself, just so she could accompany Dawan. One reason was to supervise him, and the other was to learn herself so she could assist Dawan. Without consulting Juncheng, she rented a small house to avoid the constant scolding from her daughter-in-law. The house was old, with the water tap located outside, and the toilet was in the alley. Inside the room, there was only a worn-out mat spread on a kang bed that could fit two people, along with a lonely broom standing in the corner. There was a dilapidated chair paired with a table missing one corner, and nothing else. Yaozhi said that this simplicity could bring peace of mind and allow for focused studying.

Outside the house, there was a coal stove with a fire shovel, an iron kettle for boiling water, and an iron pot for cooking.

Juncheng felt neglected as he saw Yaozhi completely disregarding him, wholeheartedly focusing on their son Dawan's exam preparation. They were even planning to move to a rented house together for the sake of Dawan's college entrance exams. Juncheng understood that Yaozhi was doing it all for their son's future, but the feeling of being neglected, along with the mistreatment he experienced in the second son's house, made his temper flare up.

As a result, Juncheng had an argument with his daughter-in-law. He saw Yaozhi buying a rolling suitcase and making multiple trips to the small house to move things, which made him feel jealous. Juncheng rushed over and grabbed the suitcase from Yaozhi, saying, "You can't leave, but if you're leaving, take me with you."

Yaozhi pushed Juncheng's hand away and said, "Stop messing around. It's already this late. We have less than a year left. The main obstacle in our family right now is Dawan's college entrance exams. If he gets in, I'll come back to be with you."

Juncheng pleaded, "I can also help tutor Dawan. I can cook for you both."

Yaozhi replied, "You? Just not having to take care of you is already a relief. Besides, the place can't accommodate three people. You'll just cause chaos if you come."

Juncheng still refused to let Yaozhi go and said, "Then, are we practically living separately? This won't work!"

Yaozhi, feeling embarrassed, said, "I will consider your feelings. How about I come back every weekend to be with you?"

Juncheng had no choice but to let Yaozhi go. So, Yaozhi promised to return to their second son Xiaodi's home every weekend to spend two days with Juncheng. Dawan would also come back, and they would all spend the weekend together.

Apart from the weekends, Yaozhi primarily took care of their son's daily life, accompanying him for meals, bedtime, and attending the tutoring classes together. She helped him find study materials and answered his questions.

Yaozhi had changed a lot over the years and was no longer the proud princess she once had been. She grew accustomed to listening to her three daughters-in-law criticize her and her husband, and her sons often questioned them about why they abandoned the three brothers and allowed the eldest to work in the countryside for many years before returning to the city. He only recently secured a job at a plastic decoration production factory, while his wife's household registration remained in the rural area. The second son had been involved in fights and was taken to the police station multiple times, but he was now starting to make some progress in his self-employment. The third son was irresponsible and relied on his wife's family even after getting married. Aunt Chen took care of the three brothers for many years, but eventually stopped caring for them because of their constant troublemaking and excessive demands. Once Yaozhi sent Dawan off to university, the last piece of stone in her heart finally fell, and she began spending time with Juncheng, taking walks, playing chess, cards, and mahjong.

Then the daughters-in-law started flattering their mother-in-law again, hoping that she would help tutor their grandchildren with their schoolwork. However, Yaozhi didn't want to tire herself out again. So she was once again criticized and blamed by her three daughters-in-law. They talked behind her back, calling her a heartless and ungrateful old witch, and this language eventually rubbed off on her grandchildren.

In 1988, with the support of his uncle, who worked in investment banking in the United States, Dawan went to study in the United States. Yaozhi wrote a letter to her son, who was studying for a Ph.D. at the University of Texas in Austin, seeking help. Dawan's income was limited at that time, but he remembered the promise he made when he was a child: to ensure that his mother would live a good life and have her own house. So he worked two jobs, saved money, and bought a two-bedroom apartment for his parents in Yingkou. Yaozhi and Juncheng spent their remaining years there.

## 3

I later visited Shihezi, where there was a military colonization museum built in 1952. At the entrance, there was a unique hoe called "Kantouman" used by the people of Xinjiang, tied together with an old rifle, symbolizing the integration of soldiers and farmers, which was the essence of military colonization. Across the street was the Cultural Square, where a statue stood of a military colonization soldier, holding a towering steel sword, showcasing Shihezi as a city that turned swords into plowshares. The museum's admission ticket was only three yuan. The visitors in the museum arrived by bus, all of them being from groups enthusiastic about red tourism. In fact, the museum had only a few exhibits, and some of them even indicated the donors. These exhibits were the authentic representation of that era. There were plows and hoes used by those pioneers in the early days, old tractors once driven by military colonization soldiers, daily life items they used, as well as some sculptures and yellowed old photos of military colonization figures. From these photos, I could see the hardships of the life endured by my Aunt Yaozhi back then.

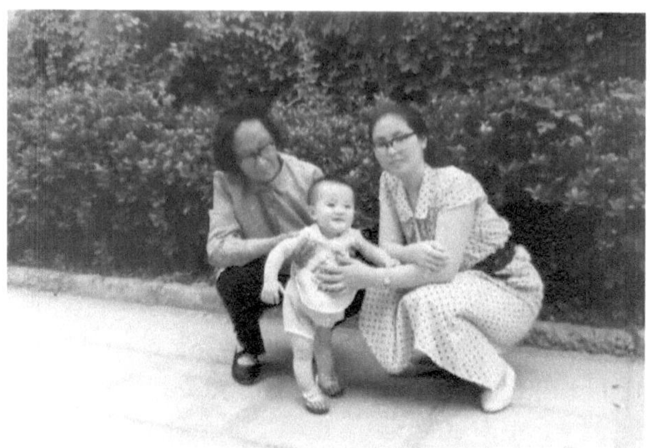

Yaozhi, Mingyu, and Yang Xi

In the autumn of 1992, my father Guangzhong went abroad for postdoctoral studies, and my mother Yang Xi and I returned to our hometown. I was only a little over three years old at that time. I unexpectedly saw my grandfather Yaowei taking Aunt Yaozhi to the best hospital in Shenyang, China Medical University Hospital, for treatment. Aunt Yaozhi had ovarian cancer, and it was already in the advanced stage, spreading throughout her body. Great Aunt Yaozhi looked very old. Due to her years of labor, her back was slightly hunched, her hands had thick calluses, her complexion was dark, and her eyes had lost their luster. Her abdomen was swollen and filled with fluids. She would take a few steps and then rest to catch her breath.

Aunt Yaozhi chatted with my grandfather, and when she talked about her son Dawan, her face was filled with a look of happiness. She said, "Eighth Brother, even if I die today, this life would still be worth it. Last year, Dawan invited me to the United States, and I saw my grandson. Dawan even gave him an American name, which I didn't approve of. Later, at my strong request, I gave him a Chinese name."

She chuckled proudly as she reached this point.

During great aunt Yaozhi's hospitalization in Shenyang, Uncle Dawan specially returned from the United States to take care of her for a month. Later, we heard that she passed away not long after, at

Yaozhi and Yaowei

the age of seventy. Two years after great aunt Yaozhi's passing, Wu Juncheng also left, accompanying his lifelong partner.

From the white mountains and black waters, having experienced the tribulations of life,

Yaozhi and Juncheng, bound together for eternity, embracing the sentiments of love.

In this life, never giving up, exchanging bitterness for sweetness,

After death, becoming two birds with intertwined wings, wandering between love and hate in the boundless heaven.

Part Six

# *The turbulent life story of Li Yaoxin*

# Chapter One

## A difficult farewell to hometown and the painful loss of an unborn baby

### 1

In 1999, when I was ten years old, I returned from Norway to mainland China to meet my great aunt Li Yaoxin, who came back from Taiwan to visit my grandpa. That year, my family went to the United States. It was during this trip that I met great auntie Yaoxin's daughter, Shulan. She was born in the year 1960, during the Republic of China era, and was older than my father. I called her aunt Lanlan. It was during this time that I learned a huge secret: Li Yaozhi had passed away. Shulan looked at the photo of her mom's sister Li Yaozhi hanging on the wall and said to her mom Yaoxin, "I don't resemble you much, but I look a bit like Aunt Yaozhi!"

Li Yaoxin looked at Shulan, gently caressed her head, and slowly began to reveal her story and the long-hidden secret in her heart.

It was the year 1948, a leap year in the Gregorian calendar, and the year of the Rat in the Chinese lunar calendar. February 10th marked the Spring Festival, without an intercalary month, and it was also the thirty-seventh year of the Republic of China.

The weather on that February day in 1948 was clear and sunny, with a gentle breeze. It didn't feel as cold as it did during the Lunar New Year in Yingkou. Li Yaoxin was about to celebrate her first Spring Festival in Taiwan. Walking the streets of Taipei, everything felt unfamiliar. It had been three months since she arrived in Taiwan, and she constantly missed her family, especially Yaoguo, Yaowei, and Yaozhi, her two younger brothers and older sister. She wondered how they were doing.

Yaoxin had arrived in Taipei the previous November but hadn't yet taken the time to explore the city's streets. On this particular day, she decided to walk to the Tamsui River Bridge instead of taking a bus. It was said that the sunset along the Tamsui Riverbank and the view of the harbor were the most enchanting. Standing on the bridge, Yaoxin gazed into the distance. The fishing docks were filled with boats of various sizes, and fishermen returned with their white sails, unloading their day's catch. Yaoxin observed Taiwanese fishermen wearing rubber overalls and boots as they unloaded the fish into large wooden crates, which were then lifted onto trucks and carts. As dusk approached, many men and women gathered at the fishing docks to admire the seascape. Some stood still, watching, while others walked along the wooden boardwalk or sat in front of small restaurants below the boardwalk. The sun was starting to set, and the night gradually unfolded. The white streetlights illuminated the boardwalk, casting shadows on the people. The sun hid behind the distant mountains, but the horizon was tinged with a golden hue. In the reflection of the sunset, the Tamsui River shimmered with golden light. At that moment, the world became a grand stage, encompassing all those who admired the sunset. Yaoxin felt as though she had become part of the scene. The sky grew darker, and the radiant golden glow suddenly vanished. Yaoxin looked up at the starry sky, where the twinkling stars seemed to be telling her that everything in the world is constantly changing. The distant mountains and rivers, the nearby pavilions and towers, all seemed to mimic the appearance of her hometown under the night sky. However, to Yaoxin, it all seemed futile. None of it could evoke the sense of familiarity she felt for her hometown.

Yaoxin went to a nearby grocery store and bought some fruits and vegetables. Compared to the turmoil and scarcity during the war in Northeast China, there was a wide variety of vegetables and fruits available here, and they were reasonably priced, especially in February. Yaoxin had never seen "Shijia" (*Annona squamosa*) before, a fruit with a green color resembling the shape of the Buddha's head. Perhaps that's how the fruit got its name. These days, Yaoxin would buy a few kilograms of ripe "Shijia" every time she went fruit shopping. The fully ripened "Shijia" had plump and juicy grains, with a soft and sweet taste. Sometimes, when the "Shijia" she bought was not fully ripe, it would be a bit firm. Yaoxin would wrap the "Shijia" in tissue paper, spray some water on it, and let it sit for two to three days. Once it became slightly soft to the touch, she would peel off the skin with a small knife and place the fruit in a bowl, complemented with red pomelo juice for consumption.

Lin Shunyi also loved eating "Shijia" and described the combination as visually appealing, delicious, and sweet. He said, "Yaoxin, we didn't come to Taiwan for nothing. At the very least, we have such delicious fruits. Where in Northeast China can you find anything like this?"

Yaoxin replied, "If you love eating it, I'll always buy it for you."

Because Shunyi rarely talked about food and ate his meals in a hurried manner, it felt like he was on a military march. He would often finish eating at the stove while Yaoxin was still preparing the meal, and then he would leave to attend to his own business. This made Yaoxin feel like she didn't have a sense of home. Fruits piqued Shunyi's interest and he would sit down with Yaoxin to enjoy them, praising their taste, giving Yaoxin a warm and comforting feeling. To satisfy Shunyi, Yaoxin became very picky when buying fruits.

Later, Yaoxin saw a vibrant and beautiful dragon fruit. She had never eaten dragon fruit before, but the name alone was enticing. When she cut it open, revealing the red flesh interspersed with small black seeds, she couldn't resist taking a bite. It truly lived up to its reputation as the king of fruits, combining beauty and deliciousness. There were many other fruits that Yaoxin couldn't even name. Shunyi told Yaoxin that from now on, they should try every type of fruit. He also hinted that their stay in Taiwan was temporary.

The fruits and vegetables in Taiwan whetted Shunyi's appetite, and Yaoxin found joy in being a homemaker. One day Yaoxin discovered a unique vegetable called "baby cabbage." It was incredibly sweet and delicious, reminiscent of the small bok choy in Yaoxin's hometown in mainland China. However, the baby cabbage was tender and vibrant, making it a perfect ingredient for cooking with exceptional texture. Unbeknownst to Yaoxin, she spent a whole hour meticulously selecting vegetables in the store.

As Yaoxin stepped out of the grocery store, it suddenly started pouring rain. She hailed a tricycle, and the driver, wearing a straw hat and a white smock, helped her open the canopy above the passenger seat to shield them from the rain. The sound of raindrops hitting the canopy filled the air. Yaoxin noticed that the driver's back was getting wet, and she felt a sense of empathy. However, to her surprise, the driver moved swiftly and fearlessly in the rain. He was quite talkative, introducing himself as Mr. Meng and mentioning that his family had immigrated to Taiwan from Shandong during the Qing Dynasty. He shared that he enjoyed going to a small tavern for a drink after work, as it helped him relax and forget the fatigue of the day. He also mentioned that he liked driving in the rain, stomping in the puddles, finding it the most delightful experience during hot summer days. However, it was a bit chilly today, considering it was February, and such heavy rain was uncommon. He even remarked that the best time for him was during a typhoon when many drivers wouldn't work, allowing him to earn two to three times the usual fare and take a break for two or three days. Listening to him, Yaoxin occasionally asked, "Don't you find this profession to be difficult?"

Mr. Meng replied with a cheerful tone, "Life may be filled with hardships, but I practice Buddhism, which has taught me to find joy in suffering! Running in the rain brings me happiness, listening to music and drinking are also my sources of joy. In reality, how can life be truly bitter?!"

Yaoxin said, "So, I've encountered someone who practices Buddhism, and you must be the happiest person!"

The two of them continued their conversation throughout the journey. After a short while, they arrived at the entrance of Yaoxin's home. She paid the driver double the fare and went upstairs to her apartment. They lived in a high-end residential area, and Shunyi had secured a position as a professor in the History Department of National Taiwan University, ensuring their livelihood. Their home was located in the middle section of Zhongzheng Road in the Siling District. It was a three-story building with a charming old-fashioned appearance, constructed with red bricks. At the entrance, two white marble pillars supported a spacious balcony on the second floor. The building accommodated six households. The corridors were wide, and the rooms were to Yaoxin's satisfaction. When she opened the windows, the outside view was delightful. The large bed in the bedroom provided her with a peaceful sleep, easing the anxieties and worries she had when she first arrived in Taipei and soothing her longing for her family.

Yaoxin sat at her desk, spreading out the stationery to write a letter to her family. She had already written ten such letters. As she gazed up at the night sky of Taipei, she wondered if her family back home was also missing her. When would they be able to reunite?

It was getting late, and Shunyi hadn't returned yet. He had just started his job, and there was a lot to handle at the university. He had to prepare for new courses, write lesson plans, and seemed to be happily engrossed in his work. Yaoxin was having some difficulty adjusting and experiencing a bit of homesickness. That's why she had started looking for work in the past few days.

Fortunately, her job search had been successful. A few days later, Yaoxin accepted a position at Taipei Private Taibei Senior High School on Fulin Road in the Shilin District. She would be teaching Chinese classics and *Guoxue* to high school students.

Talking about Guoxue, some people said it was just a general term for traditional Chinese culture and thought. However, its scope was extensive, and its connotations were rich, beyond anyone's ability to fully articulate. It encompassed ancient Chinese thoughts, ethics, literature, philosophy, history, geography, politics, and economics, and extended to music, calligraphy, religion, astrology, medicine, architecture, and many other aspects. Yaoxin believed that Guoxue was the embodiment of the national essence, flowing in the blood of the Chinese people. Moreover, after the Taiwan government took over the schools at all levels, it fully implemented Sinicized education, emphasizing the Three Principles of the People and national education spirit, and Japanese-style education was forcibly prohibited. Although Yaoxin wasn't as quick-witted as fifth sister Yaozhi, she had always been diligent in her work since childhood. Her lesson preparations were filled with detailed notes, and she completed her assignments diligently. She spent at least twice the amount of time preparing for each class compared to the actual class time. As a result, she quickly became well-known among the students at Taibei Senior High School.

## 2

In 1957, while Yaozhi went to Xinjiang for reform through labor, Yaoxin was promoted to the position of Dean of Academic Affairs at the school. Her classes were loved by the students, and she began to be somewhat famous in Taipei. She was frequently invited to other schools to give lectures.

Shunyi was also promoted to a tenured professor, and his career flourished. Yaoxin wanted to have a baby with him. Over the past few years, they had both thought about having children, but they were both too busy! Shunyi was so focused on his career that he forgot about the family. What was even more frustrating was that he often brought students to their home to discuss academic matters. Yaoxin had to prepare dinner for them, and their discussions would continue until late into the night. Yaoxin was a light sleeper and even the slightest noise could wake her up. Although their bedroom was on the second floor of the house, she could still hear the voices from downstairs. Over time, Yaoxin developed insomnia.

In the morning, Yaoxin prepared hot milk, boiled two eggs, toasted bread, and made two sandwiches, waiting for Shunyi to come downstairs for breakfast. She sipped tea while waiting.

When she heard footsteps upstairs, Yaoxin stood up and saw Shunyi carrying a briefcase and straightening his suit collar, looking busy and rushed. Yaoxin said, "Come and have breakfast!"

Impatiently, Shunyi replied, "I don't have time, I have a class in the first period!"

After saying that, he walked to the shoe rack at the entrance, threw his shoes on the floor, and without even putting them on, he hurriedly left the house.

Yaoxin was feeling disappointed; Shunyi was always so busy and didn't care about their family at all. Whenever he had any free time, he would spend it writing books, not knowing what relaxation meant. It had been ten years since they came to Taiwan, and they hadn't even watched a movie together or strolled on the streets. They rarely went out to restaurants for meals together. Yaoxin felt a sense of injustice. She was already an outsider in Taiwan, and her relatives were mostly on the mainland. She had no one to share her joys and sorrows with, and she felt it was time to have a child. Yaoxin mentioned it to Shunyi several times, but he always said he was too busy and had no time for a child.

Shunyi bought boxes of condoms and they used them every time they were intimate. It seemed like he was really afraid of having a child. When Yaoxin saw their neighbor with a little girl, who was taken out to bask in the sun every day, her desire to have a child grew stronger. Taking advantage of Shunyi's absence from home, she used a needle to poke a small hole in each condom. Three months later, her menstrual cycle was delayed, and two weeks had passed without it coming. It happened to be a day when primary and secondary schools were on vacation, so Yaoxin went to a nearby private clinic to find out what was going on. When she received the test results, she happily exclaimed, "It's positive, I'm pregnant!"

The doctor looked at her excited expression and smiled, saying, "Congratulations! Go and share the good news with your husband!"

Yaoxin picked up her bag and got into the bus, heading straight to Shunyi's school. Shunyi was teaching in a tiered classroom, wearing a brown suit and a neatly tied brown tie, earnestly delivering the lesson to his students. Yaoxin looked at Shunyi and felt that his seriousness in teaching was not much different from her own dedication to Guoxue. Shunyi was of average height, slightly overweight, and in his forties. His hair had started to thin, and he had indeed worked hard over the years. With thoughts on her mind, Yaoxin checked her watch and realized there was still over half an hour until the end of the class. She decided to sit down on a bench in the corridor and close her eyes to rest. She dozed off and had a dream. In the dream, her belly was large, and she walked unsteadily before giving birth to a daughter. The baby was small and delicate, with big, bright eyes. Her tiny hands were not as big as Yaoxin's palm, but once she grabbed onto her mommy's finger, she held on tightly and wouldn't let go.

"Yaoxin, what are you doing here?"

Shunyi's question, along with the ringing bell signaling the end of class and the noisy footsteps of students, interrupted Yaoxin's beautiful dream. She opened her eyes and saw Shunyi leaning down, looking at her. Rubbing her eyes, she suddenly remembered that she came here to tell Shunyi about her pregnancy. She was about to reveal her secret when Shunyi said, "Yaoxin, do you need something?"

Before Yaoxin could answer, Shunyi glanced at his watch and continued, "I have a meeting with my doctoral student to discuss work. If you don't have anything urgent, you can take the car back."

The words stuck in Yaoxin's throat, and she felt a sense of resentment and disappointment. Her husband was highly intelligent but emotionally unaware.

She returned home alone and spent the whole afternoon feeling down. She had no appetite and didn't even feel like eating. She felt lethargic and wanted to sleep. She covered her head and slept for the entire afternoon until Shunyi returned around 8 p.m. He asked why she hadn't cooked dinner.

Yaoxin put on her clothes, tied her apron, and started washing vegetables and cooking. The smell of cooking oil made her nauseous, and she knew she was experiencing morning sickness. However, Shunyi sat in the study, grading student assignments, completely oblivious to his wife's changes. Yaoxin finished cooking, placed the dishes on the table, set the tableware, and called Shunyi to come and eat.

While Shunyi ate and continued reading academic reports, he completely ignored the fact that Yaoxin hadn't taken a single bite. Yaoxin looked at her husband, who was absorbed in reading, and said, "Shunyi, we're out of rice at home. Could you buy some tomorrow?"

Shunyi looked up and stared at Yaoxin, puzzled as he asked, "But don't you usually buy it? Why can't you go this time? You can handle it."

Yaoxin replied, "The bag of rice is heavy, and I'm afraid I won't be able to carry it."

Confused, Shunyi asked, "Why? You used to be able to carry it before, so why not now? Yaoxin, are you feeling unwell?"

After thinking for a moment, he continued, "Alright, I'll ask my student to help you. How about that? I really don't have the time."

Tears welled up in Yaoxin's eyes. She dropped her chopsticks, stood up from the table, and retorted, "No need! You're always busy! Do you ever spare a thought for this family and me?"

A few days later, as expected, Shunyi sent a tall young man to their home asking if there was anything Yaoxin needed help with, but Yaoxin had already bought the rice herself. She carried it to the doorstep of the rice shop and then hired a rickshaw to bring it back.

On this day, Yaoxin, who was over three months pregnant, carried a basket of vegetables and climbed the stairs to their home. She felt the weight and struggled to climb the stairs. Exhausted, she returned home and lay down on the sofa to rest. But suddenly, she felt a sharp pain in her abdomen. She sensed warm liquid flowing onto her underwear—it was blood. Yaoxin rushed to the bathroom, her hand pressed against her belly. She walked to the phone and called an ambulance.

In the hospital, after undergoing a miscarriage and dilation and curettage (D&C) surgery, Yaoxin was being wheeled back to the ward by a nurse when Shunyi hurriedly arrived, carrying his briefcase. He said to Yaoxin, "I'm sorry, I just found out!"

He muttered to himself, "How could this happen? I was being careful!"

Yaoxin turned her face away, unwilling to look at Shunyi. Tears welled up in her eyes.

In the following days, Shunyi took a few days off to accompany Yaoxin. Although he was not good at household chores and often burned the food, Yaoxin felt that as long as they were together, they were the happiest, even if the food was burnt. But such days only lasted for a few days! Afterwards, Shunyi started to go to work early and return late. In fact, over the years, Yaoxin felt that Shunyi had changed. The Shunyi who used to pursue her had a romantic side. He took Yaoxin to watch precious movies, brought her to restaurants, and bought her hair accessories. However, as time passed, they were engulfed by work and the trivialities of life, and romance had long left them. What Yaoxin couldn't bear the most was Shunyi's indifference towards her. He didn't speak, their married life lacked passion, and they had no common ground in their work. Their spiritual world became dull, and the communication between them was almost nonexistent. Yaoxin used to enthusiastically share classroom anecdotes and students' different interpretations of the topics she taught in her Chinese culture classes at the high school. She hoped that Shunyi would also share his opinions, perhaps as examples for the students to ask questions. At that time, Shunyi would also engage in conversations based on Yaoxin's questions. But now, he was completely immersed in his own work world, and he couldn't even be bothered to argue with Yaoxin. Yaoxin hoped to receive attention, and she felt frustrated in her heart, wanting to say a few words. However, whenever that moment came, Shunyi would either remain silent or leave, not speaking to Yaoxin for days.

## Chapter Two

# Farewell to Shunyi; Yaoxin entrusts her worries to Amitabha

### 1

During these days, Shunyi would cough in the middle of the night and early morning. He didn't pay much attention to it himself because he had previously had tuberculosis when he was on the mainland. Yaoxin urged him to go to the hospital for a check-up, but he kept putting it off, claiming to be busy.

As the Lunar New Year approached, Shunyi's cough worsened, and Yaoxin grew more worried. Without Shunyi's consent, she made an appointment for him at the National Taiwan University Hospital, to see Dr. Liu in the Internal Medicine department next Tuesday morning.

On Friday, when Shunyi returned home, it was already past nine o'clock. He coughed while saying to Yaoxin, "I need to go on a business trip to Taichung on Monday. Prepare a suitcase for me."

Yaoxin became anxious and said, "Your cough is so severe. I made an appointment with a doctor at the National Taiwan University Hospital for you, to have a medical check-up next Tuesday! Why didn't you inform me about the business trip earlier?"

Nonchalantly, Shunyi grabbed a freshly steamed large bun from the kitchen and ate it while saying, "I'm not sick. It's just a little cough, nothing serious."

He continued, "The business trip is already scheduled, and there are three other professors involved. I can't inconvenience them just because of a medical check-up. I didn't tell you earlier because the trip was confirmed only these past two days."

Yaoxin shook her head helplessly.

On Monday morning, after Shunyi left, Yaoxin was about to call Dr. Liu to cancel the appointment. At that moment, the rotary phone hanging on the wall rang. Yaoxin picked up the receiver, and an urgent voice on the other end said, "Is this Mrs. Lin? Your husband fainted on the train today. The ambulance took him to the Emergency Room at the National Taiwan University Hospital. Please come quickly."

Yaoxin knew that something would happen to Shunyi, but she didn't expect it to happen so soon. She quickly put on her clothes, grabbed some toiletries, as she knew that Shunyi would most likely be admitted to the hospital. Then she took Shunyi's medical card, some cash, turned off the lights, locked the door, and called a taxi downstairs, rushing to the National Taiwan University Hospital.

The emergency room doctor at the hospital was performing resuscitation on Shunyi. After about ten minutes, Shunyi regained consciousness. The doctor said he needed to be transferred to the Internal Medicine department for further examination. At this point, Yaoxin hadn't canceled her appointment with Dr. Liu yet.

When Shunyi regained consciousness, he wanted to leave the hospital. The nurse held him down on the hospital bed, with an intravenous drip needle inserted into his arm. He asked Yaoxin, who was sitting by his bedside, to bring his briefcase over. He had a manuscript that he still needed to revise. Yaoxin wiped away her tears and said, "Yi, what have you been working day and night for? Now that you've fallen ill, don't exhaust yourself too much. Take good care of yourself and focus on getting better."

Shunyi asked Yaoxin, "Could you ask the doctor if I can be discharged tonight?"

Yaoxin reassured him, saying, "Don't worry, the doctor will let you know when you can leave. Since you're here, just accept the situation."

Finally, Shunyi nodded obediently. He also felt that he might have a serious illness. He hadn't told Yaoxin about coughing up blood these past few days, nor about the chest pains when he coughed, which were causing him some concern. What worried him the most was that recently his right hand sometimes didn't obey his commands, and he couldn't lift it to write. So he didn't argue with Yaoxin and agreed to stay in the hospital for a complete examination.

Shunyi stayed in the hospital for further examination. The hospital was designed by the Japanese in the Renaissance-era Victorian countryside style. The architecture featured a combination of red bricks and pebbles, giving it an antique and grand atmosphere, resembling a large villa. The inside of the hospital was clean, comfortable, spacious, and well-lit. The arched hall was intricately divided, adorned with colorful wallpaper and decorated with Greek-style columns and crystal chandeliers, creating a warm and peaceful ambiance. Through the bright glass windows of the hall, Yaoxin could see the beautiful scenery outside. There were patients enjoying the coconut trees, admiring the lotus flowers in the small pond, and watching the fish swim, seemingly forgetting their illnesses for a while. Yaoxin felt as if she were looking at people in a painting, while she stood outside the painting, but then she quickly reminded herself that she needed to go to the doctor's office to inquire about Shunyi's condition. These past few days, Yaoxin had been telling herself that Shunyi's condition was just an emergency, and he would recover soon.

## 2

Dr. Liu sat behind his desk, and after Yaoxin sat down, he said, "Your husband's condition is quite complicated. You need to be mentally prepared."

Yaoxin felt her scalp tighten as she watched Dr. Liu take out Shunyi's medical records. He pulled out the X-rays and several lab reports, saying, "Based on the current assessment, his primary tumor is in the brain, and it has already metastasized to the lungs, forming secondary tumors. It's now in the advanced stage. Cancer cells have spread to other organs through the bloodstream and lymphatic system. Due to the brain tumor, he will soon be paralyzed and experience severe pain. We will use morphine to alleviate the pain, but surgery won't be of much significance anymore."

Gritting her teeth, Yaoxin asked, "How much time does he have left?"

Dr. Liu pondered for a moment and said, "Approximately three months, maybe up to six months at most."

Yaoxin was dumbfounded. She hadn't anticipated such a bleak outcome.

Yaoxin believed it was her duty to inform Shunyi. It wasn't an act of cruelty but his right. If he knew his condition, he could better arrange the remaining time he had.

Returning to the hospital room, Yaoxin saw that Shunyi's students had arrived. There were about six or seven young people, joking and laughing. Shunyi didn't look like someone who was ill. He was still discussing papers and other academic matters with his students, holding their articles in his hand. On the small table beside his bed, there was a large vase filled with fresh and colorful flowers sent by the students. Shunyi's complexion did appear somewhat pale, and he had lost a lot of weight recently. His eye sockets had sunken a bit, but his spirits seemed fine.

After a while, the students left, and Yaoxin contemplated how to discuss Shunyi's condition with him. However, Shunyi spoke first. He asked Yaoxin to sit down and calmly said, "Xin, my dear wife, I accidentally saw my medical report. I know I won't live until next year."

Shunyi paused for a moment, looking at Yaoxin in tears, and continued, "Xin, I may have less than half a year left. I want to tell you something. Please don't be angry with me. Before you, I had a wife back in my hometown in China, and we have a child together. My cousin, who was also my student in China, brought him to Thailand in 1948. The child is almost thirteen now, and I want to bring him here before I pass away."

Shunyi looked at his wife with hopeful eyes, but in truth, Yaoxin already knew. Over the past ten years, she had often discovered remittance receipts in Shunyi's suit pockets, and she had even copied down the address in Thailand. However, she didn't know that those were for the living expenses of his child from his previous marriage. She had already suffered greatly because of it. At this moment, she felt rather calm, staring into Shunyi's eyes and nodding her head.

Yaoxin left the hospital room and arrived at a small bridge by the flowing water, attempting to calm the surging waves in her heart. Her life was about to undergo significant changes. Shunyi would leave her, and the continuation of his life, his son, would enter her life. Yaoxin felt that there must have been an inseverable connection between her and Shunyi from their past lives. The karmic ties of this lifetime, the debts from their past lives, if there was no mutual owing, how could they have encountered each other? It had long been predetermined in the depths of the universe!

As Buddha said, "The bond between husband and wife is the result of 500 lifetimes of cultivation, and becoming husband and wife is to fulfill the accumulated karma from past lives." Yaoxin silently recited in her heart, "Amitabha Buddha." She knew that from now on, only Amitabha could dissolve the perplexities in her heart.

## Chapter Three

# Yaoxin takes in Shunyi's son Xianglong from cousin Su Meichen. She meets Gao Hongying and adopts Shulan

### 1

In Thailand, Yaoxin met Shunyi's cousin, Su Meichen. She was petite, with a boyish haircut, dressed casually, and had a very easy-going and approachable personality. Yaoxin and Su MeiChen immediately became good friends.

Shunyi's thirteen-year-old son, Lin Xianglong, was somewhat reserved and didn't speak much. Perhaps he didn't fully trust his father and Yaoxin yet; he always avoided them and rarely engaged in conversation. He did not address Shunyi as "dad," and didn't call Yaoxin "aunt." Yaoxin was concerned because she knew that Shunyi was waiting for Xianglong to call him "dad" in his own words. Shunyi had mentioned more than once to Yaoxin, "Xianglong doesn't call me dad, and I know I don't deserve it."

Yaoxin reassured him, saying, "Don't worry, he's still young, he will call you that eventually."

Shunyi's sleep was troubled because Xianglong refused to call him "dad." Seeing Shunyi's distress, Yaoxin couldn't bear it and sought out Su Meichen behind his back. Yaoxin referred to her as "little sister" and asked, "Sister, do you know why Shunyi is in a wheelchair?"

Su Meichen replied, "Sister, I asked my brother, and he told me. I never expected it, I'm sorry."

Yaoxin said, "It's okay, I know Shunyi has prepared himself, and I have prepared myself too. But there is one thing that Shunyi is struggling with, and now only you, little sister, can help him."

Su Meichen turned her head, looking at Yaoxin with determination, and said, "I will do whatever I can to help!"

Yaoxin shared Shunyi's wish for Xianglong to call him "dad."

After contemplating for a while, Su Meichen said, "Let me give it a try."

A few days later, Su Meichen asked Shunyi and Yaoxin to come to her house. She said Xianglong wanted them to see his room. As Shunyi and Yaoxin pushed open the door, they were stunned by the sight inside. There was a large banner hanging on the wall in front of them, with the words, "Dad, I wish you a speedy recovery! I love you! Xianglong."

Xianglong, tall and slim, stood in front of the door, holding a bouquet of flowers. He shyly walked up to Shunyi and handed him the flowers. Clearly and distinctly, he said, "Dad!"

Shunyi stood up from his wheelchair, accepting the flowers, and tightly embraced the son he had longed for over the past decade! This scene moved both Shunyi and Su Meichen to tears, and they applauded vigorously. Su Meichen arranged for Shunyi and Xianglong to stay in the same room. They started talking more and more, with Shunyi sharing stories of Xianglong's childhood, his birth mother in the mainland, why he was entrusted to Aunt Su, and how he came to know Aunt Yaoxin. Shunyi told Xianglong that once they returned to Taiwan, he would have more time to spend with Aunt Yaoxin and encouraged Xianglong to accept her.

The night was calm and quiet, with the faint sound of crickets outside. Shunyi was in pain and couldn't sleep, and he could hear Xianglong tossing and turning. He knew that his son was awake too.

Shunyi tried his best to bear the pain silently, but it was difficult for him. Xianglong turned on the light and walked to his father's bedside, concerned, as he looked at Shunyi covered in sweat. Xianglong took out a handkerchief and gently wiped the sweat from his father's forehead. He reached into Shunyi's shirt pocket and took out a strong painkiller, then brought a cup of water. Supporting Shunyi to sit up, he placed the pill in his open mouth and held the cup to his lips, slowly raising it to allow him to swallow the medication. After a while, Shunyi's pain eased a bit, and the father and son turned off the light and prepared to sleep.

Shunyi asked Xianglong, "Xiaolong, if you have any questions, ask me now while my mind is clear. I can answer complex questions."

Xianglong cautiously asked, "Dad, can you tell me how you left my mom?"

Shunyi cleared his throat and slowly replied, "Child, your mother and I had an arranged marriage. I am a few months older than her. However, later, I left home to go to school, and we were hardly together. Your mother is a good woman. She took care of your grandparents on my behalf, fulfilling their needs in their old age. I owe her a lot in this lifetime."

Xianglong interjected, "Do you have a photo of my mom? I want to see what she looks like."

Shunyi said, "When you come with us to Taiwan, I will have a photo of her. She may not be highly educated, but she embodies the traditional virtues of a Chinese woman."

Xianglong wanted to uncover the mystery of his identity, unraveling the thirteen years of doubts. At first, he didn't want to acknowledge his father because of Su Meichen. Xianglong knew that his existence led to Auntie Su's marriage and subsequent divorce, and he believed it was all caused by his father. Xianglong was aware of his blood relationship with Su Meichen, so he called her Auntie.

Xianglong asked again, "So why did you entrust me to Auntie Su?" Shunyi remained silent for a while and slowly said, "At that time, I was teaching in Yingkou, and I only returned to my rural hometown once every six months. I wanted you to have a good environment to grow up in, so I brought you to Yingkou. As a grown man, I didn't know how to take care of a child. Auntie Su is my elder cousin, the daughter of my aunt, and my student. She was only 18 at the time, and she volunteered to help take care of you. She was great with children. In October 1947, she went to Thailand, and I agreed to let Su Meichen take you with her. By then, I was already planning to marry your Auntie Yaoxin, and I hid the fact that I was married to your mother and your existence. That was my mistake. At that time, the situation was chaotic, and I didn't consider many things. I thought I might go to Thailand too, but later, after I got engaged to Auntie Yaoxin, we hurriedly fled to Taiwan."

Xianglong nodded and said, "I know Auntie Yaoxin. She also came to Bangkok, and she has been very kind to me. Auntie Su has been good to me as well. She loves me, but you came at a difficult time for her when she was about to get married. I didn't want to burden her."

Shunyi said, "That's why we came to pick you up this time. It's fate. I hope my cousin, your Auntie Su, finds a good marriage."

Suddenly, Xianglong asked in an excited tone, "Then why did you marry Auntie Yaoxin?"

Shunyi replied, "Son, you'll understand matters of the heart when you grow up. I can only tell you that Auntie Yaoxin is the best woman in the world. She is kind and wise. You will experience it when you are with her."

Xianglong stopped asking questions, and after a while, Shunyi heard him murmuring "Mom" in his sleep. Xianglong began to try and accept Yaoxin as his mother, and they started talking. Yaoxin also tried to take care of this child who had faced so many hardships.

In the second month after Shunyi and Yaoxin brought Xianglong back to Taiwan, Shunyi passed away. Yaoxin looked at Shunyi lying peacefully in the coffin, silent and still. She reminisced about the many years she had spent with Shunyi. Shunyi was someone she had once loved deeply, and she had also been deeply loved by him. The emotional bond between them was undeniable, and even after Shunyi's departure, it continued to tug at Yaoxin's heart. Her closest person was gone, and she wondered if he had gone to another world after death. She fervently recited "Namo Amituofo" in her mind countless times, hoping to guide him to the Pure Land.

From then on, Yaoxin lived with her stepson, Lin Xianglong. She enrolled him in her own school, and they went to school together every day, maintaining a harmonious mother-son relationship. Xianglong was very intelligent, with a strong self-learning ability. He had a keen interest in mathematics and astronomy but lacked enthusiasm for other subjects, barely showing any interest. Although he was not talkative, his teachers considered him the most inquisitive student in the class. He loved digging deep into things and had remarkable concentration. He could observe ants moving for over an hour.

When Xianglong came to the family, Yaoxin hired a nanny to help take care of him. The nanny, named Basong, came from Thailand and was recommended by Su Meichen. Yaoxin gave her a name,

Taiqi. Basong and Su Meichen were good friends before, and she had known Xianglong for a long time. Basong's presence was like a miracle, and Xianglong called her Aunt Tai. Although Basong didn't speak much Mandarin, she was eager to learn. She often studied Mandarin with Xianglong and diligently wrote down everything in a little notebook. Besides buying groceries, cooking, and tidying up the house, Basong spent the rest of her time learning Mandarin and practicing Buddhism. Xianglong seemed to enjoy teaching her Mandarin. Seeing their harmonious relationship, Yaoxin felt relieved and spent her days with Xianglong, although she still felt the pressure. Xianglong was a genius, and he didn't particularly enjoy learning Mandarin or the Chinese classics that Yaoxin taught him. He had learned Mandarin from Su Meichen since childhood and had a solid foundation, which made him confident in front of Taiqi. He started to develop a liking for Mandarin, which gave Yaoxin and Xianglong some topics to discuss. Sometimes, even Taiqi sought Yaoxin's guidance, and Yaoxin patiently taught her. She used vivid teaching methods, gentle words, and colorful pictures, making learning interesting for Taiqi. Taiqi became the harmonizing force in this family, bringing Yaoxin and Xianglong closer together. Yaoxin was grateful that Taiqi had blended their relationship so well.

What was more important was that Taiqi was a devoted Buddhist. Every Sunday, rain or shine, she went to Longshan Temple. It was located at No. 211 Guangzhou Street, southwest of Taipei City, along the Tamsui River. The temple was built in the fifth year of the Qing Dynasty's Qianlong era and featured a three-section architectural layout in the shape of the character "回". It consisted of a front hall, a rear hall, east and west treasure halls, and a central main hall. Numerous deities were enshrined there, with the main deity being Guanyin Bodhisattva. The gold-plated Guanyin Bodhisattva sat on a lotus throne, radiating a majestic and solemn presence.

When Yaoxin was in mainland China, her family members were devout Buddhists, and she followed the same faith. However, since moving to Taiwan, she had only practiced Buddhism at home, offering incense and prayers in front of the Buddha statues but rarely visiting temples. This time, she accompanied Taiqi to Longshan Temple and was immediately surrounded by the serene, elegant, peaceful, and warm atmosphere of the jungle-like temple. Listening to the sound of the bell and drum, she felt the passage of time and had a sudden awakening. In this atmosphere, Yaoxin recalled the verse by Lu You: "The morning bell and evening drum toll ceaselessly, a shared sorrow spanning a hundred years." How appropriate it was in this setting.

She and Taiqi walked into the Buddhist hall, knelt on the cushion, clasped their hands together in front of their chest, bowed, and began to pay homage to the Buddha. Yaoxin performed three prostrations, confessing to the Buddha Bodhisattva: she would nurture Lin Xianglong with the infinite compassion of the Buddha; she asked the Buddha to grant her a tranquil heart, to help her overcome the grief of losing Shunyi; she prayed for a pure heart, to free herself from the endless yearning for her family in mainland China. She silently recited the Great Compassion Mantra, aspiring to transcend life and death, accumulate boundless merits, and cultivate great compassion.

From then on, Yaoxin became a devout Buddhist. She practiced Buddhism at home, became a lay Buddhist practitioner, and adopted the Buddhist name "Fuxin." Her innermost being had taken refuge in the Three Jewels.

## 2

Time flew by, and it had been eleven years since Yaoxin started teaching. She began receiving invitations to give lectures at other private high schools. One day, right after she finished her lecture on stage, she suddenly heard someone shouting, "Yaoxin, you're Yaozhi's sister, right! I finally found you!"

Yaoxin followed the voice and recognized the person immediately. It was Gao Hongying. During their school days, Yaozhi often brought Gao Hongying to their house to play. Later on, both Yaozhi and Gao Hongying became female officers in the military intelligence, gaining fame and recognition. People even said that Yaozhi and Gao Hongying resembled each other, with high foreheads and oval faces. At that time, Yaoxin idolized Gao Hongying because she was not only beautiful but also often treated Yaoxin with kindness, buying her delicious food. Even Yaozhi couldn't compare to Gao Hongying's thoughtfulness.

Now Gao Hongying looked thin, with messy hair and an unhealthy complexion, a yellowish tinge. Yaoxin couldn't believe that this was the same vibrant military officer she used to know.

Meeting an old acquaintance in a foreign land was truly a pleasant surprise! After the big class ended, Yaozhi went with Gao Hongying to her house. Gao Hongying said she worked at the Education Bureau of the Republic of China government in Taipei City. When she saw a poster at the school advertising a lecture on Chinese classics by a teacher named Li Yaoxin, she wondered if it was Yaozhi's younger sister, and indeed it was!

Yaoxin looked at her daughter Shulan and said, "Lanlan, you must remember what I'm about to tell you. Mommy is sorry for not telling you about your birth until now."

Shulan looked at her mother with a blank expression. It was the first time she had heard her mother talk about her origins. Her mother's love for her had always been selfless, and she had never doubted that she was her biological mother.

She remembered when she was six years old and had a high fever of 40 degrees Celsius. It was midnight, and there were no taxis on the silent streets. Mommy carried her to the hospital, running all the way. Mommy was exhausted and out of breath, collapsing at the hospital. The doctor had to rescue both mother and daughter. Afterward, Mommy stayed up all night, taking care of her until she recovered and was discharged from the hospital. And throughout her childhood, whatever she liked, Mommy always found ways to fulfill her desires, never making her feel the absence of a father.

Yaoxin continued speaking.

That day, she had a long conversation with Gao Hongying. They felt that they had met each other too late. They talked about their childhood experiences, how they came to Taiwan, and so on. Eventually, Yaoxin invited Gao Hongying to stay overnight at her house. Taiqi prepared dinner, and after they finished eating, Yaoxin and Hongying lay in bed, continuing their conversation until late at night.

Gao Hongying told Yaoxin that she was sorry for what happened to Yaozhi. Back then, it was she who reported to the authorities that Yaozhi's older brother and sister were members of the Communist Party, which led to Yaozhi losing his position as a section chief. Gao Hongying continued, "We were so young back then! I also liked Director Wu, but he fell in love with your sister. We were always competing secretly. Your sister was smart and beautiful, but I wasn't any worse! I even had fairer skin than her."

Yaoxin remained silent, realizing that Gao Hongying carried a heavy burden of negative karma and lived a weary life.

Gao Hongying continued, "But she didn't suffer any losses either! Director Wu took her home directly. Speaking of which, I didn't gain much either. It's true that I became a section chief, but Director Wu made things difficult for me at every turn. My life wasn't easy, and eventually, I had to resign. I wanted to find someone to marry early on, but I misjudged and ended up with a scoundrel!"

Yaoxin had heard from her fifth sister Yaozhi that Gao Hongying had betrayed her, using despicable means to take away her position as a section chief. However, looking at Gao Hongying's subsequent fate seemed to confirm a saying: "Good deeds are rewarded, evil deeds are punished." After hearing about her hardships today, Yaoxin silently prayed for her in her heart.

Lying in bed, Gao Hongying shared a secret with Yaoxin. She had a daughter whom she had sent to an orphanage a few months ago. Her boyfriend was unaware of the child's existence, and he had gone to the United States without any contact between them.

Yaoxin was surprised and asked Gao Hongying, "Why didn't you raise the child yourself?"

Gao Hongying replied, "I don't believe in love! My first husband left me for another woman. Later, I was in a five-year relationship with this boyfriend, but I didn't dare to get married. Last year, before he officially broke up with me, he was already with someone else, and they quickly went to the United States. But I unexpectedly got pregnant."

As Gao Hongying spoke, she started crying, and her tears became uncontrollable. Yaoxin handed her a tissue, and Gao Hongying wiped her tears, gradually calming down. She continued, "After giving birth to a baby girl, I started experiencing significant discomfort in my body. When I took my child for a six-month checkup, I also had my own health examined."

Gao Hongying paused, staying silent for a while.

Yaoxin gently patted her shoulder and asked, "Amitabha! Is it severe?"

Hongying said, "My autoimmune system malfunctioned. It's a rare case of primary biliary cirrhosis. By the time I discovered it, it was already in the advanced stage, with cirrhotic ascites. I don't have much time left to live."

Hongying continued, "After learning the diagnosis, I sent my child to Tzu Chi Children's Welfare Home. I couldn't burden the child. I hope that she will find a good family to take care of her in the future."

Hongying couldn't continue speaking.

Upon hearing Hongying's words, Yaoxin fell into contemplation. It was getting close to dawn, and she could hear Hongying's steady breathing, but she still couldn't sleep. She thought about Shunyi and thanked him for giving her a child like Xianglong. Although Xianglong wasn't her own flesh and blood, Yaoxin now considered him her own son.

Yaoxin asked Hongying to move in with her and Xianglong. Privately, Yaoxin brought back Hongying's daughter from the welfare institution, so that they could spend time together as a family. After Hongying passed away, Yaoxin adopted her daughter and named her Lin Shulan, with the nickname Lanlan.

During this time, Xianglong developed a passion for singing. Yaoxin sent him to a children's choir. While the choir didn't charge any fees, the training and performances were demanding. When Xianglong turned fifteen, his voice started to change, so he joined a mixed choir. His performances became more frequent, and Yaoxin often had to pick him up and drop him off for rehearsals and shows. Sometimes, Xianglong had performances on weekends, and Taiqi stayed at home taking care of Lanlan. Yaoxin had to wake up at six in the morning to drive Xianglong, which was truly exhausting. Yaoxin was also not good with directions and often took the wrong routes when driving Xianglong, causing many detours before finding the right way. Every time that happened, Yaoxin would get anxious and her palms would sweat.

Later on, Xianglong helped Yaoxin tremendously. It turned out that despite being silent, he had a natural sense of direction. Unless the choir went to a new location, once he had been to a place, Xianglong could give Yaoxin directions. He would say, “Turn left in about 500 meters ahead, then take a right for two kilometers…” and so on, speaking in a tone resembling that of a navigator.

Initially, Yaoxin was skeptical, but after a few times, she fully believed in Xianglong. While driving, she would earnestly say to him, “Xiang’er, from now on, you’ll be my map. If I had asked you earlier, I would have saved so many detours!”

Xianglong chuckled and replied, “You didn’t ask me before, and I didn’t dare to say anything! I was worried when I saw you taking the wrong routes.”

Yaoxin asked, “Aren’t you worried?”

Xianglong calmly answered, “Worrying won’t help! After all, I can’t drive.”

Yaoxin laughed and said, “Well, it’s because Mom is absent-minded and overly confident. From now on, we’ll implement family democracy.”

Xianglong said, “Thank you!”

Suddenly, Xianglong said, “Mom!”

This was the first time in two years that Xianglong called Yaoxin “Mom.” Yaoxin was so excited that she almost took her hands off the steering wheel to reach out and hug Xianglong. From then on, Xianglong also changed; he became more daring in speaking with Yaoxin. Their relationship became like being glued strongly together.

Later, Xianglong went to the United States to perform in a joint concert with the American Crystal Children’s Choir. This choir had many connections with Taiwan, and many of their members were children adopted from Taiwan to the United States. They would sing many Chinese songs. The choir also came to Taiwan to perform multiple times, which became one of the reasons why Xianglong insisted on going to the United States for further studies. Thinking about Shunyi, Yaoxin realized that Shunyi shouldn’t be considered as having betrayed her. In fact, he was the one who had owed allegiance to his original wife at home. But isn't being in a loveless marriage a kind of purgatory?

Yaoxin felt that she had a mission in this world. First, it was Lin Xianglong, and then it was Lin Shulan. By then Shulan was two and a half years old and very intelligent.

## Chapter Four

# A trickle of maternal love nurtured by kindness as classical dolls reveal true feelings

### 1

Listening to her mom's words, Shulan began crying uncontrollably. Since childhood, many children envied Shulan for having such a loving mother. She did not lack maternal love, nor did she feel insecure due to the lack of a father's love. Every birthday, her mother would write cards with her and invite classmates and friends to come to their home to celebrate Shulan's birthday. At that time, many of Shulan's friends celebrated their birthdays by eating longevity noodles and boiled eggs.

However, once, when Shulan saw a foreign movie where children celebrated their birthdays by eating beautiful cakes, her mother began buying birthday cakes from the cake shop for Shulan's birthday. Later, her mother learned how to make large cakes and wrote on them with colored cream: Happy Birthday Shulan! Shulan's birthday was in June, which was the time for harvesting strawberries and mangoes. Her mother liked to make strawberry cakes that Shulan liked, with a light pink cake decorated with circles of red strawberries, which looked very beautiful. Her mother also learned how to make mango mousse cakes, just because Shulan said she liked them. These lovely cakes were made according to Shulan's preferences. The light-yellow cake had a layered texture, and the mango flesh was like flowers blooming on top of the cake, very cute and beautiful. Cutting a small piece and taking a bite, the mango filling tasted refreshing, and the mango flavor instantly filled the mouth. The children loved it very much. Every time it was Shulan's birthday, her small room was crowded with children who came to celebrate with her, singing birthday songs and eating cake, which was very lively. Her mother also took her to the photo studio to take pictures on Shulan's birthday. Shulan put on the pretty clothes her mother had bought for her and captured the warm and beautiful moments of her life.

Her mother, a seemingly frail woman standing at 1.59 meters [5'2"], shouldered the burden of a household. She raised two children at home and taught her students at school. At home, her encouragement was always spot-on, and she could always find Lanlan's shining points.

Once, Shulan got the lowest score in the physical exam at school and was so upset that she didn't have the courage to attend physical education classes anymore. She said to her mother in great distress, "It's so embarrassing. All the other students reached the finish line and watched me run over."

Her mother comforted her gently, "Lanlan, you are shorter and have shorter legs than them, so of course you run slower. Besides, you haven't trained for long-distance running, so you didn't do well this time. But you know your weaknesses, and with targeted practice, you will surely make progress next time!"

Later, her mother actually hired a long-distance running coach to guide Lanlan, teaching her how to warm up and how to breathe during running to help coordinate her pace. Sure enough, in the later long-distance running exams, Lanlan achieved better results, joined the school's long-distance running team, and even won good rankings. With her mother around, Lanlan was never alone and never afraid of difficulties. Her self-esteem came from her mother's praise and encouragement.

Lanlan had a talent for literature, which was, of course, related to her mother's guidance. She won first place in the school's speech preliminaries. Mom said, "Congratulations to my little Lanlan for winning the championship! Whether you win or lose in the next competition, as long as you try your best, you've already succeeded halfway."

Then Lanlan entered the top three in the semifinals in another city, and she happily went out to party with her best friend. Mom reminded her, "Lanlan, there are wins and losses in life, don't take it too seriously!"

Finally, in the finals in Taichung, there were thirty candidates, and Lanlan ranked twenty-first. She felt a little disappointed and even cried. Mom said again, "You just didn't perform well this time. Winning and losing are inevitable in life, and no one can always win."

Mom's words always made Lanlan feel warm to the bottom of her heart. When she lost, she could let it go, and when she won, she didn't become complacent.

## 2

The most unforgettable thing for Shulan was when her mom bought her a doll. When the little girls visited each other's houses, they always showed off their beautiful dolls, but Shulan's mom was too busy with school work and didn't pay attention. When the girls came to Lanlan's house, she was the only one without a doll. Taiqi saw this and quietly told Yaoxin. Yaoxin said, "Why am I so careless? Girls all love dolls, and dolls can stimulate their maternal feelings, cultivate their kind and patient nature, and also play with other children, promoting their harmony."

Yaoxin said to Taiqi, "Thank you so much for being attentive and telling me early."

That day, Yaoxin let Lanlan choose the doll she liked. She asked Lanlan, "Mommy will take you to the mall, what kind of doll do you want?"

Lanlan said, "My friends all have fairy dolls. Their hands, feet, arms and legs can move, they wear beautiful chiffon skirts, with pretty flowers in their hair, and some even hold pockets or fans."

Yaoxin and Lanlan went to the mall and visited the biggest Mingyao department store in the city. At that time, it was the first and best in Taipei, with good quality and low prices. It had a fashionable spiral escalator and Yaoxin often came here. Compared to mainland China, life in Taiwan was much more abundant. Mainland China was still a planned economy, and many people couldn't even get enough food to eat. But Taiwan had not only achieved adequate clothing and food but had also entered the era of high-end consumption.

This market was a favorite of mothers, and many memories were left here. On both sides of the market were the Top Good Shopping Center and the Top Good Aiqun Mall. At that time, the singer Chen Sheng sang in his lyrics, "Walking along Zhongxiao East Road, do you recognize anyone?" Everyone called it "Celebrity Lane." This department store was a large shopping center at that time, attracting full-time mothers, female employees after work, and underage girls.

There were famous and delicious "Eastern District Rice Balls," ice cream taro balls, crispy beef rolls, and full and juicy flower and vegetable dumplings. There were also the best-looking and most useful household items, the newest and most novel branded clothing, and the rarest children's toys, including the most beautiful and fun classical dolls!

Standing in front of the doll counter, Yaoxin let Lanlan choose her favorite doll herself, always exercising her independent thinking and building her own confidence in making decisions. Lanlan fell in love with a music box doll that could sing, and the doll turned around with the music, full of vitality. Yaoxin said, "Lanlan, you chose the best doll." Then they bought several classical dolls, including Lin Daiyu, Xue Baochai, and the Four Beauties dolls, Yang Guifei, Xi Shi, and Diao Chan, as well as the decorated Zhongjun Chusai doll.

Lanlan had set her sights on another big doll. The doll could blink its eyes and looked lifelike, but sensible Yaoxin hesitated when she saw the price tag. Still, she believed it was worth it and picked up the doll, saying, "I'll take this one too. Lanlan can give her a name and make her your daughter, how about that?"

Lanlan was overjoyed that day and bought many dolls. The one she liked the most was this big doll, which she later named "Nongnong," after the sound babies make when they drink milk. She combed her hair, washed her face, put makeup on her, changed her clothes, and even slept with her, telling her stories every day. The doll accompanied Shulan as she grew up. Later, Lanlan really grew up, and the doll's clothes became worn out after being washed so many times. But, since that kind of old-fashioned doll was no longer produced, Mommy and Lanlan worked together to make her several outfits. Although the clothes were not as fancy as the store-bought ones, they were all sewn carefully by Mommy and Lanlan, with carefully chosen fabrics and lace added.

Now, the doll is locked in the closet at home, and sometimes Lanlan will remember to hug her. Students at school often come to Yaoxin to solve their emotional problems. She was initially a teacher of traditional Chinese culture, then promoted to the position of academic affairs director, and later experienced ups and downs, returning to being an ordinary teacher, and then teaching traditional Chinese culture again. When she was the academic affairs director, Yaoxin bought a game console to play with the boys to understand their psychology and family situations and then to provide tailored solutions. After graduation, groups of students came to visit her at home and said that having a good teacher like Yaoxin when they were students was their happiness. Shulan felt that having a mother like Yaoxin was her good fortune and that she was her chosen mother in this life.

# Chapter Five

## Siblings reunited after many years separation by the Taiwan Strait

### 1

I knew that great aunt Yaoxin was a devout Buddhist, and she said Taiqi was like her family. Taiqi took care of all the household chores for her, went to the temple and made offerings with her, and meditated with her at home. Over the years, whenever great aunt Yaoxin had troubles and felt scattered or restless, she would recite the "Amitabha Sutra" once, and it had a magical power to calm and focus her mind! She and Taiqi cultivated their hearts and virtues together, and everything that happened was met with a calm and peaceful attitude.

After that everything seemed very natural. Great aunt Yaoxin was promoted, given a raise, then demoted, and finally she retired and returned home. Through all the ups and downs, great aunt Yaoxin felt her heart was always bright and free from idle thoughts, and her inner self was serene and comfortable. Her body and mind became one, and she entered a state of meditation. The wonderful thing about this was being "selfless, desireless, egoless, and unattached."

In fact though, there was one thing that she could never let go of — her siblings. That's also why she couldn't follow Taiqi's path and become a nun. Her worldly affections were still present, and she didn't want to escape from them. She wanted to see her siblings.

At last the cross-strait relations seemed to have eased a bit. The mainland went from Mao Zedong's era of red communism to Deng Xiaoping's era of reform and opening up. The mainland stopped firing at Kinmen on the Taiwan Strait, and Taiwan's official side no longer talked about counterattacking the mainland. On New Year's Day of 1979, the mainland issued a "Message to Compatriots in Taiwan" which changed its tone for the first time. The transformation went from the original insistence on "liberating Taiwan" to "peaceful reunification, one country, two systems". On April 4th, President Chiang Ching-kuo responded with the Three-No policy of "no contact, no negotiation, and no compromise". The following year in June, President Chiang proposed "Three Principles of the People's Reunification of China". Taiwan wanted democracy, and the mainland needed reunification. In 1981, a historic turning point occurred in cross-strait relations. The first batch of Taiwanese-funded enterprises settled in Fuzhou, and four ports were opened for Taiwan businessmen to park ships and receive Taiwanese compatriots.

Yaoxin had been waiting for this day to come, but after multiple inquiries, she found out that ordinary Taiwanese citizens were not allowed to visit the mainland. She had to find other ways to meet her relatives in the mainland.

Her eldest son, Xianglong, went to the United States to study at the age of 20. When he left, Yaoxin withdrew $5,000 from the bank for him to carry with him, and then sent him a monthly living allowance. He graduated, took the postgraduate entrance examination, pursued a doctorate, became a professor, and finally started a family. Yaoxin was very pleased in her heart, and she could finally say to her beloved deceased husband in heaven: "I have fulfilled your wish!" Thanks to the blessings of Amitabha, your son, who is also my son, is doing very well!

Once Taiqi became a nun, Shulan took care of Yaoxin at home. Eventually her 21-year-old daughter opened her own clothing store. She had been living with Yaoxin all along, refusing to leave her mother's side. On opening the store, Lanlan said that it was when she made clothes for big dolls with her mother that she fell in love with cutting and sewing clothes. Half of the credit belonged to her mother.

In 1978, Xianglong returned to Taiwan with his wife and child to visit Yaoxin. Yaoxin saw Xianglong's family of three, heard her granddaughter calling her grandma, and knew that this was the blessing of Buddhism that changed her life philosophy. She held good thoughts in her heart and ultimately received good karma. Xianglong's family was going to fly to Thailand to visit his aunt, Su

Meichen. Yaoxin had been in contact with Su Meichen for many years, sending her greeting cards with Xianglong's photos during holidays. After all, Su Meichen had raised Xianglong for ten years, and Yaoxin knew that this kind of affection was hard to cut off. She was also pleased that Xianglong had shown filial piety and hadn't forgotten Su Meichen's kindness. She said Xianglong was worthy of being the child she, Li Yaoxin, had raised.

## 2

Su Meichen operated a clothing business that had just started doing business with mainland China. She customized clothes from mainland China and shipped them to retail stores in Thailand. When Yaoxin told Meichen over the phone about her family's situation, saying they were not able to reunite, Meichen said, "Sister-in-law, do you treat me like an outsider? If not, leave this to me. Let's try a roundabout strategy. I'll have you meet in Thailand."

Yaoxin chanted "Namo Amitabha," thanking the Buddha for giving her hope. Yaoxin arrived in Thailand and stayed at Su Meichen's home, waiting for Meichen to return from mainland China with good news. Would her wish to see her brother and sister come true? She hoped her wish could be fulfilled. A month later, Yaoxin received her brother Yaowei's first letter from the mainland.

The letter read:

> "Dear Sixth Sister Yaoxin, your friend Su Meichen found us through our local police station registry. We are all very happy to hear that you and your family are doing well! I am married now, and my wife's name is Liu Fengyun. We have a son and a daughter, which means you have a nephew and a niece. Guangzhong is 17 years old, and Guanghua is only nine years old. Su Meichen gave us an invitation letter inviting us to Thailand to meet you, and we are currently processing the paperwork. I hope you can be patient, as getting the necessary approvals and documents to leave the country is a complicated process. I hope we can see each other soon!

Enclosed is a family photo of us."

Missing you, your eighth younger brother Yaowei

March 3rd, 1981

Finally, they were about to meet. Yaoxin read her eighth brother's letter over and over again, tears streaming down her cheeks. She looked at the family photo. Her sister-in-law looked younger than her eighth brother, with short hair and a gentle appearance. She must have been a virtuous wife. The young man with black round glasses to Fengyun's left was her nephew Guangzhong. He was dressed in black and was almost as tall as her eighth brother. Standing in front of her eighth brother and Fengyun was a dark-skinned girl with pigtails and a skirt. She must have been Guanghua. The whole family was dressed simply. Her sister-in-law wore a white shirt, black pants, and flat cloth shoes. Her eighth brother also wore a white shirt, black pants, and a pair of black loafers. Yaoxin thought this was the lifestyle of mainland Chinese people. After that, every two or three weeks, her eighth brother Yaowei would write to her, updating her on the progress of his travel documents:

> In the previous letter, I mentioned that I had paid a deposit of 1000 yuan to prove that I wouldn't stay abroad illegally. With the help of an introduction letter from my employer's personnel office, I obtained a non-criminal record certificate from the police station and a household registration certificate from the local police station. Although the process for obtaining the household registration certificate was slow, I managed to speed things up by giving a police officer a pack of Zhonghua cigarettes. I needed to go to the public security bureau to apply for a private passport, take passport photos, and pay the fees. Despite the tedious process, the thought of reuniting with my sister made everything seem small.
>
> Missing my sister, Eighth Brother
>
> Dated March 18th, 1981

In Yaoxin's letter, she worried that Eight Brother didn't have much money, as she heard that people in mainland China earn very little, only about 60 yuan per month, which is approximately 8 US dollars. She asked if he needed any financial assistance from Su Meichen. However, Eight Brother replied that he had borrowed money from someone and didn't need any help. But she still wasn't at ease, so she transferred 4,000 US dollars from her Citibank account in Hong Kong to Su Meichen, who then passed the money on to Yaowei.

In the third letter, there was progress. Eighth Brother said he was waiting for his passport and would be able to obtain a visa at the Thai embassy about a month later.

Three months later, Su Meichen's visa expired and she returned from the mainland. She told Yaoxin that her younger brother had obtained his passport and Meichen brought Yaowei's letter with her.

Yaowei's letter read:

> "Dear Sixth Sister, I have received my passport. It took some time because the background check process was longer. My next step is to apply for a visa. After my visa is approved, I can buy a plane ticket to Thailand!
>
> Sixth Sister, you asked last time if Fifth Sister could come with us. I'm afraid it's not possible because she just returned from a labor camp in Xinjiang and her household registration has just been settled. It's likely she won't pass the background check. And as for your younger brother, my Sixth Brother can never come. He died in the war in Korea in 1951..."

Yaoxin was prepared for this. She had been searching for Fifth Sister Yaozhi and Fourth Sister Yaoxian in Taiwan. She knew that Yaoxian was a member of the Communist Party and not having news of her in Taiwan was expected. However, Yaoxin was disappointed that she couldn't find Yaozhi. Yaozhi's husband worked for the Military Statistics Bureau, and most of the people from there came to Taiwan in 1948. Did Yaozhi and her family not come to Taiwan? While searching for Yaozhi and Yaoxian, Yaoxin found her eldest brother, Yaozhong, but they didn't have much contact. He worked in investment banking and had a large business, so he was often out of Taiwan and didn't have time to keep in touch.

Yaoxin didn't dare to leave Thailand because she was afraid that she wouldn't be able to see her brother Yaowei again if she left. After receiving Yaowei's eighth letter, he finally said he had bought a plane ticket and was waiting to board the plane in a week.

## 3

Yaowei had to buy a plane ticket and shook his head as he looked at his clothes. It was the first time he had ever gone to the store with his wife Fengyun to buy some fashionable clothes.

They went to Zhongjie in Shenyang, which is the earliest and longest pedestrian commercial street in Shenyang with a history of more than 300 years and the title of "Northeast First Street". It was built in the fifth year of the Tianqi period of the Ming Dynasty, and was rebuilt and expanded by the Later Jin dynasty from the tenth year of the Tianming period (1625) to the fifth year of the Tiancong period (1631). Later Jin rebuilt and expanded the imperial palace of the Ming dynasty.

In the Warring States period, there was a record in the "Zhou Li Kao Gong Ji":

> "The craftsmen camp the country, nine square miles, three gates on the side. In the country, there are nine classics and nine weaves, and the classics are painted with nine tracks. The left is the ancestor and the right is the society, facing the rear market, and the market is facing one man. One of the three rooms."

The meaning of "left ancestor, right society, facing the rear market" is that the left side of the imperial palace is the ancestral temple, where the emperors worship their ancestors; the right side of the imperial palace is the altar of the God of Land and Grain, where the emperors worship the God of Land and Grain; the front of the imperial palace is the court, where the emperors hold court; and the back of the imperial palace is the market, where the people of the imperial city trade. In short, all of this was designed and implemented around the center of the imperial palace, fully reflecting the sacred dignity of the ancient imperial power. Based on this concept, the Later Jin dynasty changed the original 'ten'-shaped (十) two streets of Zhongjie into a 'well'-shaped (井) four streets.

This is also the origin of Siping Street in Zhongjie, with a clock tower and a drum tower on both sides, like two guard towers guarding the sides. At that time, Zhongjie was over 1,000 meters long and nearly a dozen meters wide, and carriages could pass through. In fact, since the end of the Ming Dynasty, the horse market trade in Liaodong's Kaiyuan, Guangning, and Fushun has been quite prosperous, which has greatly promoted the prosperity of Shenyang Zhongjie Commercial Street located in the three major horse market centers.

When Yaowei first came to study in Shenyang, there was still a horse market on Zhongjie where horses and horse feed were bought and sold. There were even farriers who shoed horses there, making it a very lively place. Now Zhongjie is located at 83 Zhongjie Road in Shenhe District, and it's very convenient to get there by tram.

On both sides of Zhongjie, there are many department stores, and there are many different types of small commodity stores in the alleys along the street. It's a great place for shopping. Young people can spend a whole day here and if they get tired, they can find a small restaurant along the street to rest and eat some dumplings or noodles. After eating, they can continue to shop. Nowadays, some of the small shops along the street are state-owned and collectively owned enterprises established after the founding of the People's Republic of China. In recent years, individual businesses have been allowed to take over some of the shops, which has made business on Zhongjie flourish again.

If it were not for the sake of meeting his sister whom he hadn't seen for over thirty years, Yaowei would not have bothered to buy new clothes. At the department store, he bought a light-yellow Dacron shirt, a pair of polyester pants, and a pair of black leather shoes. Fengyun suggested, "Buy two shirts so you can have one to change into." He hesitated for a while, looking at the ten yuan left in his wallet. Fengyun snatched the money and went to the counter to pick out a large white shirt. After paying for the clothes, they also bought a suitcase, but there was only enough money for the tram ride back. They didn't go into any of the small restaurants in the alley but went home with empty stomachs.

Time passed quickly. On July 2nd, he was about to leave for Thailand. Yaowei had never been on a plane before, it was his first time in his life. He felt excited about the novelty, but even more so about finally seeing his sixth sister.

Yaoxin woke up early in the morning for the flight that her younger brother was taking, which was scheduled to land at 3 pm. She dressed in her favorite clothes, got ready, and called a taxi to the airport. She waited for more than four hours at the airport, and finally heard the news of her brother's flight landing through the announcement in the airport hall.

## 4

Yaoxin spotted her brother appearing at the airport exit from out of the bustling crowd. He was wearing a yellow shirt, bronze-colored suit pants, a brown belt, and black leather shoes. He looked brand new and well-dressed. His square face was not big, but his eyes were shining brightly. He had shaved his beard cleanly, and his mouth had a resolute expression. His tanned face had a sense of many vicissitudes. He ran towards Yaoxin with his suitcase and the siblings hugged each other. When they last had said goodbye, Yaowei was a thirteen-year-old child and Yaoxin had just been married; now her brother was close to fifty, and she was already fifty-six. White hair had quietly climbed up their temples, and wrinkles had gradually formed at the corners of their eyes. Yaoxin had practiced Buddhism for many years, which made her face look gentle, and she didn't get too excited or worried when things happened. But today, she couldn't help shedding tears of joy.

The eighth brother brought special products from his hometown in Northeast China to give to his sixth sister: large black fungus, dried mushrooms, and especially two boxes of old ginseng from the mountains of Northeast China, to help her maintain good health.

The sixth sister was also concerned about her younger brother, and she brought two large travel bags full of clothes, many of which were fashionable ready-to-wear from the Shulan store! Looking at the colorful clothes, Yaowei said, "Your younger sister-in-law Fenyun is so unsophisticated that no clothes will look good on her. Let me take them back to give to our relatives and neighbors."

The sixth sister Yaoxin criticized Yaowei in a slow and measured tone: "How can you say that? You should love my younger sister-in-law. Let her choose the clothes she likes first. How do you know she doesn't like beautiful clothes?"

Yaowei felt a little embarrassed saying this. Over the years, he had never taken the initiative to buy new clothes for Fengyun. She had been wearing the same white shirt for seven or eight years, which had become thin and yellowed from washing. But Fengyun never said she wanted new clothes.

It was said that nephew Guangzhong had been admitted to college, so of course, his aunt brought a very useful gift, a multifunctional calculator, and a Swiss plum-shaped watch to help him keep track of time. Yaowei tried to refuse, saying, "The gift is too much, I can't accept it."

Yaoxin, who seemed angry, said, "Since the child was young, I, as his aunt, haven't done anything to help. This time, you can't deprive me of my rights!"

Brother Wei seemed to have returned to his childhood, where he listened to his elder sister for everything, and obediently said, "Okay, I'll listen to my elder sister!"

His elder sister laughed, "That's my good little brother."

Yaoxin then asked her younger brother, "Guess what gift I brought for my niece Guanghua?"

Yaowei shook his head and said, "How could I possibly guess?"

Yaoxin mysteriously took out a doll from the box. Of course, it was a doll! Since buying a doll for Lanlan, Yaoxin had personally experienced the needs of girls.

Years later, I went to grandpa's house and saw a pile of lively Barbie dolls in Aunt Guanghua's room!

Sixth sister also brought many Taiwanese specialties, such as Taiwanese wife cake, pineapple cake, delicious and sweet exploding coconut candy, and the beautiful and delicious Taiwanese-style Snowy Love dessert made by Uncle San. They all had very exquisite packaging bags or boxes, which were very delicate and beautiful.

Yaowei looked at them and said, "This box is also too beautiful. I have never eaten such high-end snacks. In the mainland, packaged snacks are only available for high-ranking officials and old revolutionaries. For us ordinary people, we just need to buy them by the pound and wrap them in butcher paper and tie them with paper string."

Yaowei looked at Sixth sister and added, "But it has clearly changed in recent years. There are more small vendors and people's lives have become more convenient. The packaging of goods has also become more beautiful." The siblings continued to talk and eventually got to the topic of their home country.

**Part Seven**

# *The Li family sons of the generation named "Yao": Yaoguo, Yaoyou, and Yaowei*

## Chapter One

# Heroic Li Yaoguo is filled with patriotic spirit to go to Korea and give his life for his country

1

Yaoguo and Yaowei were different. Yaoguo was mischievous and did not like to study. So, he didn't graduate from elementary school, and because his mother Wan'er had passed away, he spent his days with a group of delinquents in the streets, smoking and fighting. His father didn't like him. Later, Yaoguo's two sisters, Yaozhi and Yaoxin, both left home, and his father went to live with his first wife in the front yard, so the two brothers were really free for a while.

It was a turbulent time. After Japan surrendered to the United States and two atomic bombs were dropped, the Soviet Red Army followed into Northeast China. Then Yaozhi, the fifth sister, who had gone to Changchun, disappeared. Later, someone came to Shanghai to investigate Yaozhi's husband, and Yaowei then learned that Yaozhi had gone to Shihezi, Xinjiang. And Yaoguo's closest sister, Yaoxin, went to Taiwan and disappeared without a trace. The family was scattered!

Yaoguo and Yaowei grew up together, eating when they could and going hungry when they couldn't. No matter how difficult it was, they grew tall and strong.

Yaoguo and Yaowei became independent and became cynical. In 1949, the People's Republic of China was founded! Everyone celebrated on the streets, banging drums and gongs. The two brothers were also in the parade, holding little red flags and shouting slogans. They played landlord and capitalist with everyone, driving them around and grabbing their property, smashing their antiques. It was so exciting. But in the end, they ended up robbing their own home. It turned out that they too were capitalists and were fundamentally different from those who came from pure working-class and peasant backgrounds.

Yaoguo felt inferior and ashamed of his family background because he was born into an exploitative class family, he wanted to change his fate. His opportunity came when he heard on the radio in 1950 that the American imperialism had started the Korean War, trying to use North Korea as a springboard to bring the war to the Sino-Korean border, hoping to strangle the newborn Communist China in the cradle! Chairman Mao Zedong issued a call to resist the United States and aid Korea, and the Chinese People's Volunteers for Anti-US Aid Korea issued a call to the whole nation to contribute money and efforts. The Northeast's Peking Opera performer, Xin Fengxia, led a charity performance and donated a MiG-15 fighter plane all by herself. This kind of charity act was highly motivating, and people on the streets and in alleys actively donated money and goods. Young men enthusiastically signed up for the military to defend the country and become volunteer soldiers, rushing to the Korean battlefield.

Yaoguo, full of youthful zeal and patriotic fervor, was the first to sign up for the military at the age of 19. At that time, Yaowei was only 16, but under the influence of his elder brother's patriotic enthusiasm, he also signed up. The two brothers were assigned to different units, with Yaoguo as an infantryman and Yaowei, a junior high school graduate, serving as a tank communication soldier, a more technically advanced type of soldier.

In October 1950, under the command of General Peng Dehuai, Yaoguo and Yaowei wore big red flowers and entered North Korea secretly by crossing the Yalu River from Andong (now Dandong) as members of the Chinese People's Volunteers.

Yaoguo clasped his hands together and silently recited "Namo Amitabha Buddha," listening quietly as his younger brother Yaowei recounted tales of bloodshed and violence.

## 2

Yaowei slowly narrated, "Sixth brother Yaoguo and I were not in the same battalion. He was an infantryman, the most dangerous type of soldier. Yaoguo was the kind of person who was not afraid of death in battle. He always charged at the front. Before he left for Korea, he told me to do well in the army, as our fate might change because of this war. But neither Yaoguo nor I knew that I would later be transferred and not be reemployed."

"Yaoguo had just arrived at the front lines in Korea when he participated in the famous Battle of Wonsan. In this battle, the volunteer army occupied Wonsan and prevented the United Nations forces from approaching the Yalu River near the Sino-Korean border. Later, he also participated in the Battle of Chosin Reservoir. It was bitterly cold during that time, and the battle lasted for nearly twenty days. Many of our soldiers were frostbitten, and combined with the lack of resources and inferior weapons, the volunteer army fought bravely and tenaciously, relying on their large numbers and eventually emerged victorious. Yaoguo was awarded the third-class merit twice within six months. Due to their consecutive battles, they captured three American machine guns and several automatic rifles, which earned them commendation from the military.

"When they were preparing for the third battle to capture Seoul, Yaoguo and the other new recruits were extremely excited during the pre-war mobilization. It must be said that at that time, the United Nations forces, led by the Americans, had advanced weaponry. They had airplanes and paratroopers, as well as the support of the South Korean army. The volunteer army had no planes, only several hundred thousand infantrymen and a small number of light artilleries. Of course, we had assistance from small units of the Korean People's Army. Each volunteer soldier carried dozens of hand grenades. When the battle cry was sounded, a group of fearless soldiers threw hand grenades like rain and charged forward. In the first two battles, MacArthur misjudged the size and combat effectiveness of the volunteer army, resulting in significant casualties on both sides. Yaoguo's 39th Army of the volunteer army directly confronted the

Li Yaoguo with head wound a few days before he died.

United Nations forces for the first time in the Battle of Yunsan. In this battle, they captured a lot of heavy equipment from the American forces, including tanks, armored vehicles, artillery, and heavy machine guns.

"Yaoguo became a little excited and said, 'In war, you become numb and don't know where to run to protect yourself.' Moreover, Yaoguo was a reckless person who never knew how to retreat in battle. This battle lasted for a long five or six days, until the lunar New Year of 1951. Our army advanced into the defensive depths, leaving the trenches in front of the bunkers filled with bomb craters, scattered with shrapnel and bullet casings. During the battle to capture Seoul, Yaoguo and his army fought together. It was during this battle that Yaoguo was promoted to squad leader. He led six new recruits in a firepower reconnaissance mission but was discovered by concealed enemy positions. He was seriously injured, and five out of the six soldiers in his squad died. A few days later, Yaoguo passed away in a field hospital due to his severe injuries. His life ended at the age of 20."

革命軍人犧牲證明書

烈字第零貳[illegible]號

李耀國同志於一九四八年十月參加革命工作在三七三团三連任战士不幸於一九五〇年十一月十五日在三〇七高地战斗光榮犧牲除由我軍奠祭英靈外特懷哀悼之情敬報貴家屬並望引榮節哀持此證明書向遼東營口市人民政府領取撫邮[illegible]及革命犧牲軍人家屬光榮紀念證[illegible]屬得享受烈屬優待爲荷

此致

中国人民志願軍 司令部 政治部

一九五一年八月五日

Martyrdom certificate for Li Yaoguo

Yaoxin's hands were constantly clasped together in front of her chest, repeatedly chanting, "Namo Amitabha, Namo Amitabha, Namo Amitabha!"

Yaowei said, "I was the first one in the family to be informed of sixth brother's sacrifice, followed by my father. Father received a martyr's certificate, a pension, and Yaoguo's first-class merit certificate. But the person was gone!"

He also said, "In fact, during the early years of the founding of the country, my father was not criticized, and our family was not searched, all because we were martyrs' families. However, Yaozhi and her husband always remained stuck in the Chinese Communist Party's throat, making them distrust the Li family."

Yaowei rolled up his pants and pointed to a scar, saying, "I'm lucky. Tank crew members have the protection of steel shells. But there was one time when a mortar shell hit me. I was hit by three shell fragments, and this one in my ankle was never removed. It aches faintly on cloudy days when it rains."

Yaoxin looked at the scar on her brother's ankle and said, "It's better to remove that shrapnel sooner. The body can't tolerate a piece of steel hidden in the flesh."

Yaowei nodded in agreement and said, "I'll take some time off to visit a doctor in Beijing."

Yaowei suddenly remembered something and slapped his forehead, saying, "Oh, how could I forget about the fourth brother Yaojia? He's a senior-level official. When I go to Beijing for medical treatment, I'll look for them, and my sister-in-law knows people at the hospital."

Yaowei and Yaojia

Yaoxin said, "You must promise Sixth Sister that you'll go. If I have the time, I'll also visit the fourth brother Yaojia."

She urged Yaowei, saying, "The matter of getting medical treatment is settled. Now, continue telling me about your story with Fengyun. As an older sister, let me catch up on those years when I wasn't part of your life. Life is full of regrets!"

Yaowei took a sip of water and continued his story.

## Chapter Two

# Yaowei pursues his dreams, passes the college entrance examination, and meets the other half of his life

### 1

After the end of the Korean War Yaowei, having completed junior high school, served as an instructor in the army for a year. Then, due to family reasons, he was discharged in December 1954. His military career had strengthened his will and cultivated a tall and upright posture. He always walked with his head held high and took confident strides.

Yaowei was assigned to work as a junior staff member in the district government. On his first day of work, he quickly understood the nature of his job: fetching water, delivering newspapers, political study, and assisting the section chief in drafting speeches. Writing those speeches was relatively easy. He could copy some grandiose and clichéd phrases from the "People's Daily" and ensure a proper understanding of the current policies of the central government without deviating from the main direction. As a junior secretary with an elder secretary overseeing his work, Yaowei was not particularly worried about the quality of his writing.

The head of the department, Cheng Kezhang, loved to crack jokes, and the office was always filled with laughter and joy. Several female staff members would gather to knit sweaters and chat about personal matters. In general, everyone would also take a nap for over half an hour during the day, making the days quite comfortable. After three years, Yaowei was promoted to deputy section chief, and he began to notice people trying to curry favor with him. Some even presented him with stewed chickens as gifts. With a monthly

Li Yaowei, army enlistment 1951

Above & left: Li Yaowei, army discharge 1954

salary of 38 yuan, Yaowei felt financially secure. His living expenses were easily covered—rent was only three yuan, and with an additional one yuan for utilities, he could eat at the canteen using food ration coupons. He didn't buy anything else and felt quite wealthy. However, he sensed that life was becoming somewhat stagnant. Was this how the rest of his life would be?

The members of the Li family all possessed stubbornness, ambition, and a determination not to give up until they achieved their goals. It was during this time that the fervor for the national college entrance examination in the 1950s arose. Yaowei was unwilling to settle for his comfortable job and wholeheartedly focused on preparing for the exam. At that time, the acceptance rate for the college entrance examination was quite high since the country was in need of talent for its development. Yaowei locked himself in his room, often skipping meals or reducing them to focus on his exam preparation. A neighbor's aunt, seeing Yaowei's dedication, voluntarily started bringing him meals and said, "Young man, you're working too hard. If there's anything you need from Auntie, just let me know."

Yaowei replied with a simple and sincere smile, "Okay, thank you, Auntie. If I become prosperous, I won't forget you!" Afraid of disturbing Yaowei's studies, Auntie left with a smile.

Yaowei had to work extremely hard because he had decided to take the college entrance examination, and there were only six months left until the exam. He had 180 fewer days than others to prepare, so he knew he had to push himself relentlessly. Time flew by, and when the results were announced six months later, Yaowei was too nervous to look at the list. He felt that he hadn't performed well and most likely hadn't been accepted. He spent the whole morning struggling with the decision to look or not. Then, the phone rang. It was Guo Jianshe, who had also been discharged from the military. His voice on the phone was filled with excitement as he shouted, "Yaowei, you made it! Liaoning University, Department of Physics!"

Yaowei's heart leaped into his throat, and he asked, "Jianshe, how about you? Where did you get accepted?"

The voice on the other end of the phone sounded distant, "I got into the College of Mechanical and Electrical Engineering, Yaowei. I'm coming to find you right away."

It seemed that Guo Jianshe had hung up the phone and immediately rushed over to see Yaowei.

Guo Jianshe was Yaowei's fellow townsman and one year older than him. They were not only from the same hometown but also comrades in the same platoon during their time in the military. They were very close. During their preparation for the college entrance examination, they had studied together, meeting once a month to discuss any questions they didn't understand. Now, both had been accepted into university. They celebrated the occasion by staying up all night, drinking beer and eating peanuts.

## 2

Yaowei lived on campus during his university years. He felt that his foundation was weak, so he worked hard every day, immersing himself in the library until closing time. Every day, there was a girl who would leave the library right after him. One day, it was pouring rain, and the girl didn't have an umbrella. Yaowei held his umbrella over her head. She felt a bit embarrassed and smiled at him, saying, "Thank you!"

From that day on, they started walking back to the dormitory together. Yaowei first accompanied her to the women's dormitory and watched her enter the building before leaving. After that, they frequently bumped into each other at the library and often walked back to the dormitory together. Through their conversations, Yaowei learned that the girl's name was Liu Fengyun, a freshman in the Chemistry Department, and she was five years younger than him. Liu Fengyun was quiet and serious, excelling in her studies. She didn't stand out in terms of appearance and wasn't socially adept; one could even say she was a bit of a bookworm, solely focused on studying. Yaowei liked her; she gave off a sense of reliability and steadfastness.

Now at 25 years old, Yaowei began to have thoughts about finding a partner.

Liu Fengyun came from a background of small landowners and belonged to a criticized social class, which made some men hesitant to pursue a romantic relationship with her. But Yaowei wasn't afraid. He said, "My family is already complicated enough, I'm not afraid of making it even more complex."

Another significant factor was that Yaowei once fell ill with viral dysentery, experiencing vomiting and diarrhea. Liu Fengyun took care of him meticulously, cooking meals for him, washing his soiled clothes, and staying by his bedside. Her care and concern made this young man, who had lost his mother at the age of seven, feel an extraordinary warmth.

One of the young teachers who shared a dormitory with Yaowei, Xiao Wang, was about to get married. Yaowei helped him prepare for the wedding. On the evening before the wedding, Xiao Wang approached Yaowei for a drink. Seeing Xiao Wang's anxious expression, Yaowei sought advice from him and asked, "Xiao Wang, you seem honest and straightforward. How did you win over your fiancée?"

Blushing, Xiao Wang shyly replied, "To be honest with you, my future wife is quite down-to-earth and not at all romantic. She comes from Wusangong Commune and has a rural background. I met her when I was assigned there. I liked her sincerity and simplicity."

Holding a beer bottle, with a flushed face, Xiao Wang half-drunkly said, "But I suggest that you confess your feelings before proposing and add a little bit of romance! Take her to watch a movie or buy her a beautiful dress, anything romantic will do!"

Yaowei asked, "What would be considered romantic?"

Xiao Wang replied, "Taking her to a movie or buying her a nice dress would be good options!"

Yaowei and Liu Fengyun were both unfamiliar with the concept of romance. Liu Fengyun didn't have any specific demands or take the initiative in that regard. This time, Yaowei wanted to be romantic in his own way. Seeking inspiration from Xiao Wang's suggestion and romantic love stories from foreign novels that often involved roses, candles, and cakes, Yaowei felt that he lacked the ability to create such gestures. Additionally, at that time social circumstances in China didn't emphasize this bourgeois kind of romance. He asked Liu Fengyun, "What kind of date do you prefer? Watching a movie or going on an outing?"

Liu Fengyun replied, "Watching a movie can be dull, surrounded by people. Let's go on an outing together instead! I enjoy the fresh air and natural scenery."

On a Saturday morning, both dressed in what they considered their best outfits. Liu Fengyun even tied her hair in a small braid. She carried a canvas shoulder bag containing a lunchbox with steamed buns from the previous night and a container of canned lunch meat. Yaowei wore a yellow military uniform and had a belt around his waist, giving him the appearance of a soldier. Liu Fengyun was amazed by his handsome looks. The combination of Yaowei's military demeanor and his tall posture truly exuded the aura of a heroic fighter. Yaowei brought several boiled eggs he had cooked the previous night, a military flask filled with water, a map, and a few yuans. He rode a 28-inch bicycle while Liu Fengyun held onto his waist, sitting on the back seat. Excitedly, the two of them embarked on their first countryside adventure.

The weather that day was clear and refreshing, with the autumn air invigorating their spirits. They rode their bicycles along the way, frequently stopping to admire the scenery. As they traveled on the road leading to Qipan (Chessboard) Mountain, they passed through fertile fields, often overtaking horse-drawn carts driven by farmers. The journey took over three hours, and they had been cycling for more than four hours when they reached the foot of the mountain and started to feel hungry. They spread out a plastic sheet on the ground and began to have their lunch. Yaowei opened the can of lunch meat, and Liu Fengyun used chopsticks to feed Yaowei. Yaowei peeled the boiled eggs for Liu Fengyun. Each of them had a boiled egg. At that moment, the two of them felt like a family.

After lunch, they prepared to climb the mountain. Yaowei, concerned that Liu Fengyun might get tired, carried her shoulder bag on his shoulder as well. The path up the mountain was difficult to walk, but Yaowei had strength and often lent a helping hand to Liu Fengyun. When they reached halfway up the mountain, Liu Fengyun said she was tired, so they decided to rest in the vicinity. As they looked out, the houses below seemed much smaller, like toy building blocks. It was autumn, and the maple trees on Chessboard Mountain were ablaze with red leaves. The pine trees were lush and there were many fruit trees as well. Yaowei climbed a hawthorn tree and picked a ripe hawthorn. He put it in his mouth and found it to be both sour and sweet, a delightful taste. He picked several larger ones and handed them to Liu Fengyun. She told Yaowei that such good-sized hawthorns couldn't be found in the city. She suggested picking more to make hawthorn cake, as she remembered her mother making square-shaped hawthorn cakes when she was a child. It was her sweetest childhood memory. Yaowei climbed another sturdy hawthorn tree and picked hawthorns from there, while Liu Fengyun stood on the ground, looking up with one hand gripping a branch and the other busy picking. They filled the entire bag. Then, they began to hike on foot. More people joined them, and it became lively. The hiking trail had pavilions and stone steps, making the climb easier. When they reached halfway up the mountain, there was a snack bar where people stopped to enjoy the view or take a short rest before continuing to the summit.

Unbeknownst to them, time had passed, and it was getting late. Yaowei and Liu Fengyun walked and rested along the way, realizing that they wouldn't make it to the summit in time. People who had already reached the peak were making their way back down the steps, preparing to go home. Yaowei and Liu Fengyun decided to avoid the crowd and took a detour to the back of the mountain, descending through a small grove. Unexpectedly, they arrived at a small village. The village was tranquil and elegant. The corn in the fields had fully ripened. Yaowei and Liu Fengyun walked through the cornfield, surrounded by the sound of rustling corn leaves. Suddenly, Yaowei heard Liu Fengyun's stomach growl. He asked her with concern, "Are you hungry? We got a bit lost, and this place isn't marked on my map. How about having a meal first?"

Fengyun gladly said, "Sure, I was thinking the same."

So they went to a restaurant with a small inn and had a meal. Wanting to test the waters, he said, "Yun, how about we stay here for the night?"

Fengyun was already contemplating how to go back, but upon hearing what Wanting said, she went along and replied, "Alright, after dinner, let's each book a room."

The two of them followed this conventional arrangement and went to their respective rooms. Fengyun, with her inherent girl's reserve, went back to her room and said to Yaowei, who was trailing behind her, "Get some rest. We're quite tired today!"

Yaowei nodded and replied with a smile, "Alright, we did walk a long way today, and we need to rest well. You should also get some rest and head back to school early tomorrow. Goodnight, Yun." After saying that, Yaowei bid Fengyun goodnight and returned to his own room, preparing to rest.

Yaowei took a shower and lay on the bed, unable to fall asleep. He went to Fengyun's room next door and sat there for a while. He sat beside Fengyun, inching closer to her, feeling his breath quicken. The air seemed to thicken, and he felt his legs trembling. Fortunately, he was sitting next to Fengyun. His hands felt uncontrollable, but Yaowei still stood up, lifted Fengyun, and she patted his back, asking him to put her down.

Yaowei said, "If you don't want me to, then I won't let go!"

At first, Fengyun was a bit shy and stiff, but after a while, she obediently rested her head on Yaowei's shoulder, their heads touching. Yaowei gently said, "I want to hold you like this forever!"

Fengyun shyly replied, "As long as you don't find it heavy, then hold me."

Whispering in Fengyun's ear, Yaowei asked, "What do you like about me?"

Fengyun said, "Your integrity, your handsomeness, your honesty, and your straightforwardness."

Fengyun asked Yaowei, "Da Wei, what do you like about me?"

Yaowei answered, "Your intelligence, your simplicity, your perseverance, and your ability to live life."

Fengyun lowered her head and said, "Yaowei, actually, I've admired you for a long time. I like your optimism, generosity, and willingness to help others. Someone who loves others must have a kind heart."

Yaowei let go of Fengyun, and he understood the meaning behind her words. So, he earnestly asked, "Yun, let's get married, okay?"

Fengyun didn't answer, but she held Yaowei's hand. At that moment, their hearts seemed to be closely connected.

The next morning, after having breakfast, the two of them rode the bicycle back to the school. At the school gate, to their surprise, they saw Fengyun's roommate and classmate Xiao Li. Now, their relationship became known to others. They had been secretly dating for about half a year, and now they were finally bringing their relationship out into the open.

## 3

Every time they were together, Fengyun would go to Yaowei's dormitory because Fengyun's dormitory had six roommates, and two of them were openly in a relationship. Whenever Fengyun finished her classes or self-study and returned to the dormitory, there would almost always be a couple inside the room. Fengyun was not good at small talk, but she was considerate and would promptly leave the room after putting down her backpack. She would often say, "Sorry!" and rush out of the dormitory to Yaowei's place.

By that time, Yaowei had already started working at the university. He was assigned to the Physics Teaching and Research Office and moved into the male faculty dormitory. Each faculty dormitory room accommodated four people, with bunk beds. When Fengyun came over, the younger teacher who shared the room with Yaowei would make room for her.

Fengyun wasn't very skilled at cooking. She and Yaowei had an electric stove, which they used to boil noodles and cook eggs when no one else was around. Due to the large number of students and the poor quality of the university cafeteria food, there were often instances of power outages caused by everyone using electric stoves. The dormitory management turned a blind eye to this issue because the dormitory manager also had a child studying at the university, and he told them to take care of themselves. However, he also feared the possibility of a fire breaking out one day, which would be his responsibility. Therefore, the dormitory manager didn't use overly thick fuses. He prepared a roll of 20-amp fuses so that if a power outage occurred, they could simply replace the fuse.

In 1960, before Fengyun graduated, she encountered the devastating famine that followed the Great Leap Forward. Everyone was suffering from food shortages. The situation was particularly dire for Mr. Xiao Wang, who had married a woman from a rural area. His wife did not have an urban household registration, which meant she couldn't receive food rations. However, during this time, Mr. Xiao Wang's wife became pregnant, which meant three people had to share the rations meant for one. Without food coupons, it was impossible to buy food in the city, and the situation was even worse for people in the countryside, where starvation was rampant. Many people died of hunger, and Mr. Xiao Wang's wife's family was also struggling to survive.

Mr. Xiao Wang and his wife lived in the school dormitory. When his wife was five months pregnant, she fainted due to hunger and low blood sugar. After being rushed to the hospital, both the mother and the baby were lost. Seeing Mr. Xiao Wang grieving and sobbing uncontrollably, Yaowei couldn't help but think about how fortunate he was to have found someone like Fengyun. They started sharing meals, combining their food rations. Fengyun ate less, and Yaowei rarely went hungry. It was at this point that Yaowei started thinking about having a home.

In the early 1960s, before getting married, young couples usually needed a fashionable velvet suit. Some relatively affluent families would give their children a dowry ranging from tens to a couple of hundred yuan. Most parents were more practical, providing food coupons and fabric vouchers, along with preparing a simple wooden trunk and a bedsheet, which was sufficient for starting a household. The trend for marriage emphasized new customs and practices, with no emphasis on astrological compatibility or the traditional formalities of a proper wedding. However, Yaowei came from a traditional large family, and deep down, he still valued those traditional rituals. However, now both their families were no longer in Shenyang, and Yaowei's parents had already passed away. Yaowei hoped to receive the blessings of their elders and gain the approval of Fengyun's parents. That's why they were determined to visit Fengyun's hometown in Jinzhou. Yaowei also had another idea swirling in his mind; he wanted to trace his roots and visit the Li family's fields in Yingkou.

Jinzhou is over 200 kilometers southwest of Shenyang. To reach Jinzhou, one must first take a slow train from Shenyang West Station, which takes about three to four hours to reach Jinzhou Station. Sitting on the slowly moving train, Yaowei overheard two people from Jinzhou sitting across from him, speaking in the Jinzhou dialect. Fengyun started conversing with them as well. Yaowei found it quite fascinating as it was the first time he heard Fengyun speak in her hometown dialect. The Jinzhou dialect has an upward inflection, sounding almost like singing.

The two individuals opposite them were brothers who were working in Shenyang and returning home to visit their parents. They were eating roasted sweet potatoes, tea eggs, and cracking melon seeds that they had bought at Shenyang West Station. People from Northeast China are hospitable, and the two brothers warmly invited Yaowei and Fengyun to join them. So, they all cracked melon seeds together, chatting and laughing, enjoying a pleasant conversation. As they talked, the four of them became acquainted and started playing cards. After a while, train attendants came to sweep the floor, clearing away the melon seed shells scattered on the ground. The attendants also kept coming by to sell snacks and bring hot water. The two brothers had a large enamel jar with Mao Zedong's waving portrait printed on it, along with the slogan "Long Live Mao Zedong Thought!" The jar could hold enough water for the four of them to drink from.

Along the way, as the train passed various locations, Yaowei saw remnants of the numerous fortifications left behind by the Kuomintang (Nationalist Party). These fortifications had thick reinforced concrete walls. When the People's Liberation Army attacked Jinzhou in 1948, it took a significant loss of personnel to break through the Kuomintang's fortifications. History was not pleasant to recall, as the Kuomintang was eventually defeated and forced to retreat. By then, Yaowei's sixth sister Yaoxin had already moved to Taiwan, following her husband. Time had flown by, and it had been over a decade since that time.

After getting off the train at Jinzhou Railway Station, Yaowei and Fengyun went to a small restaurant to have lunch. There were many small restaurants around the train station, offering various types of food. They had heard that Jinzhou barbecue was famous, but because time was limited, Yaowei and Fengyun opted for a simple meal of dumplings. At the West Station, there were many individual operators of minibusses trying to attract passengers. They boarded one of the minibusses, which had available seats, for a fare of two yuan, and headed to Mangniutun, a suburban area of Jinzhou located about ten kilometers away.

Upon arriving at the entrance of the village, they noticed a large stone monument with the words "Mangniutun" carved in red. Beside it was another black stone monument. Curiously, they walked over to take a closer look. The inscription on it narrated an ancient legend:

> "It is said that a long time ago, there was a ferocious tiger on Cuiyan Mountain, known for preying on the villagers' livestock during the dark nights. The villagers both hated and feared the tiger. One day, a Taoist priest informed the villagers about an object capable of subduing the tiger. Perplexed, the villagers watched as the priest pointed towards a grazing bull at the village entrance, saying, 'It is this creature.' Everyone focused their gaze and realized that it was just an ordinary bull. The priest proclaimed, 'To bestow it with divine objects is the key to vanquishing demons.' The villagers then bound a pair of mandarin duck-shaped daggers with a red rope onto the bull's horns. When night fell, they drove the bull into the mountains. In the middle of the night, a resounding roar echoed through the mountains, causing sand and stones to fly, and obscuring the stars and moon. At dawn, the villagers discovered the tiger lying dead at the foot of the mountain, while the robust bull stood tall, raising its head and bellowing... The bull had eliminated the

> menace, possessing unparalleled divine power. It came to be known as the 'Mangniu' (牤牛) or 'Divine Bull.' For centuries, the villagers have revered the Mangniu as their totem and named the village in commemoration."

Yaowei was amazed by this enchanting legend in such a small mountain village.

Fengyun's family used to be modest landlords and were considered part of the exploiting class even after liberation. Now, her mother and one of her younger brothers lived in the eastern part of the village. Following the dirt road into the village, not far on the right side, was the fifth house, where Fengyun's mother resided. From a distance, it appeared as a single-story house with adobe and brick walls. The house was not tall, but it had an arched roof to facilitate the flow of rainwater during rainy days.

As Fengyun called out "Mom," a small, wrinkled woman in her mid-sixties, wearing a simple black dress made of coarse cloth and with her hair tied in a bun, emerged. It was afternoon, and the sunlight was intense. The elderly mother raised her hand to shield her eyes from the glaring sun. Fengyun approached and held her mother's hand, affectionately calling her "Mom." She immediately introduced Yaowei to her mother, who looked at Yaowei, tall and dignified, and smiled, saying, "Good, good!"

Mom said, "I heard that you're coming back. Your younger brother went to buy lamb meat. We'll have lamb skewers when he returns, and we also bought some clams. You don't have those in Shenyang."

Fengyun's sister-in-law came over to greet them, directly referring to Yaowei as her brother-in-law. Mom invited everyone to sit on the kang (a heated brick bed). She sat cross-legged on the kang, and Fengyun also took off her shoes and joined her. Yaowei felt a bit awkward taking off his shoes, so he sat on the edge of the kang with his legs hanging down. Fengyun's sister-in-law added fuel to the stove in the kitchen and prepared the meal.

After a while, Fengyun's younger brother, Zhiqiang, returned. He brought back lamb meat and some large yellow clams. He called out to his sister and brother-in-law and then set up the barbecue pit to start grilling. Soon, the fragrant aroma of cumin filled the air.

The meal consisted of steamed white sorghum rice and various dishes, including dried cabbage with shredded tofu, cucumber and mung bean vermicelli tossed in Jinzhou shrimp sauce, stir-fried shrimp shells, and sautéed yellow clams. There was also radish with dipping sauce. It was a simple farm-style meal. Yaowei and Fengyun's younger brother, Zhiqiang, enjoyed a few bottles of Snowflake beer.

While they were eating, Fengyun's mother secretly said to her, "I agree for you two to get married. Seeing you with Yaowei makes me happy."

She added mysteriously, "Make your brother-in-law eat more yellow clams. They have a powerful aphrodisiac effect and can replenish vitality and nourish the body."

Fengyun playfully nudged her mother and said, "Mom, who told you that?"

However, during the meal, Fengyun kept putting yellow clams into Yaowei's rice bowl.

In the evening, Fengyun's mother brought out her family heirlooms and said to Fengyun and Yaowei, "Our family used to have some valuable possessions, but they were confiscated during the liberation. When your older brother got married in Jinzhou, I gave him some to help with their household expenses. He had a hard time initially, working as a coal stoker on trains for ten years. Luckily, your sister-in-law had connections, and your brother eventually became a regular railway worker, securing a stable job. Your second sister, just like you, has a degree. She graduated from university and now works in a big city. When she got married, your father and I didn't treat her unfairly. As for your younger brother who stayed in our hometown, he earns less as a private school teacher, and his wife helps me with farming, so they get a bit more. Now it's just the two of you left, and this is all our family fortune."

Fengyun's mother spoke with a serious tone, "Don't think it's too little. This is your dowry from your late father and me."

Fengyun felt her eyes welling up with tears as she watched her mother open a handkerchief bundle and take out a pair of gold earrings and a set of solid gold bangles. Her mother handed them to Fengyun and Yaowei. She also took out 300 yuan in cash, tightly bound with rubber bands, containing many small bills. It was evident that her mother had diligently saved every single yuan. As she unfolded the money, she said, "This is all my savings. Take it and live a good life."

Yaowei gave Fengyun's arm a gentle squeeze, and Fengyun understood. She said, "Mom, we can't accept this money. You need to keep it for your old age!"

But Zhang Yuzhen, Fengyun's mother, replied, "This girl, you're being polite to your mom now!"

Fengyun still didn't relent.

At that moment, Fengyun's younger brother and sister-in-law brought out 100 yuan and said, "Sister, we don't have much money, but please accept this."

Seeing her younger siblings wearing patched clothes and with their bellies protruding, Yaowei and Fengyun didn't take their money but symbolically took out only a 10 yuan bill. Fengyun's sister-in-law said, "Don't worry about it. When we got married, you gave us 200 yuan as a betrothal gift. We wouldn't have been able to earn that much in two years."

Fengyun said, "Consider it as the celebration money for our future nephew's one-month-old celebration!"

Fengyun's younger brother and sister-in-law put the money away. Then, her sister-in-law brought a basket of apples from Jinzhou and said to Yaowei and Fengyun, "Jinzhou produces apples, and our apples are big, round, and delicious. Take some back with you."

This time, Yaowei and Fengyun gladly accepted.

Before leaving, Zhang Yuzhen, Fengyun's mother, and her younger brother's family accompanied them to the bus station. Across from the bus station was the former headquarters of the Liaoshen Campaign Field Army, and seeing it firsthand, Yaowei finally understood why this small village had such a reputation.

A hand-operated tractor came toward them, loaded with bricks and tiles. They were going to build a brick house. The tractor driver saw Fengyun and Yaowei and said to Zhang Yuzhen, "Congratulations! The third miss has found her match."

Zhang Yuzhen proudly replied, "Yes, they came, and now they're leaving. They eat state-supplied food, and we can't keep them here."

Zhang Yuzhen asked, "Lao Nian, are you building a brick house?"

Lao Nian replied crisply, "Yes, my son is getting married, and the village has allocated a plot of land. We'll start by building a Beijing-style house for the wedding."

Zhang Yuzhen immediately said, "Congratulations!"

At the bus station, Fengyun's younger brother, Zhiqiang, looked at the schedule board and said, "The bus will arrive in about ten minutes."

At that moment, a group of children, around ten years old, came over playfully. They were wearing old clothes, and some of the children's clothes didn't fit properly. It was clear that they were wearing hand-me-downs from older siblings or adults. At that time, China had not yet implemented the one-child policy and encouraged having multiple children, celebrating the concept of heroic mothers. Every family had several children. The children came over to see Fengyun and Yaowei and asked them, "Are you city folks?"

Before Yaowei could respond, they confidently said, "Definitely, just by looking at how you're dressed. We don't have such nice clothes here!"

The children left, and the bus arrived. At this hour, there were no minibusses available. It was a blue-colored large bus with some paint peeling off. People on the roof of the bus were handling their luggage, and others were getting off and retrieving their packages using the handrail. Fengyun and Yaowei bid farewell to their mother and younger brother's family, boarded the bus, and left. Inside the bus, Fengyun saw her mother standing there, wiping away tears with her hand, her eyes also moistened.

During their trip to Jinzhou, Fengyun's mother agreed to their marriage. After Fengyun graduated, she stayed at school and became a chemistry teacher. Their belongings were moved together. Without large suitcases, each of them had a woven bag and a bed sheet. They moved into the staff dormitory, officially starting their married life.

After getting married, Yaowei and Fengyun took advantage of the summer break to visit Yaowei's hometown in Yingkou.

Their ancestral house in the hometown no longer belonged to them! They walked around outside the old Li family courtyard.

Yaowei really wanted to go in and touch the walls of the room he used to live in, to see the markings on the door frame where his father had recorded his growing height each year. But no matter how he looked from the outside, he couldn't see his room. The courtyard had been transformed, with layer upon layer of additional structures, and many other families were living there. It had been altered so much that its original appearance was no longer recognizable.

They also went to the ancestral grave of the Li family, and even there, everything had changed completely. Yaowei and Fengyun stood in the approximate direction, both kneeling down and bowing three times towards the Li family's grave. Yaowei said, "Ancestors of the Li family, today I, Li Yaowei, am here with my wife Liu Fengyun to pay our respects! Today, I can consider myself finding my roots. I swear: From this day forward, in marriage, our love will be eternal!"

## Chapter Three

# The birth of Guangzhong continues the family line; Grandma's ways of raising children

### 1

My grandfather looked at me and said, "Mingyu, the next part of the story involves your father, Guangzhong. There are parts that I haven't covered, and you can add them." I, along with my great aunt Yaoxin, my mother Yang Xi, and my father Guangzhong, all focused our attention on my grandfather, eagerly awaiting the continuation of his narrative.

My grandfather continued, "The schools were empty, and students stopped attending classes during the early stages of the Cultural Revolution. Many desks, chairs, windows, and doors in the universities were vandalized by the students. Professors were criticized and denounced, forcing the schools to suspend classes. The statues in front of the schools had their right arms chopped off, resembling the disarmed Venus de Milo of ancient Rome! The plaques hanging on the school gates were slashed several times, and the character 院 in the word 学院 ('college') lost its left ear, becoming 学完 ('finished studying'). Fengyun saw this as a good thing, as she needed time to take care of our son."

"Motivated by his old comrades and other young teachers, Yaowei went to Tiananmen Square and finally had the opportunity to meet our revered leader, Chairman Mao. He returned home filled with excitement. Later, he also visited Yan'an, Hunan, and even Xinjiang's Shihezi, where Yaowei had the chance to meet his long-lost sister, Yaozhi, who had experienced many hardships."

Yaowei and Fengyun lived in a high-rise building with a staircase connecting the upper and lower floors. Each small room had a door, and every family's room was adjacent to one another. The rooms were not soundproof, so there were no real secrets among the neighbors. The kitchens of each family were in the corridor, and everyone had to go to a communal water room to wash clothes and vegetables. It was easy to see what each family was cooking. On each floor, there was only one public restroom, separated for males and females, located on opposite sides of the building. Inside, there were over a dozen squatting toilets, but fortunately, they were flush toilets, so the smell was not too strong. During the Chinese New Year, families would gather their dishes onto a large table in the activity room, making the atmosphere lively and bustling.

Yaowei's favorite activity was to have dinner, and after that, he would join a group of elderly men sitting on small stools under the streetlamp in front of the building, playing chess. Only two people played at a time, but there were many onlookers who offered advice. Of course, there were always some people who would loudly exclaim, "Terrible move! You're doomed!" Sometimes, when someone lost after following someone else's advice, they would get angry, destroy the chessboard, and shout, "A true gentleman does not speak while observing a game!"

However, not everyone agreed, and they collectively grabbed him from the stool, forcing him to give up his seat. Then, another person would challenge the winner to another game. Yaowei took great pride in this activity. If Liu Qing from the third floor didn't come, he would often occupy a seat until the end. The joy of playing chess together with everyone was about having fun, and Yaowei's face would light up if he played well.

But playing against one person was a way to improve and refine their chess skills. So, the competitive Yaowei often brought his chessboard to Liu Qing's apartment, requesting to play several rounds. Even if he lost, he would still improve his chess skills. Over time, Yaowei became the runner-up in the annual chess competition among the school's faculty and staff. Then, after three years, he astonished them all and reached the top spot.

Another game Yaowei loved was playing poker. There were some teachers from the southern region who lived in the school's bachelor quarters due to their long-distance relationships. After work, with nothing else to do, they often gathered four people to play poker. Although Yaowei had a family, his love for games led him to join these young single teachers or those who lived apart from their spouses. They would play poker until late at night, sometimes even forgetting to bring his home keys. The knocking on the door would disturb Fengyun's sleep. Eventually, there were times when Yaowei returned too late and forgot to bring his keys, so he ended up sleeping in the bachelor quarters.

One time, he took his four-year-old son, Guangzhong, to play. Guangzhong curiously climbed up and down the bunk beds in the bachelor quarters for a while but soon grew bored. He ran out of the room and headed home to find his mother Liu Fengyun. However, being a young child and in the darkness of the night, he got lost. Yaowei realized it was already past 9 p.m. when he finally thought about Guangzhong and realized he was missing. This filled him with a sense of panic, and he immediately went out to search for him. When he returned home, he pretended as if nothing had happened and casually asked Fengyun, "Did Guangzhong come home by himself? Is he already asleep?"

Fengyun was puzzled and asked in astonishment, "Didn't he go with you to play? What happened?"

Yaowei could only say, "The child is missing!"

At that moment, both hurriedly went outside to search for Guangzhong. The two of them searched the entire school campus but couldn't find the child. They were about to report to the police when a neighbor came running towards them. It turned out that the child had gotten lost and ended up at a nearby grocery store. Knowing that his mother often came there to shop, he believed she would come looking for him. However, it was already 10 p.m., and the store was about to close. A kind-hearted farmer from the nearby Wusan Commune accompanied Guangzhong back to the school gate. With the information provided by Guangzhong about his parents' names, the security guard helped locate Yaowei's apartment number, and then the guard escorted Guangzhong home. The neighbor promptly came to inform them.

After this incident, Fengyun didn't allow Guangzhong to accompany Yaowei to play poker anymore. However, Guangzhong still secretly went with his father because there was something he couldn't let go of—cigarette boxes discarded by the young teachers. Empty cigarette boxes fascinated Guangzhong. Every time he went, he would empty a whole box, fold the cigarette box into a triangle. At that time, all the kids loved playing with fan-shaped cigarette boxes. If there were "Dazhonghua" or "Daqianmen" cigarette boxes, all the children would be envious.

Guangzhong also enjoyed riding on his father's broad shoulders to the park to see the animals. He loved going to the movies with his father as well. At that time, they had to walk for over half an hour to the Shengli Cinema at the DaNanmen (Great Southern Gate). To be able to ride on his father's shoulders, Guangzhong would pretend to be tired and say he couldn't walk anymore. Then his father would swiftly lift him up and let him ride on his shoulders. In young Guangzhong's heart, his father was a tall and strong, mighty hero. He had heard from his mother that his father was a hero who fought in the Korean War. Proudly, he would tell his little friends that his father was amazing and the most extraordinary father in the world.

## 2

Fengyun no longer taught chemistry classes. She was assigned to the school library to manage the shelving and retrieval of books. She worked eight hours a day and remained busy throughout. Yaowei no longer taught physics classes, so he applied for access to the school woodworking workshop to make tables and chairs for the college.

Fengyun initially disagreed with the idea of going to the woodworking workshop, and she raised a concern, saying, "Are you sure about this? If you do it, your professional title will change from a cadre to a worker."

Yaowei responded, "I've thought about that too. I went to the personnel department yesterday and they said that this temporary reassignment won't affect my professional title."

Fengyun asked, "What about the food coupons? Workers receive 45.5 jins* of grain per month, while cadres only receive 31 jins! If you do the work of a worker, naturally, you'll need more food."

Yaowei nodded, realizing something, and said, "Darling, you've considered everything so thoroughly. I can't believe I didn't think of that. I'll go and clarify this today."

Fengyun said, "This probably doesn't fall under the school's jurisdiction. Take the reassignment order with you, and let's go to the neighborhood office together."

The two of them soon arrived at the Fumin Neighborhood Office, which was two blocks away from their home. At that time in China, there was a hierarchical management system for the public, and the neighborhood office was the smallest administrative unit. It was commonly referred to as the "street office" or "community committee" as it governed a specific area known as a street or community. The neighborhood offices had a complete set of management personnel, mostly composed of proactive and progressive middle-aged women, often referred to as the "neighborhood aunties." They were familiar with every household and individual within their jurisdiction, and their actions were under their control. Sometimes, they also handled minor disputes among residents. The neighborhood offices were described by the people as the "work team of the community committee," consisting of aunties and sometimes uncles from our community. Every day, they would wear red armbands and roam the streets and alleys, listening to the gossip and resolving neighborhood disputes.

The Fumin Neighborhood Office was in a small alley where the two of them couldn't walk side by side. They walked in a single file, with one in front and one behind, until they reached a small door with a sign indicating the Fumin Street Office. Fengyun used to come here every month to collect various vouchers.

Inside the neighborhood office, there was a woman in her forties wearing a red armband on her arm. She was sitting, drinking tea, and reading the newspaper. She was the director of the neighborhood office, Yu Min. As they approached her, Yu Min recognized Fengyun and asked, "Teacher Liu, do you need something?"

* 1 jin = 0.5 kilogram

They explained the situation in detail, and Yu Min looked at the reassignment order and said, "We need to study this matter and also conduct an investigation at your school. Please wait for further notice."

Fengyun, noticing Yu Min's official tone, spoke up, "If we are reassigned as workers with a fixed grain quota, we only need 43 jins per month. The remaining 2.5 jins can be given to those who need it more."

Upon hearing Fengyun's words, Yu Min happily agreed, saying, "Alright, no problem. You wait for the news."

On the way back home, Yaowei said to Fengyun, "Why did you say only 43 jins? We should take as much as we deserve. I can't stand it when they have a little power and take more for themselves!"

Fengyun replied, "If you don't do it that way, this whole thing might fall through. You won't get even an extra jin."

Due to his straightforward temperament, Yaowei had suffered some setbacks in the past. He knew he had to listen to his wife this time, so he had to bear with it.

Sure enough, after one week, the grain quota for Yaowei was adjusted to 45.5 jins. Fengyun's family didn't consume much, and Yaowei was the biggest eater, consuming around 40 jins of grain per month. After deducting the 2.5 jins withheld by the neighborhood office, there were still 3 jins left. At that time, grain coupons were equivalent to money, and the remaining coupons could be exchanged for valuable items. Fengyun liked to exchange them for eggs.

The student dormitories at the school were vacant, with no students. Buildings 1 to 5 were repurposed for other uses. One of the buildings became an office building, housing a medical room and a finance office. Fengyun visited this building frequently. On one hand, she brought her children to the medical room when they had headaches or fevers, seeking medical treatment and medication. On the other hand, she came to collect her salary every month. Yaowei earned 56 Chinese yuan, while Fengyun earned 49.50 yuan. Together, their salaries totaled 105.50 yuan. Despite living month to month, they were still better off than workers who earned just over 20 yuan per month.

Fengyun's job in the library, managing books, was relatively relaxed. She had time to read books every day, and over the past few months, she had read many books during her free time. However, a few months later, the No. 2 workshop of the Shenyang Smelting Plant moved into the school campus. The Soviet-style pointed roofs of the school buildings were replaced with flat ones, and elevators were installed inside to facilitate the transportation of lathes, planers, and milling machines. There was an urgent need for personnel relocation, and some teachers from the School of Metallurgy and the Department of Chemistry were transferred to the No. 2 workshop, including Fengyun.

Suddenly, Fengyun became the busiest person at home. She jokingly said, "You see, my dear, you can't compete with me in woodworking. My job is where dreams are cast."

Yaowei replied, somewhat dismissively, "I don't believe I can't do well as a woodworker! Lately, working with the workers, I feel they are more down-to-earth. Yun, it's not without reason that people say we 'stinky old ninth' have a bit of a sour smell."

Excitedly, Fengyun responded, "Yes, now we are also members of the 'Red Five Categories.' We are workers now, and Chairman Mao said the working class leads everything!"

During the Cultural Revolution era, China classified people into several categories, with the most prestigious being the "Red Five Categories": workers, revolutionary soldiers, revolutionary cadres, poor peasants, and lower-middle peasants. They were considered the most dedicated and loyal to the revolution and enjoyed special privileges from the state.

On the other hand, there was a tragic group of people known as the "Black Nine Categories." They included landlords, rich peasants, counterrevolutionaries, bad elements, rightists, traitors, spies, capitalist roaders, and intellectuals. Among the "Black Nine Categories," intellectuals were ranked last and derogatorily referred to as "stinky old ninth."

Now, both Yaowei and Fengyun underwent a transformation. They went from being the lowest-ranking intellectuals, the "stinky old ninth," to becoming workers in the "Red Five Categories" at the school, receiving cadre salaries.

Initially, Fengyun was assigned to transport thyristors for the No. 2 workshop. The frail woman often shuttled through the beautiful campus, pulling a cart carrying several thyristors. She would transport the thyristors to the designated location, and then personnel from the smelting plant would use a large truck to transport them back to the Tie Xi District factory area. Later, Fengyun was assigned to operate machine tools in the workshop. After a few months, the clever Fengyun became proficient in operating various lathes. She later said that during her two years as a lathe worker, her proudest work was making a pair of dumbbells for Guangzhong at the casting workshop. Thanks to those dumbbells, Guangzhong acquired a new nickname.

When Fengyun brought the pair of dumbbells home, Guangzhong couldn't let go of them and would lift them for half an hour every day. Over a month later, Yaowei noticed that his son's biceps had developed and were noticeably bulging—a remarkable result.

Yaowei jokingly teased his four-year-old son, saying, "Since you love this pair of iron blocks, let's call you 'Iron Egg.'"

Still looking bewildered, Guangzhong, Fengyun answered with a smile, "Iron Egg, I like that name. From now on, let's call Guangzhong by the nickname 'Iron Egg.'"

After that, the name "Iron Egg" caught on. Teachers, students, and family members in the school campus all called Guangzhong "Iron Egg." Over time, fewer and fewer people called him by his formal name, Guangzhong.

Fengyun never changed her job title to a worker; she retained her cadre title. However, she received a two-jins meat ration supplement every month. Don't underestimate those mere two jins of meat ration. Guangzhong benefited greatly from it. After all, he was in the stage of growing up and needed to replenish his protein intake.

## 3

Guangzhong was sent to the daycare, and Yaowei was responsible for picking him up and dropping him off every day. Since there was only one bicycle in the family, and buying a bicycle required a bicycle ticket, they could only afford one bicycle. So, Yaowei became the designated driver, shuttling little Guangzhong to and from the daycare. He would place Guangzhong on a wooden triangular seat tied to the bike's crossbeam and reach the daycare in just a few minutes.

The daycare had two teachers. One was surnamed Yang, known as Auntie Yang, around 37 or 39 years old. The other was surnamed Guo, referred to as Grandma Guo, as she was nearing 50. These two teachers oversaw about twenty children in different age groups: big, medium, and small classes. They also had to prepare lunch for the children, making their workload extremely busy. Sometimes they couldn't attend to a child who got hurt or bumped into something. Later, in response to parents' feedback, a young teacher named Xiaomeng was assigned to take care of the small class and handle cooking. As a result, Auntie Yang oversaw the medium class, while Grandma Guo solely looked after the children in the big class.

At the age of 4, Guangzhong was just old enough to attend the big class, but he was a picky eater. One day Yaowei arrived at the daycare to pick up Guangzhong at 5 p.m. and saw him standing in a corner, crying with tears and snot, looking at his father with a pleading gaze.

Yaowei asked Grandma Guo what had happened. Grandma Guo said, "You better not send this child anymore. Why is he so delicate? He refuses to eat this and that. If all the children were like him, how could we manage?"

Yaowei then learned that Guangzhong hadn't even eaten lunch. Without saying anything to Grandma Guo or blaming the child, he picked up Guangzhong, placed him on the bike's small seat, and asked, "Why didn't you eat your meal?"

Guangzhong cried and said, "There was sand in the food."

Yaowei straightened up the bicycle, returned to the daycare, and asked Grandma Guo, "What did the children have for lunch today? Why did Guangzhong say there was sand in it?"

Grandma Guo was surprised and said, "That's impossible! Children shouldn't make up such things!"

Saying that, Grandma Guo brought some leftover rice and shrimp-stir-fried potato slices for Yaowei to taste. After eating,

Yaowei indeed felt a sandy texture in the rice. He realized it was the heads and antennae of the dried shrimp. He apologized to Grandma Guo and went back to Guangzhong, telling him to eat well tomorrow. Guangzhong nodded in agreement.

The next day, Yaowei arrived at the daycare earlier and saw other children playing games, but Guangzhong was sitting on a small stool in front of a small table with a bowl in front of him. Apart from two whole steamed buns, there was also a half-eaten bun in Guangzhong's hand.

Grandma Guo walked over and said, "Look, he has been eating these three steamed buns for two hours and still hasn't finished them. Are they really that bad?"

Yaowei asked Guangzhong, "Didn't you promise Dad that you would eat your meal? Why is it different this time?"

Guangzhong, like a child who had committed a grave mistake, whispered, "The buns taste bitter."

Yaowei asked what filling was inside the buns. Grandma Guo replied, "They are filled with radish and radish leaves. Other children find them delicious, so why does he say they're bitter?"

Yaowei realized that the bitterness came from the radish leaves, and he couldn't blame Grandma Guo for being upset. Guangzhong indeed had picky eating habits.

Unable to say anything, Yaowei went home and discussed with Fengyun what to do. He said, "It seems like Grandma Guo at the daycare doesn't understand child psychology. Guangzhong has this picky eating problem, and it's not good for him to go hungry every day."

Fengyun thought for a moment and said, "Why don't we ask my mom to come and help take care of Guangzhong?"

So, a few days later, Fengyun's mother, Zhang Yuzhen, arrived by train from Jinzhou, carrying a bag. Yaowei went to the train station to pick up his mother-in-law.

With the arrival of his mother-in-law, Yaowei faced another dilemma. They only had one bedroom, so they used two bookshelves to divide the space. They set up a foldable bed near the entrance, where Grandma and Guangzhong would sleep together. However, Yaowei and Fengyun felt somewhat inconvenienced.

Guangzhong was happy because he had more freedom now. He happily followed Grandma around every day, and Grandma showered him with love and care. When Guangzhong refused to eat, Grandma would chase after him with a bowl and keep saying, "Darling, eat your food, or Grandma will leave!"

That statement worked wonders, and Guangzhong would immediately come over and take a bite.

Grandma, being from a rural background, had some habits that Yaowei found a bit uncomfortable. If a grain of rice fell on the table, Grandma would pick it up and put it back in the bowl for Guangzhong to eat.

Fengyun couldn't tolerate her mother's actions and said, "Mom, if the rice falls, we shouldn't eat it."

Grandma Yuzhen said, "I've heard you teaching the child Tang poems. 'Who knows the hardships of every grain of rice on the plate.' If it falls, what's the big deal? It's still food, and we shouldn't waste it. You don't know that the grain we just harvested is from the ground, and the land is not easy either."

The old lady continued with a serious tone, "You were also raised by me like this."

Fengyun didn't want her mother to feel upset, so she remained silent. Yaowei couldn't say anything either. After all, the elderly lady came to help, and she was nearly 70 years old. Yaowei advised Fengyun to clean the table thoroughly every day.

Furthermore, whenever Guangzhong had a runny nose, Grandma Yuzhen would pinch his nose and make him blow hard. Then she would flick the mucus onto the floor and wipe off any remaining residue on her hands onto her clothes, the wall, or a tree trunk. Yaowei and Fengyun asked her to use tissue paper to wipe her hands, as well as to blow her nose into it. However, the elderly lady said, "What a hassle."

Fengyun told Yaowei, "Let it go. My mom won't change her habits."

Yaowei understood. Besides, with Grandma Yuzhen's presence, they saved a significant amount of money on daycare fees. Yaowei and Fengyun decided to give all the saved money to Grandma Yuzhen, as she deserved it.

Three years passed, and Guangzhong started primary school. With Grandma Yuzhen around, the miscellaneous school fees were reduced from five yuan to three yuan because the family had one more member, and the average income per person decreased. In fact, many children from the rural areas of Wusi Township didn't have to pay any fees to attend school because farmers were considered part of the population without a stable income.

In the early 1970s, Yaowei began teaching classes to workers, peasants, and soldiers again. They also had their second child, Guanghua, making their living situation even more inconvenient. Grandma Yuzhen helped during Fengyun's postpartum period for a month, but once their granddaughter turned one month old, Grandma Yuzhen returned to her hometown. She never came back again, and a few years later, she passed away in her hometown. Fengyun's younger brother and his family also went to work in the south, so from that point on, in Mangniu Village, Liu Fengyun's family had no relatives nearby.

## Chapter Four

# Teachers struggle with housing. Neighbors have trouble with oil

### 1

Professor Shi's family who lived in the same building unit were from the southern region and enjoyed eating homemade black bean paste. They fermented their own bean paste and distributed it to the neighbors every year, and this generally maintained good neighborly relations. However, one day, it was heard that Professor Shi's mother-in-law was arrested. It was reported that she used a newspaper that happened to have Chairman Mao's portrait to wipe her grandson's runny nose. Unaware of the implications, she caused trouble with this innocent act. Then the street director escalated the situation and labeled the elderly woman as a counter-revolutionary, so she was sent back to her hometown in Sichuan, causing Professor Shi to be suspended pending an investigation.

This incident left the household in a state of constant anxiety, feeling as though they were under constant scrutiny in the communal building. It felt like there were countless eyes watching their every move, and they became overly cautious. Yaowei and Fengyun were both relieved that Yaowei's mother had returned to her hometown!

One day, Guo Jianshe called with good news, announcing the birth of his son and his mother coming from their hometown to help with the new mother's postpartum recovery. Upon hearing the joyful news, Yaowei and Fengyun bought a mother hen and went to visit them.

Guo Jianshe was also a university professor, and he faced a similar housing situation without a proper house. He lived in a residential building converted from student dormitories. Each two dormitory rooms were connected, with a door in between serving as an entrance to the inner and outer rooms. The kitchen had been transformed from the student cafeteria, giving each family a small space and a stove. Every stovepipe was connected to a large duct on the cafeteria's roof, which led outside the building. When everyone cooked at the same time, the stoves would emit roaring flames, posing a potential fire hazard.

Guo Jianshe complained to Yaowei, "Wei, look at this. We fought on the frontlines for the country, but in the end, this is where we have to settle down. I just can't understand it!"

He continued, "Have you heard that some of our old comrades have been labeled as rightists?"

Yaowei replied, "Of course. Hu Zhipeng's wife even called on me to borrow money and make connections!"

Guo Jianshe sighed and said, "If you ever need me, just let me know. If there's anything we can do to help, we'll do it!"

Yaowei responded, "Alright, after all, we crawled out of piles of dead bodies in the same trench."

Guo Jianshe held Yaowei's hand, nodded, and advised him, "Speak less, focus on self-preservation. It's also about protecting the whole family. I know you have an honest character, but if you can endure, endure. Don't jeopardize our larger plans for the sake of small grievances!"

Listening to Guo Jianshe's heartfelt words and seeing his worn-out face while taking care of his family, Yaowei felt a sense of melancholy. But then again, when he thought about it, his own situation wasn't much better.

At that time, there were hardly any civil engineering projects, and schools hadn't built new buildings for decades. Teachers had no homes to live in. However, their old comrade Yang Wei, who stayed in the military, was different! He had already been promoted to a regimental commander, had service personnel, and owned a large house of over 100 square meters. The furniture in his house was all made of mahogany, exuding a faint woody fragrance. And the kitchen in his house was high-end. They had piped gas, unlike

Yaowei's family who used liquefied gas cylinders. Their stove had four burners, making cooking much faster. Moreover, the ceiling lights in their house sparkled like shining gems. There was a bathtub in their house, unlike Yaowei, who had to go to the school's large communal bathhouse, which only opened twice a week. The school's bathhouse had a large square-shaped pool that could accommodate hundreds of people bathing together. However, there was no personal privacy there. Your body was fully exposed to everyone in the pool. Looking at Regimental Commander Yang Wei's house, there was even a private bathroom, clean and tidy, without the need to use the public dry toilets.

Yaowei felt somewhat uneasy in his heart. He had once thought about what his fifth brother Yaocheng had said to him: "being in the military is not only about protecting the country but also for one's own future."

Yaowei thought, "Yang Wei had found a way out, but what about me?" His mother-in-law had to live with them separated only by a bookshelf. It seemed that his family background meant that he might never have a way out. However, his mindset was as broad as his nickname, "Black Judge." He hoped for a better future, as the saying goes, "May I have a thousand houses, bringing joy to all the underprivileged in the world." But now, all housing was uniformly allocated by the school, based on seniority and rank. Faculty members had no priority over other staff members and had to stand in line together. This put them at a disadvantage because their time spent in school wasn't considered as work experience. However, Yaowei took a big advantage at that time because military service counted as work experience, and when calculating his seniority, the four years of university were not deducted. As a result, when their daughter Guanghua was born in 1971, they were assigned to a unit with a shared kitchen.

On moving day, Yaowei borrowed a cart from the school and had some chess buddies help him. With a few back-and-forth trips, they moved most of their belongings. In fact, they didn't have many things: a hardboard bed, a five-drawer chest, a bookshelf, a large wardrobe, and the willow baskets each of them had when they got married. Of course, they also had a dining table, which was made by removing the tabletop from a discarded desk, planning it smooth, adding four legs and crossbars, and then applying a coat of varnish. It became a perfectly usable dining table. Later, Yaowei wasn't satisfied with the ordinary appearance of the table, so he turned the table legs into cylindrical shapes, carved patterns on them, made them detachable with bearings that could rotate or be locked. He also changed the tabletop to a round antique design. After painting it with dark red lacquer and varnish, it truly looked like an antique round table. The carpenter, Xiao Li, who helped with the move, was so impressed and immediately wanted to apprentice under Yaowei. He said, "Teacher Li, we are relatives. Please accept me as your apprentice. I believe knowledgeable people should do something worthy."

Unexpectedly, Yaowei took on an apprentice, and because of him, this devoted apprentice started to study academic subjects earnestly. After the resumption of the college entrance examination in mainland China, Xiao Li even got admitted to Shenyang Construction University to study architecture.

## 2

The neighbors of the new unit were surnamed Zhu. The lady of the Zhu family worked at a small restaurant in the grain station. They often had some extra soybean oil, eggs, pork, rice, and flour, and so on. At that time, everything was distributed in fixed quantities. Each family would only receive 3 liang (roughly 150 g.) of soybean oil per month, which was barely enough to fill the gaps between their teeth. It was said that in other provinces across the country, people received about half a jin, or 5 liang (250 g.), but in Liaoning, there was a provincial leader nicknamed Chen Xilian (Liaoning people called him "Chen Three liang"), who automatically deducted two liang from the allocation for the people of Liaoning, making it three liang instead.

Liaoning people would go to Beijing and carry pork back home like oxen because in Beijing, there were no fixed quantities, and meat was sold freely. However, one had to wait in line, and each person could only buy two catties (a Chinese unit of weight). If someone from Liaoning went to a grocery store in Beijing, they would have to wait in line for several hours. Each time they could only buy two catties, and if they did this ten times, they would get twenty catties. In this way they would most likely end up buying all the fatty meat in the store. At that time, the people of Beijing referred to Liaoning people as "Northeast Tigers."

Uncle Zhu, the neighbor, was fatter than anyone else in the building because someone from the family worked at a restaurant. Having the advantage of being close to the source brings rewards. They stored their soybean oil in large barrels. Sometimes, when Fengyun cooked, she would only use a few drops oil, and Uncle Zhu would give her a spoonful of oil as a gesture. Fengyun would usually say, "No need, you keep it for yourselves."

However, Fengyun also wondered in her heart: No matter what, the Zhu family couldn't possibly have so much oil! The neighbor's eggs were also very abundant. Every morning, they could hear the neighbor using chopsticks to stir the eggs, "kaka," a crisp sound, followed by the sound of the eggs hitting the pan, "cila," and then the fragrance of the fried eggs would drift into the Li family's bedroom through the door crack. This sound would wake up little Guangzhong, and the aroma would entice his appetite. He would always raise his head and shout to Fengyun, "Mom, I want to eat scrambled eggs too."

However, at that time, each family would only receive one catty (500 g.) of eggs per month, so there were no eggs for Guangzhong. Therefore, he clearly looked thinner than the neighbor's child, and he often fell ill. He would catch a cold and have a fever almost every single month, and when he got sick, he would take tetracycline. That's why Guangzhong had a mouthful of teeth stained yellow by tetracycline. Later, Fengyun came up with an idea: to raise chickens herself.

Fengyun raised a total of three chickens: two Luhua and one White Lehe. Guangzhong and his younger sister Guanghua gave them names: Huahua, Honghong, and Da Bai (Big White). Every morning, the three chickens were allowed to roam freely in the residential courtyard of the school. They would peck at worms on the ground, and the yolks of the eggs they laid were bright red with a sheen of oil. Guanghua was luckier than her older brother. During her tooth-changing phase, she could eat one egg every day. The two siblings carefully cared for the three egg-laying hens. They would go to the riverbank to catch dragonflies and grasshoppers for them, encouraging them to lay more eggs.

However, one evening, they couldn't find Big White no matter how hard they looked. In the dark, Guanghua frantically called out Big White's name, nearly in tears. The neighbor downstairs informed them, "Teacher Li, don't let your child search anymore. I saw several worker-peasant-soldier students taking the chickens away. I heard they often kill the courtyard's chickens for meat. Now, there might be only bones left!"

Since Big White went missing, Fengyun and the two siblings no longer let the chickens out. Huahua and Honghong were confined to a cage, deprived of sunlight. Gradually, the shells of the eggs they laid became soft, and their combs slowly lost their redness. Soon, they stopped laying eggs, and eventually, both died. Fengyun wanted to eat the meat, but Guangzhong and Guanghua strongly objected. They found a small mound and buried the chickens there, where green grass and insects were abundant. Huahua, Honghong, and Big White, who had disappeared, should be satisfied in that place.

In fact, the neighbor's family didn't have a good time for long before something happened. Teacher Zhu would carry a thermos to and from work every week, and everyone thought it contained hot water. However, one day, as she was carrying the thermos and locking the restaurant's door with one hand, the thermos broke, and yellowish soybean oil spilled out. Unfortunately, the Party branch secretary of the restaurant saw it and elevated this act to the level of class struggle, accusing Teacher Zhu of undermining socialism. Eventually, the Zhu family moved away.

The utilization rate of the faculty housing was very high. As soon as the Zhu family left, a new neighbor named Xu moved in. Her husband was transferred to Liaozhong County, and she stayed in Shenyang with their two children. Their life was difficult, to the extent that they couldn't afford the school fees, and the children had to attend school for free. Xu was an honest person. Fengyun suggested to her, "Have you thought about building connections at the school to get your husband transferred back?"

Xu opened her hands and replied, "I have no connections and no money. What can I do?"

Fengyun gave her an idea, "You see, Mr. Hu's husband at the school was transferred back after only six months. You can ask him how he did it."

Xu shook her head and said, "I asked, they not only used connections but also spent money and gave some good liquor as gifts." Xu continued, "Building connections requires money. I rely on picking up old newspapers, cardboard, and bottles to earn some money, but it's not much. After buying groceries, there's hardly anything left."

Seeing the plight of Xu and her two children, Fengyun tried to help them in every possible way. Sometimes, she secretly provided assistance to them. Guangzhong and Guanghua would see other children eating cookies and get tempted to have some as well. So, when Fengyun made dough, she would add some sugar and make triangular-shaped dough pieces. Then she would stack two triangle pieces together, deep-fry them until they puffed up, forming a hollow space in the middle, resembling chubby little cookies. The children would munch on them with a crispy "crackling" sound. Fengyun called these cookies "Li Family Cookies." Every time she fried the dough pieces, she would have Guangzhong invite the neighbor's two children. The four children would gather around Fengyun, eagerly waiting to eat the Li Family Cookies. When Fengyun heard the children chewing the cookies with a "crunching" sound, she couldn't be happier. Those days of making the best out of a difficult situation were also moments of happiness.

## Chapter Five

# Ways of returning from the Countryside; making laboratory equipment for teaching

### 1

Then came the period of suspended classes and the revolution began. The authority of teachers was criticized, and the propaganda teams composed of workers entered the school's leadership committee, sidelining the former principal, Zhang. Instead of teaching, he went to the school's woodworking workshop to repair and make desks and chairs for the school.

Not only did universities stop recruiting recent graduates, but high school students also responded to Chairman Mao's call. They graduated and answered the call by going to the countryside to receive reeducation from the poor and lower-middle peasants. It was deemed necessary. In fact, this was a corresponding policy implemented by China at that time to address the problem of youth unemployment in cities. Some students expressed their determination, saying, "We respond to Chairman Mao's call and go to the places our motherland needs the most with a red heart and passionate enthusiasm. We also have two hands and won't idle away in the city!"

During that time, there was a large-scale, organized movement of educated youth going to the countryside and settling there. It was known as the Up to the Mountains and Down to the Countryside Movement. They accounted for one-tenth of the urban population, and almost every household had educated youth going to the countryside.

In the building, there were two graduates who completed the nine-year compulsory education, one male and one female. They were dressed in green military uniforms, but without any insignia or caps, giving the impression of being in military attire. They held Chairman Mao's quotations in their hands, wore Red Guards armbands, and wore large red flowers on their chests. They gathered at the school gate with backpacks, shouting deafening slogans like "Youth with no regrets! Glory in going to the countryside!" and singing the song "Learning from Lei Feng is a good example." They then boarded military trucks and left. They were later sent to various places' Youth Homes through the train station. Many parents watched the departing trucks with tears in their eyes, while some parents went directly to the train station to see their children off.

The son of the Party Committee Secretary on the third floor used to be a student cadre. He took the lead in signing up to undergo training in remote rural areas in Guizhou. However, he returned from the countryside after only half a year, claiming to be sick and needing treatment at home. But judging from his lively appearance, it seemed that there was nothing wrong with him. It's probably because his father pulled some strings to have him transferred back to the city. He was a sensible young man. When he saw people moving liquefied natural gas cylinders upstairs, he came over and offered to help. Yaowei asked him, "Did you get transferred back to the city?"

He smiled and said, "I'm waiting for the placement office's notification. I have to take it step by step!" He added, "But it's almost there. My dad has already made arrangements, and I'll probably start working at the school's factory next month."

The child wasn't lying. Later, Yaowei did see him working at the school's factory.

The daughter of the family downstairs didn't go very far away to join her assigned rural work team and she often came back home. Every time she returned, she would argue with her parents, and the shouting would echo through the thin floorboards up to our floor. I heard her mother say, "Look at those officials' children, they've all returned to the city. Why can't we spend some money and use connections to bring our daughter back?"

The father of that family replied angrily, "Easy for you to say. We are ordinary folks and can't even find the right connections."

Then there would be the incessant sound of the girl's sobbing.

In years following, the arguments gradually subsided. It turned out that the girl got married to the son of the village chief there, so she probably had no hope of returning to the city. Later, during the Chinese New Year, I saw the neighbor girl again. She had transformed into a rural woman, accompanied by a sturdy and short husband and a two or three-year-old boy when she visited her parents' home.

## 2

In 1966, the college entrance examination was abolished in mainland China, and universities stopped enrolling students. In 1971, the system of recommending and selecting workers, peasants, and soldiers as university students was implemented, allowing them to study in universities for a few years before returning to practical work. At that time, the universities became busy again, with various workers, peasants, and soldier students shuttling around the campus. Among them were many model workers of different ages, including those with only primary school education.

In the carpentry workshop, there was one student who stood out. He liked to give seats a smooth and rounded appearance, rather than the usual square shape. Yaowei's comfortable days in the carpentry workshop lasted for over two years. When the school began to admit workers, peasants, and soldier trainees, due to the lack of teaching staff, he was reassigned to the physics teaching and research office and even given the title of office director.

Many said that educating workers, peasants, and soldier trainees was a waste of time. Since the incident involving Zhang Tiesheng, the "blank paper hero" who wrote a letter, there were no closed-book exams in universities. Therefore, nobody prepared their lessons properly; they just went through the motions. The laboratory equipment was incomplete, but how could physics be taught without experiments? If it were not for one peculiar worker, peasant, and soldier trainee who repeatedly requested to do experiments, it seems that nobody would have cared.

Yaowei preparing a lesson

This trainee's name was Zhang Hongbin, and he was recommended by the army to attend university. He studied diligently and kept his notes neat and tidy. Among the many trainees who had only graduated from primary school and couldn't understand or take notes during lectures, Zhang Hongbin stood out as a special individual. Yaowei thought that just for him, the physics laboratory should be established.

He recalled, "The most headache-inducing issue was the lack of funds, so everything had to be done by ourselves. I found every available prop I could get my hands on. Iron wire, iron bars, clotheslines, wooden blocks, plastic bottles, glass cups, steel pipes, rubber hoses, magnets, and more were all put to use. Even the old pocket watch at home was used as a timer. Fengyun complained a lot; things would often go missing at home. Today, a light bulb would disappear, and tomorrow, a teacup. She would tell me that our home was being emptied because of me! Every time she said that, I would reply that these things were of little use at home but could be very useful in the laboratory."

Yaowei worked with Zhang Hongbin for a whole semester, and they improved the laboratory. The subsequent trainees had experiments to do, and even if something broke, they could fix it themselves. Zhang Hongbin said, "That kind of dedication comes from the heart, the joy of being immersed in it, and selflessness."

Due to the varying foundations of the worker, peasant, and soldier university students, Yaowei had to provide them with extra classes, starting from high school physics. They did experiments and witnessed sunlight being refracted into a spectrum by a prism. They conducted acceleration experiments and learned about the magic of gravity. They performed Archimedes' principle experiments and quickly measured the volume of irregular objects. They were exploring the mysteries of nature.

In 1977, during the Deng Xiaoping era, when the college entrance examination was reinstated, Zhang Hongbin was admitted to the Department of Physics at Harbin Military Institute of Technology. He came to thank Teacher Li with excitement, saying, "The physics laboratory classes at that time showed us the power of knowledge. The natural world is so amazing, and there's no way we could continue living aimlessly every day. All the efforts were not in vain. From that time on, I started studying diligently, and the college entrance examination was a breeze for me."

Yaowei paused and proudly told his sister Yaoxin, "My students come to visit me every year during the holidays and bring me gifts. They are like my children."

Glancing at his sister, Yaowei let out a sigh. It seemed like he was talking to her, but also to himself, "I never thought that I would spend twenty years in the teaching profession!"

Sister Yaoxin smiled and replied, "Isn't it the same for me? In fact, most of our siblings in the 'Yao' generation of the Li family have entered the ancient and noble profession of teaching. As the ancients said, a teacher imparts knowledge and dispels doubts. Teaching is a respected profession, and we should set an example as educators!"

Years later, when I returned to the mainland, my grandfather asked me, "Mingyu, do you know why I have been a teacher all my life?"

I looked at him and said, "Because you teach and educate!"

Grandfather shook his head and said, "Not entirely correct! It's because when I see those successful students, I feel the mission of being a teacher! It's about the transmission and sublimation of knowledge."

I understood then, during the difficult decade of the Cultural Revolution from 1966 to 1976, what supported my grandfather and prevented him from leaving the teaching profession. Now that he is old, over eighty years of age, when his students come to visit him and he engages in conversations with his accomplished disciples, he seems to return to the earnestness of his youth, teaching with dedication.

# Chapter Six

## Yaoyou chases his dreams and achieves his goal — attending Tsinghua University

### 1

I looked at the photos of my grandfather and his two older brothers when they were young, and I pointed to my grandfather and asked him, "You often tell stories about your other brothers, but you rarely mention Uncle Yaoyou. How is he doing?"

My grandfather pondered for a moment and said, "Uncle Yaoyou and his older brother and sister were all members of the Communist Party. His path was different from your great uncle Yaoguo and your Great Aunts Yaozhi and Yaoxin's . Even his path was not the same as that of your Great Uncle Yaojia . However, he also faced some hardships."

As my grandfather spoke, he began to tell me about Uncle Yaoyou's experiences.

Great Uncle Yaoyou and my grandfather Yaowei, judging by their names, should have been inseparable brothers who achieved success together. However, that wasn't the reality.

Yaoyou and Yaowei were born in the same year and played together since they were in open-crotch pants. Yaoyou was smart, sharp, and liked to show off, while Yaowei was honest, simple, and enjoyed helping others. Most of the time, they had a competitive relationship—neither would let the other have their way. Yaoguo, who was three years older than them, often found himself in the middle, trying to balance their relationship. However, they also had harmonious moments. They would go together to pick wild fruits on the mountain, catch frogs in the river, and climb trees to find bird eggs. During those times, they were very in sync.

Yaoyou always had grievances against his father. His father treated his Er mother Wan'er better than his own mother. Er Ma (2nd wife in Chinese) was beautiful, and his father liked her more. As a result, Yaowei received more paternal love. From an early age, Yaoyou felt a sense of unfairness, and he often expressed his dissatisfaction with Yaowei.

When Yaowei was seven years old, his mother passed away. At that time, Yaoyou felt a sense of balance in his heart. Although he felt sorry for Yaowei, who had lost his mother, but Yaoyou gained more fatherly love. But even though his childhood wish of seeing his father every day came true, he realized that life wasn't as beautiful as he had imagined.

His father and his mother were not as close as they seemed. They would argue and quarrel about big and small things. In the end, his father stopped consulting his mother on anything and would often speak to her in a commanding tone, without room for negotiation. Yaoyou felt sorry for his mom. She had relied on his father her whole life, and she was straightforward and would frequently anger his father. This made Yaoyou feel that it was difficult to stay in this family. However Yaojia, who was 10 years older, once said that his parents were like that, and there was no hope for their relationship to improve. They were enemies in a previous life and enemies in this life, yet they ended up becoming a family, living under the same roof, eating from the same pot, and sleeping on the same kang bed. Because of this, Yaoyou sought the true meaning of life early on and seemed to have found it: communism.

Yaoyou found a book titled "The Communist Manifesto" in forth brother Yaojia's bookcase. It was written by Karl Marx and Friedrich Engels and served as a guiding principle for the Communist League. Yaoyou would hide in the firewood shed every day, secretly reading the book from cover to cover. In the book, he came across Yaojia's notes, where he wrote about his own reading experience. Yaojia expressed, "This book is the guiding light of my life, illuminating the path forward. It has answered my doubts about life, my family's perplexities, and the country's uncertain future! China will eventually become a socialist republic following the model of the Paris Commune."

Yaojia also wrote, "The Paris Commune was an early experiment in socialism and a glorious milestone in the rise of the world's left-wing political movement. Just as Marx believed, it was a powerful proof of his communist theory."

Yaoyou discovered that he enjoyed reading Yaojia's annotations, and he was surprised to find annotations by his sister, Yaoxian, in the book as well. He began to be influenced by his older siblings and developed an interest in this elusive communist society. The depiction in the Communist Manifesto was so beautiful, the highest state of humanity! Equality for all, distribution according to needs—how could anyone resist the allure of this liberal radiance!

Yaoyou remembered the first time he became the liaison officer for Yaojia and Yaoxian. That day, he was hiding in the firewood shed, secretly reading the Communist Manifesto, when his sister Yaoxian pushed open the door and entered. Instinctively, he hurriedly hid the book behind his back, but Yaoxian walked straight toward him and snatched the familiar book from behind. She looked at her bewildered brother and asked, "Do you like reading it?"

He nodded vigorously.

Yaoxian asked, "Why?" to which Yaoyou replied, "Because it gives me hope."

Yaoyou noticed a flicker of joy in Yaoxian's eyes, and she said, "Little Brother Seven, it's not enough to just watch; you have to take action. But do you know how dangerous it can be?"

Yaoyou confidently said at that time, "My determination is firm!"

From that day forward, in addition to being a student, Yaoyou took on the role of being a junior liaison for his older brother and sister in the underground Communist Party station. He directly communicated with Mao Chunyu, a shopkeeper at the hardware store. Being young, each time he received a task, it felt mysterious, and Yaoyou felt a sense of fulfillment and validation. He completely forgot about the danger until one day he was followed and narrowly escaped being arrested, which made him feel a bit scared. Later, when his older brother Yaojia and sister Yaoxian were exposed and had to leave for the interior, then later went to Yan'an, Yaoyou truly understood the true meaning of the danger involved in this work, as it eventually turned into underground operations.

Yaoyou studied diligently. He was the type who combined intelligence with hard work. Although he wasn't exceptionally brilliant, he grasped things quickly. His grades were better than his younger half-brother Yaowei's, which served as a remedy for the imbalance in his heart.

Because of his excellent academic performance, Yaoyou even skipped two grades and entered a prestigious high school. In 1950, after the signing of the Sino-Soviet Treaty of Friendship, Cooperation, and Mutual Assistance, Yaoyou, as a recent high school graduate, had the opportunity to study in the Soviet Union. In 1952, he spent a year in a preparatory class for studying Russian. During that time, students like him had access to milk, eggs, and sometimes even crabs and large shrimp. By the end of the year, Yaoyou had gained about ten kilograms of weight. Then he had to go through a rigorous political screening before being allowed to travel abroad.

The conditions for studying abroad at that time were indeed very generous. Just a few months before departure, each student in the preparatory class received two large boxes containing clothes and daily necessities for all seasons. The daily necessities even included small items like nail clippers and fruit knives. All of these were provided free of charge, thanks to the concerted efforts of the whole country.

However, in the end, Yaoyou was disappointed because he failed the political screening. The reason was that his half-sister Yaoxin, who had a different mother, had gone to Taiwan. When the party organization talked to him, they said that they couldn't do anything about it. They acknowledged that he had been with the party since childhood, and his older brother and sister had been his guides to communism. However, the political screening process was extremely strict, personally overseen by Comrade Liu Shaoqi. The comrades who talked to Yaoyou said that they had done their utmost, but they couldn't change the decision.

Yaoyou didn't let this setback discourage him or leave him in a state of despair. He never forgot the words that Yaojia said to him before he entered the preparatory class: "We need to build our country and urgently require a large number of professionals in construction and management. Yaoyou, you can't embarrass me. You must make a name for yourself."

Although the situation had taken an unexpected and sudden turn, Yaoyou couldn't help but question himself and wonder if he had chosen the wrong path. He felt uncertain about the future and asked himself whether he had made a mistake. However, deep down, he still held onto the belief that his dedication to communism and his pursuit of knowledge were valuable and meaningful.

Yaoyou knew that setbacks and doubts were part of any journey, especially one as challenging as building a socialist society. He reminded himself of the greater cause and the importance of contributing to the construction of a better China. He drew strength from the words of his siblings and the ideals they instilled in him.

Instead of letting himself be consumed by doubt, Yaoyou used this unexpected turn of events as an opportunity for self-reflection and growth. He became more determined to prove himself and make a positive impact in his chosen field, regardless of the obstacles he faced. He understood that setbacks were temporary and that his commitment to the communist cause remained strong.

With renewed determination, Yaoyou set his sights on other avenues for contributing to the revolution and the development of his country. He sought alternative ways to utilize his talents and knowledge, always keeping in mind the ultimate goal of building a socialist society.

## 2

First, Yaoyou was assigned to Tianjin Military Unit as a civilian staff member. Later, due to his experience working at the Li family's hardware processing factory and his political background, he was reassigned to a forging factory where he worked as a laborer for several years. The factory primarily produced automotive components and was a nationally recognized military-industrial enterprise. He was appointed as the Communist Party branch secretary of the factory. Seeing advanced precision stamping and spiral press machines, he felt the need to further his education. The dream of pursuing higher education resurfaced in his mind, and his aspiration was to study advanced scientific technology and contribute to the country's progress.

After a day's work, covered in oil stains, he would take off his work overalls, return to his dormitory, and embark on late-night study sessions, delving into cultural knowledge. His perseverance paid off. In 1958, the Ministry of Education submitted a document to the central government proposing the selection of students to study computer and automatic control disciplines at Tsinghua University. In June of the same year, Vice Premier Nie Rongzhen endorsed the proposal in the Ministry of Education's report: Approved!

Finally, with the recommendation of the organization, this revolutionary hero who had participated in the War of Liberation was admitted to Tsinghua University as a transfer student. He and other transfer students were being cultivated as future teachers in the fields of computer science and automatic control.

Arriving for the first time at the beautiful Tsinghua University, Yaoyou felt an immense sense of pride. It was his first-time setting foot on the soil of Beijing, the capital city. As he stood in front of the school gate, admiring the four prominent characters of "Tsinghua University," a teacher in his fifties, with a round face, kind eyebrows, and gentle eyes, approached him. The teacher asked, "Young man, are you a freshman? Which department are you in?"

Proudly, he answered, "I'm in Class 102 of the Automation Control Department."

The teacher's eyebrows raised, and he smiled, saying, "Haha, then come with me."

He truly followed the teacher into the Electrical Engineering Building. The teacher pointed to the teaching building and said, "You'll have most of your classes here in the future."

Later, during his first class, he saw the teacher he had encountered earlier walking into the classroom to teach. It turned out to be the renowned Professor Zhong Shimu, the head of the Automation Control Department. It was fate. Eventually, he became a proud disciple under Professor Zhong's guidance, pursuing his graduate studies while working. It was his first time attending this prestigious Chinese university.

He received a school emblem engraved with the eight characters "Self-discipline and Social Commitment" as the motto, and he solemnly pinned it to his chest. In the department's party branch office, the party branch secretary said, "Comrade, you were recommended as a transfer student, and we have reviewed your file. Your qualifications are impressive, and we need someone like you. Join us."

And so, as the eldest brother among the students and a senior party member who had been involved in the revolution from a young age, he became a party branch committee member of the Automation Control Department as soon as he entered the university. In addition to his party work, he also took on social roles such as being a class advisor.

Yaoyou projected a slightly serious but still amiable image. Being impatient by nature, he walked quickly and spoke rapidly. He wore a pair of glasses on his slender face, and his bright eyes sparkled. Due to his previous work experience in the factory, he often wore a blue uniform, and it seemed like he never changed his clothes since he had multiple sets of the same uniform. His daily schedule was packed, and he approached his studies with the same enthusiasm as he did his work.

As a university student, he became a resident on campus. In those days, each dormitory housed at least eight to ten students, most of whom were much younger than him. The young students loved to sleep, but he was the first one to wake up and head to the Automation and Electrical Engineering buildings to study in the mornings. During the afternoon nap time, while everyone else was asleep, he would review what he had learned, complete his assignments, and prepare for the next chapter. He saved some time for others because in the afternoons and evening, he had many student and social responsibilities to attend to.

Whenever he silently picked up his backpack and left the dormitory for early self-study, the youngest student in the dorm, Xiao Zhao, would mutter, "Brother Li is going to devour books again. The books have their own golden house, and within the books, there is a beauty like jade."

He looked at the lunchbox on his bedside table, grateful that Brother Li had prepared breakfast for him in case he overslept. This eldest brother was full of drive and served as an example for his studies. However, he was used to laziness, and he would either arrive late or skip the first class. Fortunately, the first class was the "Principles of Automatic Regulation" taught personally by Professor Zhong Shimu, the head of the department, who never called attendance. Often, when other students returned from lunch, Xiao Zhao would still lazily lie in his upper bunk. He would borrow notes from his older brothers and review them. As a result, he managed to pass most of the mid-term exams.

In the morning, Yaoyou looked at Xiao Zhao, who was still lying in bed and said, "Little Nine, it's time for you to get up! Chairman Mao said we are the sun that rises at eight or nine in the morning. Where is the sun that doesn't get up?" Xiao Zhao chuckled and covered his head with a blanket.

As the semester was coming to an end, one night, Yaoyou fell ill and had a slight fever. Feeling heavy-headed, he went to bed early and slept soundly until the next morning after nine o'clock. When he woke up, the dormitory was quiet, and his classmates had already gone to class. Realizing he was late, he hurriedly got up to get dressed, but his head felt heavy, and he nearly stumbled. He steadied himself by holding onto the pillars of the bunk bed. He noticed someone had placed breakfast at his bedside, and under the lunchbox, there was a note that read: "Brother Li, I brought your meal back for you. I noticed you were sick. There's medicine I bought for my last cold next to the lunchbox. Taking it will help you recover faster. I'll take good notes during class, and you can copy them later. From Little Nine."

It was Xiao Zhao! He finally went to his early class! He felt delighted that Little Nine had finally turned over a new leaf. It wasn't just a passing impulse. From then on, Xiao Zhao never skipped a class again.

During the final exams, Xiao Zhao bought a gift to thank Yaoyou. Professor Zhong didn't adhere to the specified exam time; instead, he conducted flexible in-class assessments. Along with the scores from the regular quizzes and the midterm exam, these assessments made up the final grades. On that day, Xiao Zhao passed, but several students from other classes who often skipped the early morning classes failed. A similar situation occurred in the electronic technology fundamentals course taught by Professor Tong Shi Bai, where a few students also failed.

Xiao Zhao brought a bottle of wine and invited Brother Li to have a few drinks at the student canteen. He filled their glasses, raising his own and said, "Brother Li, I am so grateful to you for lending me a hand. I'll spare you the other words of gratitude. Here's to you, my first toast!"

After saying that, Xiao Zhao downed his first glass happily, and Yaoyou did the same.

Xiao Zhao patted his chest and said to Brother Li, "Brother Li, I can guarantee that you will become a great teacher in the future! Honestly, I've always been willful since I was young, and my mom couldn't control me. But your words and actions have had a powerful impact on me. I feel like I can't move forward without listening to you. This might be the power of sincerity, breaking through the hardest stone. Brother, I admire you."

Yaoyou replied, "Little Nine, it's not easy for you to change your habits. I have a newfound respect for you. I firmly believe that 'Black hair knows not the diligence of studying early, but white hair regrets the tardiness of learning.' Compared to you, I no longer have the advantage of age."

Yaoyou added, "Actually, everyone has flaws and shortcomings. Sometimes, I can be self-righteous and unwilling to listen to others' advice. But you are like my own younger brother, who will keep me on track in the future."

Xiao Zhao smiled, bowed with clasped fists, and said, "Li brother, I am truly grateful for your kindness."

Li Yaoyou, who had a bit to drink, unexpectedly became talkative. He said, "Little Nine, in reality, our party made mistakes during the Anti-Three Campaign and the Anti-Five Campaign.* I know that

* Instituted by Mao Zedong in 1951 and 1952; Anti-Three targeted corruption, waste, and bureaucratism; Anti-Five charged people with bribery, theft of state property, tax evasion, cheating on government contracts, and theft of state secrets. Hundreds of thousands of business and property owners were prosecuted and punished or driven to suicide.

people are reluctant to admit their mistakes, and the party won't easily acknowledge its errors either. But too many innocent people have suffered, some even losing their lives or becoming disabled."

It was the first time Xiao Zhao heard the organizational committee member of the party branch speaking negatively about the party. Xiao Zhao dismissed it as mere words.

In the dormitory, the eldest and youngest became the best of friends. Xiao Zhao called Brother Li as if he were his own brother, and Brother Li took great care of his younger brother Xiao Zhao.

At that time, the Department of Automatic Control belonged to a confidential discipline, and the Department of Automation at Tsinghua University was the first department of automatic control in China, with Professor Zhong Shimu serving as the department head. The students were proud to engage in national key projects in the fields of automatic control and computer science. As President Jiang Nanxiang said, the computer and automatic control majors at Tsinghua University were oriented towards military applications, primarily for aerospace and nuclear industries, with some civilian applications as well. Therefore, their research projects were subject to confidentiality agreements. Each student received a confidential notebook from the school to ensure compliance with the agreements.

The young students of Tsinghua University were filled with vigor and a sense of mission upon entering the campus. In addition to taking Professor Zhong Shimu's mandatory course on automatic control principles, they also had the option to choose Professor Tong Shibai's course on digital electronic technology fundamentals. Upon entering their third year, they would attend Professor Zhou Shouxian's course on pulse technology and Professor Wu Qi's course on automatic control systems, among others. China's computer industry started ten years later than the West, and at that time, the first-generation vacuum tube and transistor computers were still in the stage of imitation followed by innovation.

Yaoyou learned how to design circuits, write early computer machine code, and study computer architecture alongside his classmates. They had to design their own logic circuits, arithmetic units, controllers, and memory units. They attempted to use domestically produced semiconductor devices to develop small-scale transistor computers and address the issue of unstable transistor performance. They worked hard to improve computer processing speed, extend the average continuous stable operation time, and reduce power consumption. All of this filled Yaoyou with immense delight, as he became one of China's earliest talents in the field of computer and automatic control systems, one who possessed advanced skills.

Who wouldn't enjoy such an opportunity for work and study? Yaoyou, with his dedication, diligence, and excellence, earned the respect of his classmates, who referred to him as "Big Brother," while the teachers saw him as an outstanding assistant. Therefore, after graduating, Yaoyou easily stayed at Tsinghua University to teach and continue his academic career in graduate school.

## 3

With his diligent studying and outstanding academic performance, combined with Tsinghua's rigorous education, Yaoyou was fortunate to be accepted as an on-the-job graduate student by Professor Zhong Shimu, becoming a disciple under Professor Zhong's guidance and continuing to deepen his knowledge in automatic control technology, bringing him closer to his ideals. He still held onto his temperament and belief from childhood: "A spirited steed can't leap ten steps; a sluggish horse can't cover ten rides. Success lies in perseverance."

As an on-the-job graduate student, Yaoyou held weekly Q&A sessions for students every Wednesday afternoon. Each week, a female student named Zhu, with a polite demeanor, would attend and ask Yaoyou questions. Every time, she brought small gifts for Yaoyou, such as candies or cookies. Eventually, when there were no other students waiting in line for the Q&A session, the two would chat about daily life and personal experiences. Yaoyou learned that the girl's name was Zhu Xinqin. Her father was a professor at Tsinghua, and her mother was a high school teacher. She came from a genuine intellectual family. Half a year later, the two went on a date.

During the Lunar New Year, each grade at the school started organizing Spring Festival gala evenings, and Yaoyou was invited to participate. He went to Zhu Xinqin's class to attend the event. Everyone played the game of passing a flower while drumming, and when the flower landed in Yaoyou's hands, the drumming stopped. Yaoyou held the big red flower, stood up with a smile, and everyone shouted, "Teacher Li, it's your turn! Teacher Li, it's your turn!"

Yaoyou didn't know how to perform, so he looked at Zhu Xinqin and handed her the flower, asking her to sing on his behalf. Xinqin graciously sang "My Motherland." As she sang, Xinqin came over and held Yaoyou's hand, and they sang together. The entire class stood up, gathering around, holding hands, and singing loudly in unison. The clear voices echoed through the classroom's doors and windows, resonating inside and outside the building.

From then on, Yaoyou had Zhu Xinqin by his side.

In 1966, when Yaoyou was still a graduate student, the Cultural Revolution broke out! The Red Guards at Tsinghua High School were the first to put up big-character posters titled "Long Live the Spirit of Revolution and Rebellion," proclaiming that revolution is synonymous with rebellion and that the essence of Mao Zedong Thought is rebellion. As a result, on August 1st, Mao Zedong responded, endorsing the revolutionary act of "rebellion is justified." With this, cultural and educational activities in China were set aside, schools were closed, and teaching activities came to a complete halt.

From 1966 to 1976, Yaoyou experienced the most tumultuous decade of his life. He married Zhu Xinqin, and in the 1970s, they had a lovely daughter named Li Guangmin. His focus shifted to his family, particularly in nurturing their obedient and adorable daughter, causing his teaching and research career to stagnate. Seeing Yaoyou, once so diligent and ambitious, feeling a bit down, Zhu Xinqin tentatively asked him, "Don't you want to pursue research anymore? If that's the case, I'll clear the shelves and put something else there."

Surprisingly, Yaoyou didn't object! Zhu Xinqin felt disappointed, and she packed up Yaoyou's old books. However, she noticed that Yaoyou would often go and rummage through those boxes of books. Xinqin understood what was going on and secretly bought some books on computer science, placing them on Yaoyou's desk. At first, Yaoyou hesitated to engage with them, but before long, he couldn't resist.

After the reform and opening in 1978, Yaoyou, who had remained unnoticed, was remembered once again. Tsinghua University always needed elite individuals to take on the responsibilities of research and teaching, and Yaoyou was reappointed as a professor.

In 1990, when I first met Great Uncle Yaoyou, I didn't remember anything. Later, before I accompanied my mother to Munich, Germany, she took me to visit him. I was a little over three years old, and he lived in Tsinghua University. At that time, he was the director of the Tsinghua Computing Center, and he was busy. During the one hour we spent at his home, phone calls kept coming in, inquiring about matters related to the center, and students would come seeking his guidance. According to my grandpa — Yaoyou's younger half-brother, the eighth of the same father, "Your Great Uncle Yaoyou is a busy man. Even when I'm in Beijing and want to meet him, I have to make an appointment! Time never comes back, and he wishes he could split a minute in half to reclaim the lost ten years."

Grandpa continued, "Your Great Uncle Yaoyou has always been stronger than me. His determined character keeps him from falling behind in any aspect. Among the Li family's younger generations, the first person I admire is your Great Aunt Yaozhi, and the next one is your Great Uncle Yaoyou."

Grandpa also said to me, "Your Great Uncle Yaoyou once said that being a person means never giving up, giving twelve times the effort when you have ten times the ability, and not doing things you will regret."

Listening to Grandpa, I realized that Yaoyou dedicated himself to his work for over twenty years, and his influence spread far and wide, making invaluable contributions to China's higher education sector.

## Epilogue

# After half a century apart, the brothers and sisters on both sides of the strait finally reunite

### 1

After November 1987, when the Taiwanese authorities lifted martial law and opened the door for people to visit the mainland, China, which was experiencing rapid development, also began to welcome their Taiwanese compatriots.

In 1990, the day when Yaoxin obtained her ticket to Beijing was a scorching hot day in July. The colorful hues in the sky reflected the vibrant emotions in her heart. Yaoxin silently recited "Amitabha Buddha" and suppressed her racing heart. As soon as she arrived home, the first thing she did was to call her fifth sister Yaozhi and eighth brother Yaowei. The phone conversation lasted for over an hour, and in the end, they decided to save their stories for a week later when they would meet again in the illuminated city of Beijing. They eagerly anticipated this reunion after nearly half a century.

### 2

Guangzhong and his family lived in a rented courtyard house in Beijing. In recent years, Beijing had been witnessing a boom in real estate development, with many tall buildings under construction but few completed. Therefore, since his marriage, Guangzhong had been living in student dormitories. A few months ago, the school no longer allowed Ph.D. graduates to stay in the dormitories, so they had to move out.

In the evening, Guangzhong was holding their nine-month-old

son and, along with his wife Yang Xi, taking a stroll in the hutongs (narrow streets). Their landlord, Aunt Song, called out to Guangzhong, "Dr. Li, there's a phone call for you!"

Guangzhong turned to Yang Xi and said, "You go ahead with the baby; I'll catch up with you."

The mid-July sun in Beijing was scorching, even in the evening. Air conditioning was a luxury few households could afford, and the electric fans provided little relief. However, not using the fans made the heat unbearable, so everyone sought solace outside. Besides the people strolling around, by the walls and under the big trees, uncles and aunties shook their large handheld fans while shooing away mosquitoes and flies, enjoying the breeze and chatting. Occasionally, cyclists skillfully weaved through the crowd, as if performing stunts on their bikes.

Yang Xi walked slowly along the narrow Beijing hutong, holding her son in her arms. She hummed a nursery rhyme. Her son, Mingyu, who was still babbling, seemed to be singing along with his mother's voice. Guangzhong caught up with them and excitedly told Yang Xi, "On July 22nd, which is next Sunday, my aunt from Taiwan is coming to Beijing."

Yang Xi stopped and looked at Guangzhong, asking, "When is her flight? Where will she be staying?"

Guangzhong proudly said, "Dad said she will be staying with us!"

Yang Xi joyfully exclaimed, "Then what are we waiting for? Let's go home and tidy up the house. We can let them stay in the main room we rented. Let's also talk to the landlord and see if they can clean up the other two storage rooms and rent them to us for a month."

Aunt Song, the landlord, had recently reclaimed her old ancestral home due to a change in national policy. She had just started renting out the house. It was quite a coincidence that the first tenant was Guangzhong's family. As soon as she heard that it was a Taiwanese compatriot coming to reunite with family on the mainland, she didn't hesitate and started cleaning the house with her son. She even offered free accommodation during the days when Guangzhong's great aunt would be in Beijing. Guangzhong and Yang Xi were extremely grateful.

Guangzhong didn't go to school, and Yang Xi didn't attend her classes either. They both took time off and cleaned and tidied the house together.

The architectural style of the Beijing courtyard, known as the *siheyuan*, originated in the Ming Dynasty. The siheyuan typically faces north and is surrounded by narrow hutongs on the east and west sides. The basic layout consists of a main house (*zhengfang*), a south-facing house (*daozuofang*), and east and west wing rooms. The quadrangle is enclosed by high walls, with a single gate, and the courtyard is in the center. The siheyuan is usually symmetric along the central axis, with the main gate opening towards the southeast. According to traditional Feng Shui beliefs, Beijing locals believe that opening the gate in the southeast direction ensures a continuous flow of wealth and money.

As Aunt Song organized the rooms in the storage area, she began talking about the siheyuan. She said, "This is our old ancestral home. Our family used to be a large extended family, and all the sisters-in-law lived in this courtyard. In the past, there was only one street entrance to the courtyard, and when the door was closed, it was completely sealed off from the outside world. Only our large family lived inside. The courtyard used to have crabapple trees, grapevines, and a large fishpond. In the summer, we would relax under the grape trellis, enjoying the beautiful natural surroundings bestowed upon us. Later, my family scattered in different directions, some stayed on the mainland, some went to Hong Kong, and perhaps some went to Taiwan."

Aunt Song continued to share her past with Yang Xi, saying, "Every summer, the grapevines in the courtyard were lush and abundant. When the grapes ripened, I would eat my fill under the trellis! The grapes didn't need to be washed; the naturally green fruit was the best. And there were crabapple fruits, much smaller than apples. I would pluck them from the tree and rub them on my clothes a few times before eating them. They were sour, sweet, and mouthwatering."

Aunt Song said, "At that time, I was only five or six years old, often sitting under the grape trellis listening to my grandmother tell stories. Later, my grandmother passed away, and my father went off to

Yaozhi and Yaoxin

serve in the military and never returned. It was only my mother who raised me. Later, the house was collectivized, and my mother and I were allocated the coldest and smallest west wing room. My mother would take me to different households every day to wash clothes and earn a living. A few years ago, my father found us, but he already had a new family. I wouldn't go to Hong Kong with him. As long as my mother is alive, I will protect her."

Aunt Song mentioned that since the courtyard was divided among five families, the space became cramped, and as a result, the trees and grapevines were cut down, and the fish pond turned into an open-air water pool for the five households to share. Aunt Song said she missed the spacious and sunny courtyard with its lush greenery.

This time, Aunt Song came with great enthusiasm and decided to undertake a major renovation. The broken tiles on the roof and the damaged bricks on the walls were replaced, and the interior of the house was freshly painted. The fish pond was gone, replaced by a large goldfish tank. The goldfish swam freely, gracefully wagging their tails. Just as people rely on clothes and horses rely on saddles, the siheyuan also relied on decoration. After the cleaning and renovation, the siheyuan sparkled and radiated brilliance.

## 3

The day arrived, and on July 20th, the schools started their summer vacation. Guangzhong first picked up his father and Great Aunt Yaozhi, and upon their strong insistence, they also brought along his half-brother Yaoyou, who used to play with him as a child. Yaoyou had now changed his name and become a distinguished professor at Tsinghua University. The courtyard became lively, instantly feeling smaller with the addition of more people. They had even proposed inviting their fourth brother Yaojia to join, but he was visiting his eldest son in Japan and wasn't in Beijing at the time.

On the 22nd, at the capital airport, Yaoxin walked slowly out of the airport exit, following the crowd towards her loved ones.

She wore reading glasses, a brown and white silk blouse, a black wide-skirted long skirt, and black leather shoes with moderate heels. With a benevolent smile on her face, she walked forward. At the moment she walked out of the exit, her composure vanished. She dropped her luggage and opened her arms to embrace her sisters and brothers. After forty-three years, what a long wait it had been! Since their separation at the end of 1947, they had all experienced different trials and tribulations. This was a long-awaited reunion after the vicissitudes of life. Yaoxin thought:

> Forty-three years, longing through one's eyes,
> Crossing mountains and oceans, separating siblings on both sides,
> How many times have we dreamt of wandering in the homeland beyond,
> How many times have we yearned for a meeting, the anticipation of reunion.

Guangzhong. Yaowei, Mingyu, Yaozhi, and Yang Xi

Today, embracing each other with joy, all four siblings now
with streaks of white in their hair.

The four siblings went to a Northeastern cuisine restaurant in Xisi. Yaoxin said, "In Taiwan, most restaurants cater to the tastes of southern people. As a northerner, I really miss the rich flavors, vibrant colors, and distinct sweet-salty taste of my hometown dishes. Today, let's savor them again." She noticed a private room in the restaurant that resembled the Eight Immortals table from their old home. Yaoxin walked straight to it and said, pointing, "Let's have this room!"

Everyone agreed that Yaozhi, being the eldest sister, should sit in the seat of honor. Yaozhi declined, saying, "How can I bear that! Yaoxin has come all the way from Taiwan, she is the guest of honor and should sit at the head."

So, the two younger brothers drove Yaoxin to sit in the center, facing the entrance. Then Yaozhi sat in the position of the vice host, facing Yaoxin. Yaoyou sat on the right side of Yaoxin, and Yaowei sat on the left. The elder siblings settled into their seats, and Yang Xi put the sleeping Mingyu into a stroller. She and

Guangzhong also took their seats. In an unprecedented move, the elder siblings ordered a bottle of Shengyuanchun Baijiu. After all, it was a reunion after more than forty years. How could they celebrate without alcohol?

Yaoxin reminisced, saying, "I remember when we used to have meals together in Yingkou. At that time, Yaoyou wasn't with us, and we had Yaoguo. It was also the four siblings dining together."

Yaowei also remembered the past, saying, "Yes, I remember it vividly. At that time, what I loved the most was the mud loach stuffed tofu that Yaoxin made!"

Yaozhi nodded and said, "Who doesn't agree? It was during that time that I learned how to cook, thanks to Yaoxin!"

Yaowei raised his glass, standing up with a slightly trembling hand, and spilled some wine. He was extremely excited, saying, "I never dreamed that after forty-three years, I would still be able to sit at the same table and share a drink with my sisters and brother! I am so happy. I raise this glass to toast my sisters and brother, and I finish it. Cheers to all of you!"

After saying that, he tilted his head back and drank the first glass. Yaozhi, Yaoxin, and Yaoyou had no reason not to follow suit. After a few more glasses, the four siblings' faces were flushed, and their conversation became livelier.

The food arrived, and the four siblings ordered several hot dishes, all of them Northeastern flavors: Braised Pork with Vermicelli, Sour Cabbage Ribs, Stewed Chicken with Mushrooms, and Stir-Fried Pork Strips, among others. There was also a cold dish: Northeastern Jelly Noodles. Yaoxin asked the waiter for dumplings with a mixed filling.

While eating the dumplings, Yaoxin asked Guangzhong, "Do you, the younger generation, know the significance of dumplings?"

Guangzhong smiled and replied, "Yes, I do."

He picked up a dumpling and continued, "Eating dumplings symbolizes the anticipation of reunion, the wish for peace and unity, and the hope for a swift return."

Yang Xi added, "The shape of the dumpling resembles ancient Chinese gold ingots, symbolizing wealth, prosperity, and auspiciousness."

Great Aunt Yaozhi added: "Yes, making dumplings means

encapsulating good fortune. Moreover, the word 'jiao' in 'jiaozi' sounds similar to the word 交 (jiāo), and 'zi' represents the 'zi' hour, which refers to the time between midnight and 1 a.m. on New Year's Eve, the moment when the old year transitions into the new. We call it 'jiaozi' to signify this exchange."

Yaoxin's skilled at summarizing: "When we put all these meanings together, it becomes comprehensive. As Han Chinese, we value family bonds. On New Year's Eve, with the cold wind outside, the house warm with a blazing fire, and a pot of boiling water with dumplings shaped like ancient gold ingots, we enclose our longing for distant loved ones and heartfelt blessings within these small dumplings. As these plump dumplings float to the surface, accompanied by the sound of firecrackers bidding farewell to the old and welcoming the new outside the window, we serve ourselves these rich and plentiful dumplings, overflowing with our blessings for our family and hopes for a bright future."

Yaoxin, deep in thought, said, "Do you know how much hope I have in these small dumplings on every New Year's Eve?"

Yaozhi replied, "I understand, sixth sister. Haven't I felt the same way too? Every New Year's Eve, I wonder, how are my brothers and sisters? How are my children? Are you cold? Are you hungry?"

She looked at Yaoxin and continued, "You still have dumplings to eat during the New Year. In the labor reform farm in Shihezi, I couldn't even dream of having dumplings."

Saying that, Yaozhi wiped away tears from the corner of her eyes with her hand. Yang Xi handed her a tissue, and Yaozhi took it with her rough and withered hands.

Seeing his sisters getting emotional, Yaoyou suggested, "Let's have some Beijing-style hot pot with lamb, enjoy the meal, and chat at the same time."

The restaurant owner also offered a complimentary specialty dish, "Four Happiness Meatballs," symbolizing the joyous reunion of the four siblings. They enjoyed their hometown dishes, drank their hometown liquor, sang their hometown nursery rhymes, and missed their loved ones back home. It felt as if the elder siblings had returned to the past. The scenes from forty years ago were vivid in their minds—the courtyard gate of the northeastern quadrangle house, Yaoxian, Yaozhi, and Yaoxin playing shuttlecock and jumping rope. Yaoxian was the best at playing shuttlecock and could perform various tricks. The shuttlecock seemed to stick to her feet. Yaozhi was the smartest; whenever she played jump rope, she never lost and even came up with many new tricks herself. Yaoxin, the youngest, followed behind, picking up the shuttlecock. Yaoguo and Yaowei played with rolling iron hoops and slingshots. Yaowei was the champion at rolling iron hoops, always rolling it for the longest time among the boys, earning praise from the other children. Yaoguo excelled at using slingshots; he was accurate when targeting sparrows at home and later became a sharpshooter in the army.

Yaoyou asked Yaozhi, "Do you still keep in touch with Yaoxian, our fourth sister?"

Yaozhi replied, "Of course, we've reconciled! Her son just graduated with a Ph.D. and went to Australia. He's now an architect. She went to visit him. She sent me a letter last year, saying that life there is good, and she has a grandson to take care of. Perhaps she won't come back."

Yaowei added, "Yaoxian has had a difficult time these years. Both her husband and she made mistakes in their political views, and their whole family was sent to Langfang and not given important positions. Yaoxian even suffered from depression and almost attempted suicide. According to Yaojia, a few years ago, they returned to Beijing and then went to Australia."

Yaozhi said solemnly, "Ten years ago, when I moved back to Yingkou from Shihezi, Yaoxian wrote me a long letter. She talked about her involvement in confidential work and how she had no choice in the matter. In these years, she has dedicated herself to the Party with all her passion and neglected her closest family members. She apologized to everyone!"

Yaozhi looked at everyone, seeing their focused and attentive gazes. She continued, "Yaoxian visited me several times in Yingkou. She knew I loved chocolate and would bring a lot of it each time. We slept in the same bed, and she personally cooked steamed egg cakes for me. It felt like we were back in the Li family's courtyard, eating egg custard from the same bowl."

Yaoyou said, "I haven't met our fourth sister often, but I have seen Yaojia sometimes. He has a keen political mind and has come through various political movements unscathed. He is now the Party Secretary of a university. He's doing well in life, although he's a bit bald."

Yaowei added, "However, Yaojia has also said that engaging in politics is like walking on thin ice sometimes! That's why he didn't allow any of his three children to pursue a political career. He never sent them to Beijing No. 4 High School or No. 6 High School, which are attended by the children of high-ranking officials. His eldest became a teacher, the second settled in Japan, and the third returned from studying abroad and now works as an ordinary employee in a foreign-owned company."

Yaowei jokingly remarked, "It seems that Yaojia, with his collection of books by Marx, Engels, Lenin, Stalin, and Mao, doesn't have an inheritor!"

As they chatted, time passed unnoticed, and more than two hours had gone by. They had to end their conversation and hailed two taxis to go to Guangzhong's quadrangle house. Yaoxin looked at the character "口" (courtyard) and thought of her old house in Yingkou. It was a typical northeastern quadrangle house with multiple courtyards. The four siblings spent the night reminiscing about their old house, grandparents, father, mother, brothers, sisters, and the ups and downs of their lives. Tears streamed down their faces one moment, and laughter filled the air the next. Their life experiences had weathered storms but also enjoyed bright spring moments.

Yaowei said with deep emotion, "Mainland China has changed, experiencing an unprecedented level of openness. Guangzhong had the opportunity to study in France and received the Humboldt Foundation scholarship to Germany. After completing his studies in France, he'll go directly from France to Germany for postdoctoral research."

Yaoyou said, "My daughter Guangmin followed in my footsteps and went to Tsinghua University for graduate studies. I was so focused on my studies that I got married late. You all have three generations living together, and I'm lagging behind."

Yaozhi added, "Dawan, in the first year of the 1989 democracy movement, went to the United States for study. He recently sent a letter saying that he is pursuing a Ph.D. and everything is going well. He's also applying for a U.S. green card. He longs for a country that values freedom and democracy."

Yaoxin also spoke, "My daughter Lanlan went to study in Japan. Actually, I didn't agree with her going to Japan due to the high cost of living there and some historical grievances."

Yaoxin looked at Yaozhi and said, "But Lanlan is just like you, Fifth sister Zhi. She didn't want to miss this opportunity. She has always been proud of Aunt Zhi. She has passed the Japanese language proficiency test and said that if she has the chance to meet Aunt Zhi, she would definitely seek advice on Japanese."

Yaozhi looked at Yaoxin and nodded, saying, "I was curious about Japan back then, and a strong thirst for knowledge drove me to go and see for myself."

Yaozhi sighed and said again, "Ah, those are all stories of the past."

Yaoxin added, "Xianglong obtained American citizenship. I don't blame him; it was his choice."

After a pause, Yaoxin continued, "A few years ago, Xianglong found his birth mother on the mainland. That is his roots, and I wish him well!"

She clasped her hands together and chanted, "Namo Amituofo!"

The night grew late, but the four siblings continued to excitedly chat around the table. Guangzhong brought a pot of Tie Guanyin tea to invigorate them. Through the doors and windows, he saw the silhouettes of the four siblings projected on the wall under the lamplight, frozen in a moment of eternal happiness.

## 4

Yaoxin took to heart the teachings of Buddhism and devoted herself to solitary practice, guarding the Buddha's lamp. In her heart, she chanted the mantra of the pure lotus, striving to detach herself from worldly attachments. But she knew deep down that the pure heart of a Buddha, free from any lingering concerns, was difficult to attain. Today, however, she could finally find solace.

光中姪:

收到你從Nancy寄來的明信片賀卡,無限的欣慰,我知道你一定在百忙中寄出的,謝謝你!

公堂在公事陪同[illegible]在11月7日送你出發,一定非常担心你這次出國進修。在一所知之下,一定会满心不安的到了一個異民族國家中,語言雖然可[illegible]國語言相通,但是还有有限的隔閡,但是也不必过分緊張,放心大胆的去尋找人情的温暖,積極的学習法語,因法國人不欢迎美(英)語的,他们雖然懂但是还[illegible]心的不喜欢。我想法國一定也有不少来自大陸的学生,不管他学识的高低,还是要注重他们的人际關係,比如暑寒假日可以找到點餐館的打工机会,這是我欧洲觀光時見到的,瞭解的情形,我想你都可以做得到的,以后若是能够熟習了一切,也可以藉假期坐火車和伙伴们遊覽一番,法國是一個文化氣息相当高的地方,知道一些民俗習[illegible]生活的態度,也可以增加一些個人生的趣味和氣質!

你現在的情形如何,我也非常惦念,願你能安心向学和工作,不久的未来才能带妻子團圓共住一起!我最近还好,勿念!祝

健康,事事如意

[illegible] [illegible]

12.27

Yaoxin's letter to Guangzhong, who was studying in Nancy, France

Afterwards, Yaoxin returned to the mainland several times to visit. In 2002, she returned from the mainland to Taiwan one last time. The teachings of Buddhism finally granted her liberation from worldly desires, and within her heart rose the profound words of Zen. With her mundane concerns left behind her mind regained purity. The lotus in her heart blossomed, and she found a glimpse of peace in the world. Striking the wooden fish, she sat amidst the wafting incense, silently reciting in her heart: "A grain of sand encompasses the world, a flower is a paradise. Infinite realms reside within a palm, a moment becomes eternal."

How long is a lifetime? Life exists within the realm of heaven and earth. Yaoxin, at her virtual age of 78, closed her eyes and gradually fell into a peaceful sleep.

One summer day in 2002, when our family was in the Midwest of the United States, my father received a phone call from my grandfather in China, informing him of Yaoxin's passing. Grandfather said, "According to Lanlan, her mother woke up in the morning and said she wasn't feeling well, mentioning that she might be going to the Pure Land."

Lanlan wanted to take her mother to the hospital, but Yaoxin said, "Call me by my Dharma name, 'Foxian,' and there's no need to go to the hospital."

Later, she went to her own Buddhist shrine. After a while, when Lanlan saw her mother again, she was sitting up, her face serene and peaceful. She departed gracefully and happily. From that moment on, she bid farewell to all the worldly troubles.

Lanlan looked at a poem written by her mother, a eulogy to the Pure Land, and softly recited:

Towards the setting sun in the west,
Gazing at the compassionate countenance from afar.
Purifying the waters of the Four Seas,
Radiant amidst the purple-gold mountain.
Diligent chanting ensures rebirth,
Hence the name "Ultimate Bliss."
The spiderweb becomes a precious treasure tree,
The heavenly flower disperses fragrant essence.
These images fill my vision,

As I wish to seek refuge in that sacred place.
Through these boundless merits,
May we receive the blessings of the netherworld.
Eighty billion kalpas of sins,
Like a breeze sweeping away frost.
May we witness immeasurable longevity,
Constantly seeing the brilliance of the jade-like hair.

Later, my grandfather and grandmother took care of the funeral arrangements for Yaoxin. When they returned, they brought back a stack of family letters that Yaoxin had written in her earlier years but had never sent.

## 5

After my mother, Yang Xi's Chinese version of "Batiandi" was published in the United States for a year, on July 5th, 2021, my grandfather Yaowei passed away in his sleep. It was a time when the novel coronavirus was wreaking havoc, and China was on high alert. Our ten-year visas were temporarily invalidated, and we couldn't return to mainland China. My father was left with a lifelong regret of not being able to see him one last time. His nephew wrote a poem that encapsulates my grandfather's life,

In Memory of Uncle Li Yaowei:

Since childhood, he aspired to uplift China,
With intelligence and wisdom admired by all.
Defending home and country, aiding Korea,
Received awards for valor, returned to his fold.
Self-taught, he excelled and entered university,
Teaching and nurturing, achieving great success.
His children, products of his guidance, exemplary,
Friends and relatives never ceased to be impressed.
His home became a tutoring center, bustling,
Students like a continuous stream, on the move.
Providing food, shelter, and quality teaching,
Wholeheartedly dedicated to everyone's improvement.

The younger generation made strides in their studies,
Thanks to Uncle and Aunt's tremendous contributions.
An exemplar as a teacher, a role model indeed,
Integrity permeated his entire life's conclusions.

We planted a pine tree in our backyard to commemorate my grandfather. My father wrote this poem in memory of my grandfather, Li Yaowei, and let's conclude this book with that poem:

A Pine Tree in Remembrance

In our backyard, a pine tree stands tall,
A symbol of reverence for my grandfather's soul.
My father penned this poem, a tribute to recall,
The cherished memories of Li Yaowei's role.

A man of honor, strength, and grace,
Through his actions, he left a lasting trace.
A life dedicated to family and nation,
Guiding us with love and inspiration.

Like the branches that reach for the sky,
His wisdom and guidance never denied.
Rooted in values, firm and true,
His legacy lives on, forever anew.

With every rustle of the pine's green leaves,
His presence lingers, a comfort that never leaves.
A testament to a life well-lived,
In our hearts, his spirit thrives.

As seasons change and years go by,
The pine tree stands strong, reaching high.
Batiandi family — A symbol of our eternal bond,
Forever united, in memories fond.

## Afterword

Upon completing this novel, I feel incredibly honored and fulfilled. This story is based on the real history of Li family, although I have changed the names of some characters, they all have real counterparts. Through artistic techniques, I have transformed the rise and fall of this family into a novel, hoping to inspire and provoke thought in readers.

The novel spans from the Daoguang period of the Qing Dynasty to the early 21st century in the present day. Through the story of this family, I attempt to depict the impact of historical changes on people's lives. The Li family is an ordinary prominent family, and their fortunes and misfortunes represent the ever-changing times. I hope readers can gain some enlightenment from it.

During the writing process, I have included some illustrations to better depict the settings and characters of that time. These images serve as a tribute to the deceased main characters and a gesture of respect towards them.

I want to make it clear that this book does not intend for readers to directly associate the characters with real individuals. The viewpoints I describe are based on oral accounts from some members of the Li family and limited resources, and they do not represent my personal opinions. While I respect historical facts, I am fully aware that the compilation of family history inevitably involves subjectivity and partiality.

Finally, I want to emphasize that the copyright of this book belongs to me, and any unauthorized reproduction is prohibited. I hold deep affection and respect for this story, hoping it brings value and inspiration to readers.

Once again, I sincerely thank everyone who has supported and read this novel. I hope you enjoy this story.

Thank you from the bottom of my heart!

Xi Fu

## Acknowledgments

I would like to express my sincere gratitude to all those who have contributed to the completion of this book.

First and foremost, I would like to thank my family for their unwavering support and understanding throughout this journey. Their love and encouragement have been my constant motivation.

I am immensely grateful to my friends, Yu Zhang, Sue Zhu, Yuannan Xia, Suping Lu, Bao Wang, Katie Ge, Alexandra Zheng Harner, RongBiao Zhao, Li Liu, Xiulian Han, for their remarkable work in proofread the Chinese version of "Batiandi." Their talent and dedication have brought this story to life and touched the hearts of many readers.

I would also like to extend my appreciation to Xingzhong Li for his invaluable insights and for penning the beautiful poem in memory of his father, Li Yaowu. His words capture the essence of our beloved patriarch and serve as a testament to his remarkable life.

A special thank you goes to my brother-in-law Li Guangpei for his contribution of the poignant poem that encapsulates the achievements and virtues of my father-in-law, Li Yaowu. It serves as a fitting tribute to his exemplary character.

Thank you, Lily Li for helping proofread the English errors so that this book can meet readers in a more standard English form, and thanks to David Li, whose design reflects profound cultural heritage.

I would like to express my thanks to Paul Royster for proofreading, editing, and illustrations who worked tirelessly to bring this book to fruition. Thanks to him, as an outstanding editor for bringing this book to English-speaking readers.

Lastly, to everyone who has played a part, no matter how big or small, in the creation and publication of this book, I extend my heartfelt appreciation. Without your support, this project would not have been possible.

Thank you.
Xifu

## References and Sources

"Genealogy of the Li Family in Batiadi, Yingkou, Liaoning"
"Genealogy of the Li Family in Laiyang, Shandong"
"Genealogy of the Li Family in Li Jiagu, Pingdu, Shandong"
"Yingkou Chronicle, Old Place Names of Yingkou/Batiadi"
Baidu Baike (Baidu Encyclopedia), "Zhuzhuma in Pingdu"
"Yulin City Chronicles (County-level), Spring and Autumn Period and Qingming Festival"
Baidu Baike, "Huanghekou Town"
Baidu Baike, "Lijin Tiemenguan"
Baidu Baike, "History of Huludao, Liaoning"
"Old Place Names of Yingkou/Yingkou Matou" by Li Guichun, March 20, 2017, original article URL: https://kknews.cc/history/en424lr.html
Yingkou Daily, October 29, 2017, "Historical Stories: Yingkou Liaodong River Wharf in the 1920s and 1930s (Part 1)"
"The Complete Works of Guo Songtao, Volume Eight"
Introduction to Tashan Revolutionary Martyrs Cemetery in Huludao: History of Shandong Coastal Development
"Discussing Marriage: Trendy Wedding Comperes and Fortune Tellers" by Huang Zhenyu
Wikipedia, "Foot Binding"
Baidu Baike, "Taiping Heavenly Kingdom"
Baidu Baike, "Eight-Nation Alliance Invasion of China"
Baidu Baike, "Self-Strengthening Movement"
Ancient Porcelain Academy, September 16, 2019, "Old Shengjing/Shengjing Stories: 'Four Towers'"
Northeast News Network, "The 250-Year-Old Wall near Shenyang City"
Baidu Baike, "Japanese Invasion of China"
Baidu Baike, "Bengbengxi (a traditional Chinese performance)"
"Modern Political History Series - Land Reform History"
Huasheng Forum, "Past Memories," February 29, 2012, Picture Story: Fengtian 1900-1910

WWDZnet, "[Repost] Liaodong: Don't Forget 1905" by Yiye Bianzhou, December 1, 2006

Baidu Baike, "Fengtian University"

Meiri Toutiao, "History and Space: The Ancestral Home of Liaoning University is in Yingkou,"

Baidu Baike, "Public-Private Partnership"

Baidu Baike, "Nara Women's University," and http://www.nara-wu.ac.jp/nwu/faculty/index.html

Wikipedia, "Big Character Poster"

Archive Library, "Key Events of the Anti-Rightist Movement," URL: [link]

Wikipedia, "Investigation and Statistics Bureau of the Military Commission of the National Government"

Wikipedia, "Siege of Changchun"

Wikipedia, "Xinjiang Production and Construction Corps"

Xinjiang Old Li Collection, "Shihezi Has a Military Reclamation Museum"

"Modern History Research," 2015, Issue 5, Xu Zhimin, "Enemy State Study Abroad - The Living Reality of Chinese Students in Japan during the Anti-Japanese War"

Baidu Baike, "Xinjiang Uygur Autonomous Region Library"

Wikipedia, "Kashgar Clash"

Baidu Baike, «1976»

Baidu Baike, «Rensselaer Polytechnic Institute»

Wikipedia, "Reform and Opening-Up"

Baidu Baike, "Shenyang Zhongjie"

Baidu Baike, "Beijing Siheyuan (Traditional Beijing Courtyard)"

Baidu Baike, "Korean War (Historical Event)"

Wikipedia, "Korean War"

Baidu Baike, "Mangniu Tun"

Baidu Baike, "Shangshan Xiaxiang"

Baidu Baike, "Workers, Peasants, and Soldiers Students"

Wikipedia, "Street Office"

People's Daily Overseas Edition, June 11, 2018, "College Entrance Examination Changes the Destiny of Hundreds of Millions of Chinese People"

Baidu Baike, "Longshan Temple"

Wikipedia, "Battle of Kinmen"
Xinhua Net, September 29, 2009, "The 'Three Links' First Proposed in the 1979 'Message to Compatriots in Taiwan'"
"Shandong Historical Materials," 1982, Issue 2
Baidu Baike, "Pingdu County"
"Local Chronicles of Liaoning Province," Shenyang City
"Local Chronicles of Liaoning Province," Yingkou City
"Yingkou Chronicle" Journal, British Consulate General in Yingkou, June 14, 2012.

www.ingramcontent.com/pod-product-compliance
Lightning Source LLC
Chambersburg PA
CBHW020423030726
47495CB00006B/1629

* 9 7 8 1 6 0 9 6 2 3 5 6 2 *